SUZANNAH ROWNTREE

# Dark & Stormy

*Miss Dark's Apparitions, Volume III.*

First published by Bocfodder Press 2023

First edition

ISBN: 978-0-6454668-2-9

Cover art by MiblArt

This book was professionally typeset on Reedsy.
Find out more at reedsy.com

*For Irina.*
*Congratulations—you're Vasily's godmother now.*

# 1

# Chapter I.

The tea ought certainly to have put me upon my guard. That it did not, I can only attribute to a deplorable want of excitement in the humdrum events of our modern life. Which of us, upon receiving a cup of tea, expects it to contain ampoules of poison, or smuggled diamonds, or even so small a thing as calculating intentions? This cup certainly contained the last—or so I am told; but of this I was not, at first, conscious.

Indeed I was conscious of very little. At the moment the tea arrived, I was gradually returning to life in my cramped cabin aboard the Königsberg to St Petersburg boat. I am an indifferent sailor, and the unfortunate choppiness of the voyage had violently disagreed with me for most of the previous day. Since awakening this morning, however, my indisposition had begun to pass off. Now feeling only about half, instead of mostly, dead, I staggered from my berth to the porthole and observed in the golden light of the late spring afternoon that we had passed into calmer water, across which I could see a low green shore crowned with the roofs of noble mansions and far off, the gilded tip of some church spire.

This must be the imperial Russian capital; and I must make myself presentable for disembarkment.

Only the prospect of soon getting myself onto *terra firma* could have induced me to act. I wedged myself into my berth and began feebly to tidy my hair. This task was complete, and I was looking about muzzily for my boots, when a knock came at the door. In answer to my call, the cup of tea entered in the company of a German steward and a Russian Grand Duke. The steward was dressed in a blue uniform with brass buttons, and looked very respectable. The Grand Duke's slim grey trousers and blue coat, however, had been cut in long, lean lines that made his every attitude seem impossibly elegant; the effect was not helped by a slim silver-topped walking-stick which he had rested carelessly across his shoulder, nor by the red silk ascot under his chin. Gentlemen ought not to roam about in such a manner; it's almost indecent. Someone ought to write a sternly-worded letter to the *Times* about it.

Vasily Nikolaevich Romanov would have paid no attention if they had. "Miss Dark, you look ravishing," he said quite untruthfully from where he lounged, louchely, in the doorway. "We dock in ten minutes. I have brought you tea."

Strictly speaking, it was the steward who had brought me the tea; and I made sure to render my thanks to the man, for after the unpleasant few hours I had passed I was sorely in need of nourishment. As I brought the life-giving brew to my lips, I regarded Vasily narrowly through the rising clouds of steam.

As those of you who have read the previous volumes of my memoirs will recall, my association with the wicked Grand Duke was purely professional in nature. An imposter I may be—and a diamond thief—and someone who throws paper darts at the opera—but I have been properly brought-up, all the same. Vasily Nikolaevich Romanov was *not* the sort of gentleman a well-behaved young lady from Brixton should find herself consorting with on any terms but those of the strictest propriety. The chasm which divides the scions of Royalty from the daughters of the mercantile class is absolute, and those who seek to cross it are soundly punished, they and their children, unto the fourth and fifth generations! Such was not *my* ambition. Why should it be? Vasily was presently in deep disgrace with his Imperial relatives, and had spent the larger part of our acquaintance attempting to evade the secret policemen employed by his cousin, the new Tsar. Nor would he have been any more eligible had he been on the best of terms with his family. From the earliest age, like every good Englishwoman, I have been taught to shudder at the mention of autocratic Russia, whose millions of peasants are ruled with reddened fang and naked claw by its vampire masters. Vasily might no longer be one of these; indeed, it was due to his having assisted in defanging some of the monstrous royalties of the Continent that he was now a wanted man— yet still he was acutely conscious of the privileged position to which he had been born. Beyond that, if I may be frank with the reader, there was something about the man that reminded one irresistibly of a house on fire, or a train wreck, or a large nursery on a rainy day when Nanny has a cold and everyone has got out of bed on the wrong side. He was, in short, a *mess*.

Yet he had for a week or two—ever since we had left London, and all the way by rail to Vienna and then north to Russia—been quite puzzlingly attentive. Cups of tea, warm blankets, and steadying arms had been offered at regular intervals. He had also been in indecently good spirits, for a

3

fugitive returning to a native land that had put out a warrant for his arrest. Some weeks ago I might have viewed all this with suspicion: until quite recently I had been convinced that Vasily was plotting to betray me. That was all over now—and yet this solicitude was extremely surprising! What could be the reason for such an alteration in his manner?

All I said, as I breathed in the steam from my tea (scented faintly with woodsmoke, in the Russian manner), was: "How very considerate you've become, your grace!"

"It's a trick," he told me, with a gesture I can only describe as *preening.* "I mean to win your confidence."

Since Vasily and I had buried our differences, I was not alarmed. "So long as it results in tea, I shall be happy," I said tranquilly. With a reminder to be ready to disembark shortly, and to call upon him should I require any assistance, Vasily departed. The door closed. There was a ghost standing behind it.

I believe I have mentioned that I am in the habit of catching glimpses of the departed; a proclivity which I was recently surprised to learn I had inherited from my mother's side of the family. Ordinarily, these visions of mine are little more than the silent memories imprinted by the dead upon the scenes of their life, and may be grisly or humdrum. At a glance, I recognised this particular apparition as my latest client and the reason for our present visit to St Petersburg.

"Ah! it's Mimi's Annushka," I said, swallowing a sip of tea before it had quite cooled sufficiently. Blinking back my tears, I sought a clearer look at the young woman—a pale figure in a short dress of fluttering white *tulle* which showed a pair of extremely sinewy legs. "Now: I wonder what happened to you?" I added in an undertone.

"My name is *Anna*," retorted the ballerina, in accented French. "It is rude to address a perfect stranger by her diminutive."

It was an excellent thing that I had swallowed my tea, or else my surprise might have been expressed in a manner authentic, but unladylike. As it was, a generous helping of the liquid found its way into the saucer.

"I beg your pardon!" I stammered in the same language. "I thought—that is, I did not expect—"

I halted, labouring under a feeling of acute social embarrassment. Imprints never speak at all. Those who do are either very much alive or very recently dead—what I refer to as *shades*. Only I could not possibly be speaking to a shade! Annushka—*Anna*—had first appeared to me approximately two weeks ago, on the boat crossing the Channel, and I had never met a shade older than a day or two, let alone a week. The spirits of the dead, in my experience, never remain in this world for very long. Perhaps this was not Mimi's dead friend at all—perhaps a real, flesh-and-blood ballerina had secreted herself in my cabin while I was preoccupied with the cut of Vasily's trousers! There was a lump of sugar on my saucer and I felt the wild urge to shy it at my visitor. This, however, would scarcely have improved the situation.

"I beg your pardon," I said weakly, "but are you by any chance Anna Sorina, who is acquainted with my friend, Mimi Laine?"

"I am."

"Then allow me to introduce myself. I am Miss Mary Dark. Miss Laine is a—hem!—a colleague of mine." I did not add that Miss Laine was in the habit of assisting me in any tasks requiring the skills of a circus-acrobat, or a cat-burglar. "What brings you to my cabin, mademoiselle? You observe that I am about to disembark."

Indeed, the view from my porthole now showed that we had steamed into the Petersburg docks, where navvies were going to and fro outside, hauling at ropes and manhandling gangways. Anna glanced towards them with a look of bewilderment. Her mouth opened, and her stiff manner softened into confusion.

"I—I really don't know how I came here!"

A shade, then, and *not* a flesh-and-blood ballerina. "I see," said I sadly. "Perhaps I might be able to assist you. What is the last thing you remember?"

She considered this with knit brow. "I remember last night's performance at the Maryinsky Theatre," she said at last. "I have a rôle as one of the swans in *Swan Lake,* so I am dancing every night. I don't remember anything that happened this morning. How strange!"

"Do you remember returning to your lodgings after the performance?"

"I don't think so."

This left me somewhat at a loss. Had Anna's shade been able to recall the circumstances of her death, the information might not only have been of great assistance to *us*—for I was, of course, anxious not to spend any more time in Russia than was absolutely necessary—but it might also have helped Anna herself to move on to a better world.

"Is there anyone who might wish you harm?" I asked her, very gently. "Have you any enemies?"

"Enemies! How could I have enemies?" She reddened. "What are you pretending to say? Why should you wish to know of my enemies?"

I took a deep breath, seeing that I might as well make a clean leaf of it. "Anna, I'm afraid that someone might have done you harm."

"What nonsense!" she said, now quite up in arms. "You can see for yourself that I'm perfectly well. Indeed I've never felt better in my life!"

"No," I said as soothingly as I could. "I imagine you haven't. You have been dancing every evening, and rehearsing every day, and yet this morning your feet are as light as air."

She frowned down at her feet, which were encased in little stiff pointe shoes.

I rose from my berth. "Come here, my dear. Take my hand."

She put her hands behind her back. "What are you saying?" Her lips were trembling; I think she felt that I was right. I think she knew what would happen if she tried to take my hand. "For God's sake, just *say* what you mean!"

"You're a shade, Anna," I said reluctantly. "I very much fear that you're dead."

"What nonsense!" she repeated, but her voice had gone high-pitched and tremulous. "Dead? How can I be dead? I'm only twenty-three!"

This was horribly awkward. "Pray don't distress yourself—"

"You tell me I'm dead, and ask me not to distress myself?"

I attempted to pat her on the shoulder, but failed. The dead appear so solid that it is often difficult to remember how intangible they truly are. "In the world to which you are going there is, I hope, a Friend who will wipe away every tear," I said. "Don't cling to this world when there is a better one waiting for you."

"I've never heard such a lot of nonsense in my life," Anna said, quite as stubbornly as myself.

"Then you don't feel an—an urge to move on?"

"I feel an urge to do *this*," she said, and had she been tangible, she would have delivered rather a spiteful little pinch to my arm. As it was, her hand passed through me, quite harmless except for the horrible little chill that accompanied it. This, it seemed, was too much even for Anna to overlook. Her eyes grew very wide indeed.

My door rattled under a salvo of blows. "Dark!" called an imperious voice—Miss Nijam, another of my confederates. "Don't dawdle about in there! It's time to go ashore!"

"All right; keep your hat on! —I truly am sorry to have been the bearer of bad tidings," I told Anna hastily, pulling on my boots and stuffing my comb and book into my valise. "I hope you can soon move on to your eternal rest. Mimi and I and our friends will see justice done, so don't be anxious. And now, I do hope you'll excuse me."

Although it meant leaving my teacup behind—with all that it contained, including the calculating intentions which Vasily had so plainly announced—I was glad to be out of the cabin, which had been close and frowsty. I was gladder still to totter onto the deck of the steamer to find myself in a blaze of May sunshine. The Petersburg docks were bright with people in gay summer apparel, and everywhere were billboards and bunting in honour of the forthcoming Imperial coronation. On the deck, my four companions awaited me near the gangway beside a pile of luggage, most of it belonging to Vasily. I have described that gentleman's attire already. Mimi Laine had produced a new summer frock in a shade of lilac that suited her pink-and-white complexion and ashy-blonde hair to perfection, and even Alphonse Schmidt, who as the Grand Duke's valet did not usually dress in a manner likely to call attention to himself, had donned a pair of light flannels. Only Miss Nijam, a statuesque beauty of Indian descent, had made no concessions to the festive mood. She wore a sensible bombazine in black, and had a black straw boater planted very squarely on her head. The effect was that of a very small thundercloud that meant to commence thundering and lightening at the first opportunity.

"Where the dickens have you been, Dark?" she said upon seeing me. "You ought to be paying attention to the time, not getting lost in that Anthony Trollope nonsense. Now we shall be caught in the crowd going through customs."

Nijam herself did not read, unless it was something with a jolly title like *Practical Chemistry* or *Metals in the Service of Man.*

"There's no harm done," Vasily said expansively. In the sunlight, his silk necktie shimmered in a self-satisfied manner as he offered his arm. "Allow me do the talking at customs; and don't forget, please, that upon this occasion I am plain Baron Dragomir Smilets."

"Oh, *slava!*" said an awed voice at my elbow. "Is that *Grand Duke Vasily Nikolaevich?* The beard and pseudonym are not going to fool anyone; I hope you know that. Oh! and there's Mimi Laine! How well she looks in that frock!"

I perceived with a sinking heart that Anna Sorina was still in our company.

# 2

# Chapter II.

Anna's alarming prediction did not, I was greatly relieved to find, come true. Vasily had no extraordinary trouble coaxing us past the Russian customs officials, although the liberal quantity of gold British sovereigns surreptitiously passed beneath the counter may have had something to do with this. Having presented the supposed Grand Duke with a sheaf of official-looking papers, we were waved towards the freedoms—such as they were—of the Russian capital.

"There!" Vasily said, as we waited for a cab. It was not the time of year for the celebrated sleighs, so the *troika* horses were hitched to carriages. "That was not so difficult as I feared. Here, Mimi; your papers."

Mimi accepted the sheaf with a scowl. "This is very troublesome, Vasya, and dangerous to all of us. You ought to have given them more gold."

"I am not *made* of sovereigns, my dear, and there may be many more bribes to pay before our business is done."

"What's the matter with Mimi's papers?" I inquired, for being unable to speak Russian, I had not been privy to the conversation at the customs booth.

"She's been issued with an internal passport," Vasily explained, "as she is the only Russian subject among the party. You know, Mimi, that this was the compromise. He very much wanted to issue *all* of us with passports."

"Well, you've been cheated," Mimi said. "Look here! *The bearer is required to register with the authorities in every city and town where she means to remain for any longer than three days.* As long as I am with you they will be able to keep a close watch on all of us. You might as well have kept your money, for all the good it did!"

"Ah! No one knows the value of a *rouble* better than Wilhelmina Laine," Anna said affectionately.

*Wilhelmina!* Well—we never truly know anyone, do we?

"Whom do you mean," Nijam asked, setting down the large trunk fitted with a pair of wheels at one end, which she had been trundling behind her, "when you say *they will be able to keep a close watch on us?*"

"Oh! the police, of course," Mimi said with a sniff, tucking the papers into her reticule. "Hullo—what's been slipped in among these? A leaflet for a monarchist organisation? *Autocracy—Orthodoxy—Nationality!* What made him think I would be interested in *that?*"

"Wait a moment—the *police?* Why should the Russian police want to watch *us?*"

"My dear Miss Nijam," Vasily said, "pray don't let it go to your head. In Russia the police watch *everybody*. They mean nothing by it, except to discourage the anarchists, and the socialists, and the suffragists."

Schmidt, having deposited Vasily's pile of luggage upon the pavement, made a sound of surprise. "Suffragists? You mean

11

they're asking for votes for women? Russia has become more liberal than I thought!"

"Ha!" Mimi cried, tearing up the leaflet, and scattering the pieces on the breeze. "No, you turnip, they're asking for any votes at *all*."

"That needn't concern us, and neither does the passport, just yet," I said brightly. "Let us hope that it will take no more than three days to complete our business here, and in the meanwhile I'm sure the police will be much too busy with the Emperor's coronation to bother about *us*."

Still, I could not help a feeling of distinct worry. Vasily was wanted by the very same police whose attention we had attracted merely by entering this country. Beyond that, what was I to make of Anna's shade? Once, in my school days, I had been taken by a well-meaning history mistress to visit a poor madwoman in a lunatic asylum, who had once been gifted like me with the ability to see the unforgotten dead. Hopeless insanity had been the result; and in the ravaged face and incoherent mutterings of the poor prisoner I had caught a glimpse of my own future. Thus far, despite all the horrors I had witnessed, I had been able to keep my wits about me. Yet for how much longer would I do so? Anna was starkly different to any other shade I yet encountered; it made no sense that she should be able to cling to this world for so very long a time. I almost thought my reason had at last begun to give way. Was Mimi's friend indeed dead—or had I led us all into peril for a figment of my own imagination?

Schmidt having at last attracted the attention of a cabman, who drew his three ponies to a halt at the curb, we addressed ourselves to the business of getting our luggage aboard. There was an awkward moment when Schmidt seized upon a valise and had his knuckles rapped for it. "Where are you going with that?" Nijam protested, snatching the bag from his hand. "This one is *mine;* yours are over there." Schmidt reddened, but relinquished the valise.

None of this was lost upon Mimi; and since one carriage was not enough to carry us, she very ably arranged matters so that Schmidt and Nijam were sent off together in the first carriage with the luggage, and Vasily was obliged to summon another. "I don't think it will help," I told Mimi in an undertone. "Nijam is very obstinate, you know."

"I can't see why she should be," Mimi said, shrugging. "What is wrong with her? Does she not have eyes?"

Miss Nijam was, of course, almost painfully conscious of Alphonse Schmidt's attractions. I did not, however, think that she had noticed that he returned her feelings with interest. "She's bound to figure it out sooner or later," said I. Then Vasily captured a carriage, thank goodness, and off we went.

We crossed many canals on our journey north towards the heart of the city, where the Winter Palace and the great fortress of Peter and Paul face each other across the sparkling expanse of the Neva. After a short trip through the poorer neighbourhoods about the docks, which appeared shockingly squalid and dirty, the city became as elegant and graceful as any I had known. It was, to my disappointment, quintessentially European. Nowhere in the city could be seen the onion-domes or red-brick ramparts one might expect from a Russian scene. Like Paris its broad and expansive streets were lined with elegant tenements, Baroque mansions, and neoclassical churches; and many of these were painted like wedding-cakes in mint-green or pastel-pink, with quantities of gold leaf and white plaster moulding. At first, especially about the train stations and the docks, there had been a quantity of traffic; but this quickly cleared up and our three ponies whisked us merrily through well-nigh abandoned streets.

"Have you ever seen it so empty, Vasya?" Mimi asked.

"Never." Vasily sighed, and I thought the sound was a little wistful. "Everyone must be in Moscow for the coronation. So much the better for *us*," he added, "for there's much less chance of my being recognised. Look over there, Miss Dark!" He pointed towards a house in yellow stucco. "That's *my* old place. It would have been confiscated after the affair at Coburg, of course. I wonder who has got it now."

The house, which in London would have put Marlborough House or Carlton House to shame, had been separated from the road by a great wall topped with spikes. "It looks like a fortress," said I. "Look at the bars on all the windows!"

"One wouldn't want a bomb dropping into one's samovar over breakfast," Vasily said with a shrug. He must have been waiting for my look of horror, for he chuckled happily when he received it. "Why, Miss Dark, surely you don't think I removed to London because I enjoyed the weather?"

I shuddered. I had been scarcely half an hour upon Russian soil, and already the place was living up to the dreadful stories I had heard in England. As our journey continued, and Vasily pointed out more of the city's landmarks—the residences of his brothers and cousins, a church endowed by one of his aunts or a fortress built by his forefathers—I could not help noticing that despite the smiling sun and the summer heat, not a window or a door stood open anywhere: everywhere were locks and bars, walls and gates, and wary, unsmiling faces. Though beautiful and superbly grand, the city was thoroughly unwelcoming.

"To hear you speak, Vasya, anyone would think you owned half the city," Mimi said, when Vasily waved towards a block of elegant flats and declared that in better days, all the inhabitants had paid their rents to him.

"Dear me, no," Vasily said with a very poor affectation of modesty. "But really, before I was obliged to leave the country, I don't think there can have been many men with a larger portfolio here in Petersburg. I fancied myself as a businessman."

"He means that people let him have their property for less than it was worth," Anna said in my ear, making me jump, "because of who he was."

"As for outside the city," Vasily went on, perfectly unconscious of our ghostly companion, "there was the estate in Moldova, and the dacha in Karelia, and the palace in Moscow, and the shooting-box in the Urals, and the little summer place in the Crimea. All gone now, of course, except for the villa at Cannes, and that's been mortgaged to the hilt. How the mighty have fallen! Once, Miss Dark, I might have given your friend Vandergriff a run for his money!"

I winced. The pursuit of the American millionaire had *not* been one of my prouder moments, and I did not like to be reminded of it.

Perhaps Mimi perceived my discomfort, for she said, "Well, Vasya, if it is such a great misfortune for you to do without your six palaces, perhaps you should go and tell the Emperor how sorry you are, and beg him nicely to give them back to you."

"That would solve a great many problems, would it not?" Vasily said, laughing softly. The rest of the journey passed in silence.

Our hotel was a long, palatial building of white-painted stone just south of the river, opposite a very fine park and an imposing cathedral in the neoclassical style. Had our travel arrangements fallen to my lot, I should have sought a more modest resting-place; but alas! I had not a word of Russian, and we were quite in Vasily's hands.

The Grand Duke's ebullience had not deserted him, despite Mimi's attempted repression. "Well, Schmidt!" he said, as that young man followed us into the hotel, fanning himself with his hat, "what do you think of my Russia?"

"Warm, sir."

No sooner had we been allotted our rooms, than I retired to mine pleading illness; and indeed the ordeal aboard the boat had left me with a sick-headache. To my annoyance, Vasily insisted upon escorting me to the door, and carrying my bag, and asking if I would like my dinner sent up to my room in an hour or so, when it was due. "Indeed I want nothing but a little quiet," I said, "and once I have rested for an hour or so I'm sure I shall be quite equal to dinner."

Not that I was likely to get much in the way of quiet, for Anna was still my constant companion. No sooner were the two of us alone, than she let out a chuckle and went pirouetting about the room, for all the world like a great, fluttering white butterfly. "Ah! Have you ever seen such luxury?" she crowed. "Look at that silk bedspread, and that lacquered screen! What it is to be a Grand Duke's dainty!"

I saw that I must correct her at once. "Oh dear, no! The Grand Duke and I are only professional acquaintances."

"Oh, is he?" she said with an arch look that I did not much like. "Well, I should very much like also to be the professional acquaintance of a Grand Duke! But I am only a ballerina, and must take what I can get."

I shuddered, remembering what Mimi had told me, that the staff of the Imperial Ballet were treated more or less as a dinner menu by the vampire princes of the empire. "You *wish* to be a Grand Duke's dainty?"

"Why not?" Anna deposited herself upon the red armchair by the window—or rather, hovered at a distance an inch or two from the cushion. "I am no great dancer; I am no Legnani or Preobrajenska. If I cannot snare a rich lover I will never get out of the chorus. I will subsist upon a pittance for the rest of my life, and be obliged to take in laundry in my old age."

At the beginning of her speech my mood had been rather censorious; but by the end of it I could not help pitying the poor creature. I knew what it was to have no respectable means of supporting myself. Nor would it be any consolation to reflect that Anna was now almost certainly dead, and would not therefore be requiring any support, respectable or not, in the near future. "I think you need not fear *that*," I said instead, pouring myself a glass of water, and hunting through my valise for an aspirin.

Hearing the words I had refrained from speaking, Anna scowled. "I'm not *dead*," she insisted. "I'll tell you what *I* think. I think this is all a very tiresome dream."

I swallowed the aspirin and thought that the dream was proving a great deal more tiresome for me than it was for her. I wondered again whether the dream was hers, or my own. Well, it could not be helped. I had embarked upon this journey on the assumption that I was sane; and I could only go on as I had begun.

17

"Well," I said, "we mean to find out if there is anything wrong; and to help you if we can. Have you any family?"

"Yes; but they're peasants in Rostov."

I had not the faintest idea where Rostov was, but from the way Anna said the name it sounded somewhat remote. "And with whom were you accustomed to spend your time in Petersburg?"

"Mostly with Oksana Yurievna, since I shared a room with her," Anna said with a shrug. "There is the rest of the corps de ballet, of course. *Particularly* Mathilde Kschessinska."

This last name she pronounced as though it ought to mean something. "I'm afraid I haven't had the pleasure," I said, fetching a pencil.

"You don't know Little K! Why, she is only the tsar's personal dainty, and one of our most celebrated dancers! *And* a particular friend of mine. But you won't find her in town. By this time she will have gone to Moscow for the coronation."

"Then we'll try to speak to Oksana. You'd better give me her address." This Anna did, and I was still attempting to get the spelling approximate when a knock came at the door. When I opened it, I found a round little man with a round little head standing outside. Although the dinner hour was near, his chin was shiny and pink, as though very recently shaven.

His mouth split into a smile that did not reach his eyes. "Welcome to our beautiful country!" he announced in heavily-accented English. "Allow me to introduce myself. I am Maksim Pavlovich, tour guide. Anything you may require in Russia I am happy to arrange for you."

My complete astonishment was relieved when Anna appeared soundlessly at my elbow and said, "Oh, this is your Okhrana man. You might as well say yes; he'll know all the best restaurants."

*My* Okhrana man? The thought was appalling. "But I don't *want* to know the best restaurants," I said, stammering a little under the exigencies of the two-sided conversation.

The secret policeman—if such he truly was—scarcely blinked at the *non sequitur.* "But what a shame!" he said. "You ought to experience our wonderful Russian hospitality. Or perhaps you like sightseeing? Shopping? I am qualified interpreter. There are many confidence men about, who will give you poor bargains. Don't risk it, eh?"

"Thank you, but really," I said, when I was able to get a word in edgewise, "I'm here on business, not pleasure, and I don't require a guide." And I shut the door very firmly in his face. Just how many confidence tricksters were currently in the city he had, I devoutly hoped, no notion. *"My* Okhrana man?" I repeated to Anna in a high-pitched whisper. "Why do *I* have the secret police on my track?"

Anna shrugged. "Why does anyone? It's easiest just to go along with it."

Seeing that the dinner hour had come, I washed up, changed my frock, and went downstairs to meet the others. The hotel restaurant was more lavish even than that at Claridge's in London, where I had once eaten a very memorable lunch in the company of Mr Vandergriff and Grand Duke Vasily. My heart sank, all the same, to see that my confederates had not been able to gather in privacy. There, lurking behind a newspaper at the very next table, was Mr Pavlovich.

I did not sit down even when Vasily got up to pull out my chair. "Do you all mind very much moving to a table further from the window?" I asked. "I still have a slight headache, and the evening light is so strong." Vasily was more than eager to oblige, and, since the restaurant was nearly empty, there was no trouble in making a migration. As he settled me at another table, with my back to the distant windows, I leaned forward and added, "Don't stare, but I think that gentleman with the newspaper has been following us."

"Well, he's certainly following us *now*," said Mimi, ignoring my instructions. With this observation Anna concurred. Indeed, within a moment or two the jovial Mr Pavlovich ambled across the room and settled himself at a new table beside our own. Up went the newspaper, and a profound silence settled across both tables.

It was Vasily who broke the silence. "I shouldn't worry about the weather if I were you," he said very coolly, with a tip of his head towards the Okhrana man. "It's unlikely to rain, and so long as we carry umbrellas, we shall have nothing to fear." This I took to mean that we ought to behave ourselves circumspectly and allow the police to continue breathing down our necks. "What are our plans for tomorrow?" he added, nodding towards myself.

"I thought Miss Laine might like to pay her friend a visit," I said, hoping that this did not give away too much as I slid the paper, with the address on it, across the table.

Mimi's eyebrows rose. "An address! Where did you find that?"

I found that I was, after all, grateful for the presence of the Okhrana man, for I did not like to confess that I was being haunted very assiduously by a shade for whose prolonged existence I could not account except by my own madness. "I don't know if it will be of any use," I said nervously, imagining how foolish I should look if the address proved to be a false lead. "As for the rest of us, someone ought to visit the school. Baron, you could no doubt gain admittance."

"I could," he said, "but my face would tell against me. *You* should do it, my dear Countess."

"Me?" I said in surprise, unsure which of us he was addressing. I had come ashore under the name of Miss Mary Angelica Dark.

"Yes, you." With that, he changed the subject, and we finished our dinner. This was excellent, although the dishes would not have been at all out of place on an English dinner-table, which disappointed me. Afterward, the others returned to their own rooms, but Vasily leaned across the table and asked if I felt well enough to take in some of the sights. Since the aspirin had done its work, I consented.

Our promenade was a short one, for we merely went across the road to the park, and looked in at the domed cathedral, which, with its pink neoclassical columns, rather resembled a smaller version of Saint Paul's in London. The interior was splendid in the Baroque manner, being richly decorated with gilded moulding, and great frescoes, and panels and ornaments of coloured marble; and Vasily said with pride that it had been built by his great-uncle, the first Emperor Alexander. I should have enjoyed it all immensely, had our stroll really been a tête-à-tête; but with Anna making a voluble third in our party, and with Mr Pavlovich never out of our sight, and a little clergyman in a cassock who first offered to take us over the building and then invited us to a lecture by someone named Prince Lvov on How to Improve the Peasant's Lot, I cannot say that I was able to do the place justice.

"Tell me about this Countess you wish me to impersonate," I asked in a low voice, when the clergyman had departed.

"Oh! that!" Vasily said. "Believe me, you will get farther in Russia as a Countess than you will as an English governess. I think you had better be French, since you speak the language almost like a native. In that guise you could quite easily gain admittance to the Ballet School; indeed there would be nothing more natural."

"I think you're going to a ridiculous amount of trouble," Anna said fretfully, "when I tell you there's nothing in the least wrong with me."

With Vasily smiling down at me, I resisted the urge to react to the spectre's protests. "Isn't that likely to make Mr Pavlovich ask awkward questions, if I suddenly begin calling myself a Countess?"

"Oh! I don't think so. People of our station adopt transparent aliases all the time, you know." We emerged from the church door. It was now about sunset; and as usual at that hour, the imprint of my father appeared, kissed my forehead, and passed on. The golden light of late afternoon had mellowed to twilight; the air cooled rapidly; and I shivered.

Vasily must have felt my shiver, for he quickly removed his coat and put it around my shoulders. It was warm and carried the sharp scent of pine that always hung about him. As he pulled the lapels close at my chin, I found that his gaze lingered upon mine, and suddenly my cheeks were as warm as the rest of me.

"You are tired, and cold," he said, slowly, as though to himself. "If you were not, we should walk about together all night, and I would show you the White Nights of Petersburg."

Feeling that this was going somewhat beyond the limits

of a merely professional relationship, I shrugged away from him and uttered a somewhat shaken laugh. "On no account! What if you were to be recognised?"

"You are right," he said, with a faintly jeering tone to his voice, to which I had become accustomed. "Imagine Vasily Nikolaevich spending the nights wandering the streets, like a poor devil of a university student with barely two kopecks to rub together! And with a governess, no less! I should never live it down."

I could not, at that moment, have said why this little speech, light with self-mockery, should have galled me so. Nor could I think of any rejoinder. Vasily smiled and took my arm, and we returned to the hotel.

# 3

# Chapter III.

I was woken from my sleep by an imperious knock at the door. There was light coming in around the edges of the curtains, which were heavy and made of velvet, and for a moment I presumed that it must be morning. But then I remembered that I was in Petersburg upon the threshold of summer, where during the White Nights of which Vasily spoke, the twilight persisted all night long. Indeed: when I peered at my watch, the hour was barely past midnight. Realising at once that there must be something wrong, I hurried from my bed and put on my slippers and nightgown.

Anna flitted to my side, a ghostly pale shape in the dim light. "It's bad," she said. "You must have slipped up. There are four Okhrana men in the passage."

When Mr Pavlovich had come to visit, Anna had taken it as a matter of course. The agitation in her voice now filled me with nameless fears. "For heaven's sake, Anna, tell me what you suspect."

"I don't know. If you're lucky, they're only here to arrest you. But it might be a liquidation."

"A liquidation!" I said faintly. I did not know what this might signify, but it sounded unpleasant. What could I do? My window was a good two storeys distant from the street. No doubt, were I Mimi, I should have no trouble in making my escape. But I had no head for heights, and I had not so much as climbed an apple-tree since I was a little girl in pinafores.

The door rattled again under the force of the knocking, and a stern voice bade me open up in the name of the Emperor. With no choice but to comply, I found myself face to face with four very stern-looking men, one of whom immediately ordered me to get dressed and accompany them.

"Wonderful Russian hospitality, my foot!" I muttered, having closed my door.

"Keep your head," Anna advised, regaining a little of her composure as I hurried into my clothing. "Mostly the Okhrana don't beat people, unless they're quite clearly revolutionaries. Just answer everything they ask you, and if they ask you to *do* anything for them, don't hesitate to comply. It's murder on your reputation if anyone finds out, of course, but the money's quite good."

My heart stood still. It took me a few tries before I could get out any words. "If they ask me to—to *do* anything for them?"

Before Anna could answer, there was renewed knocking at the door, and, consigning myself to the care of my Maker, I opened it and handed myself over to the secret police. The corridor was full of them now; I saw Vasily's door standing ajar, and men inside, searching the furniture and tossing through his clean shirts. Poor Schmidt! thought I. What a job he would have to tidy everything! And then I hoped that he would get the opportunity, for now it was clear that the whole party was to be arrested, and I still had no notion why.

Really, had I not been so absolutely terrified, I might have been ready to weep with vexation. Last month in London, having stolen away the most famous diamond in the world from under the nose of a prosthete detective, I had felt almost certain that I was to be arrested and exposed to the world's censure. Now, within hours of setting foot upon Russian soil, I *had* been arrested—and without having done the slightest thing to deserve it! It was not at all fair!

Black carriages awaited us in the street outside the hotel. The sky was a deep and dreaming purple, fading to a delicate lemon-yellow in the north. Stars spangled the heavens like diamonds. I wished I had accepted Vasily's offer, and remained out with him all night in this endless twilight. Instead, I was bundled into a windowless carriage and made to sit opposite Nijam. Two police officers joined us, and with a jolt we were trundled away.

"Nijam!" I said, grasping her hands. "Where are the others?"

"How should I know?" she replied, disengaging my grip. Nijam was never happy when her sleep had been disturbed. "I suppose they're in one of the other carriages."

"Oh, Nijam, I wish we had not come." Then one of the policeman made us to understand that we must be silent. As the carriage sped through the twilight, I felt all the more certain that we had been arrested for Vasily's sake. It was as Anna had said—his alias and beard must not have fooled anyone for a moment. Since the affair at Coburg Vasily had been a wanted man, and now we were all to pay the price of associating with him.

Our journey was not a long one, taking us north to the river

26

and then across a long, echoing bridge. At length we reached solid ground again; and after a few minutes' drive the carriage halted and we were made to alight in a very narrow cobbled alley between frowning walls of yellow stone. I did not know it at the time, but this was the famous St Peter and St Paul Fortress—an evil place, of which everyone in the city lived in fear.

We were hurried inside, and in a shadowy room with massive whitewashed walls and a ceiling of round vaults, a gentleman behind a desk took down our names. We did not see the others. Very quickly Nijam and I were parted, and I found myself in a small cell lit by one small, arched window at the end. I might have seated myself upon the bare, narrow bed, but it was already occupied by the imprint of a sadly thin and shivering prisoner. Instead I paced the room and wondered what the future might bring. I could not bring myself to believe that I would be immured in this prison very long: for our employer, Franz Haber, would not allow much time to elapse before employing his considerable wealth in retrieving us. But would he be able to help Vasily, who had done so much to make himself odious to the Russian Emperor? and in the meantime, what might happen to Nijam, and Schmidt, and Mimi, and myself? I did not think they knew of such things as Habeas Corpus here, or Trial By Jury, or Innocent Until Proven Guilty.

Anna, my constant companion, was at my side. "Sooner you than me," she observed, looking about the interior of the cell with a shudder. "What a depressing place! If you don't mind, I think I'll go and stroll by the river." So saying, she passed through the solid wall beneath the window and left me to my own devices. Happily, I had not long to wait before

27

the key rattled once again in the lock, and I was taken down a long hallway studded with cell doors, and then marched upstairs into a small office where a mustachioed gentleman sat at desk, affixing his signature with a fountain-pen to the pages of a typed document. Another desk, to the side, hosted the typist himself.

"Ah, Miss Dark," the policeman said in French, getting up and gesturing towards a seat which faced him. "Please be seated. I have a few questions for you."

He seemed affable enough, and gentlemanly. His kindly manner did much to put me at my ease, but I took my seat reminding myself not to forget that I had been dragged from my bed at midnight in order to answer those few gentlemanly questions.

At first the interrogation seemed harmless enough. I told him my name and place of birth, forgoing the fiction about the Countess, and upon which boat I had arrived in the country, and where I had been before that. I said that I had been a governess but was now employed by a Viennese nobleman in finding philanthropic causes and individuals to support; which in a way was true.

All this was noted down by the typist in shorthand; and when we were done with these questions my interlocutor stretched a little and said, "And now, Miss Dark, when were you first approached by the Finnish nationalists?"

This was the last thing I expected to hear. "I beg your pardon?"

"Just answer the question," he said encouragingly.

"But I've never been approached by Finnish nationalists," I said, laughing in spite of myself.

"You are travelling in the company of Mimi Laine, are you

not?"

Good Lord—did this nocturnal arrest have something to do with *Mimi?* "Well, yes," I said, "but our association is merely professional. We've never discussed politics at all."

The policeman clicked his tongue as though somehow disappointed in Mimi. "Did Miss Laine never tell you the circumstances under which she departed Russia?"

"She only said she had been expelled from the Imperial Ballet School for saying something in favour of Finnish independence," I said quite truthfully. "But of course in any empire such sentiments must be common among the subject peoples. I thought no more of it, and we never spoke of it again."

"My dear young lady, I disagree entirely. I don't know what it is like among your British colonies, but such sentiments are quite out of the ordinary in the great Russian Empire." I refrained from asking why, in that case, so many of the windows in Petersburg were locked and barred. "The ordinary Russian, Miss Dark," he added impressively, "is a simple soul who loves his God and his Emperor. But there are a small number of malcontents—anarchists, socialists, populists, and bigoted nationalists—to whom the very existence of Holy Russia is an insult, one which they mean to wash away in her own blood. Considering this, you cannot blame us for taking such attacks very seriously."

Could it be true? I wondered. Could Mimi *really* have been such a radical? Or did it really take little more than a grumbling allusion to the subjection of one's nation to mark one out as a bigoted nationalist and a devoted enemy of Holy Russia?

"I quite understand," I said in my most placating manner,

"but sir, you are really quite mistaken if you think that my association with Miss Laine is in any way political. I assure you that my own feelings towards your great Empire are entirely friendly."

The policeman sat back in his chair, clasped his hands, and regarded me thoughtfully. I felt that I was being weighed, very shrewdly, by someone who was not sitting in that chair by accident. I wondered whether I ought to have fetched out my handkerchief and scattered a few tears about; but before I could do more than flutter a little and look plaintive, he sat forward again and said, "Miss Dark, I want you to do something for me."

"Oh?" I asked, feeling the grasp of fear tighten about my heart. This was what Anna had warned me of!

"I want you to keep your eyes and ears open," he said, "and, if you hear anything—from Miss Laine, or anyone—that might be construed as nationalistic in sentiment, I want you to report to me at once. You will be well paid; you may be sure of that."

"Oh," I repeated, blankly. What—he meant me to spy upon my friends—to work as an agent of a foreign power? The very calm with which he made this monstrous suggestion shocked me. "Oh, sir, I couldn't possibly do that. It wouldn't be proper. I'm a British subject, you know."

"That makes no difference. It would be a secret between the two of us."

I rose from my seat, allowing all my agitation to show. Spy on my friends—put myself in the power of these people—perhaps be forced to betray Vasily, if there was any hope whatever that he had not yet been identified! "Really, I can't! Please don't ask me."

"But I do ask you. You are a guest in our country, Miss Dark, and in all civilised countries it is understood that a guest must show his host appropriate respect."

"I don't think it's appropriate at all!" I cried, and, judging the time to be ripe, permitted myself the luxury of bursting into tears. "I never heard such a thing in my life!" I wept into my handkerchief. "I wish to see the British Ambassador! Let me send a message to him at once!"

The man behind the desk watched me impassively. "I'll pass your request to my superiors," he said, when I had delivered my little speech, "but I'm afraid that unless you are willing to show your goodwill towards the Emperor in the customary way, they may not be inclined to look favourably upon your request."

With that he struck a little bell which stood upon his desk; and the interview was over.

\* \* \*

Later, I heard that Nijam had been interviewed in much the same manner. "That's ridiculous," said she, when it was suggested that she ought to spy upon her confederates. She was aware, as I was not, that the atmosphere of terror created by the Okhrana had less to do with the number of their policemen—which was not large—than it had with the number of agents whom they had recruited from among the general populace, so that they could be said to have eyes and ears everywhere. "We aren't a revolutionary cell, and there is nothing to report. It would be a complete waste both of my time and of yours."

"Not a revolutionary cell? How do you expect us to believe

31

this, given your travelling companions?"

Nijam, who had learned of the business at Coburg, had believed from the moment of the knock upon her door that Vasily was the one responsible for our predicament; but she was too cautious to admit to this. "I haven't the faintest idea to whom you refer."

The policeman shuffled through the typed papers on his desk—the transcripts, Nijam guessed, of interviews conducted with the rest of our crew. "It seems," he said mildly, "that you are travelling in the company, not only of a known Finnish nationalist, but also of the celebrated Alphonse Schmidt."

Nijam prided herself upon being able to keep a straight face under great emotional strain; and this she did now, but her hands found the edges of her chair, and gripped so tightly that her finger-nails ached from the pressure. She was grateful for the pain; it seemed to give her something to cling to.

"Alphonse Schmidt?" she asked.

The policeman rose to his feet, drew a cigar from his pocket, and lit it. "We know a great deal about Mr Schmidt," he said, drawing on his cigar with evident satisfaction. "We know, for instance, that he was present at Coburg during a certain subversive act which was carried out against a number of very highly-placed personages. We also know of certain… experiments, which he and his brother conducted with great success on that and other occasions."

Nijam closed her eyes in something akin to despair. She had always known that this day would come—that the secrets which had been buried along with Alphonse Schmidt's memory would not be permitted to fade quietly into oblivion. Sooner or later, the empires of the earth would come looking for them.

Perhaps, after all, it was a mercy that she had not succeeded in restoring that memory.

"Schmidt knows nothing of such matters," she said. "He has amnesia. These days he can barely make a salt-water solution, let alone do anything in the field of chemistry."

"You say that you are yourself a dabbler in scientific pursuits," her interlocutor said. "Perhaps *you* can help us with the information my Emperor seeks?"

"I really can't," Nijam said with finality. To all further blandishments she turned a deaf ear, and soon found herself once again in her cell.

Alone, she put both hands to her head, like a woman distracted, and began to pace from one end of the low, arched room to the other. Had she been familiar with Tennyson, she might have felt some kinship with the Lady of Shallott, when the curse had come upon her. She had always known that if Alphonse was to regain his memories, there would be a cost. His brother's experiments had never sat very well with him, and even in those days he had had a tendency to allow others the government of his own conscience. She thought that the cost was worth it; she herself had done things of which she was not proud, and still she would never desire to buy oblivion at the price of all the love she had ever known, nor the hard-won learning she had achieved. Yet she had expected to *be* there when Alphonse learned of his past: to her it would have fallen to tell him of his sins, and to explain in what ways he had already made expiation. To her, he had always been something very close to a saint, not least because of his tender conscience. And now—what if this policeman had callously informed him of past misdeeds, quite baldly,

33

without any of the extenuating circumstances?

They would never let him go, surely, if they thought they could recover the secrets which had once been in his possession. Unless—and once again, Nijam thrust her fingers through her hair, careless that it must make her appear like a madwoman. Unless she, *she,* told what she knew.

The world had never known her name. The world had never guessed the truth. The world, even now, would find it difficult to believe that a female, and a coloured one at that, should have been privy to the Schmidts' awful knowledge.

Yet Alphonse had kept no secrets from her. Even now, with a few strokes of a pencil, Nijam could release his knowledge once more upon the world…and with it, doubtless buy her own liberty, and that of the man she loved.

But at what price? Nijam had kept her secret for good reason: because such knowledge was better off forgotten, because the world would without a doubt be a better place if she and Alphonse took their secrets to the grave. What destruction, what misery, what evils would she be releasing upon the world, along with that secret? What a rod would she create for her own back? She would never again be permitted to leave Russia; she would become at once the target of every other Empire which desired to know her secret.

Nijam paced a little longer; and then, shuddering, she smoothed her hair down again, and fixed it once again into a single smooth coil at the nape of her neck. What did it matter if *she* remained in this trap, so long as Alphonse was set free of it? And what good did it do, if *she* flew this terrible place, leaving Alphonse behind her? No, it was better this way: for Alphonse would escape, perhaps never knowing the price she paid for his liberty, and certainly never knowing that she had been driven to it by the terrible burden of her love for him. He would be happy; and her misery in confinement would be nothing compared to the misery she would feel, even in liberty, knowing that she had purchased that liberty at the price of his.

One of them must disgorge the secret; and Nijam knew that it must be herself.

To this resolution she had come when the door of her cell opened. The cigar-smoking policeman stood in the doorway.

"Sir!" she began sternly. "I have something to say to you."

"As do I to you," said the policeman. "I'm delighted to inform you that you and your friends are not considered to be a threat, and therefore are free to go."

Nijam opened her mouth, and then closed it again. Almost dizzy with relief, she followed him from the room. Two minutes later, I followed my own guards into the reception-room, where I found her sitting on a wooden bench looking utterly bloodless. Schmidt bent over her, asking if she was feeling well. A moment later, Mimi joined us, and the clerk behind the desk, who had taken our names upon arrival, informed us that we were free to return to our hotel.

There was, however, one of our number missing. "But where's the Baron?" I inquired blankly.

# 4

# Chapter IV.

Schmidt must have had about the worst half-hour of his life, and I myself was filled with the most horrible misgivings, for the cigar-smoking policeman had disappeared into the shadows of the building's upper storeys, and the clerk at the desk was determined to give us no information as to Vasily's whereabouts.

"There was no Baron Smilets brought in tonight," he insisted.

"That's nonsense," Schmidt protested. "At the hotel, your men searched sir's rooms. He has certainly been arrested."

"I'm afraid I can't help you."

"Perhaps you have him under a different name," Schmidt began, desperately. At that, Mimi seized his arm, and perhaps gave it a spiteful pinch, for he broke off with an exclamation.

"Come *away*, Schmidt," she hissed. "It won't help the Baron to get yourself re-arrested for disorderly conduct."

"She's right, you know," Miss Nijam added, and between them they marched poor Alphonse out into the lane, whither I followed them all too reluctantly.

"For God's sake, calm yourself," Mimi muttered, when we were shivering beneath one of the lamp-posts which shed an ineffective light upon the twilight air. "If there's the smallest chance they don't know about Vasily already, then we mustn't enlighten them. It's as much as his life is worth."

"But what shall we *do?*" I protested, unable to keep silence any longer. "They certainly *have* him—"

"Do they?" Nijam put in. Had I not seen her a moment ago in the waiting-room looking nearly grey with shock, I might never have thought she had anything on her mind but the present mystery. "Vasily was not in *our* carriage when we were brought to the prison; was he in yours?"

Schmidt and Mimi shook their heads.

"Then they took him in a carriage of his own," I said. "They certainly searched his room at the hotel."

"Which is where *we* ought to be," Mimi put in, impatiently. "Or should we ask the commandant to step outside, the better to listen in upon all our secrets? *Come!*" And she set off at a walk nearly fast enough to be a run.

There were, of course, no cabs about, for despite the twilight it was still the dead of the night, about three or four in the morning. Moreover, as became clear when Mimi led us through an enormous open gate and across a great bridge to the southern shore of the river, we had been conducted to the heart of a massive, star-shaped fortress situated upon a small island in the Neva. Looking back at the frowning stone walls, and the golden spire rising from the cathedral at its centre, my heart nearly failed me to think that Vasily might be imprisoned there. How easy would it be for anyone in this city to vanish within—and how impossible to fetch them out again!

37

Alphonse Schmidt seemed instinctively to understand my feelings. "Take heart, Miss Dark," he said as we made our way across that long, long bridge. "We snatched the Noor-Jahan from the British Museum; surely we can rescue sir from the Peter and Paul Fortress... Why, Miss Nijam, you're shivering with cold! Let me call you a cab!"

Schmidt's attention fixed at once upon a vehicle that was approaching us, and he ran out into the road, waving his arms. Indeed; it was a *troika* cab, and within a very few minutes we were back in the warmth and comfort of our hotel, and the clerk on duty, having congratulated us upon our quick release from gaol, was desired to send a hot-water-bottle to Miss Nijam's room.

"The first order of business," Nijam whispered as we stood in the hallway preparatory to retiring, "is to find whether the Grand Duke *has* in fact been arrested."

"That will be costly, but not difficult," Mimi said, with a shrug. "There are people I know who might be able to find us information—that is, if we really need it."

"What do you mean?" Schmidt said eagerly. "Have you another lead?"

"Something like that," Mimi declared, marching down the corridor a short way, and pounding upon one of the doors. The sound made me jump; it was like a cannon going off in that quiet building.

"What are you doing?" Schmidt gasped, but Mimi held up a finger. The next moment, the door opened, and you could have knocked me out with a feather, for there in the shadows beyond, arrayed in a splendid dressing-gown of figured silk and with his hair charmingly disarranged, was the wicked Grand Duke himself.

"What a racket!" Vasily said, stifling a yawn. "For a moment I thought you were the secret police come to round me up at midnight!"

This observation, given the events of the morning, did not pass off particularly well. "Very funny, Vasya!" Mimi said, throwing the door wide open, and marching in. Vasily's room was still in a shambles from having been tossed about by the police. "I suppose you've no idea how *this* happened? No notion that the rest of us were liquidated?"

"Were you, indeed?" Vasily murmured, going a little pale. "I confess, the notion did not occur to me that this was the doing of the police."

"Explain," Nijam said, entering the room upon the heels of the rest of us, and closing the door behind.

"My dear Miss Nijam—"

"I am *not* your dear," Nijam said icily. "Explain."

Vasily looked from one to another of us, startled and (I thought) a little offended. "Very well," he said with a charming smile. "In fact, I supposed that one of *you*, having discovered my absence, must have been going through my things."

I very nearly choked upon my own indignation. "Your grace! Do you suppose that one of *us* would sink to such depths?"

"We would certainly have concealed our tracks a little better," Mimi added, scornfully. "You had better confess, Vasya, because I would *very much* like to know *exactly* who it is that set the police upon me, and how you came to have the very wonderful good luck not to have been arrested along with me!"

"Why, Mimi! You don't imagine that *I* would go to the Okhrana—of my own accord!"

"I don't know! Perhaps you thought it was worth your while. Perhaps you thought it was safer to sell me, before I could find the chance to sell *you*."

There was something ragged in her voice which told me that she, too, had been deeply shaken by the night's events. "Mimi," I said, putting an arm about her shoulders. She was quivering. "Let us have Vasily's explanation first, before we accuse him."

I confess that my relief upon finding the fugitive Grand Duke safe and sound—and free—had quite overwhelmed every other feeling. At that moment I could even have forgiven him, had he in truth betrayed us to the police. Yet feminine intuition whispered he had not.

"Very well," Vasily said with a shrug, "it is true that I had business of my own in the town, and that I slipped away after dinner to see to it."

"Without *me?*" Hitherto, Schmidt had been silent. This outburst, however, was surely justified. Vasily never went anywhere without his valet, who doubled as his bodyguard; a precaution which I could not imagine Vasily willingly forgoing in the Russian capital itself.

"My business was of a clandestine nature, I admit, but it was not with the police." Vasily shuddered. "I must have returned to the hotel only once they had departed. Had I known...*Bozhe moi*," he added, seeming suddenly to recollect something. "They did not harm you, did they? Miss Dark, for God's sake—"

"I am well," I said. My arm was still about Mimi. "I was only asked some questions. I cannot speak for the others."

"We are well," Mimi said shortly. "But you were saying?"

"As I was saying, I was absent upon business of my own.

40

But really, my friends, I am covered in shame. There was a time when the police would *never* have dared to bother the travelling companions of Vasily Nikolaevich, no matter what you were suspected of! But why *did* they suspect you?"

"They thought Mimi was a nationalist," I said.

Nijam held up a quelling hand. "Don't evade the question, your grace. If you weren't in the hotel, where *were* you?"

Vasily gave a disbelieving laugh. "I gave you my word as a gentleman I was not with the police. Of course you distrust me."

"Naturally," Mimi muttered, but Nijam said very coolly: "Since it seems clear to me that Miss Laine was identified by the customs official, I don't distrust you; but I may begin to, if you refuse to answer my reasonable questions."

"There is no great mystery," Vasily said, a trifle defensively. "I went to the house I pointed out to you, on the Nevsky Prospekt—the house that was once my own. I was looking for a French painting I used to own—Meissonier's *Musketeer*—and I thought that if I was alone it might be easier to pass myself off as an ordinary pedestrian. The picture is worth a fortune in America, and I had an idea of retrieving it."

"Of course," Mimi said bitterly. "My Annushka is dead, but you are only interested in your own pocket. I should have known!"

"Miss Dark knew of the painting," Vasily said, with an appealing look.

I was covered in remorse. For the past two weeks we had all been preoccupied with the danger to Vasily that might come from a return to Russia; and none of us had thought to ask Mimi whether there she, too, might have reasons to fear.

"I knew of the painting," I affirmed, "and if Vasily wishes to steal his own painting in his own time, I've no objection; I'm sure he'll take care not to be caught. But, Mimi, I *am* sorry. I ought to have remembered that you had been in trouble in Russia. We ought to have forged your papers, or something."

She threw off my arm. "Don't be sorry," she said gruffly. "I should have remembered what it was like here before I showed my face as Mimi Laine again." But I thought that my words consoled her, all the same.

"In the meantime," I added, "for one thing we may be grateful, at least—that the police still seem to be ignorant of the Baron's true identity. They didn't question any of *you* about him, did they?"

"No," Schmidt volunteered. "They only asked me about Miss Laine."

Nijam cleared her throat. "In fact," she said, "they also asked me about Schmidt."

"About *Schmidt?*" Vasily repeated.

"Yes," Nijam said heavily. "They know he is the brother of Stefan Schmidt."

A blank silence followed. "I don't understand," Schmidt said.

"I do," said Vasily. His lips had gone white.

Nijam turned to Schmidt. "Your brother, before his death, was Europe's foremost authority upon the topic of revivification." She hesitated. "In fact, it was he who created the revenants."

Poor Schmidt! He said nothing, but I could see that this came to him as a very great shock. He sat very suddenly in the armchair behind him. I, too, was horrified. Until two or three years previously, the gendarmerie of the Continent had been staffed by dreadful undead creatures—the revenant corpses of wretched criminals, who, having been executed in the course of justice, had thereupon been revivified by the application of some strange electrical charge and added to the ranks of the police. Mindlessly devoted to following orders, prone to going into a terrifying rage when defied, the revenants had been not only the scourge of revolutionaries and anarchists, but also the terror of ordinary citizens.

And then, one ordinary summer evening just two years previously, revenants across Europe had lost the malevolent spark which had animated them. The streets were dotted with uniformed corpses. Once the first shock was past, I think that even respectable and law-abiding people were glad to see the revenants picked up and carted away for a decent, if long-overdue, burial.

Personally, as an Englishwoman, I had always shuddered at the sight of the grisly reanimated corpses, and the blood-stained life-preservers with which they were armed. How could *Alphonse Schmidt* be in any way associated with their creation? "Impossible!" I said, shuddering.

Schmidt shuddered also. "This, then, was the reputation which proceeded me into the University College in London!"

The silence was unbearable. Even Mimi seemed horror-struck. "Oh, Schmidt," I said, "I'm sure that no matter what your brother might have done, it can have had nothing to do with *you*."

"The Okhrana do not think so," Nijam said with a sigh. "The secret passed away with Stefan Schmidt, but naturally they believe Alphonse may have been a party to his research. Of course they want to get their hands on it. If Russia was to gain revenants, it would give them an insuperable advantage, not only over their own people, but over the rest of the world as well."

Schmidt buried his face in his hands. "They *did* ask a number of questions about my scientific research, which I told them plainly I could not answer. When I told them I had lost my memories and ended up in custody on the *Akbar,* they told me I might go. But—revenants? Are you sure?"

Not even I could tell him I was not. Too plainly, the Russians would jump at the possibility of reviving the revenants, if they were given half the chance.

"Look on the bright side, my dear fellow," Vasily said. "It must have been the mention of the *Akbar* which saved you. That would have warned them not to meddle about trying to jog your memory. Your memories must have been removed by a siren, and you must have been sent to the *Akbar* on the orders of the Kabale itself—which is, or used to be at any rate, a body of the highest royalties in Europe. No, they will not harass you further without orders from the Emperor himself; and if I know my cousin Nicky, he will not be inclined to set all Europe by the ears, even to restore the revenants. All the same," he added after a moment's silence, "the police will certainly be keeping an eye on us now, and it will behove us to take care."

"Perhaps," I said slowly, "the wisest thing to do would be to leave Petersburg in the morning, and go back to Vienna."

"*You* may go home if you like," Mimi said, "but *I* have come all this way and been arrested and interrogated, and I am certainly not leaving without doing what I can for Annushka."

"Then it's settled," Vasily said, stifling a polite yawn, "and now, if you please, I'd like to snatch a little more sleep before morning."

Mimi left, and so did Nijam. Schmidt poked unhappily at some of the clothes and shaving-brushes lying about, still looking thunderstruck from Nijam's revelations, but Vasily told him to go and rest, and that he would not be wanted before noon on the following day.

With the others gone, I lingered in the doorway; I was not quite sure why, except that I was still shivering a little with the knowledge of how close Vasily had come to discovery, and I felt that every moment I could spend with him was somehow impossibly precious. "And was the painting where you left it?" I asked.

At that, his teeth flashed in a grin, and he came to lounge against the lintel, near enough that his pine-scented cologne tingled in my nostrils. "No," he said. "but I know where it is, thanks to my old housekeeper, who is still in residence. Nicky made a gift of it to the French ambassador."

"Do you mean to steal it back?"

"Why not? A painting is light, and portable, and easy to conceal," he said, shrugging. "Vandergriff said a Meissonier might be worth as much as fifteen thousand francs. With that, a man could rebuild his fortune. Wait a moment," he added, disappearing into the darkness of his room. "I found something at my house that reminded me of you."

Something that reminded him of me! Not many moments must have passed, but I was in a fever of anticipation until he returned with something small and shining in his hand. "Here," he said, opening his palm. "For you, little mouse."

And it *was* a little mouse: a beautiful, shining Fabergé trinket carved from one solid block of some translucent brown gemstone the precise colour of a mouse's fur. The tiny creature had two bright little rubies for eyes, and its tail and ears, which were studded with diamonds, must have been made out of silver, or more likely of platinum. The thing was astonishingly lifelike; one half expected it to start nibbling at whatever it held in its paws.

"Oh!" I said, enchanted. I could not help putting out a hand to touch the sleek little head, with the faint grooves that suggested fur. "Oh, I've never seen anything so beautiful."

"It ought to have been my mother's, you know." There was a note in his voice I had never heard before—soft, and I should have said vulnerable, if you can credit such a thing from Vasily Nikolaevich. "I bought it for her birthday, but she died before I could give it to her."

Words failed me. "How old were you?"

"Thirteen," he said with a pensive smile. "At least I can remember her. People said she was not beautiful, except for her fair hair, but she had a kind face, and that was all that mattered to me. Father didn't allow me to attend the funeral. So instead I held a funeral in the garden, for the mouse."

His eyes were like deep pools; and mine, perhaps, were brimming with tears for the boy he had been. I remembered the thing he had said to me, not three weeks ago on the staircase in my mother's house in Brixton: that his mother had died when he was a boy, because his vampire father had drained her blood. I did not know what to say; I did not know what to make of the fact that he had, it seemed, dug up the mouse and offered it to me. Instinctively, I glanced about for the Grand Duchess' imprint, which must surely be hovering somewhere near, summoned by these recollections; but of any such thing there was no sign at all.

"Vasily, I don't know what to say."

"Then don't say anything," he said, taking my hand as if to

46

place the mouse within.

I resisted. "But your mother's birthday gift—how can I?"

"My dear, it was languishing in a biscuit-tin under the elm-tree in the garden. I should not have gone to the trouble of unearthing it if not for you."

"But it must be worth a fortune. Really, you ought to keep it. It wouldn't be proper to accept such a gift."

"Why not? You accepted Vandergriff's pearls."

"And I wish to heaven I had not, for people thought very ill of it!"

But that only provoked him to a wicked grin. "You mean that people might think I am your lover? Perhaps you are right. Perhaps I should give you something you can wear in public. Hand it back, then, and instead I'll fetch you my mother's earrings. They are made of rubies the size of hazel-nuts, and everyone will think me the luckiest man alive."

It was at this moment that Anna's shade strolled up the hallway and remarked, "Be a sensible girl. Take the rubies, and the lover. Who cares for a little brown mouse?"

I bit my lip, caught between mortification and laughter. "Oh, very well! I'll take the little mouse, since you insist. But I will keep it safe and secret, for I'm sure that one day you will want it back, to remind you of your mother."

Indeed, I felt quite guilty as I slipped the lovely little thing into my pocket and fled back to my room. What a ridiculous gift! Surely he had only made it to tease me. I knew Vasily all too well—certainly the coincidence of the *little mouse* had been much too entertaining to ignore. If he had once been a broken-hearted little boy, that was long past: he did not even carry a clear memory of his mother with him, enough to inspire an imprint. And yet, once the door was closed and

I was alone with Anna in my room, I could not help taking the mouse out of my pocket and examining it in the glow of the electric light. It was wonderfully beautiful, not merely because of the gemstones with which it was studded, but because of the skill with which it had been carved.

"*I* should have held out for the ruby earrings," Anna observed. "So you managed to get out of the Peter and Paul Fortress! I *thought* you would very quickly do so—if you did so at all."

And *I* had thought that Anna would very quickly move on to a better world—yet here she was, once again. "I hope you had a very pleasant walk," said I, with brittle politeness.

"I did." She cast herself with a tragic air upon the counter-pane. "I walked about for hours and I don't feel a bit tired."

"Well," I said, "I'm afraid that I do. May I?"

Obligingly, Anna moved over. I hid the *little mouse* in my valise, turned out the light, and sank into my pillow with a sigh. Perhaps the presence of a shade—or a hallucination—in my bed would have given me more to think about, had it not been for the great weariness I now felt.

I was yielding gracefully to the arms of sleep when Anna gave a sound very much like a sob. I jerked to a sitting position. "Anna? Is something wrong?"

"I can't sleep," she whispered. "I've walked ever so far, and I'm not tired, and I can't sleep. I don't...I don't know what's happened to me."

"Oh," I said muzzily, lying down again. "Well, I hope that we shall know more in the morning."

Anna sniffed once or twice more. Then she said, "That Grand Duke would take you if you would have him."

Take me—perhaps, as his mistress! thought I. And then

48

discard me when it suited him, leaving me unfit for any respectable match. Good sense would absolutely forbid such a thing even if my principles did not. Well, after all that had passed between us it was in no way surprising to be told that Vasily fancied me, perhaps even preferring me to other women. For that matter, I fancied him—had done so from the very first. My life had been full of such fancies, yet I had acted upon none of them, as was right and decent. Indeed, in a way I might find it in me to fancy each of my confederates, except possibly Schmidt, for embracing him would have been a little too much like embracing a Greek statue. Even Anna was a very pretty girl, with a very graceful way of moving—yet upon such things I tried not to dwell, for it is no use tormenting oneself with what one can never have.

By the same token I ought not to torment myself with the thought of Vasily, either. He was so shockingly ineligible! and I did not for a moment imagine that he *meant* anything by what he had already described to me as *a little harmless flirtation.* Only, at this moment I began to feel that the flirtation might *not* be harmless. It would be so shockingly easy to be in love with Vasily; and who knew what folly I might not commit, if I allowed myself to do *that.* Even now I could not help feeling absurdly pleased at the look on his face when he had declared his willingness to be thought my lover. Oh, I thought, shame on you, Molly Dark, you ought never to have accepted that mouse!

It was close to noon before I awoke. Anna was a ghostly form near the window, standing upon one toe while the other one stretched elegantly towards the ceiling. When I stirred, she dropped at once to two feet and said, "At last you are awake! Mimi has gone away on business; I think she went to

49

see Oksana."

An anxious thrill went through me: what if Mimi arrived at the place and there was no Oksana? Hastening to wash and dress, I quickly joined Vasily, Schmidt, and Nijam in the restaurant downstairs, where each of them was very blearily eating what appeared to be either a late breakfast or an early lunch. Our friend, Mr Pavlovich, was installed behind his newspaper at the next table. I made sure to wish him a cheerful good-morning, to which he responded with unblushing affability.

The strength and smokiness of the Russian tea was precisely what I needed that morning; and I was beginning my second cup of it in a companionable silence when Mimi strolled in out of the glaring sunshine, looking as fresh as a daisy.

"Mimi!" I greeted her. "What news?"

"Nothing, except that my coffee tooth is aching," she announced, pulling up a chair. "What is that? Tea! Not strong enough." Vasily elbowed Schmidt, who summoned her a waiter. With the coffee duly ordered, Mimi leaned forward with a sigh, and tossed the piece of paper with Oksana's address on it onto the table before me.

"Wrong address," she said. "Or at least, no one of that name was living there."

My tea, to say nothing of the bacon and eggs it had washed down, sat suddenly very uncomfortably on my stomach.

"Anna?" I inquired under my breath.

The shade peered over my shoulder. "Well, you copied it down very badly, but that is the right address."

Doubtless something of my perturbation showed on my face, for Vasily touched my hand. "Miss Dark? Did you say something?"

"Oh," I said, forcing a smile. "No, no, not at all." What was I to tell the others? That Mimi's Annushka was behaving very oddly for a shade, and that I feared I had brought them all to Russia on what promised to be a horribly costly wild-goose chase?

"It doesn't matter, at any rate," Mimi put in, helping herself to a cold piece of toast. "Our friend may have moved house, but I have no doubt of finding her at the theatre—or at the very least, someone who can tell us where to find her."

I bit my lip, but remained silent. There was no need, quite yet, to give ourselves up for lost.

# 5

# Chapter V.

Boxes at the Maryinsky Theatre were cheap this season because anyone who was anyone had gone to Moscow for the coronation. Most of the star dancers had gone, also, the box office clerk told us, because the Moscow and Petersburg theatres would be putting on a joint gala performance for the new Tsar. Legnani was away, and so was Johanssen, and Kschessinska, and any number of other names that ran in melodiously at one ear and out the other. But a skeleton company was still putting on the new Petipa-Ivanov *Swan Lake* to a skeleton audience.

"There's almost no one here," I observed as we entered our box. There was a crowd of chattering students in the "gods" high above, and a sprinkling of well-to-do bourgeois in the stalls far below, but the boxes themselves were practically deserted. "That's good!"

"It's *necessary,* is what it is," Nijam said over the transmitter which reposed in my ear. Caring for neither music nor dance, she had elected to stay in the hotel tonight and work on some invention or other. "The fewer of Vasily's old friends get a look at him, the better."

"Put yourself at ease, Miss Nijam," said Vasily, who was also wearing a transmitter. "I'm sure that the darkness and the beard will do all that is necessary to conceal me."

"Ah!" said Anna gloomily, in my other ear. "An optimist!" This was disconcertingly close to my own thoughts.

"The boxes are always empty to begin with," said Mimi with a sniff as the great red velvet curtain rose on the ballet's first act. "It's unfashionable to be on time, you know. Hand over that opera-glass, Schmidt; the performance is beginning."

"Just don't take any foolish risks," Nijam cautioned us, "and for heaven's sake, Dark, *don't* go throwing any paper darts." With that she cut the connection, so anxious not to be bothered by the divine strains of Tchaikovsky that she did not even wait for my indignant rejoinder. Of course I would take no risks. Vasily had promised that by arriving and leaving early he would certainly avoid any old acquaintances, most of whom—with the entirety of his nearest family—were in Moscow anyway; yet I myself was not quite set at ease by his assurances. Vasily had been equally certain of his safety in London; and look how *that* had turned out.

But the lights had dimmed, and we were for the moment safe. I gave myself up to the performance. I had never seen the famous Russian ballet before, and I found myself utterly entranced. As for the story, I gathered that there was a handsome young prince who wished to shoot some birds, and later, a graceful lady who had been enchanted into a swan by a sort of swamp-monster. Abandoning crossbow and swan-shape, the two of them embarked upon a tender *pas de deux*. It was all splendidly romantic, though somewhat at odds with the handsome princes I had so far been privileged to know.

I caught my breath as the tall and elegant swan-maiden made a graceful leap and was lifted—apparently effortlessly—into the air by the prince. Both dancers' movements were impossibly strong and controlled; their costumes could not help displaying an impressive musculature. Beside me, Mimi was perched on the edge of her seat, scrutinising the stage through her opera-glasses. "Can *you* do that?" I whispered.

"If I could, do you think I would be wasting my time up here?"

"No sign of Oksana?" Vasily inquired of Mimi under his breath.

"Of course not; we've only had Act One," Mimi said as a flock of white-clad swans entered the scene, moving in dizzyingly symmetrical geometries. "I suppose she might be in Moscow for the gala, of course! That was Preobrajenska dancing Odette. How she's improved! Her knee is scarcely troubling her at all. As for the others, they're very indifferent. Poor Anna! At a performance like this she might have made her fortune!"

"That's unlikely, with so few rich lovers in the audience," said poor Anna, with a laugh. I wondered whether I was to spend the rest of my life going slowly mad in the company of a cheerfully unprincipled *danseuse*. "Oh!" Anna added, "there's Oksana!"

Mimi, who of course had not heard Anna's comment, made no sound of recognition. For a moment I tormented myself wondering if there was no such person as Oksana Yurievna, after all. But then Mimi dropped her opera-glasses and said softly, "I have her! Look, Vasily: the swan on the right, at the front."

"I see her," Vasily said, peering through the glasses. "Excellent; I shall approach her after the performance."

Presently the second act ended, and the lights went up for the intermission. Throughout the performance thus far it had been possible to see doors opening in the boxes up and down the theatre, and ladies and gentlemen entering to take their seats. When the lights went up, I saw with some relief that they were in large part prosperous-looking bourgeois: others beside ourselves had had the notion of engaging boxes while all the great people were away in Moscow.

Yet, latest of all, just as the theatre welled with light, a lady entered the box exactly opposite. She cut a dashing figure indeed against the white and gold of the box, for she was dressed in a gown of black velvet; which, however, was softened by a softly draping shawl collar of white satin, as well as golden appliqués of lilies and a great many strings of pearls. As for the rest of her, her hair was caught up into clouds of black curls at her forehead, and her young, softly rounded face was held proudly aloft upon a long white neck. I was unable to stifle a sound of admiration; and Vasily, beside me, turned from the stage to catch a glimpse of the one other undeniable aristocrat present.

For just a moment the Grand Duke was still; and then, with a casually unobtrusive gesture, he removed his transmitter from his ear.

"A change of plans is advisable, I think," he murmured. "Here, Miss Dark; look after this, will you? Come, Mimi; let us pay Oksana Yurievna a visit—now—at once."

Was this, then, another of Vasily's former acquaintances? It stood to reason that if Vasily was obliged to flee an old friend, it would of course be one of the most elegantly beautiful creatures I had ever laid eyes upon.

"Who is that lady? Do you know her?" I asked, at the same moment that Mimi protested, "In the middle of the performance? Vasya, it's impossible."

"Nothing is impossible, given sufficient amounts of money," said Vasily. "Come, Mimi, if you wish me to do the thing at all, you had better let me do it now. Unless you fancy having Schmidt arrange a tryst with a ballerina, while I pay my own visit to St Peter and St Paul."

At this suggestion Nijam's Alphonse turned upon us all a look of such horror that not even Mimi could insist. "Very well," she said with a scowl, "come along, then."

I had solemnly promised Nijam to throw no paper darts; nor did I mean to, of course. But as Vasily brushed past me, the demon of mischief seemed quite strongly to take hold of me; and switching on the transmitter which Vasily had given me for safekeeping, I dropped it very adroitly into his coat pocket. I am quite sure that under the circumstances *you* would have done the same, dear reader; for I was in a fever of impatience to learn what Oksana Yurievna had to tell us about Anna. In addition, it seemed only sensible to remain in communication with Vasily, when at any moment he might run into someone who knew him!

The door closed. In my seat beside Schmidt, I laced my fingers together, listening to all the sounds that fill a theatre during intermission. Around the theatre, people were leaving their boxes to visit others. The lady in black velvet had twisted around to speak to someone behind her, and nothing could be seen of her face. There was a hum of pulleys and wheels from behind the red curtain masking the stage. From my transmitter, there came a brisk sound of footsteps, and of doors opening and closing. Presently I heard Mimi say, her voice a little muffled, "I'll help you to question her, but it's your task to get her alone. She won't throw up a performance for an old school-mate."

Schmidt, who could also hear this, touched his ear. "Mimi," he said in a low voice, "you're transmitting."

Mimi, of course, did not answer. "That's Vasily's transmitter; Mimi must have switched hers off," I confessed. "I slipped it into his pocket in case something goes wrong and he needs you. For heaven's sake keep your voice down, or he'll know."

Schmidt looked first shocked, and then conflicted, and at last resigned. I reassured myself that in the interests of Vasily's safety, my inquisitiveness was justified even in Schmidt's eyes. In some quiet corner, Vasily must have been putting on the dentures, and the false lenses, which gave him the appearance of a vampire Grand Duke: "How do I look?" he asked Mimi.

"Like a very pretty bloodsucker!" she replied, which was rather impolite of her. "Look, there's our woman. Try not to let anyone else get too clear a look at you."

I heard a sound of milling and chattering, and imagined some cramped backstage area full of girls in fluttering white dresses. After a moment, rather nearer and clearer, I heard a gasp: I imagined Vasily pulling Oksana Yurievna behind a pillar or a bit of scenery.

"My dear, I'm Vasily Nikolaevich," he said in French, the language of the imperial court. "Why don't you invite me home with you?"

Oksana Yurievna hardly seemed perturbed by this. "I can't leave just yet, your grace. But if you'll be quick about it, there's a quiet corner over there, and I can ask my friend Lydia to see that we aren't disturbed."

Schmidt very carefully did not look at me, but his ears had gone red as fire, and he fumbled in his haste to switch off his own transmitter. I, however, felt rather sorry than embarrassed. What a tawdry exchange! Pity the man who could make such a bloodless request, and the woman who could so bloodlessly accept!

"I'm not the man to gnaw on a woman in a corner," Vasily said, with a lazy note of amusement in his voice that might have made me contemplate murder, were I less in command of myself. "And whether it's business or pleasure, I prefer to linger. Call your understudy and tell her you've been taken ill. I'll make it well worth your while."

Oksana considered this a moment before muttering her consent. "All right, but be sure you do."

I touched Schmidt's shoulder. "Come on," I whispered. "She's taking him home."

We emerged from the box to find ourselves face to face with the lady in black velvet, who was trailing a retinue of black silk hats and scarlet uniforms down the corridor behind her. *"Bonne nuit, mon ami,"* she greeted us with a childishly breathless eagerness. "I beg your pardon, but the gentleman who was sitting in your box just now—was that by any chance Grand Duke Vasily Nikolaevich?"

At her words, my blood absolutely congealed in my veins. Schmidt looked at me in abject panic; I did not know whether he spoke much French, but he could not have missed the name. Seized by terror, I said the first words that came into my head. "Er—I'm terribly sorry," said I in German, "I don't speak Spanish." And then I grasped Schmidt's hand and rushed away, leaving the lady and her retinue in a cloud of confusion behind us.

Outside the theatre—which, like so many of the buildings in Petersburg, resembled nothing so much as a great round wedding-cake in white and mint and gold—Mimi awaited us by the carriage. "Where is Vasily?" I asked, momentarily alarmed to see her alone.

"He's taking a *troika*," she said, pointing behind her. Indeed, there was the Grand Duke's familiar figure, handing the ballerina into a cab.

"Oh, thank goodness," I said, nearly ready to sob with relief. "That woman in the black velvet recognised him at once, Mimi, and very nearly caught us as we were trying to leave. Follow the *troika*, Schmidt!"

"Trust Vasily to fall afoul of a woman!" Mimi said scornfully, as we dashed away on Vasily's trail. "He will need to be more careful after this."

"With any luck she'll go to Moscow and the coast will be clear," I suggested.

"With Vasily's luck, she will stay here in Petersburg and make life much too interesting," Mimi responded.

The drive was a short one, and silent in both carriages. We crossed the river to what proved to be a small island in the Neva river's delta, which was much built up with old and shabby tenements. In a dark and narrow street the *troika* came to a halt, and Oksana led Vasily in at a door; their footsteps echoed in a stairwell, and after a short time, Oksana's key rattled in her lock.

"Which of the Grand Dukes are you?" she asked, still in French. "I thought I had seen most of you."

"Oh, I have been living abroad for some years. My father is Nicholas Nikolaevich the elder, and my brother is Nicholas Nikolaevich the younger."

"Ah, you are the exile." Oksana's door creaked open. "Enter, then."

The door closed again, sealing them in together. In the carriage, I put up a hand to adjust the transmitter, and Mimi's eyes narrowed at me. "Are you *listening?* How—"

"Hush," I said, holding up my hand. "He's about to start questioning her." Or so I very devoutly hoped.

"Turn it off, Dark," Mimi said, very wearily, but kindly. "You won't hear anything to his advantage, I'm afraid."

"She's right," Anna put in. "Turn it off, you goose."

But if I turned it off, then I would always wonder, and I had much rather know the worst about Vasily than torment myself with wondering. Besides, the less I liked Vasily, the better for both of us!

In the rustling quiet of Oksana's flat, Vasily asked, "Do you live alone?"

"Yes, and no one will disturb us. Do you want vodka?"

"Thank you, but I prefer cognac."

"Well, I don't have any of that." There was a clink as the lip of the bottle touched the glass, and a slosh of the spirits into the cup, and a gulp as the woman tossed them back. "Here are the rules: you pay for my time, and if you want a feed, that's extra, because I won't be able to dance for as long as it takes me to recover."

Vasily cleared his throat in a gentle, deprecating sort of way. "My dear, I'm afraid you seem to be labouring under a misunderstanding. I'm not here to buy anything more than a little information."

"What?" The glass slammed on some hard surface. "You aren't...you said you wanted me to invite you home!"

"For a little chat, as I said. Don't pretend to be disappointed,"

Vasily added, with that sly amusement that so often made me dream of putting something unpleasant in his tea. "You've drunk a quantity of very bad vodka, and that is hardly the action of a woman pining for my embrace."

"You," Oksana said thickly. No doubt she was about ready to break the vodka bottle over his head. "All right, then. I'll give you a taste of my blood free of charge."

"I very much regret, my dear, that circumstances forbid it."

*"Bozhe moi,"* she said, and I heard the clink of the bottle again, and then something like a scuffle. "Give that back! *Slava!* You drag me away from my performance on the one week of the year I might show to some advantage and make a little more money—and now you won't even bite me? If they find out I walked off with a man halfway through a performance, I'll be thrown off the stage!"

"There's no reason in the world why they should find *that* out, if you'll answer my questions like a good girl," Vasily said, and I gasped, seeing how neatly he had turned poor Oksana's reproaches into a knife to hold to her throat.

A dead silence followed, broken only by the ballerina's quick, angry breathing. "Dark," Mimi warned me again.

"Hush," I said. "It's nothing. She's angry he won't bite her; that's all."

Mimi's fingers went to the high neck of her dress, which hid the scars on her own skin. "That's why I made him wear the dentures," she said; but there was a note of regret in her voice. The ballerinas of the Maryinsky vied with each other to catch the eye of the vampire princes of the land; not just because a Grand Ducal lover promised wealth and comfort, but also because their bite would increase a dancer's strength and agility, and with it her fame.

61

From the transmitter there was a sound like a marble rolling across a tabletop.

"That, my dear," Vasily said pleasantly, "is a spinel ruby worth quite enough to start you in a new life, should that become necessary, or to smooth your path in this one. There will be another for you when you've answered my questions; and now, tell me what you know about Anna Sorina."

"Anna Sorina?" Oksana repeated, her voice wary.

"I understand that until recently you shared a room, for instance. Is that true?"

Again, there was a long silence. At last, Oksana said lifelessly, "I know nothing about Anna Sorina. You had best take your ruby and go."

"Sorina is dead," Vasily said. "Are you quite sure you know nothing? Whoever did it ought to be brought to justice."

Oksana only laughed derisively. "I'm sorry. If you don't know what happened to Anna, you won't learn from me."

Despite her words, there was a tremble in her voice, and I understood perfectly what she must feel. Oksana was frightened—frightened at having invited this duplicitous stranger into her home, frightened to answer his question, despairing of how to satisfy him when there was nothing she could do to make him leave against his will.

Perhaps she was afraid—but to me her fear was like life itself: for if Oksana was afraid, then something had certainly happened to Anna, for why else should she fear?

*Something* had certainly happened to Anna; and my mind, after all, was not playing tricks on me.

In the carriage, Mimi made a sound of disgust, and I realised that she must have been listening in, too. "This is hopeless. She will never speak to a Grand Duke. Perhaps I should go up."

"Let me," I told her. Anna was still sitting beside me in the carriage. "I can do better."

I darted into the tenement, which was as squalid as anything I had seen in London or Vienna, and dashed up the first flight of stairs. Beyond, a hallway of closed doors greeted me. Anna, whom no door or wall could bar, fleeted in at one door and then out at a second. "This one," she told me.

I knocked, seized the doorknob, and stumbled in upon a very unprepossessing apartment, dark and mildewed. Its occupant had evidently been to some pains to make it look nice, however, for there was a small African violet on the windowsill and the armchair beside it had been draped with an old scarf to cover up the places where the upholstery had worn through. Oksana—dark-haired and sinewy—stood by the table with an angry flush in her pale cheeks.

Vasily turned when I entered. For a moment he beheld me with absolute stupefaction; and then, although it is too much to say that he blushed, his face certainly darkened with wrath.

"Eavesdropping, my little mouse?" he inquired, with menacing softness. "But how?"

"I can explain," I said, in my most winsome manner. "Miss Yurievna—"

"Who are *you?*" the ballerina demanded, her lip trembling.

"Molly Dark," I said, putting out my hand. "I'm so sorry for your spoiled performance. Anna sent us, you know. She said she roomed with you, before…"

"Anna sent you?" Oksana whispered. Her eyes grew very wide, and then she broke down completely into tears. "Then she is alive, after all!"

"If you tell her I'm dead I shall never speak to you again,"

Anna said, severely, as I put a comforting arm around the sobbing ballerina. I was tempted to take Anna at her word, for I did not much care to have her haunting me for the rest of her days. But, poor Oksana! She had had a *very* trying evening.

"That's what we hope to discover," I said soothingly. "Don't be afraid: anything you tell us will be as safe as houses. Just sit down and tell us what you know."

Oksana fished a handkerchief from her pocket and blew her nose. "The Grand Duke won't like it," she said, with a distrustful glare at Vasily.

Vasily at that moment was not looking particularly trustworthy, for he uttered an exclamation of outrage as he fished the guilty transmitter from his coat pocket. All the air seemed to flee the room as his brows knitted together and he gave us a very sharp-toothed smile.

"Proceed, my dear Oksana Yurievna. It isn't *your* murder I wish to commit tonight." With that he leaned forward, his hand caressing my cheek, his blood-red gaze fixed upon mine. "Anon, my love," he said; and with that his clever fingers tripped the switch of my own transmitter, so that it would broadcast anything spoken within the room. The next moment he turned and left the apartment.

I found myself short of breath and comprehensively flushed. Oksana and Anna stared at me.

"Ah," said Oksana. "All becomes clear."

Feeling extremely foolish, I cleared my throat. "Go on, then. Tell me about Anna."

Oksana slumped into her battered armchair and pillowed her chin on her drawn-up knees. "You are not familiar with the workings of the Maryinsky ballet?"

"Not at all, I'm afraid."

"Very well. Then the first thing you should know about is the contract which binds us here."

Oksana explained how young dancers, once enrolled in the Imperial Ballet School by hopeful parents or wealthy sponsors, entered upon a life of strictly defined limits. Female students at the school were kept in almost nun-like seclusion, prohibited even from mixing with the male students. Upon graduation, unless they were dismissed sooner, they would enter the corps de ballet at the Maryinsky under a twenty-year contract. The terms of this provided that a dancer would become eligible for a pitifully small pension at the end of twenty years; but woe betide the dancer who departed the company, married, or bore a child before those twenty years had passed. Even if she served her twenty years in perfect obedience, a ballerina often had few prospects for her declining years unless she had been lucky enough to catch the eye of a rich lover or an imperial monster. Then, and only then, she might amass sufficient fortune to carry her through the years of her retirement in comfort; and it was this, said Oksana, that Anna had attempted to do.

"That's why she was toadying to Mathilde Kschessinska," Oksana said dolefully. Anna gave a muttered protest. "You know Kschessinska, of course? The Emperor's dainty? She is under the protection of some other grand duke now. But it's still the case that you are more likely to meet with rich men if Kschessinska takes a liking to you. That was Anna's undoing. She *did* catch the eye of a man; of a Grand Duke, in fact."

"I *did?*" Anna said, startled. "What a stroke of luck! Who was it?"

I thought of Vasily as he had appeared tonight, with

lengthened canine teeth and blood-red gaze; I thought of his brother Nikolasha, whom I had met once, briefly, in Vienna. I could not think that a chance meeting with such a man could be described as in any way lucky.

"That night, before the performance, Kschessinska asked Anna to go fetch something from her dressing-room," Oksana said slowly. She took another sip from the glass of vodka on the table, as though she did not like to go on. "The Grand Duke left her there in the passage, bleeding all over the floor. There was a terrible uproar, and the director sacked her that very evening. Anna ran out of the theatre, still bleeding, and that is the last anyone heard of her. I was on stage; I only learned of it after, but by that time it was too late. I haven't seen Anna since."

Anna herself did not say a word, but when I glanced up at her I saw a look of sickened horror upon her face.

The transmitter crackled in my ear and Vasily spoke in a low growl. "His name?"

"Do you know which Grand Duke it was?" I asked.

Oksana's lips pinched together and drew down, a look of utter distress. "Your friend, the Grand Duke—"

"Vasily won't hurt you," I promised. "We already know it was a Grand Duke; you might as well tell us which one."

Oksana passed a hand over her eyes with a curiously despairing gesture. "It was Grand Duke Nicholas Nikolaevich," she whispered. "The elder one, the father."

# 6

# Chapter VI.

"Nicholas Nikolaevich? *That* old goat?" Anna wailed.

Mimi, on the transmitter, was more philosophical. "I can't say I'm surprised," she said with a sniff. But from Vasily I did not hear a word. When I had thanked Oksana for her confidences, and once again assured her of our discretion, I found the Grand Duke standing in the corridor outside the door in an attitude of the most profound absorption, his arms crossed and his chin sunk upon his breast. I had to touch his arm before he looked up and saw me. Then he darted me a look that made my heart quail, for his eyes were all red and bloodied with the lenses Nijam had made to give him the appearance of a vampire, and his teeth had curled back in a mirthless smile from his elongated teeth. For a moment the scent of pine which always hung about him seemed less fresh and invigorating, than it was cold and obliterating, something a monster might draw about himself to conceal the stench of blood...

I drew my hand back as though it had burned. "I beg your pardon!"

"For what?" Vasily asked. That dreadful smile did not falter, and his voice was low and full of some emotion which was difficult to identify.

I did not quite know, myself, how to answer. Did I beg his pardon for disturbing his reverie; or for implicating his father in a horrible crime; or for eavesdropping upon him?

I was still hesitating when, uncrossing his arms, Vasily gave an elaborate bow and extended his arm. Vasily, I found, had a dreadful habit of pretending not to be in the least perturbed when he very clearly *was,* and I could not help feeling that I was walking downstairs arm-in-arm with a ticking bomb. Nevertheless, I had very clear and recent memories of a similar occasion upon which it had served me well to play along to Vasily's moods; and I had reason, too, to trust him better than I once had.

We returned to the carriage, and Schmidt drove us back to the hotel, but no one had much to say. Vasily's brooding mood hung over us like a cloud and prohibited any easy conversation. At the hotel, he wrenched the transmitter from his ear and went at once, soft-footed and intent, to his room. He had barely disappeared when Nijam popped out of her own room in a cloud of peppermint scent, wearing the intricate pair of spectacles, with its shades and dials and magnifiers, low on the bridge of her nose. "What news?" she asked.

"We have identified our culprit," I informed her, "and it's Vasily's father. He's taking it hard, I think."

Mimi emerged from her room holding an empty bowl. "Where are my peppermints?" she demanded, thrusting the bowl under Nijam's nose. "I know you've taken them; I can smell them on your breath!"

Nijam regarded the ballerina scornfully. "Then how do you propose I should give them back? Just wait for the hotel to replenish the bowl, Mimi."

"But you can't have *eaten* them all."

Nijam thrust a grimy hand into her pocket and came out with a handful of empty papers. "Well, it appears that I have. Oh, no; there's one left."

"Don't worry, Miss Laine, you can have mine," said Schmidt.

"As a matter of fact, I believe this *is* one of Schmidt's. And since we're keeping such close accounts of whose peppermint is whose—there, Schmidt; have it back, with my compliments." Having tucked it into the breast-pocket of the astonished Alphonse's coat, Nijam withdrew, closing the door behind her.

Could it be? Was Nijam learning to *flirt*?

With a sound of disgust, Mimi flounced away into her room. Schmidt retrieved the peppermint with a look of bewilderment.

"Good-night, Schmidt," I said rather wearily, for the evening's events had left me feeling quite wrung out, and the previous night had not been a restful one. Any further talk could wait until morning. In my room, which was also quite devoid of peppermints—what a busy evening Nijam must have had!—I found Anna lying across my bed staring sightlessly at the ceiling.

"Are you well?" I asked her gently, for the interview with Oksana could not have been a comfortable one.

Anna released a sigh. "Nicholas Nikolaevich! Why could it not have been a *young* one?"

This startled me. "You don't object to being savagely attacked, so long as it is by a young man?"

"Of course I object," Anna said scornfully, sitting up. "But of course one wishes to be bitten! What ballerina does not? When I awake I will be a great dancer. And perhaps the Grand Duke will like to see me again. It looks as though my fortune will be made...only I wish it had not been a stupid old satyr."

She left me quite at a loss for words, for how could she still hope to live, or to resign herself to a life with the man who had done these terrible things to her? "You do not remember any of what happened that night?"

"Not a bit. If I did not know that Oksana was my friend I should imagine that she was jealous."

Perhaps for Anna this was still only a tale that had happened to someone else. And how could I judge her? Was I so very different—I, who had been all too willing to marry Griff for his money, despite many warning signs?

"Don't get your hopes up," I said, as gently as I could. "Mimi has been vampire-bitten, too. But she has yet to become a second Legnani."

An eventful evening it had been; but of one thing I could now be quite certain. I was not going mad, like the poor woman in the Hanwell Asylum; Anna's shade was real. Greatly relieved, I relinquished my other worries—Anna, Vasily—to the morrow.

We held council the following morning after breakfast in Mimi's room—which, despite its cramped size, at least offered us sanctuary from the watchful gaze of Mr Pavlovich. Nijam uttered a triumphant cry as she entered the room.

"There!" she said. "I knew that more peppermints would be along in a moment."

"Don't touch!" Mimi said, rapping Nijam's knuckles. "Those are *my* peppermints. Schmidt went out this morning and bought them for me."

"Oh! *Did* he?" Nijam exclaimed. I noticed that she was careful not to glance in Schmidt's direction, but a little colour rose in her cheeks; my heart bled for her.

Schmidt swallowed and spoke gruffly. "I—er, I bought these for you, Miss Nijam." He thrust a brown paper bag towards her.

Nijam sniffed. "Pray don't concern yourself with me."

"No, but I bought them especially for you. I don't care for peppermints, anyway."

Nijam darted him a look of great suspicion. I stifled my laughter. Evidently Schmidt was telling a polite untruth; and she knew it perhaps better than he did himself. Rather than confess to the closeness of their former relationship, however, she accepted the bag and was soon consoling herself with the contents. I observed with delight that a woman of Nijam's severe beauty and forbidding demeanour does indeed lose some of her awesome divinity with a peppermint making a bulge in one cheek.

"Are you all quite finished?" Vasily demanded, entering the room. Although he did not look as though he had slept very soundly, the thunderous atmosphere that hung about him had certainly dissipated since yesterday.

"Peppermints, forsooth," I agreed. "What are we going to do about Anna?"

"Wait," Anna objected, for my ears alone. "I don't like the sound of this. *What* are you going to do about me?"

Vasily waved a dismissive hand. "Anna is dead and nothing more can be done for her. The great necessity is to bring home my father's crimes, and to put him beyond any possibility of repeating them. We must expose what he has done."

"What good will *that* do me?" Anna protested. "If you expose him, I'll have nothing to threaten him with! I ought to be able to get a handsome settlement, at least!'

"I agree with Vasily," I said, to the room at last. "A settlement is useless to a dead woman."

"But I'm not dead!"

"You don't *know* that," I retorted. My confederates beheld me with startled faces; and I realised that I had said the words aloud.

The others knew, of course, that the dead appeared to me; and so far they, unlike Miss Mackintosh at St Alphege's Seminary for Young Ladies, had never insinuated that an ability to see these apparitions might be the sign of an infirm mind. All the same, I was not quite sure how to explain to them that for a short time I had almost been afraid that I was going mad—or how to confess that I had concealed this from them. Nijam, for instance, had only recently admitted that perhaps I *did* see ghosts; and I did not like to push her faith in me any further by confessing that a certain class of them spoke to me—still less to admit that I had no explanation for Anna's peculiar refusal to move on.

"I mean," I added, perspiring a little, "that—ah—we don't know for certain what became of Anna. Oughtn't we to investigate a little further?"

Vasily shrugged. "For what reason? We know that she is dead, and we know that it is my father who did the deed—as he did it to my mother. Leave the dead; our business has always been with the living."

"I wash my hands of you all," Anna said, departing by way of the wall.

"But surely that would mean going to Moscow," Nijam

objected, "and for you, Vasily, that would be the height of folly."

"Indeed," I said earnestly. "Perhaps you don't know it, your grace, but you were recognised at the theatre by that dark lady in the golden lilies."

Vasily paled, but remained resolute. "It's a risk I am willing to run."

"Nijam is right," Mimi put in. "It's too dangerous if Vasily is with us. He should return to Austria."

"I'll be damned if I do that," he snarled, and although the sharp fangs had been laid aside, he managed to make quite a terrifying display of his own teeth. "There is a blow that must be struck, and no hand but *mine* shall strike it."

"That is precisely why you ought to stay out of it," said Nijam dispassionately. "This is a job for clear heads."

That stopped whatever Vasily had been about to say; and after a moment he stalked towards the credenza, where a bottle of cognac and some glasses stood beside the bowl of peppermints. Pouring himself a dram or two of the liquor, he drained it at one gulp and then turned to face us, once again the perfect gentleman.

It was very good; just like a play.

"My dear—that is, my estimable Miss Nijam," he said, as smooth as silk. "I perfectly agree with you. Certainly, if I am to be so easily recognised, it is out of the question that I should show my face in Moscow. However, it is quite impossible for you to do the thing alone. I am a Grand Duke. I have the advantage of knowing these people; of understanding their hopes and fears. I alone can instruct you on how and where to approach them. Really, you had best accept all the help I can give. I shall of course remain absolutely hidden for the duration of our visit to the city. But do not, I beg you, attempt to do the thing without me. Better to do nothing at all."

To this Nijam made no answer, for of course Vasily was correct. Without him, we should be all at sea in royal society. He might be of great assistance.

"If Vas—if his grace remains hidden," said I slowly, "and if Nijam takes over the planning, then I think it may work; but it's quite true that it would be the height of folly to go to Moscow without him. Think of how we would have fared at the Schloss Frohsdorf without him! And these people are— well, are monsters, if you'll pardon my language."

Nijam scowled. "I don't like it," she said. "But I suppose we must do *something* about Anna. Very well, then; let us all go."

Vasily looked so delighted that I wondered whether after all I had made a mistake. "Excellent!" he said, rubbing his hands. "And in the meantime I will amuse myself with thinking how to retrieve that French painting. I'm told it was sent to Moscow for the ambassador's coronation ball."

"You can amuse yourself however you like, so long as you do as you have promised, and remain hidden," said Nijam severely. Then there was a conversation about train tickets to Moscow. Mimi said that she would go to buy the tickets, as she was the only one of the party besides Vasily who spoke Russian. Schmidt, gallant as ever, offered to accompany her. At that moment Nijam, with whom the peppermints had evidently rankled, declared that she, too, would be glad for a walk. Thus the three of them set out together; and Vasily and I found ourselves alone together.

"Don't leave," I told him. "I'll order tea."

"Are you keeping an eye on me?" he inquired, throwing himself into the armchair by the window. There was a small occasional-table to one side of it, and another armchair, positioned tête-à-tête.

"I thought you would enjoy the company," said I, ringing for the tea. This was not long in coming, in a very pretty silver samovar. Vasily sat watching me with a furrow between his brows as I poured out the faintly smoky brew. "I ought to apologise," I told him at length, sliding the teacup across the table, "for listening in on you last night. I know you are angry with me."

"Indeed, my dear, you are mistaken." He took a sip of the tea and replaced the cup on its saucer. "I have nothing to hide. You know very well what sort of man I am."

I did not believe him for a moment. "I seem to recall you threatening me with murder," I teased, unable to help myself.

His brows rose, and I thought that despite himself, he was trying not to laugh. "On the contrary, little mouse, I quite plainly stated that I would *not* murder Oksana. I do not see what there may have been in those words to make *you* fear for your life."

I knew where I stood now: he was ashamed of what I had heard, and he did not mind confessing to it, so long as he could make a joke of it. Vasily is a complicated man, and one who hides himself behind a great deal of armour. Already the air seemed clearer between us; and perhaps I could have left well alone. Instead, perhaps daring, I said, "I ought to warn you that I have chosen to trust you. Not very far, I admit; but far enough not to take any such threats very seriously."

For a long moment, the room seemed to hold its breath. Then Vasily put his teacup on the table and looked at me from beneath heavy-lidded eyes, almost purring: "I warn you, Miss Dark, this flattery will get you nowhere. What is it you want from me?"

"Perhaps a little more honesty," I said, propping my chin on my hands. Something had been niggling at me for some days, and I meant to have it out with him. "Why the painting, your grace?"

"*Your grace?* You were calling me Vasily a little while ago."

"Yes, but that's not quite proper, is it?"

"We have already established your inclinations to be a deal less proper than generally thought."

"Yet still I behave with propriety, *your grace*," I fenced. "We have already one very dangerous game to play; why add theft to our troubles?"

He observed me with an indulgent smile. "Perhaps I'll tell you one day, little mouse. But there's a very specific reason I want that painting."

"To sell it—for the money. *That* much I know. But are you in such straits? Isn't Herr Haber paying us enough?"

He took another sip of tea before replying. "Money isn't merely comfort, my dear. It's also power. Perhaps, one day, it would mean enough power that I should no longer fear to show my face in the land of my birth. Can you imagine what it is like, to live one's entire life at the pinnacle of all earthly power, and then to lose it all at a stroke? There is a price on my head; a target on my back. The vultures are circling, and I cannot even protect my nearest friends. I've nearly lost Schmidt twice already—and you."

Perhaps Nijam was right, I thought. Perhaps too many of Vasily's hopes rode upon this expedition.

"Do you know," he went on, more confiding, "that I was once very friendly with my Cousin Nicky, who is now the tsar? It was the old Emperor who stopped my income, confiscated my property, and set the secret police on me. But Nicky is not his father, any more than I am mine. There was something brutal and iron-willed about the old Emperor, but Nicky is the kindest, gentlest soul in the world. Indeed I am sorry for him, for he has about as much idea as a baby might of how to go about ruling an empire. Still, this is a moment of opportunity for Russia. With Nicky on the throne, we might chart a new course."

I had never seen Vasily more unguarded, more in earnest. Indeed, thought I, he really did believe in his young cousin—love him, even. "Still, even the Emperor is a vampire, is he not?" said I. "I heard that he had a dainty among the ballerinas."

"Now, where did you hear that, I wonder? No matter," he added, before I could think of a persuasive lie. "It is true, but that affair was all over before Nicky married. And his wife Alix is at heart an Englishwoman, and the English have a passion for democracy. You may think that I have led a charmed life, my dear, and I suppose that I have; but I have also been among the people, and have heard them complain of their monstrous rulers, who maintain their bloody thrones through a labyrinth of arbitrary ministries. I can see what others among my family cannot: that without a relaxing of the autocracy, and some reform of the government according to merit rather than birth, there will certainly come a bloody reckoning. But Nicky is, as I say, gentle and innocent—a baby. There are members of the family who will do their best to keep him on the old paths."

My heart misgave me; why, I could not quite say.

For a moment Vasily beheld his teacup in silence, before giving me his sweetest smile. "What if I should have the opportunity to see Nicky? I might tell him some of what I have learned."

"Vasily!" I said reproachfully. My heart had not led me astray. "You *promised* to stay hidden!"

"I'll do anything you like so long as you call me by my name," he said, leaning forward with a smile. "Moreover I shall do nothing without your consent—but Nicky will not hand me over to the police himself; he's too much of a gentleman. And consider what good it might do all of us if I were able to patch things up between us. Surely it would be worthwhile, if only to have him call off his policemen."

I bit my lip, not knowing how to express my conviction that if Vasily and the young Emperor really *had* been such excellent friends, then surely Nicky ought already to have called off the aforesaid policemen. But there! I had never been an Emperor myself, and I did not know what a great number of things might be clamouring for my attention if I were.

Perhaps Vasily's plan might succeed. And what then? I recalled the way he had behaved ever since we first set foot in this splendid city—the lost wealth and power of which he had boasted, his insistence upon attending the theatre despite the risk, his determination to recover at least the painting from among his lost possessions. There was evidently a part of him that yet hungered for what he had lost… I had come indeed to trust this man; at the supreme moment, he had resisted the temptation to betray me. Yet it is hard for the leopard to change his spots! Perhaps even now he might see in this visit an opportunity to restore his lost fortunes; perhaps temptation would come to him disguised as an opportunity to do his friends, and his country, some real good.

"I suppose," I said, trying to mask doubt behind jocularity, "that it would not hurt if Nicky were to go the whole way, and restore your property and incomes."

"If Nicky were to do such a thing, my dear, I should at once lay it all at your feet." He said this with such drollery that I could not help laughing; I felt all at once that my worries had been ridiculous.

"I'm grateful for your confidences," I said, with a lighter heart. "But we have other confederates, too. Don't they get a say?"

"That depends," he said, with a glint in his green eyes. "Don't you mean to tell *me* what invisible spirit you were addressing, earlier?"

My heart stopped quite still. Oh, I ought to have known better than to hope that such a false step would be overlooked!

Seeing my reluctance, Vasily gave a bittersweet smile. "Trust cuts both ways, little mouse," he said; and with that he arose from the armchair and departed the room.

Frowning, I poured myself another cup of tea. Had I not shown that I *did* trust him? The interview, which had begun so well, left me feeling peculiarly dissatisfied. Once again, I found myself brooding over Vasily's confessions. If he *did* regain Nicky's confidence, and with it the fortunes he had lost, then what time would he have for his former friends?

With an effort, I dismissed these worries. I meant to trust Vasily—and if we were to brave the dangers of Moscow, trust was an absolute necessity.

# 7

# Chapter VII.

"As I understand it, you are Vasily Nikolaevich."— "Yes."— "And the Emperor is Nicholas—"

"Alexandrovich."

"Very well; but you call him Nicky. And then there is your brother, Nikolasha."

"Nicholas Nikolaevich the younger."

"So called to distinguish him from your father, Nicholas Nikolaevich the elder."

"There! You have it."

"I do *not* have it at all!" I cried. "Where does it all end? What other Nicholases am I to meet?"

Vasily laughed. "Only my cousins Nicholas Constanti-novich and Nicholas Mikhailovich—but the last will give you no trouble, for everybody calls him 'Bimbo.'"

"That," I said despairingly, "makes it no better at all. I don't know how you tell anyone apart."

"Oh, but you're only getting started," Mimi put in wryly. "There are Michael Alexandrovich and Alexander

Mikhailovich, and you had better not get those two confused because one of them is second in line to the Imperial throne. Also there are Sergei Mikhailovich and Sergei Alexandrovich, and you had better not get *them* confused because one of them is a passionate liberal and the other is a rigid conservative."

"I have great faith in Miss Dark's abilities," said Vasily with a laugh. Ever since the conversation over the samovar on the previous morning, Vasily had seemed in high spirits. Today, those spirits only seemed to rise with every revolution of the train's wheels as we were carried closer to Moscow.

My own spirits were also high, for I was almost certain that we had got away from Petersburg without the attendance of the assiduous Mr Pavlovich. Although the train was crowded with passengers—for weeks there must have been a general migration towards the ancient capital, which still served to stage the great ceremony of the tsar's crowning—Mimi had secured us a whole first-class compartment to ourselves, thanks to our numbers. It had all the usual first-class amenities, such as gold leaf, shining wood panelling, and comfortable brocaded upholstery, into the crevices of which someone had managed to secrete a little pamphlet into the cushions, titled *Young Russia.* I was charmed to observe that in addition to these, the compartment also contained a little pot-bellied stove together with a coal-scuttle to sit beside it. Both of these were, of course, empty; for the weather was very hot and sultry. We had opened the windows a little to encourage the movement of the air; yet the heat made all of us a little sleepy and careless. Nijam, having lost track of *The Practical Electrician* or whatever delightful tome she had brought with her, had been reduced to asking me for assistance, and was now actually more than halfway through

81

the first volume of *Can You Forgive Her?*

"Be quiet," she said now, adjusting her steel-rimmed pince-nez more securely upon her nose. "I want to read."

"I thought you didn't like novels," I said.

"I don't particularly," she said, turning another page, "but as I must suffer, I prefer to do so in peace."

A silence, as requested, followed. Mimi opened *Young Russia* and was soon lost within the pages.

"There's something I ought to tell you all," I said, before I could lose my nerve. My conversation with Vasily had weighed upon my mind, and I needed to get the thing off my chest. "If I've seemed a little distracted lately, it's because Anna's shade has been speaking to me."

Nijam gave me a look narrowed with annoyance. "You informed me that the imprints do not speak. *Only memories,* you said."

"That's so," I confessed, "but there is another class of ghosts as well, the shades of the recently dead, which are more than mere memories. Only they do not usually remain in the world for so long after their death, so I did not know what to think of this one—at least, not until we found Oksana to corroborate Anna's story."

"You didn't *believe* me?" Anna protested.

"You didn't know what to *think* of her?" Nijam echoed, almost at the same instant.

"I may see ghosts," I said defensively, "but I don't blindly put my trust in passing strangers."

"It rather seems that you blindly followed this one to the unfriendliest place on earth," Nijam said. "Mimi, you knew the real Anna. You ought to be able to test this one's identity somehow."

Mimi frowned a moment in thought. "Ah! Ask her what is the name of the boy who picked up her handkerchief the night we had our first rôles in *Cinderella*."

Anna responded with indignation. "Ah," said I. "She says she has no intention of answering such an impertinent question, Wilhelmina Laine."

Schmidt, who had been sitting by the window, frowned. *"Wilhelmina?"*

Mimi sniffed. "All right, all right, that *is* Anna," she declared. "She never *did* tell me his name."

"In that case I have no objections to her joining us," Nijam declared. "What is that incredulous look, Dark? I may believe that you see ghosts, but I haven't abandoned logic *entirely*."

With that she went back to her novel. I risked a glance at Vasily, who sat opposite and had listened to all this without comment. "Gracefully managed," he murmured.

I felt my cheeks warm at his words. Well: it was as he said—trust cut both ways.

"Listen to this, Vasya" Mimi told us, waving *Young Russia*. *"Soon, very soon, the day will come when we shall move against the Winter Palace to exterminate all its inhabitants. It may be that it will be sufficient to kill only the imperial family; that is, about a hundred people..."*

"That's very handsome!" Vasily said, with a laugh, but it was a trifle forced, and he was the only one of us who smiled.

*"...but it is more likely that the whole imperial party will rise as one man behind the Tsar, because for them it will be a matter of life and death. If this should happen, then with faith in ourselves and our strength, we shall raise the battle-cry: 'To your axes!' and we shall kill the imperial party with no more mercy than they show for us now. We shall kill them in the squares, if the dirty swine*

*ever dare to appear there; kill them in their houses; kill them in the narrow streets of the towns; kill them in the avenues of the capitals; kill them in the villages.* Are you paying attention, Vasya?"

He flicked a dismissive hand. "That diatribe was written thirty years ago or more—in the days of the second Alexander."

"Then what's it doing tucked into a first-class compartment in the days of the second Nicholas?" Mimi asked, and none of us had an answer to that. All I could think was that I hoped never to be compelled to witness so much death; it would be ten times worse than even the great Vienna cemetery had been.

In due course, as the sun descended towards the west from which we had come, we arrived at the Moscow train-station. We did not alight at once, preferring to hurry Vasily from the train only once the press of people had somewhat dissipated. This, perhaps, was unwise, for as we alighted from the carriage and started towards the gate leading onto the street, a sweet, musical young voice rang out in delight.

"Vasily Nikolaevich, as I live!"

It would not be too much to say that this spread panic in our ranks. Vasily came to a dead halt, and I nearly stumbled against him. Schmidt nearly dropped the luggage he carried. Nijam, who was trundling her great trunk behind her, prodded me in the back. "Keep walking!" she hissed. "Whoever she is, we mustn't recognise her!"

To this suggestion Vasily paid no attention, instead turning to face the person who had thus accosted him. It was, I saw, none other than the dark-haired beauty from the Maryinsky Theatre. This morning she once again wore black, but this time it was a crisp day dress in taffeta silk, patterned with red-and-green poppies, and opening at the front to display a shirtwaist in arsenic-green taffeta. The frills at each shoulder waved gracefully in the breeze as she hurried across the platform and seized Vasily by the elbows, beaming.

"Vaska!" she cried breathlessly. "Oh! I *knew* it was you the other night, when I saw you at the theatre! Let me kiss you!" As she leaned up to imprint a kiss first upon one cheek, then the other, I had the impression that he was drawing himself up very tall to complicate the business. So did she, for she offered him a charming pout and said chidingly, "What is this? Are you not happy to see me?"

"Ever enchanted," he said with an added measure of his own silken charm, "but, my dear, you must know that I have come *incognito,* and cannot have my name bandied about in a public place!"

"Oh, forgive me!" The young girl—or lady, for in the light of day I saw that she must be at least my own age—pressed gloved fingers to her lips, but she was laughing all the same. "What a scatterbrain I am! I had quite forgotten that you are not on the best of terms with the family. But how you've changed these past eight years!" To my horror, she absolutely pinched his cheek. "You could not deceive *me* with that beard, but I will swear no one else will know you. Won't you introduce me to your friends?"

Vasily's friends, for their part, had been absolutely dumb-struck by this most inopportune turn of events. Nijam regarded the newcomer with chill hostility. Schmidt had slipped a hand under his coat, where I knew he kept his salt-water bulbs; but he looked doubtful as to whether this would be the correct course of action. Although he had with great ability defended his master from revolver-brandishing

85

secret policemen and from bloodthirsty werewolves, a cheek-pinching young socialite was quite beyond either his abilities or his experience. As for Mimi, a scowl had settled upon her face, and she looked as though she might be about to say something we would all regret. Anxious to forestall her, I sailed forward, extending my hand to the lady.

"You must forgive our friend," said I, wielding my most dimpled smile, and the impressive title which Vasily had concocted for me: "The sight of you has overcome him, I think. I am Marie-Angelique, Countess Dubois de la Motte."

"*Enchantée,*" the girl replied at once, taking my hand and kissing my cheek. "Any friend of Vaska's is a friend of mine. I am Princess Zlata Obrenovicha. Has he indeed told you nothing about me? Why, at one time we were to be man and wife, before Vaska took it into his head to run away as far as London!"

Had an anarchist chosen this particular moment to touch off a bomb beneath my very feet I could not have been more astonished. This, then, was Vasily's former betrothed? For some moments the only thought running through my head was the memory of the words he had once spoken to me in a mood of savage fun—*I've never been even slightly interested in princesses.* For heaven's sake, why? Was the man *blind?* Certainly she must have been dreadfully young—-seventeen or so—when the match was arranged, but such disparities are barely thought of among royalties. I sent Vasily a speechless glance, and found that he had gone as white as paper.

"A word with you, madame," Vasily said, seizing the princess by the elbow, and whisking her into the shadows between a newspaper-kiosk and a slender white Corinthian pillar. I followed. For one thing, it was only proper to supply the lady with a chaperone. For another, I had a powerful curiosity to satisfy, and this morning I had not taken the precaution of slipping a transmitter into Vasily's pocket.

"Listen, my dear," Vasily said in tones of silken savagery that I quite objected to when they were being addressed to another, "I wish you to know that I'm quite serious. I cannot have my presence in Moscow generally known, and I must beg you to keep it a secret."

"You *beg* me?" Playfully, Princess Zlata tapped the end of his nose. "You are not begging very *well*, Vaska. Should I perhaps have my revenge upon you for the trick you played, running all the way to London when you ought to have married me? You know that Sergei Alexandrovich is my godfather, and he is the governor-general here in Moscow. If I speak to him—"

"Tell me," Vasily interrupted, in the very soft tones with which he signalled great displeasure, "precisely what you want of me."

She cast me a pouting look. "I am a widow now. My life is a lonely one." There was a long, suggestive silence. "Come to have dinner with me tomorrow night."

"I cannot go into society," Vasily said.

"This doesn't count as going into society," Zlata declared. "No one will be there but you and me, and the Montenegro sisters, who are quite harmless, and your father and Niko-lasha…"

Vasily seemed incapable of speech. "It is very kind of you," I said hurriedly, recalling with a shudder how very close to death I had come, one cold winter's night at the hands of Nikolasha's men in Vienna, "but indeed I believe we have a prior engagement."

"Sergei Alexandrovich was *so* unhappy with you for running

away," Zlata said to Vasily, with a look that would not have melted butter. "It's only a dinner-party. That never killed anyone—and you might reconcile yourself with your family. Ah, Vaska! You don't know how much you've been missed! I am sure that if you only showed yourself frankly…"

"You will sign my death warrant," Vasily said; yet there was that in his voice which told me he was tempted. His eyes met mine, and a wordless exchange passed between us. Zlata evidently did not mean to let him maintain his incognito; all our plans had been exploded the moment she recognised him at the Maryinsky. Now we were committed to the game, and our plans must alter with circumstances. I felt as I had once or twice before this moment, when stepping from the familiar into the unknown, and staking everything upon one wild gamble; I felt as I had the night Vasily and I had gone to steal the Noor-Jahan, or the moment at which I had chosen to follow Marie-Caroline's ghost to Vienna. The exhilaration of terror buoyed me up; and I bowed my head slightly to Vasily.

"I will come," he told Zlata, *"with* the Countess. She has remarkable gifts; I think the Montenegrins will like to meet her."

"Oh!" Zlata said, beholding me with an expression I found somewhat calculating. "A Spiritualist, is she?"

"Some would call me a medium," I said. I am not, of course, a Spiritualist. Being well acquainted with the fact that the dead are generally incapable of offering guidance to the living, being more concerned with affairs of their own, I cannot but regard Spiritualists as charlatans. Yet, if Vasily was volunteering my presence, there must already be some plan revolving in his fertile mind. I wondered for how long it had been there.

Zlata pouted. "Very well—bring her if you must. Tomorrow night, then, at my house on the Tverskoy Boulevard. Don't forget, Vaska!"

She kissed him on the cheek again and skipped away, signalling to her maidservant and to the porter with the towering trolley full of luggage, who had followed in her wake.

Vasily and I glanced at each other. "I will explain," he said, "but not here."

"Indeed not," I agreed, but could not help asking, "Is it true that you fled the country to avoid marrying her?"

"My dear, I told you I have never been interested in princesses."

"What caprice! Surely princesses are the same as other women."

Vasily sent me a serious look. "She pinched my cheek. Are you coming?"

I was not quite sure he was not laughing at me. Nevertheless, I found myself biting my lip and thinking that it served him right. Before I could think better of the thing, I reached up solemnly and tweaked his cheek.

He caught my wrist, still far too much in earnest. "Moreover, she calls me *Vaska,*" he said, with a look of ineffable distaste. "A name one would give a house-cat! Why are you laughing?"

"Because it suits you," I told him. "You are *exactly* like a house-cat."

"I am a tiger," he said, attempting a snarl. I shrugged, and we returned to the others in a silence that was to all appearances perfectly amicable. Once the warmth of my teasing passed off, however, I was astonished to discover that my thoughts

DARK & STORMY

were far from any semblance of calm. I upbraided myself
for my own agitation. But of course Vasily must have had
matrimonial prospects before. Of course, stationed as he
was in the world, his prospects must have been royal and
brilliant. Of course a young woman brought up as Princess
Zlata had been, with the best that money could buy in the way
of hairdressers and dressmakers and millinery, etiquette and
deportment masters and governesses, would be an utterly
exquisite and charming sight. I did not understand why
Vasily should have fled his country and, apparently, displeased
his powerful family in order to escape such a charming girl.
Beside her, I must appear shabby, awkward, and Amazonian.
Of course this was all to the good, if it prevented his *harmless
flirtation,* as he had once referred to it, from progressing
any further. Still, a girl *does* like to know that she shows
to advantage, especially in the company of a man like Vasily.

Only Schmidt awaited us on the platform, weighed down
with luggage. The others had gone to engage cabs, and
in one of these we were soon being driven towards our
lodgings. This time Nijam had insisted upon more modest
accommodations, and Vasily had telegraphed ahead to an
agent, who had secured the Baron Smilets and his party a
cramped attic in a genteel-shabby tenement along Tverskaya
Street. There were two cramped bedrooms at either end of
the attic, together with a sitting-room and a glass door onto
a narrow balcony; and the landlady would send up meals if
requested. It was horribly hot and stuffy, and not entirely
free of imprints; but we counted ourselves fortunate to have
found anything suitable at all in the ancient Russian capital,
which was as busy as Petersburg had been empty. Every street
was full of people and carriages; every window was gay with

90

the red, white, and blue flags of the nation; and every surface had been decorated with commemorative portraits of the young Emperor and his wife.

Schmidt soon had the windows open, and when our landlady brought up a hot samovar, the room began to feel a little more like home. Madame Kapanadzy was a tough-looking old lady in black, with a red scarf about her head, who told us not to mind the rowdy noises coming from the other half of the attic, as it was only a study circle of Populists. "How picturesque these Russians look!" I said, when she had withdrawn.

"She's no more Russian than you or I," Mimi said, in tones of indignation. "I suppose you thought Oksana was Russian, too."

Vasily sent me a droll look, and I felt sure that I had blundered into one of Mimi's hobbyhorses.

"I apologise," I said meekly. "She seemed quite familiar with the language."

"Of course she's familiar with the language. All of us are! Everywhere the Empire reaches, we're forbidden to use our native tongues, for fear we should ever remember who we were. To answer your question, Kapanadzy is a Georgian name, and Oksana is from the Ukraine."

I could perhaps imagine how this might be a sore point: it was not so very long since my own nation had attempted to stamp out the Scots tongue, for much the same reason. It was a shock to learn that such policies were still being quite openly practiced in Russia.

"I beg your pardon," I said, chastened. "And where is Princess Zlata from, pray tell?" I added, turning upon Vasily— partly to change the subject, but mainly because it was high time he fulfilled his promise of an explanation.

"Oho, so that's who she was!" Mimi said. "The two of you seemed very well acquainted, Vasya."

"I think his grace had better tell us everything at once," Nijam said. She had taken a seat in the armchair and now placed the tips of her fingers together with a rather judicial air. "I trust that for the moment we are safe from being arrested a second time, though I can't say the same for our neighbours…" (the Populists next door had begun a somewhat inebriated rendition of the *Marseillaise)* "…but I warn you that if I am not satisfied with your explanation I will be departing this city by the next train, and if the others have a spark of common sense they'll be accompanying me."

"At least I shall have my faithful Schmidt with me," said Vasily, accepting a teacup from my hands.

"Alphonse Schmidt is the *last* person who should remain in this country a moment longer than necessary," Nijam said. Schmidt opened his mouth to say something, but Nijam waved an autocratic hand, unwittingly silencing him. "Proceed."

Vasily took a deep breath. "Zlata is the daughter of King Milan of Serbia. There was a time at which the lady was my affianced bride. You understand that my family was most anxious that the match should be settled. I was most anxious that it should *not* be, and therefore I decamped with some haste to Paris, and thence to London."

Nijam raised her eyebrows. "A moment. What made your family so anxious for the match?"

"Ah!" Vasily said. "The Serbs are a brother nation. To Imperial Russia, as the great mother, belongs the duty of watching over all nations of the Slavs."

Mimi snorted. "A self-appointed duty, and one of dubious benefits."

"Wasn't Serbia until quite recently a province of the Austrian Empire?" Nijam pointed out.

"Indeed she was." Vasily scowled. "Of course we took that as a slap in the face. Serbia is *ours.* King Milan, you understand, was a selfish, fickle man who did not understand these things. But his wife—ah! the lovely Natalia was raised in Petersburg. She and my cousin Sergei Alexandrovich convinced the King to betroth his daughter to a Grand Duke. Not even King Milan would refuse such an exalted match, and the thing would bind him more closely to Imperial Russia, forbidding any return to Austria. It would have been an excellent thing, indeed—had I not been the most eligible Romanov of the summer." He broke off and brooded over his teacup. "My Emperor informed me of the great service I might render him. He assured me that I would become enamoured of my bride upon better acquaintance, but as I have said, I did not care to know the lady any better than I already did."

"In other words," said Nijam, raising a finely arched eyebrow, "you were at odds with your family long before the events at Coburg."

"As I have said, I was not in London for the clemency of its weather," Vasily said. "I succeeded in restoring myself to the old Emperor's good graces by dint of acting as his— er—agent in London. My cousin Sergei never forgave me for fleeing a marriage to his goddaughter. Queen Natalia was outraged. As for Zlata, as a consolation prize she was married off to some cadet of the family so far removed from the succession that he was not even a Grand Duke. I gather he is now deceased. In fact, Princess Zlata is yet another of the women I have betrayed."

"Yes, Vasya, we know that you are the scandal of Christendom," Mimi said, rolling her eyes. "If you want our sympathy, you might try confessing to some of your *real* crimes."

To my surprise—for I, too, had thought him only angling for sympathy—Vasily became more serious. "Was it no real crime, to abandon my brother Slavs to the Austrians?"

"Brother Slavs!" Mimi said with scorn. "If the Serbs don't want to be part of the Austrian empire, what makes you think they're so eager to be part of *yours?* Have you ever *met* any Serbs, apart from ones raised in Petersburg?"

Nijam cleared her throat. "The *real* question is, now that Princess Zlata has recognised you, how much trouble are we in? Is she likely to drain your blood? What was wrong with her, that you refused to marry her? Might she not be blackmailed into remaining silent?"

"She was not to my taste, and as far as I know she never did make the change. Princesses often do not, you know, until they are married; and since Zlata did not marry a Grand Duke, she would scarcely have been permitted to become a vampire afterward. No: we must rule out blackmail, but I am hopeful that she may be bribed. She was most anxious that I should join her tomorrow night for a dinner party with my father and brothers—"

"A *dinner party?*" Schmidt burst out; and indeed spoken out loud in that way, the thing sounded absolutely preposterous. Schmidt reddened at Vasily's haughty glance, and his voice became pleading. "With *vampires?* Sir, is this wise?"

"Nikolasha tried to arrest you *twice* in Vienna," I said with feeling. "Perhaps you have forgotten it. Centuries would not serve to dim *my* memory."

"*Bozhe moi,*" Anna put in. "I might not be dead, but you people will be soon. And this is all the help I am given!"

"Anna agrees with me!" I proclaimed. There was no point in transmitting the balance of the shade's remarks.

Nijam's eyes narrowed upon Vasily. "You are not in any way perturbed by all this, your grace?"

Truly Vasily did not seem in the least discomfited. He bestowed upon us all his most ingratiating smile. "Let us be honest with each other—"

"No speech begun in this way is ever honest," Mimi muttered, "particularly when the speaker is Vasily Nikolaevich."

Vasily coughed gently. "Let us," he amended, "*try* to be honest with each other. The cat is out of the bag. The princess knows I am in Moscow. The task before us, then, is to manage the consequences in such a way that they shall turn to our advantage. Perhaps this unfortunate occurrence could even *help* us with the job at hand."

Mimi gave a scornful laugh. "Indeed! It is all tremendously convenient, is it not?"

I, who knew something of Vasily's ambitions in Russia, might have found it tempting to suspect him of having engineered the—*unfortunate occurrence*—for his own purposes. But no—I had promised myself not to think ill of Vasily, if I could at all help it. Only I *did* wish I could rid my thoughts of the image which possessed them, of Vasily having wormed his way back into imperial favour, living here like the prince he was—and at his side a neat, modish, adorable little person in black velvet, very like the Serbian princess!

"Truly, Mimi," I said, "I cannot believe that his grace would have chosen *this* means of revealing his presence in Moscow."

Vasily regarded me with surprise. "My dear! I am touched!

Indeed, Mimi, she is correct."

"Still, oughtn't we to go away?" I added. "We might take the train back to Petersburg, and be in Königsberg in a day or two. Herr Haber will understand. You recall how earnestly he begged us not to expose ourselves to any unnecessary risk."

"In London we agreed that we must risk monsters," Vasily said with a wave of his hand. "This may be for the best. It is our goal to unmask the misdeeds of my father. Who better to perform that office than his son? If you and I should attend this dinner party, my dear, we may quickly gather all the information necessary to complete our task."

"But my dear Vaska, how do you propose we escape being arrested upon the spot?"

"My dear Mary Angelica, nothing could be simpler." He rubbed his hands with evident relish. "Picture the scene! I shall enter Zlata's drawing-room in red eyes and false fangs— and with a lovely French countess upon my arm. The last time my brother Nikolasha saw me, I was reduced to tearing out the throat of his myrmidon using these pitiful excuses for teeth. We have ample proof that the royalties of the world are desperate by any means to regain what they lost at Coburg, and now it will seem that I have done so. My recovery will astonish them. Not one of them will harm a hair of my head. On the other hand," he added, "if I attempt to leave Moscow now, Zlata will almost certainly run at once to her godfather— my cousin Sergei, who is governor-general here—and I shall be at once snatched up, with no chance of displaying my prosthetic teeth."

I wondered if my cheeks had paled, for I felt my skin congeal to ice. Indeed, it was better by far that Vasily should surprise his family with an apparent recovery, than that he should be swept up in one of the Okhrana's "liquidations".

"What do you think, Nijam?" I asked in a low voice. "It's horribly risky, but—"

"The Grand Duke has a point," Nijam said coolly. "The Emperor can't have Vasily quietly disappeared if the whole of Europe thinks that he's got a cure for defanging. The trouble will come afterward, when the whole of Europe tries to get the cure, which of course we cannot supply." She brooded on this for a moment. "Well, it's good for one thing, at least."

"And what is that?" I asked.

"It will distract attention from Schmidt. One rumour of a cure for defanging will drive all thought of the revenants out of their heads. I vote we do it."

# 8

# Chapter VIII.

The following day was almost offensively tranquil, given our state of painful anticipation. At about midday, Mimi went out to register her presence in Moscow with the authorities, and did not return for some hours. When she did, she explained her absence by planting a large covered basket upon the table at my elbow. "For tonight," she said, before going into her own room to take off her hat.

Curious, I reached into the basket and drew out a splendid gown in white satin. It had a slim, column-like silhouette with all the fulness of the skirt pleated into a train at the back, and was finished off with a pair of enormous sleeve puffs. It also came with a sash and fan, and a pair of white satin heels to complete the ensemble. "Mimi," I gasped. "I couldn't possibly—Where *did* you find this?"

"Fell off the back of a cart," Mimi called from her bedroom. I gathered that this was all the explanation for which I could hope.

Vasily got up and prowled over to me, inspecting the somewhat rumpled grandeur with approval. "This will suit you exceedingly well," he said. "Well picked out, Mimi!"

Later, once the dress had been ironed and Mimi had assisted me into it, Vasily paced over to join me at the mirror. "Permit me a finishing touch," he said, bringing out a necklace composed of several strands of sparkling gems. I recognised it at once; Vasily had had the bauble made up out of Nijam's faux diamonds. Even now it flashed brilliantly in the gaslight as he carefully pinned one end to my right shoulder, and the other—very deftly, so that not once did his ungloved fingers brush my skin—to the centre of my décolletage. "There," he said. I gazed into the mirror and found myself looking into the eyes of one who appeared in truth noble enough to be a countess. The gown, newly ironed, crisp and sculptural, with its slight pigeon-breast waist, suited my tall figure to perfection. Against that stark background, the diamonds asymmetrically festooning my bodice provided the essential finishing touch.

I caught my breath.

"There! that suits you *much* better than the frippery you normally wear," said Mimi approvingly. "Lace is too delicate for someone your size. What? I am only giving you a little useful information."

"Someone died in your bedroom, and his imprint is still bleeding on the rug. There's a little useful information for *you*," I retorted. "Thank you, Vasily; I should never have thought of the necklace."

"Just don't lose it," Nijam said with crushing practicality, from the table where under Schmidt's wistful gaze she was measuring out doses of suspicious-looking powders.

Vasily stood at my shoulder, gazing through the looking-glass into my eyes. I found myself regarding him with almost as much awe as I had myself, for although he wore quite a correct tailcoat and white tie, he had chosen one in a deliriously rich shade of dark blue. Instead of a gardenia in his buttonhole, he had pinned a flower made of pearls, diamonds, and sapphires to the lapel. More precious stones twinkled on his fingers, and above the fangs that glinted slightly between his parted lips, he had donned a pair of smoked glasses to conceal the redness of his eyes. The shameless display of wealth, the fastidious taste displayed in everything he wore, and the supreme impudence with which he carried it off, all contributed to an air of decadence so very far from English taste and English modesty that I did not quite know whether to be shocked or thrilled.

Vasily smiled, showing off more tooth. "Perfection," he said to the vision within the mirror, as much to himself as to me. Indeed, never before had I seen him so pleased with himself.

By the time we alighted from our cab and ascended the steps of Princess Zlata's house—an impressive neoclassical façade in white stone—Vasily was practically swaggering. Since the crowded traffic and the near-impossibility of securing a cab had delayed us, the butler showed us in at once to the dining-room. This was a long, parqueted apartment blazing with electric light which reflected from a dozen mirrors; there were a row of splendidly curtained windows and before each window stood a golden vase nearly as tall as me, crammed with immense hot-house dahlias in pink and orange and red.

The long table was filled with people, and the room with the hum of conversation. As faces turned to behold us, all conversation ceased; I caught the flash of the light on diamonds, on fangs, on blood-red eyes. For a moment I felt nearly suffocated, as the hot and scented room seemed to be closing in on me. Beside me, Vasily stopped dead, and I felt his arm press mine a little more tightly to his side.

Princess Zlata had promised an intimate family gathering; and we had walked into a nest of vampires.

"Best to brazen it out," Vasily murmured, and that steadied me. I had faced the melusines of Schloss Frohsdorf; surely I could face the vampires of Imperial Russia.

"Upon my soul, it's Vasily Nikolaevich!" said one of the dinner guests. I recognised Nikolasha, Vasily's brother, who had come so close to killing me in Vienna.

"Vaska!" cried Zlata, getting up at once from her seat at the head of the table, and running to kiss his cheeks. Once again clad in a magnificent black gown, it was perhaps comforting to see that her eyes were black and sparkling, and her mouth was furnished with teeth, not fangs. She pulled Vasily towards the table with some difficulty, for I would not relinquish his arm. "Look, my dears!" she said, clapping her hands with girlish excitement. "Did I not tell you I had a surprise for you? Now, I beg you all to remember that I am not blessed with the same advantages as your Royal Highnesses, and I hope that you will conduct yourselves like the little gentlemen—and ladies—that you are. Birds in their nests agree! Oh, and this lady is the celebrated medium, the Countess Marie-Angelique Dubois de la Motte. Perhaps if we are *very* good she will give us a reading later, in the drawing-room, as a treat?"

With these last words Zlata sent me an appealing smile, clasping her little hands. I was proud of how steady my voice sounded when I replied: "How could I refuse?" It was, after all, for this purpose that I had come.

I was not the only person in the room whom events had struck speechless: some of Zlata's guests were absolutely gaping at us over their wineglasses. One of them, a very pretty young girl with large blue eyes and quantities of fair hair all frizzled over her forehead, was the first to recover. "Vasily Nikolaevich, my dear!" she said, putting out her hand. "Forgive me for observing that you seem to have recovered well from your recent—er—indisposition!"

"My dear Missy," he responded, raising her hand to his lips, "surely you don't think I would have defanged myself for good! Tell me, is the Crown Prince of Roumania in good health?"

I did not quite hear her reply: it was my second shock in as many minutes. I grappled with the revelation that this fair girl, so sweet and so English in her manners, was in fact the vengeful Princess Marie of Roumania who had set the terrifying Mr Vandergriff on our trail.

"Enough of the pleasantries!" Nikolasha boomed. Where Vasily was all lithe, sinuous grace and decadence, his elder brother was quite a different proposition—a stiff, oblong man in a military tunic positively jingling with medals, with a stiff, oblong face and a ferociously waxed mustache. He indicated Princess Marie. "Look what you did to this poor little girl. If you have a cure, you ought to share it!"

"I don't care about the cure," Missy told the general with a toss of her head. "Now that I no longer have fangs I am the idol of the people. I hope that my husband will follow suit. But your brother owes me a diamond necklace, and I mean to have it back."

"And so you shall, my dear," Vasily said with a sharp-toothed smile. "Good evening, Nikolasha. Perhaps, if you are all very good to me, I *will* share the cure."

"Don't worry about the diamonds, Missy," said a handsome

young vampire who leaned close to the young princess, an arm thrown carelessly over the back of her chair. "I'll buy you all the diamonds you want."

"Good evening, father," Vasily added, bowing to an older gentleman whose seat near the hostess at the head of the table indicated his seniority.

"Oh, *Gospodin*," Anna said with some disgust—for of course she was with me. "Why could I not have had that young Boris Vladimirovich who is hanging about Princess Marie's neck?"

Indeed Vasily's father was not a prepossessing sight: he was a jowly man with a receding hairline whose side whiskers were at least ten years out of date. The heavy-lidded eyes that did so much to make Vasily look like a man one could not trust around one's young sisters made his father look at first glance sleepy and rather placid.

"I congratulate you, my boy," he said. "Where did you find this dainty?"

At first I could not imagine to whom he was referring. Then, with a sense of shock, I understood that it was myself.

"I cannot believe, sir, that you would refer to a lady of standing in such slighting terms," Vasily said in the smoothly light tones with which he masked his anger. "But no doubt you did not quite catch her name and title."

"I don't see why a French countess cannot be an imperial dainty. Dozens of them have been before. A cure, eh? They say the Emperor has had a chemist working on the problem for months. I suppose he's the one who fixed you up, eh?"

As Nicholas Nikolaevich transferred his mirthless, languid gaze from me to his son, I decided that while I would entrust Vasily with the safety of my sisters, I should feel anxious knowing that his father was in the same county as them. And then I recalled the day Vasily had met my sisters, and had bandied my own name to them. *Believe me, such things are only jests with the people among whom I am accustomed to spend my time.* I shuddered, returning silent gratitude to my Maker that my father, for all his faults, had been nothing like *this.*

"Sit down, sit down," Zlata insisted, waving us towards the two empty places that awaited us.

I found myself seated between Vasily and his brother Nikolasha, who promptly addressed himself to his fish. But the lady on Nikolasha's other side leaned forward to gaze upon me with wide and excited eyes. "Countess," she said, "you and I have not been introduced, I know, but allow me to beg that you will indeed conduct a séance after dinner! I am Anastasia Nikolaevna, but you may call me Stana."

*Nikolaevna,* thought I. "Are you another of Vasily's siblings?"

"Oh, no!" Stana said, with a self-conscious glance at Nikolasha. A lady across the table, who shared her dark and aquiline beauty, giggled behind a gloved hand. "My father is the King of Montenegro. That is my sister Militza, who is married to Peter Nikolaevich—who *is* Vasily's brother." I decided not even to try to understand all this. "You are a Spiritualist, then?"

I sighed, and said mendaciously that I was. I was soon engaged in conversation with both the Montenegrin ladies, for whom I was grateful, for otherwise I do not know who would have spoken to me at all. No doubt, like the old Grand Duke, everyone presumed me to be Vasily's mistress.

As the dinner progressed, the atmosphere became more unruly. Across the table, the Crown Princess of Roumania was quite openly flirting with the young Grand Duke Boris Vladimirovich, until I did not know where to look. Queen

Victoria's own granddaughter! and a married woman! Then, too, I *hoped* that Stana and Nikolasha were married, for the lady wore a wedding-ring and I was conscious of some billing and cooing in that quarter; but I was reminded of the wit who described flirtation between man and wife as washing one's clean linen in public. Presently, Grand Duke Boris began to make pellets out of his bread, and to flick the product into the eyes of a young lady to whom Missy referred with sisterly affection, as "Ducky". She appealed to her own cavalier, Cyril, for protection. Catching up the soda-siphon upon the sideboard, he hosed Boris with it. The next moment the party broke up into a general romp. People dashed through the house to find other soda-siphons. Jets of soda-water shot back and forth across the room, accompanied by the shrieks of the ladies and the shouts of the gentlemen. As for me, I trembled, for everywhere I looked there were red laughing mouths and gleaming fangs, and in the heat of the room I could—reader, I could *smell* them. You will say that it was my own imagination, and perhaps it was: but deep beneath the scents of hot-house flowers and bespoke perfumes, beneath the aromas of gravies and sauces was a faint, sweet, charnel-house scent which spoke only of death.

I trembled; and beneath the table, between our chairs where none of the monsters could see, the back of Vasily's hand touched mine and remained. That one warm point of contact, and the fresh astringent smell of pine that hung about him, redolent of fresh and clean faraway mountains, steadied me a little amidst the uproar.

"Ha! Vasily! Wake up! You seem to be asleep and dreaming," Nikolasha panted. He turned and aimed, but poorly. A jet of soda-water struck me square in the breast.

I could not restrain a shriek of surprise. Vasily leaped to his feet with a hiss.

Vasily's brother had for some unfathomable reason chosen to attend this dinner party got up like a robber baron, with a revolver and a dagger at his belt. Now, Nikolasha showed his teeth and put down the soda-siphon. His hand brushed the weapons at his belt.

Vasily growled; and abandoning all restraint, I seized his arm. For a moment I thought he was about to leap upon his brother with bared teeth; but then I saw a faint sheen upon his forehead, and wondered if he was actually afraid—and why, if so, he had so confidently strolled into this room.

"Vasily," I pleaded. "I'm sure the Grand Duke didn't mean it! Don't make a meal out of a molehill—"

"Hush, my dear." Vasily spoke softly, without once taking his eyes from his brother. He drew back his lips, showing all his teeth: how easily he had slipped back into the habits of the monster! "Don't interrupt. My brother was about to make you a very handsome apology."

"Come off your high horse, Vasya," Nikolasha said with a laugh. "Did you make an apology to your milkmaid?" He turned to me. "Has Vasily told you about Ioanna?"

He had not—but I did not have the opportunity to say either yea or nay, for at these words Vasily seemed to lose his head entirely. With blazing eyes he snatched up the soda-siphon and a handful of salt from the salt-cellar, brought his fist to the nozzle, and was about to direct a jet of salt-laden water directly into his brother's eyes. I caught his arm again with a shriek; and as Vasily attempted to loosen my grasp, Nikolasha reached into his belt, drew his revolver, and unloaded it in a deafening volley straight into Vasily's bosom.

I screamed; nor was I the only one. Vasily recoiled, falling back into his seat; salt and soda-siphons went everywhere. I did what, at that moment, seemed to be the only thing possible. I flung myself between Vasily and his brother, wrapping my arms about his neck and steeling myself for the impact of fresh bullets. None came: there was only the stench of gunpowder and the shocked cries of the others in the room.

"Vasily," I shrieked, pulling away and flattening my hands against his smoke-blackened shirtfront. His eyes were open and dazed, but he was breathing hard—he was *breathing*.

Understanding dawned in his reddened eyes. "I'm unhurt," Vasily said, still dazed. He tried to put me aside, but I could feel his hands trembling.

Nikolasha lowered his smoking revolver with a booming laugh.

"Ha! ha! The look on your face, Vasya! Don't tell me you thought I'd actually load my revolver for a nice little family dinner? Blanks, my dear fellow! Quite a harmless little prank, don't you think? Now then, don't try to fling salt-water at me again, and we shall say no more of it."

He took his seat amidst general merriment, for after their first moment of shock the others present seemed to think that it had all been an excellent joke. The romp, thank God, was over. For the moment I remained on my knees before Vasily, trembling nearly as hard as he did. Princess Zlata, at the head of the table, tapped her knife against her glass and said, "Now that the merriment is over, let's drink the toast and we can go to the drawing-room. I'm sure the gentlemen will be happy to forgo the cigars and come at once to join us."

From which I gathered that, despite the apparently amicable end to the matter, Zlata herself was not happy to abandon Vasily altogether to the mercy of his relatives.

The footmen began charging glasses for the toast. I scrambled back to my seat with but scant assistance from an overwhelmed and inarticulate Vasily, and received wine in my glass. I did not wish to know why, from a large silver ewer, a second footman filled Vasily's glass with a liquid far darker and more viscous; or why an imprint with sad eyes followed this second footman. The apparition was thin and very shabby, in an embroidered shirt and a heavily-patched jacket; and he held a cloth cap humbly in both hands. An unutterable weariness and resignation flowed over me at the sight of the peasant, who had evidently died to furnish this repast. Averting my gaze, I kept my eyes fixed upon my own glass as Zlata rose to her feet and sweetly begged Vasily's father to do the honours.

"Ahem!" Nicholas Nikolaevich the elder cleared his throat. "Ladies and gentlemen, I shall keep this brief—to the Emperor, long may he reign!"

To murmurs of "The Emperor!" the drinks went down. I took rather more of the wine than I had first intended when I walked in at the door, for the evening's events had left me sorely in need of something to steady my nerves. Beside me, Nikolasha drained his glass to the dregs and after a moment's hesitation, Vasily did the same. After that, Zlata had Vasily's father escort her to the drawing room, and the rest of us fell into step behind her.

Halfway across the entrance hall, Vasily squeezed my arm and said faintly, "Give me a moment," before dashing into a dark passage that opened up on our right. I followed, less from curiosity, this time, than from a strong conviction that in this house we ought to stick together. From the shadows ahead of me I heard some of the soft sounds of misery I had been making myself some two or three days since on the Königsberg boat. Rounding a corner, I found myself in a conservatory rich with dappled twilight and the shadows of orchids, palms, and orange-trees. Vasily knelt before one of these last, coughing up that dark viscous liquid into the potting-soil. When he was done, he got out his handkerchief and dabbed at his lips with some of his customary fastidious grace.

He glanced up at me with a rueful smile. "Look at me," he whispered. "There was a time when blood was like mother's milk to me. Now I cannot even stomach the taste."

Blood—*blood.* The word had been spoken aloud. All one's life one hears of the monstrous royalties of the Continent; and with the instinctive respect owed to one's betters, conceives of them as a sort of awful, august splendour. What I had seen tonight was something that was entirely awful and neither august nor splendid in the least. I shuddered, remembering the imprint of the sad peasant. Had that blood been given willingly, or taken by force? Had a human soul really been slaughtered somewhere in a dark room out of sight, and drained for the nourishment of those betters?

"I cannot bring myself to be sorry for *that*," I answered, kneeling on the spotless white tiles beside Vasily. For a moment I searched his face in the moonlight, which shone faintly through the glass of the ceiling. What little resemblance he now bore to the man who barely an hour previously had entered this house with a swagger! His mouth was drawn tight with strain, and there was something vulnerable and almost desperate in the line of his neck as he raised his head to look at me. A peculiar yearning came over me, to put my arms around him and hold his poor head to my breast, to soothe him until he ceased to tremble, and to kiss the tension from his lips—

Oh, Molly Dark, Molly Dark, how shameless you are!

"No," Vasily whispered. "I suppose you cannot be sorry for that." His fingers brushed my cheek. "I really thought he was going to shoot me like a dog."

"Your family seems—er—fond of their jokes."

His gaze did not waver: there was something utterly unguarded, utterly vulnerable in his eyes. "You feared the same thing. You would have protected me with your own body."

Indeed I had; and I was not entirely sure why. Even in the most sensational kind of fiction, that is something that gentlemen do for ladies, and not *vice-versa,* unless the lady is most desperately in love with the gentleman. I did most heartily regret my actions now, for I did not like to give Vasily any wrong notions.

"I would," I said diplomatically, "have done the same for any member of my crew."

This seemed to amuse him, for he laughed softly and said, "Naturally you would… I'm the worst kind of fool, I know. I ought never to have brought you here."

"Here?" I forced myself to smile. "I don't particularly mind this conservatory. Comparatively it's quite lovely."

Vasily tilted back his head, smiling wanly at the glass panels of the ceiling and the clouds that fleeted across the face of the waxing moon. "It's a shame we must leave it. Come, then; we have work to do."

# Chapter IX.

It was fortunate that we made our return when we did, for as we crossed the entrance hall, Princess Zlata came out of the drawing-room to find us. "There you are!" she said. "I thought we might have frightened you away, my dear Countess!"

"No," I said, "but when preparing to hold a séance, I do like a few minutes' solitude."

Zlata gave me a look of sympathy. "You must feel that I have thrown you to the tigers. Indeed they were unruly tonight, worse than I hoped; only I *did* think it might do Vaska some good, if he could but meet his father and brothers again face to face. No, truly, Vaska, don't frown—I think it *will* do you good. You know that I hate my friends to be at odds, and it is always so unhappy when families don't get along. Please don't mind them, Countess. They mean no harm; only they have been vampires all their lives, and don't know how overpowering they can be."

They meant no harm! They drank the Emperor's health in blood, and meant no harm!

Still, she meant it kindly, and I was grateful to her. It was good to feel that at least *one* person in this house would not be eager to drink my blood.

Zlata led us into the drawing-room where one of the Montenegrin princesses was playing the pianoforte for the guests. Their exertions appeared to have left them sated and quiescent, for they lounged about in a decline-and-fall sort of way. Zlata clapped her hands for silence. "Who," she announced, "wants to do a reading with Countess Marie-Angelique?"

Stana jumped up from the piano-stool, all eagerness. "Where shall we gather? What about that card-table?"

Clearing my throat, I adopted an air of portentous solemnity. "One moment! I am happy to do a reading, but I prefer to select my own subjects." This caused a little stir in the room, for the demand piqued their interest at once. It is wonderful how restorative the sensation was, of holding the attention of these dangerous creatures in the palm of my hand. I paced among them, making a show of scrutinising each in turn. I must choose Vasily's father, because it was for the purpose of "reading" him that I had come; I ought to choose one of the Montenegrins, because they would be very disappointed if they were overlooked, and would make my work all the easier for their eagerness. Nikolasha, to my surprise, seemed anxious to participate, so I chose him and Princess Militsa.

These favoured few took their places around me at the table, and although Missy and Boris remained on the sofa giggling and flirting, the other guests flocked close about us. Vasily stood at my back as though he could not bear to be parted from me. As Zlata turned down the lamps, I glanced about to ensure Anna's presence. I had begged her to be present upon this occasion, and she had consented; she saw, as I did, that our plans could not be settled until we knew a little more about the elder Nicholas—his desires and weaknesses.

Vasily had had plenty to say on that score, of course. "He thinks he's God's gift to women. He always has," he'd said, bitterly. Mimi, rather unkindly, had then put in something about apples not falling far from trees. But we had all agreed that Vasily should not be our sole source of information on this topic.

I cleared my throat, summoning up my showman's patter from the happy old days running séances in Vienna. "Ladies and gentlemen, the unseen world is a higher plane of existence, beyond our control or even our comprehension. I can open for you a path to this unseen world, but only so long as I am implicitly obeyed. Do not speak unless you are invited to do so; do not move away from the table once the circle is completed."

From the sofa, there came a little squeal of delight from Missy. "Silence!" roared Nikolasha. The youngsters subsided into whispers, and an absolute hush descended.

The room was dark, Anna just one more of the shadows that surrounded the table upon which a single, low-burning lamp lit the faces of those who sat around it. "Close your eyes," I whispered. "Join hands, and fix your minds upon those whom you have lost."

Until now, the only imprint I had encountered in this house was that of the unfortunate peasant whose blood had been quaffed as an after-dinner toast. Imprints are only memories, after all, and come only to the people and places who remember them. I did not for a moment believe that these fanged terrors, who now surrounded me so meekly with closed eyes and mouths, could not have summoned up an army of horrors should they so desire. But of course they did not. There was no place in these memories for those whom they had slaughtered; no weight upon these hardened consciences.

Instead, one by one, there appeared the ordinary kind of imprint that always did appear at this sort of gathering—a pretty child, an elderly mother, a handsome soldier who stood by the younger Nicholas and a lovely dark-eyed ballerina who I suspected might once have been a mistress of the elder. Vasily's hand tightened minutely upon my shoulder and when I cast a glance behind me I saw that the darkness about him was populated with shadows. Their shapes were indistinct, but one at least I recognised from previous occasions upon which Vasily had seemed haunted by his past—a dark-haired girl in the embroidered blouse of a peasant. For this I was prepared; but not for the strength of the impressions I received from the shades about him. The soft sensations of resignation, sorrow, pain or disappointment that hung about the other imprints in the room were absolutely overwhelmed by what I felt from those about Vasily. Their terror, fury, and despair struck me like the blast of heat from an oven. With a stifled gasp I turned away again, concentrating my mind upon the touch of Vasily's hand upon my shoulder, until the sensations retreated a little and I could apply myself to the task at hand.

"There is," I whispered, "a spirit among us—a woman. I can see her standing behind your grace's chair." I inclined my head towards Grand Duke Nicholas the elder. "Spirit, do you remember your name?"

"Anna Ivanova Sorina," Anna said promptly.

Since I was asking the question only for show, I said only, "Do you have a connection with someone at this table? The elder Grand Duke? —Sir," I added, "there is an Anna Ivanova here to speak with you. Have you any words for her?"

The Grand Duke frowned. "I can't remember any Anna Ivanova. Maybe an old nanny, I don't know. No, Nanny was an Englishwoman."

This was far from promising; yet I persisted. "She is manifesting more clearly now—oh! She is wearing the costume of a ballerina. Oh! and she is covered in blood! Anna Ivanova, who did this to you?"

There was a tense silence. I gripped the hands to either side of me a little more tightly, feeling the sweat bead upon my brow. What had seemed a sensible idea a few hours since now seemed nothing short of madness; yet I could not withdraw. Whispering, I said, "Forgive me, sir. She is pointing to *you.*"

The Grand Duke blinked, utterly astounded. "I beg your pardon?"

Nikolasha, to my surprise, came to my rescue with a diffident throat-clearing. "Anna Ivanova, Father. That was the name of the girl at the Maryinsky, two weeks ago—"

"Yes, but I never *drained* her," said his father, almost sulkily. "I know better than that. Taste but don't finish off; those are the rules for the dancers. Don't teach your father how to suck eggs, boy—or dainties, rather. Ha! ha!"

"She asks why you did it," I said, endeavouring to conceal my distaste for this cavalier dismissal of Anna's plight.

"That's rich," said the Grand Duke fretfully. He was beginning to sweat, now. Some of the ladies edged away from him a little. "What the devil was the girl doing in Kschessinska's dressing-room if she *didn't* want to be bitten?"

"It's a lie!" said Anna disdainfully. "I would allow myself to be bitten by such a man only with the greatest reluctance!"

"What made you think so?" I asked the Grand Duke, politely.

I half expected him to respond by telling me to mind my own business, but instead he became confiding. "My dear," the old roué said, leaning towards me, "I'll tell you a secret. Women find me irresistible. You feel it, don't you? Even now it's taking all your self-command not to throw yourself into my arms, begging to be bitten. Well, you're not alone. I have this fatal effect upon all your sex. Thank God, most of you have been properly brought up, or there would be no showing my face in public. As it is, I have to take the most stringent precautions. One never knows when some madwoman might accuse one of misdoing. I suppose they do it to gain attention. You understand how it was with this unfortunate girl, then?"

"Good heavens," I said faintly. At the beginning of this bizarre speech I had believed myself the subject of another bad prank, but the longer he went on talking, the more I felt that he really believed what he was saying. Why, the man was prey to the most preposterous delusions. How else could one explain the devout belief that half the human race was desperate to let him sate himself upon their blood? And as for the idea that one would provoke or fabricate such an attack for attention—what gain might that bring one? Even I knew that to be labelled as a dainty was to become soiled goods, despised and distrusted by all.

"Good heavens indeed," said he, seeing and misinterpreting the look of horror upon my face. After a moment he added, with an air of great magnanimity, "But you're a nice young lady, my dear. I'll bite you, if you are very good to me."

There was a sharp intake of breath from Vasily, behind. As politely as I could, I said, "I'm very sensible of the honour, your grace, believe me. The girl's spirit begs you, out of your generosity, to send something to her family by way of compensation."

"Send something to her family! After the trick she played on *me?* The nerve!" said the Grand Duke. "Let the theatre take care of that. I'm sure they've some money set aside for that sort of thing. My dear, I'm finished with this spirit, and if you will take my advice you won't associate yourself with young people of such bad character."

"As you say," I responded meekly. "Go to your rest, spirit, and we thank you for your presence."

For a moment there was absolute silence in the room, except for the rather huffy breathing coming from the Grand Duke, who evidently felt himself very badly used. Nikolasha and the other guests said nothing, but they seemed ill at ease. Even they, it seemed, understood the absurdity of the old man's delusions.

It would be politic to end on a less uncomfortable note, and for that I must resort to one of the other imprints I had observed. "I see another spirit," I added after a suitably impressive pause. "A military man, in a Hussar's red coat. And he's decorated, too—he's wearing a cross pattée on a black and orange ribbon."

"Oh!" said Nikolasha, "that is my lieutenant, poor Yegor—" and then he ceased to speak and went very red.

I concentrated all my attention upon the unfortunate young soldier. His emotions were faint but distinctive: surprise, reproach, a burning pain at the heart.

Nikolasha said gruffly, "Poor Yegor! He was a brave man.

If I'd known he'd a weak heart I'd never have played that shooting-blanks trick upon him!"

Stana patted Nikolasha's shoulder. "There, there," she said. "You weren't to know!"

This altogether conquered me. They were all mad, mad, and I could stand it no longer. "No, I'm afraid he's already departed," said I, releasing the sweaty grip of the elder Nicholas and the wide-eyed Princess Militsa. It did not require much in the way of acting to put a tremble into my voice. "I am overtired, I think. It is no easy thing to summon up the dead, especially with so many onlookers."

They were all very solicitous; they helped me up and put me into an armchair with a glass of port with which to fortify myself. The Montenegrin sisters settled themselves beside me and peppered me with eager questions, for they said they had never before attended a séance quite like this one. As for me, I did not know whether to laugh or cry or run screaming from the house. Instead, I drank my port.

\* \* \*

Vasily later informed me that as I was attempting to calm myself with port on one side of the room, his elder brother waylaid him at the other. The events of the evening had not gone precisely according to plan, and he found himself longing nearly as sharply as myself to flee the house altogether. Before he could pay his respects to our hostess, however, Nikolasha drew him aside.

"Listen," his brother said, "I'm sorry for playing that joke on you, before. Startled you, I shouldn't wonder. I wouldn't have liked to startle you to death, like poor Yegor Grigorievich."

"You're very kind," Vasily said dryly. Ordinarily he would have taken more pains with his words, but he was quite at the end of his tether that evening, and so the thing came out more bluntly than was perhaps wise. "You can make it up to me, if you like, by getting me an audience with Nicky."

"With Nicky—with Short Nicholas, you mean?"

"Yes, with the Emperor."

Nikolasha tugged at his beard. "I don't know if I can do that, Vasya. The Tsar summons people when he wants to see them. And you left under a cloud. If I were you I wouldn't be in a hurry to see him."

"But it's *Nicky*. You know that we were always friends."

"That was when he was the heir. He's the Tsar now. There's a difference. He can't overlook things any more." Nikolasha slapped his shoulder. "You made the right decision in coming back, Vasya. We would have caught you eventually, you know. Stay in Moscow, and keep that cure handy. Sooner or later Nicky will find out that you've returned, and when he does, you'll need to demonstrate where your loyalties lie."

With that Nikolasha went to join Stana and Militsa, and Vasily was left brooding in the shadows near the abandoned card-table. He wondered whether, after all, he had blundered into a trap of his own devising. His idea had been to dip a toe back into his old circles; yet every tentative movement had only drawn him swiftly deeper, as into a quick-sand. The appearance at the Maryinsky had exposed him to Zlata; Zlata had drawn him back to his family; and now he was exposed, helpless—and stuck. With his identity, and his presence in Moscow, no longer a secret, there was now no way out. Nicky might not actually execute the warrant for his arrest, but he might easily stalemate him merely by refusing to see or reinstate him.

He could not help but feel that he had put his head into the proverbial lion's mouth; yet at the same time the sense of peril was almost invigorating. He had no choice, then, but to go forward; to convince Nicky to reinstate him in his privileges—and then he would be a free man along with his friends; and might regain some of the power and wealth he had lost.

Zlata, who had been whispering with Missy in the corner, now left that young lady and skipped towards him. "Vaska," she said, seizing his arm with playful excitement. "Missy has been telling me *such* tales about you. She said that you stole a diamond necklace of hers! What about those diamonds the Countess is wearing? Did you steal those, too?"

"Missy is a little goose, and you're another," Vasily said, rallying his weary wits. "Why do you want to know what I have been doing in exile?"

Zlata pouted. "I wish you would steal some diamonds for *me.* It's the least you could do."

"Is it?" he said heartlessly. "At the train station yesterday, *the least I could do* was to have dinner with you, to comfort you in your lonely widowhood. But I don't find you lacking, either for company or for diamonds."

"Well, and maybe I don't! But I've never known a real, live diamond thief! It's absolutely the most thrilling thing I can think of. Don't be afraid, I won't tell a soul. Say you believe me."

"As you wish: I believe you."

"Ah! but you don't mean it." She dimpled and bit her lip. "Be honest, Vaska. You came to Moscow to steal something, didn't you?"

It was without a doubt the most trying evening of his life thus far. "Naught but somebody's favour, my dear."

"The Tsar's, you mean? I don't believe *that* for a moment." She leaned against him with an enchanting smile. "Please, Vaska. I should *so* love to steal something with you. Won't you let me help? It's the least you can do."

*"The least I can do* is growing by the minute," he said, moving away. "My dear, I'm desolated, but really I can't help you."

"Then you won't mind if I tell my godfather, Sergei Alexandrovich, that you've returned to Russia. And you know that the Emperor does everything Sergei Alexandrovich asks him to do."

Her smile was full of unbounded impudence. Miss Dark, Vasily thought, wore something of the same expression when she was putting salt into the sugar-bowl at tea-time. Would that Zlata's tricks were as innocuous!

"Sergei must learn of my return sometime. Do you mean to tell me you wish to stir up trouble for me?"

"Trouble!" she cried. "Oh, Vaska, I don't *know* what I wish. I know that I am being selfish, but cannot you humour me for once? Try to see things from my point of view. Don't you know that you broke my heart? A girl of fifteen holds nothing back when she loves; she doesn't know how to. And you fled to the ends of the earth to escape me! I am a woman now; I know that the heart has its own reasons, and you could not help it that you did not love me. But you ran away—you ran away and broke my heart, and doomed me to a marriage with a man I hated, and left my Serbia to be annexed by Austria. Am I wrong to think that I am owed some little recompense?"

There were tears in her eyes. Vasily could not meet her gaze. He had known all this, dimly, when he had chosen to flee Russia rather than tie himself to a frivolous girl. It was true. He had known that he was about to cause her pain, and that his actions would have consequences far beyond the two of them; consequences that could be drawn on maps and measured in blood. He had known, and he had chosen to disregard all this only because a marriage to Zlata was not to his taste.

Indeed, he did owe her something.

He had not yet formulated any words when Zlata sniffled a little and then reached out to touch his chest. "I ought to have told you before," she murmured. "You have blood on your shirtfront."

Looking down, Vasily realised that she was right. His misery in the conservatory had left a tiny scattering of blood droplets across the crisp white expanse of his shirtfront.

Zlata gazed up at him, her brow faintly knit. "You *are* cured, aren't you?"

Vasily cursed his bravado in trying to quaff a draught he could no longer stomach. How much did Zlata guess? How much would she know by the morrow? "What a strange question," he said, very lightly. "But I'm afraid I must bid my farewells. The Countess is coming to collect me, and I'm sure she wishes to depart."

# 10

# Chapter X.

The putative Countess, in fact, had been trying for some minutes to extricate herself from the Montenegrins' conversational clutches—the more so, once Anna had wafted over to tell me that I might regret not hearing what Vasily and Zlata were so earnestly discussing over the card-table. Naturally, with the two princesses and Nikolasha hanging on my lips, I could by neither word nor gesture beg Anna to eavesdrop upon the conversation in my stead. When I *did* get away, Vasily was in the midst of taking his leave.

"What were you speaking to Zlata about?" I asked, once we were ensconced within our *troika* cab. It was getting towards midnight, and although Moscow is not so far north as St Petersburg, the night had still something of that dreamy twilight quality about it: we seemed caught at that precise moment when there is neither sufficient light to see by, nor sufficient darkness for gaslight to do much good. Vasily sat beside me, but I could scarcely see his face.

"Old times," he said softly—a reply that left me more, rather than less, ill at ease. "I have many things to regret, my dear."

I wondered precisely what it was that he did regret, but who was I to ask, in any case? So long as Vasily could see to business, his personal affairs were none of mine.

After a moment's silence, Vasily passed a hand over his eyes and went on. "What an ordeal! They were worse than I remember. I think I have been away from them so long that I have gone soft. Well: it is over now, and we have what we came for. No doubt, after a little more of this, I shall toughen up."

It *was* over; and now, without the exigency of the moment to buoy me up, I felt myself begin to tremble with released nerves. "I do not care to be so toughened."

"I do not wish it upon you," Vasily said, with a weariness in his voice that nearly brought tears of sympathy to my eyes. "Little mouse, I am mortified. After you had invited me into your own home—to be so welcomed into mine! You have not been exposed to such manners. What you must think of me! I ought to have known it was no place for such as you."

*A nice home you must have!*—The words I had spoken with such scorn on the staircase at my own home in Brixton returned to me with interest. A nice home he *had* had—full of madness, debauchery, and unthinking cruelty. The wonder was not that Vasily resembled something out of the *Decline and Fall of the Roman Empire;* it was that he had escaped this home with any principles—with any sanity—at all!

"What I think of you!" I said softly. "Not long ago, you said that you admired me for doing right despite my worse inclinations. I should be but a poor friend to you if I could not return the compliment. I admire you for wishing to do right despite your upbringing."

Beside me there was absolute silence. I could not even hear

him breathing. Had I gone too far? Did he find my reference to his upbringing offensive? After all, he had only called it different to mine.—I reached out, blindly, and touched his hand. It was clenched into a fist.

"Vasily," I whispered, "I didn't mean—"

I could say no more. Vasily gave an inarticulate sound and slid to his knees on the carriage floor. His arms went around my waist, and he laid his head in my lap. I did not know whether he was trembling, or perhaps sobbing. I did not know what to do. In the darkness, he clung to me like a drowning man; and perhaps I was weak, for I allowed it. Nay, more—for I gave in to impulse, and stroked his head where it lay, and patted his heaving shoulders, and perhaps shed a tear or two of my own.

Vasily was calmer by the time we reached our lodgings. We went in without speaking to each other, but he kissed my hand before we went to our rooms. I closed the door behind me and stood for a long time before my looking-glass. I was pale and tired; my dress was all crumpled and stained, still damp from the jet of soda-water. I was above all conscious, with a sinking heart, that my vow to keep Vasily at a strictly professional distance was in great danger of being forgotten, if I could not be strong enough to keep it.

Anna observed me from the shadows. "Grand Dukes don't marry commoners," she said.

I started violently. "I beg your pardon!"

"Grand Dukes don't marry commoners," she repeated. "Not if they want to be in the emperor's favour. Your Vasily Nikolaevich would be punished even for contracting a morganatic marriage."

"Of course he would," I said, feeling a little hurt. "I

know very well that there can never be anything more than friendship between us!"

"I never said *that*," Anna protested, wafting herself into an armchair. "Grand Dukes marry women like Zlata, but they love women like us. They make us rich. They give us children. They even take care of their cast-offs. Just look at Kschessinska! She used to have the future Emperor, and now she has *two* Grand Dukes. If you help Vasily find his way back into favour, he'll give you anything you want. You will be secure for life."

For a mad moment I could even imagine it—could imagine spending my whole life in luxury with Vasily at my feet and real diamonds about my neck. It would be easier than marrying him, for the world of which he was a part, which would heap scorn upon the morganatic wife of the Grand Duke, would tolerate and even indulge a mistress. Principle and religion alike would forbid it; my mother would doubtless break her heart; but the world at large would not think I had committed any great sin. Only, Vasily would undoubtedly marry. I imagined having to share him with another woman— perhaps even with Princess Zlata—and I shuddered.

"Not *everything*," I said, and snuffed the lamp.

It was not until noon the following day that we gathered to lay our plans, for Vasily slept indecently late and Mimi was out most of the morning, perhaps ridding the house of the incriminating white gown. Nijam and I went out, partly for some fresh air and partly to buy bread, and eggs, and one or two other things. I am afraid that I taxed Nijam's patience, for Moscow was precisely the story-book city I had expected to find in Russia. I was continually stopping to exclaim over some little mediaeval church with wooden walls and gilded onion domes, or some far-off glimpse of a wall most beguilingly set with towers and battlements. Even the newer tenements and public buildings, with their steeply pitched roofs, their spires and cupolas, had a hint of the fairy-tale about them. In another moment, it seemed, I should turn a corner and happen upon a princess in a *kokoshnik,* or a *boyar* in bear-furs.

What we *actually* found was a gaggle of well-dressed ladies who waylaid us to collect contributions towards a new school for the children of some peasant district we had never heard of, and pressed us to attend a salon that evening where it was promised that we should all get to meet some real Social Democratic factory workers, who would tell us what the People needed.

"I cannot help feeling," said I to Nijam as we turned our steps homewards, "that there is no one in Russia who is not anxious for some kind of change—that is, except for Vasily's family."

Nijam shrugged. "The autocracy cannot build schools or roads, but they won't let anyone else do so, for that would compromise imperial authority. Meanwhile, the agricultural methods are such that the peasants can barely grow enough food for themselves, let alone for others. That's what caused the great famine of '91—a bad harvest, wasteful agriculture, and the autocracy not only refusing to help, but throwing up every obstacle to those who could. It's an antiquated system which cannot sustain a growing empire, and everyone knows it—except for Vasily's family."

"How do you know so much about it?" I asked in some amazement.

"I don't merely read Anthony Trollope," she said, intolerably smug.

I considered this in silence. Perhaps I could now better understand Vasily's hopes that a new Emperor might mean a new hope for this country. And that there was hope, I did not for a moment doubt: from the Petersburg priest and the Moscow society ladies who had assailed us to plead for the betterment of the peasantry, to the Populists singing the Marseillaise in the attic next door, the people's will for change was evidently so strong, that either the Emperor must lead them out of the autocratic prison, or else the people would drag him out of it by force. A new Emperor—one gentle and understanding—might be the very thing needed to bring about a wonderful transformation.

When we returned to our lodgings, Vasily had got up and was lounging barefoot and silk-robed in the balcony. He seemed in excellent spirits, for he was humming under his breath as he sketched one of the gilded church spires that could be glimpsed from the window. I beheld him with some confusion, for it came into my mind how his arms had felt about me in the carriage, lean and sinewy, and how his shoulders under my hands had been sculpted of warm and living stone. For a moment all I could think of was touching him again; so that I stood staring at him like a fool.

Then Schmidt wandered by with a blacking-brush in hand. He was evidently attending to his master's shoes; but he seemed distracted, and did more staring and frowning than shoe-blacking. But he broke the spell; and that was the main thing.

Mimi came home at about the time I was serving eggs, toast, and tea for lunch. She beheld Vasily sourly as he settled into the seat at the head of the table and folded his hands together.

"Shall we," he said with a pious glance towards the ceiling, "return thanks?"

"Stop that, Vasya," she said, "it's irreverent."

"My dear Mimi, I'm in earnest. I survived a whole dinner-party with my family, and I was shot at only once. I am most devoutly grateful."

"Why is he happy?" she asked me. "I didn't agree to this. If you can't keep him properly miserable I shall go back to Copenhagen."

"Who says it's *my* duty to keep Vasily miserable? See to it yourself." At this, Vasily sent me a melting look and kissed my hand. Despite my words, I felt a sense of foreboding, for it was perhaps incumbent upon me to say some very clear words to Vasily about the nature of our association.

Nijam rapped her teaspoon against the table. "If you all don't mind, I left something on the Bunsen burner and I'd like to get back to it. You spoke to Grand Duke Nicholas last night, Dark. What's his weakness?"

I cleared my throat. "Well, as Vasily said, he thinks he's God's gift to women. Indeed that is somewhat understating it. The Grand Duke seems prey to the wildest sort of delusion. He told me quite plainly that it was only my own good upbringing that prevented me throwing myself at him and begging him to bite me."

A startled silence followed. Vasily's mouth set forbiddingly.

"Delusion is assuredly correct," said Mimi.

"That's a weakness we can easily exploit," Nijam observed.

Schmidt looked alarmed. "It sounds as though what he needs is a doctor."

"Doubtless he does," Vasily said smoothly, "but he'll never seek one of his own accord. Think of it as our task to secure

129

for my father the care he needs. A *Trip to Paris* would work."

Mimi wrinkled her nose. "Vasya, you are an optimist. Do not forget that your father is a Grand Duke. Even if he assaulted someone onstage at the Bolshoi theatre during the coronation gala performance itself, what would happen to him? He is a Grand Duke who has already got away with murder twice. All the world knows that ballerinas merely exist to serve such men as dainties."

"If not a ballerina, then who *could* a Grand Duke assault in such a way as to bring about his disgrace?" I asked. "And who, moreover, would give her consent to being used as bait?"

"It's a shame he can't be made to bite a *man*," Mimi said, a gleam lighting her eyes. "That would certainly disgrace him forever! Or can he? Vasya, your father doesn't fancy boys, does he?"

"Lord, no," Vasily said with a chuckle. "That's a young man's vice, and he's well past *that* phase. What?" he added innocently, as the four of us sent him confused looks. "One would think you'd never heard of homosexuality before. Everyone goes through it."

I nearly choked upon my mouthful of toast. How casually he made this disclosure!

"No, they don't," Nijam said, plainly scandalised. "*I* didn't!"

"Nor I," said Schmidt, who had gone red. "I mean—not that I can remember."

"And how would the world be peopled if they did?" Nijam added. "Statistically speaking—"

Mimi laughed. "Never mind your statistics, Nijam," she cut in, much to my disappointment, for I would have liked to have heard her statistics. Nijam, I perceived, had a great deal of information at her fingertips, and I was not bold enough to ask her myself—but Mimi was intent upon her own argument: "For you it might be a phase, Vasya, but for a dainty like me, it depends purely on who's paying. And for the bourgeois it's unheard-of. Isn't it, Dark?"

Now she was appealing to *me*—now every eye at the table had fixed on *me*—I was utterly at a loss. For a moment I could only gaze at them all in a steadily growing panic before seizing upon the means of my escape. "I—I think that this is hardly a proper topic for mixed company!"

"I wholeheartedly concur!" said Nijam.

"But that's precisely why she ought to tell him!" Mimi persisted. "He'll believe a lady like Miss Dark!"

Mimi was too intent, and Nijam and Schmidt too aghast, to perceive my alarm. But Vasily, opposite me at the table, had gone suddenly very quiet. I made the mistake of meeting his eyes; and I knew at once with a blinding and bone-deep certainty that he was absolutely undeceived. He saw precisely why I refused to answer the question, and he was startled by the knowledge, but only a little.

"Mimi, Mimi," he said, smoothly taking the reins of the conversation. "I will believe anything you like, but let us not sully poor Schmidt's virginal ears with such talk. The important thing is to determine how we shall deal with my father."

"I wish you would listen to *me*," Anna said discontentedly. I assured her that I was all attention, and she went on. "It does *me* no good to send the Grand Duke to a madhouse. I have told you that Kschessinska is my very good friend—and she has the ear of the Tsar himself, who refuses her nothing because she was his dainty. You must go to Little K and tell her what has happened to me, and she will go to the Tsar

131

and make him send money to my family in Rostov. I can collect it from them when I awake," she added, somewhat to my discomfiture.

Recovering my countenance, I transmitted this message to the others. "I don't see why we shouldn't try it," I added. "Surely something is owed to the family."

"Yes, and all the better if it convinces the Emperor to restrain his uncle," Nijam said.

"It won't," said Mimi with a scowl. "Not on its own. If nothing has been done so far, it will not be done now, just because the Emperor's old dainty asks for it."

"Then it's agreed." Vasily smiled benignly. "We continue with our own plans. Mimi's idea is not a bad one—a *Trip to Paris* would do very nicely during the gala performance at the Bolshoi. The stage is already set, as it were."

"We'll need the help of a prima ballerina," Mimi said. "Not me; I haven't the necessary skill. Let us hope for Kschessinska. Short of the Empress herself, she's the one woman the Emperor won't allow to be molested."

"Then it's agreed," Nijam said. "Mimi, you and I must go to the Bolshoi—I take it that's the theatre here in Moscow?—and try to find allies among the performers. I will assess the backstage arrangements. Dark, you say the Montenegrins asked you to call on them this afternoon—you had better do that, to keep up appearances as the Countess. As for the Grand Duke—Vasily, I mean—you had better lie low."

"Schmidt and I have some business of our own," said Vasily, offhandedly. "Haven't we, Schmidt?"

Schmidt, who had taken a mouthful of toast, choked on the crumbs and sent himself into a coughing-fit.

Seeing his confusion, Mimi's eyes narrowed in suspicion.

"And what might this business be?"

"I'd prefer to keep that to myself, my dear, for I'm not sure whether it will be of any use to us. But on another note, I have something to tell you all, which I'm afraid you'll be unhappy to hear."

This was not a promising start. "Go on," said Nijam warily.

"Well, I think you know that last night's dinner did not quite go as planned," Vasily said. "Thanks to Miss Nijam's prosthetics, I flatter myself the majority of those in attendance believe me to be in possession of a cure, which ought to keep the lot of us safe until we've concluded our business in these parts. But I'm afraid that Zlata Milanova has taken it into her head that we've come to Moscow to steal something, and she's hinted to me that she can make things very difficult for me if I don't let her in on the affair."

Nijam's look of disbelief left nothing unsaid. "Princess Zlata wishes to *steal* something?"

"Doesn't everyone?" said Mimi with a shrug. "Nothing is holding her back. She can steal anything she likes, any day."

"Tell her no," Nijam agreed. "If the promise of a cure is as potent as you say it is, then what can she do to annoy us?"

Vasily coughed delicately. "She might spread it about that my cure is a hoax. It is possible that she may have deduced I am no longer able to stomach my blood."

A blank silence followed his words.

"Listen," Vasily said winningly, "it's true that I *am* going to steal something; a painting, if you recall. I think I do owe the child a little harmless amusement, and so long as Zlata is made to feel part of the intrigue, she will be quite satisfied. Moreover, with her connections to Sergei Alexandrovich, and through him the Tsar, she might be a very useful tool." A

133

knock came at the door. "And forgive me, but that must be Zlata now."

Nijam threw up her hands in despair as Vasily crossed to the door and ushered Princess Zlata herself into the room. This afternoon she was dressed very charmingly in black lace, with a black parasol in one lace-gloved hand. "Oh, Vaska! Is this your secret lair? What a charming place! And these are your confederates? How thrilling!"

Mimi sent the princess a look that communicated precisely the opposite sentiments.

"My friends," Vasily said with expansive charm, "this is Princess Zlata, who will be acting as our inside man—or woman, as the case may be—in the matter of the painting that is to be stolen."

With Mimi seething, Schmidt speechless, and even Nijam staring at the princess with expressionless hostility, it fell to me to rise to the occasion.

"Your highness," I said, getting up and coming forward with an extended hand, "how very fortunate we are to have your help! I wonder if you would be so kind as to accompany me on my afternoon's errand? I am going to visit the Montenegrin princesses, and you might be of very material assistance in establishing me in their society."

Zlata's eyes opened very wide. "Will that help to steal the painting?"

"It's absolutely necessary, I assure you."

"Then I would *love* to," she said, clasping her hands in girlish enthusiasm. I fetched my hat and gloves, and whisked Zlata away as quickly as she had appeared.

I did not like the thought of amusing Zlata any more than the others had; but she had left us with little other choice.

I could only hope that rather than waste the afternoon in recriminations, the others would busy themselves about the task at hand.

# 11

# Chapter XI.

With the princess' carriage awaiting us in the street, it was quite unnecessary to call a *troika.* Vasily chased us down the stairs and very gallantly handed each of us into the carriage. He kissed my hand a third time as he did so. Then, having directed her coachman to convey us to Princess Militsa's address, Zlata for a moment busied herself with a compact mirror and a powder-puff, allowing me a few moments to regulate the uproar of my thoughts.

You know, alas, dear reader—for by the time you see these lines, I shall be long dead, and my secrets no longer capable of doing anyone any harm—that I have always been disposed to find women as desirable as I have men. Since such inclinations are sanctioned neither by society nor—which is of infinitely greater importance to me—by religion, I have never chosen to indulge them; but it did not surprise me to learn that Vasily should have done so. He considered this a passing phase. I did not think it was a phase for me, but Vasily had only his own experience to go upon. He had always been desperately in search of love, and had perhaps been driven to seek it in places where his inclinations did not truly lie. *That* did not trouble me—at least, no more than did the knowledge that Mimi and goodness only knew how many others had once been his lover. What had set my face aflame with embarrassment was that wordless moment of recognition which had passed between us.

Almost I could have taught myself to hope that he had *not* perceived my secret, had it not been for that kiss upon the hand. But no: he certainly knew, and with his eyes had begged me not to suppose he thought less of me because of it. I had never spoken to a soul about what I felt; and all in a moment, without a word being spoken, he had read my heart. How dare he commit such an unpardonable familiarity? I *ought* to have been outraged—I ought to have been terrified—and yet I was not. I found, to my absolute astonishment, that after all I trusted Vasily with this last secret. All others he had known, and accepted, and had refrained from using against me. On my part, I was left with a peculiar sense of freedom. There was nothing more for Vasily to know of me: from one person in the world, I had nothing left to hide.

Zlata having finished powdering her nose, she closed her bejewelled compact with a snap, recalling me to the present— and to the troubling thought that although Vasily might be in possession of all my secrets, I certainly was not in possession of his. He had presented Zlata to us as a *fait accompli,* and we were now saddled with her; but *why* had he done such a harebrained thing?

"I know you must be surprised at my wishing to join you," Zlata said confidingly, "but really it is too kind of you to include me! You don't know what a bore it is, this endless round of parties and theatre-going! Won't you tell me more

137

about the painting? Vasily did not tell me anything last night, for he said that it was too dangerous to speak where we might be overheard."

I hesitated, for I did not know how far to trust the Serbian princess. Despite all her charm, that Zlata was spoiled and self-absorbed seemed clear; but to what degree were her declared intentions sincere, or affected? Still, there was no help for it but to do as she asked. "The painting—a Meissonier—was properly Vasily's before his property was confiscated by the former Emperor, you understand. It was in his Petersburg house, but has now been sold to the French ambassador. We have come to Moscow to retrieve it, for it will fetch a remarkable sum in America."

"Oh," Zlata said, clapping her hands. "How fortunate that *I* did not buy that Meissonier! I did consider it, you know; and then I would simply have given it back to Vasily, for it is worth very little here. Instead I let the French ambassador buy it—the dear old Marquis de Montebello—and now I shall have all the fun of helping you to steal it!"

"Very fortunate indeed!" I said, although I could not help laughing. "I don't suppose that you know where the painting is at this very moment?"

"But of course I do! Who does not know the Ambassador? He has taken the Sheremetov Palace and filled it with paintings and curios for the coronation ball next week. I can quite easily pay him a visit, you know, and sniff out the painting's whereabouts."

This was good news. Perhaps, after all, the young princess would be of some real assistance. The thought came as something of a relief, for I did not like to make enemies: on at least one occasion it had resulted in my driving a schoolmate to insanity, and I preferred not to do so again. "Please do just that," I said warmly, "it will be of very great help to us."

"It shall be done tomorrow, or the day after. What fun! I *do* hope that Vaska is not taken back into the Tsar's good graces very soon."

"I beg your pardon?"

"Why, because then everything would be given back to him and we should scarcely need to steal the painting, and that would be *too* much of a bore."

I considered this a moment. "You trust, then, that he *will* be pardoned?"

"Oh! there's not a doubt of it. His having a cure for defanging makes it absolutely certain. You saw how they all welcomed him last night—there was some little awkwardness at first, of course, but in the end everyone was perfectly cordial. Yes: I flatter myself that I have done very nicely!"

Zlata's intentions now seemed clear. I bit my lip, wondering whether I might do better to warn her, than to allow her her romantic daydreams. "It is very kind of you to interest yourself in the Grand Duke's affairs; but I beg you will not put yourself to any great inconvenience for Vasily's sake. He has already done you a very ill turn."

"Ah, but he might repair that ill turn very easily," she said.

My heart sank. This was precisely what I had feared.

Zlata leaned forward, putting a hand on mine. "Vaska knows which side of his bread is buttered. If he returns to favour, he will be expected to marry and settle in Russia. I know what you are thinking, my dear Countess. You imagine me a prey to romantic folly, supposing that a man who fled his homeland to avoid a marriage once, will be happy to accept the same match now. Indeed I do not suppose that it will

139

please him at all. He will never love me of his own accord, but Vasily Nikolaevich lost the right to make such choices when he was born so close to the greatest throne in the world. Away from Russia he is nothing but prey. He will never survive without his income, his fangs, and his family; yet I can restore them all and earn his thanks, if not his love. Help me, my dear Marie-Angelique—I may call you that, may I not? For in this matter we are sisters. Help me bring Vaska back to favour, before someone eats him alive."

Zlata spoke passionately, and with more gravity than I was accustomed to hearing from her. The ring of truth was in her words. Vasily's family was of a sort I would not wish upon a dog; yet he evidently felt that he might live more comfortably in their favour than out of it. And indeed, they were so powerful as the world reckons these things, that I did not doubt she was right. To live too near his family was risky; to live in their black books was impossible.

"Your sentiments do you credit, your highness, and I honour you for them," I said at last, after a brief struggle with myself. If Vasily was to marry, why not to Zlata? She was charming; she was beautiful; she was most in earnest about doing him good. I could not help thinking with a pang what a handsome pair they made. Why, then, could I not smile and assure her that I *would* help her? Why did the assumption of sisterhood make me feel that her face required scratching? I was no stranger to the experience of desire; I had always taken pride in being able to suppress my longings as a proper lady should. Whether Vasily chose to marry or not, it could be no affair of *mine,* and I could not allow it to become so. If I felt myself becoming weak, I must simply be more vigilant, more resolute.

With all these thoughts whirling through my head, I

retained sufficient wit only to return monosyllabic replies to all Zlata's prattle. She had changed subject and was now gossiping about the Montenegrins, informing me that Stana's husband, a Romanov cousin, had run away to Paris with his French mistress, leaving Stana quite disconsolate at home. This did not help, for it simply confirmed me in my suspicions that on the whole Vasily's bad behaviour was rather better than that of the rest of his family. Towards Zlata he might have misbehaved; but at least he had had the good judgement to run away *before* contracting his marriage and not *after*.

Mercifully, we soon arrived at our destination. Princess Militsa hurried into the entrance hall of that imposing mansion, with its acres of gleaming marble floor and soaring white columns, to welcome us in person. "How kind of you to come, Countess," she said, kissing me on each cheek. "Come at once to the drawing-room: there is a very particular personage here, who is dying to meet you."

Somewhat mystified, Zlata and I followed our hostess to the drawing-room—or perhaps the *salon* would be a better word for it, for that magnificent apartment was about as far as one could imagine from the cosy apartment that is the staple of every English home. Princess Stana was there, sitting very erect at the edge of an uncomfortable-looking French Empire divan, pouring tea for three gentlemen who rose to their feet at my entrance. One of these was familiar to me: Grand Duke Peter, Vasily's rather sickly younger brother and the master of the house. The two others were a rather slight young man in a pointed beard and a morning-coat; and a tall, imposing, gauntly beautiful gentleman in a uniform that was absolutely jingling with medals and orders. Zlata's gasp told me that this must be a very exalted personage indeed, and for a moment

I almost dreamed that it might be the Tsar himself. But no; the thin man was at least ten years too old to be the young Emperor. Besides this, the imperial portraits in every shop window showed a man with darker hair and an expression both gentle and benign; a man who much more resembled the unobtrusive young gentleman in the morning coat.

Then I heard Anna say "Slava!" and realised that Zlata had sunk to the floor in the profoundest of curtseys. The truth struck me with blinding force a moment before Princess Militsa said, "Your Majesty, please allow me to present our dear friend, the Countess Marie-Angelique Dubois de la Motte."

I hastened to follow Zlata's example, thanking Providence as I did so that at Saint Alphege's I had been taught to curtsey in the approved court manner. For the unobtrusive young man was, of course, the Emperor and absolute master of the Russian land.

"My dear Countess," said Vasily's cousin Nicky in excellent French, "I understand that you are gifted with remarkable spiritual insights."

I was; yet all the same, I felt a moment of consuming panic. I had never attempted to hoax an *Emperor.* If only Vasily were here to guide me! and wouldn't he be wild when he found that he had missed his best chance of seeing his cousin! "Yes," I gasped, "that is, your majesty, people have been kind enough to say so."

The Emperor gave me a peculiarly sweet smile. Under the gaze of his large and candid blue eyes, I felt that I could imagine why Vasily had liked this gentle young man. "My friend," he said, "will you be kind enough to perform a private reading for me? You will be paid, of course."

"*On* conditions of the utmost confidentiality," put in the tall, gaunt gentleman, with a ferocious scowl.

*He* was not an Emperor, and despite his evident hostility I felt more than equal to him. Drawing myself up to my full height, I said, "Sir, I am not accustomed to having my discretion doubted! You forget that it is not merely the living who entrust me with their secrets, but also the dead!"

"Pray don't allow my uncle to alarm you, Countess," said the Emperor hastily. "Really, Sergei Alexandrovich, you are overzealous!"

Sergei Alexandrovich—Zlata's godfather and Vasily's enemy! I wished I could recall whether it was he, or the other Sergei, whom Mimi had said was a rigid conservative. Indeed those bristling whiskers, and those deep-set eyes did not exactly suggest a broad-minded liberality; but perhaps it did not take a very liberal disposition, among the Romanovs, to pass as the most benign champion of democracy. In any case I felt very glad that I had *not* known myself to be rebuking a Grand Duke.

While I was recovering my breath for the second time in as many minutes, Princess Militsa threw open a pair of doors upon a second *salon* beyond this one, and informed His Majesty that the apartment was quite at our disposal. A moment later the doors closed, and I was ensconced alone with the Russian Emperor.

"Be seated, and I'll make some preparations," said I, seizing upon a very small side-table. I placed it before an armchair, and found myself a low ottoman upon which to perch opposite. After that, I had only to draw the curtains closed sufficiently to darken the room. None of this table-and-drawn-curtains nonsense is necessary, of course, for as the reader knows, I never have any difficulty in perceiving the dead; only it is useful for getting the living into the right frame of mind. Settling myself on the ottoman opposite the Emperor, I found myself at no loss to guess what might have brought him halfway across his capital mere days before his own coronation, in secret, to meet with a medium. He was about to be crowned supreme lord and master of one of the greatest empires in the world, and a worryingly large proportion of his subjects were in the habit of serving bombs with the breakfast. In his place I should have been terrified.

I know you will not believe it, but it *did* occur to me that perhaps I ought to warn him, as the autocrat of such a vast dominion, not to place *too* much trust in the miraculous powers of dubious adventurers. But the interview was too eventful to permit such a warning, and in any case I do not know that he would have heeded me. He did not heed others, later.

"Shall we begin?" I asked, smiling brightly.

The Emperor cleared his throat. "In fact," he said, "it isn't that I particularly want a *reading,* as such. I—in fact, I don't have difficulty hearing from the dead at all. Rather the opposite, in fact."

And he fixed a look upon me which was almost pleading.

The possibility struck me speechless for a moment. I looked around, wishing for Anna; but she had chosen to remove herself from the room and could offer me no moral support. "Could it be," I stammered, "that your Majesty suffers from— from ghostly visitations?"

The Emperor winced. "I know it sounds very foolish," he said. "But ever since the death of poor Papa, I've had these visions, and they're quite depriving me of any peace of mind."

My heart sank, for if indeed the Emperor had inherited a gift like my own, I did not know that there was much I could do for him. It was not the sort of gift that could be returned with a firmly-worded letter. On the other hand, it was quite possible that the Emperor was only being haunted by a stray imprint or two, which could be easily laid to rest. I smiled kindly at the young man, who appeared after all quite shy and good-natured.

"Why don't you show me?" I asked, extending my hands across the table.

The Emperor reached out to me, but hesitated before his hands touched mine. "I should warn you, Countess, it isn't a sight for a lady."

"Indeed, there is nothing that could shock me," said I. Alas! I spoke from ignorance. In removing herself, Anna had proven wiser than I.

Reassured, the Emperor allowed me to take his hands. Even before I could desire him to bring to mind his dead, the first of the imprints loomed over us.

This was a gigantic, burly man in a flowing shirt as red as his eyes, whose chin was graced with a luxurious beard and a very fierce set of mustaches. He spoke passionately to the young Emperor, gesturing as he did so with a pocket-flask, which sloshed liquid as he did so.

"That's my late father," whispered the Emperor, his awe not unmixed with fondness.

I could sympathise with this, for my own father had been in the habit of haunting me with great regularity for some years. "What is he saying?"

The Emperor winced. "Oh, the normal sort of thing. *You must retain the principle of autocracy as unbendingly as did I.*

145

*Anyone who says otherwise is a decadent European or a conniving Jew. Your grandfather tried it, and look where that led!"*

A pleasant sort of father to have! I did not voice this thought, because with the Emperor's final soft words, the imprint made a gesture towards the door with his flask, and a pair of men came running in carrying a stretcher with a horrible, broken, bloodied mass lying upon it. Mercifully a blanket had been thrown over the wreckage, but when the stretcher was laid down upon the carpet before us, I saw that the covering had been allowed to fall open, displaying a pair of shattered legs with the blood still spurting from the arteries; the figure's chest rose once or twice and then was still.

The Emperor shuddered, looking away. "My grandfather," he murmured. "Shall I ever forget that sight?"

I shuddered too: I dimly remembered as a girl seeing the headlines across my father's morning newspaper proclaiming the assassination of the reforming Emperor Alexander II. It was an unpleasant thing to have witnessed; but so far, Emperor Nicky's trouble did not seem hopeless. He had some bad memories, and knew himself to stand at a cross-roads in the history of his empire. I opened my mouth to say so, but the words upon my lips congealed as more imprints crowded upon us.

One of these was a tall, curvaceous lady in acres of silk petticoats, with white powder scattered across her upswept hair. She settled upon the arm of the Emperor's chair and tapped her arm with her fan. When she smiled, her sharp fangs glittered in the suddenly frigid air.

"Do you know what *she* is saying?" I asked, fascinated.

A sweat had broken out upon the young man's brow. *"Only an absolute sovereign can act with a vigour proportionate to the extent of such a vast dominion. Any other form of government would prove the ruin of Russia."* he repeated. "A saying of my ancestress, the second Catherine."

A shadow fell across us, startling me. I looked up to see another truly gigantic man towering over us, his dark hair flowing in seventeenth-century love-locks, for all the world like a Cavalier in an old painting—except that this one had a brutal, ravaged face that lacked any hint of poetry, and he carried a bloodied whip in his great knotted fist.

The Emperor spoke without prompting. *"Our people are like children who never get down to learning their alphabet unless their master forces them—*Ow!" he added, flinching, as the giant brought down his whip across the young man's shoulders— and then again. "Oh—oh—stop!"

In his attempt to evade the brutal attack, he wrested his hands from my grasp and threw them up to shelter his face. I leaped from my seat in horror. Outside I knew it to be a summer's day, with the sun a blaze of light; but the room had in an instant become frigid and absolutely dark, populated by ghosts. All light from outside had faded, and my breath hung in the air like a cloud. I was surrounded by the shadows of men and women, their expressions proud and cruel, their eyes blazing red with bloodlust. At any moment I thought the great giant would relent—but no, on he went, lashing the young Emperor in a maniacal rage. At last I reached out to catch that mighty arm, but all in vain: my hands slipped through him and I snatched them back with a little gasp of pain, for the mighty old imprint was icy enough to burn.

He stopped, however, when the cold became punishing and the light from the lamp on the table retreated to a tiny glittering glow about its flame; and with that, a withered

147

little man came stalking through the darkness. His brutal old face was wild and staring; his lips were drawn back from his lengthened fangs in a rictus of madness. In his hand he carried something that glittered with gold and blood; perhaps it was a sceptre, or perhaps it was a mace. If he spoke at all, Nicky was far beyond being able to translate. Unhesitatingly the apparation advanced upon the Emperor, hoisted the rod aloft and brought it down upon the young man's head. Nicky uttered an awful shriek and fell back, lifeless in his chair!

With that, at once the imprints vanished and the lamp blazed up, once more illuminating the entire room. I uttered a sob and tried to move, but my shoe had frozen to the marble floor in a web of ice. Unbalanced, I fell to my knees. Never before had I experienced something like *this*. The Noor-Jahan diamond had been attended by a terrible retinue of bloodied memories, which had reportedly driven more than one unfortunate soul to madness; but Emperor Nicky was not a diamond, and never before had I encountered a living man with such dreadful hangers-on.

At least, the Emperor *had* been a living man a moment or two since. At present he was sprawled bonelessly in Princess Militsa's gilded armchair, and for an awful moment I feared that the terror of his experiences had struck him dead on the very eve of his coronation!

"Your majesty! Sir!" I gasped, seizing his hand and feeling with trembling fingers for his pulse. It fluttered weakly beneath my fingers and I fairly sobbed with relief. In the same moment the salon doors were flung open and Sergei Alexandrovich stalked like an avenging angel into the room, followed by the three princesses.

"*Bozhe moi!*" he exclaimed at the sight that met his eyes—for

148

I was half sprawled across the floor, clinging to the senseless Emperor's hand at the centre of a vast web of ice.

Some of the cold ebbed from the room; and then the Emperor stirred, his hand twitching within my own. Languidly, he opened his eyes. "Ah!" he whispered through bloodless lips. "Such horrors!"

"What do you think you're doing, Nicky?" his uncle chastised him, advancing wrathfully upon the young man for all the world like one of the dreadful imprints. *"Slava!* Here you are two days before your coronation, lolling about, screaming and having hysterics like a woman! Remember who you are!"

"For pity's sake," I flashed out, climbing to my feet. Fortunately the floor had thawed sufficiently to let me move. "Just now his majesty is in no condition to play the autocrat; let me have a moment alone to calm his nerves, if I can, and then you can go about crowning him and reminding him who he is."

Sergei darted at me a look of pure venom, but the Emperor sat up and said, "Let us alone, uncle, we haven't finished yet."

The Grand Duke's eyes narrowed upon me. "For all I know she could be an anarchist! You should allow me to remain."

But the Emperor, with quiet obstinacy, persisted; and in a moment we were alone again in the room. Nicky sent me a look of quiet despair.

"What is happening to me?" he asked. "Am I going mad?"

There rose up before my eyes the image of the mad medium in the Hanwell Asylum, trembling and whispering, "Horrible! horrible!" rather the way Nicky had a moment since. I bit my lip; and instead of answering, returned another question. "Sir, did you really *feel* those blows?"

He shuddered, closing his eyes. "Yes." The answer was almost too soft to hear. "My predecessor Ivan Grozny murdered his son with a blow of his sceptre. My ancestor Peter the Great had *his* son knouted to death by his jailers. I—I am afraid I know how they felt."

"What about Catherine?" I could not help asking. "Did she have no son?"

"She did, but he survived long enough to become Tsar." The Emperor managed a weak smile. "When the officers came to tell him that he was Emperor, he thought he was about to be arrested and strangled to death, as his father had been."

I shuddered at the thought.

"You think them unnatural parents, I know," Nicky said earnestly, "but they were the parents of unnatural sons, who sought to rule in their place."

"Well—forgive me, sir—but surely it is the natural way of things for children to succeed their parents, rather than for parents to murder their children."

"Filial piety is the foundation of the motherland," the Emperor said, so solemnly that I half suspected him of joking. Now, I am not so certain. "These apparitions torment me day and night. Is there nothing you can do for me?"

"I'm afraid *I* can do nothing," I told him, very gently. "The remedy lies in your power alone. I very much fear that as long as you fear and obey your predecessors, they will always rule over you."

The Emperor gave me a look almost of terror. "But—but what else should I do? My grandfather listened to the Jews and the liberals, and look what they did to him!"

I felt something like the advent of a headache. "But then, what will *you* do?"

"I must preserve the principle of autocracy," Nicky said, rising to his feet, and beginning to pace the apartment. "I must continue the work begun by my father to restore what my grandfather destroyed, and to enlarge the empire before it is consumed by the English and the Germans. I only wish to God that I felt worthy of the task."

This rendered me speechless. He was evidently painfully in earnest, and yet—oh Lord! could he see no other way forward? Did the Emperor know *nothing* of his people's mood? Preservation of the autocracy was the last thing they wanted, and the subject peoples already within the empire were curdling with resentment, without more being added. Furthermore, I was absolutely certain that if Nicky meant to enslave himself to his ancestors he was in for a great many more extremely unpleasant encounters with the old reprobates—apart from what it might cost the empire itself in blood and turmoil.

If it had been in any way polite to tell an Emperor that he was not his ancestors' dog, to be commanded against his better judgement and whipped when he did not obey, I would have said so. However, it was plain that he would not listen to *me;* and from Sergei Alexandrovich and either Nicholas Nikolaevich he would scarcely have any better advice than what came from his ancestors.

But what if Vasily could speak to him? The two of them had been friends. Vasily himself felt sure that he could sway his cousin. There was so much *good* that Vasily might do here among his family; and was it not selfish of me to wish him well away from them?

"I regret that I could be of no greater assistance, sir," I said at last. "You asked if you were going mad: I know that the horrors of the departed dead sometimes do send people mad. Believe me that I only wish to spare you pain."

The Emperor managed one of those peculiarly charming smiles. "I do believe it, and I thank you. Sergei will make you a handsome gift."

"As a matter of fact," I said, "in lieu of the gift, may I ask a favour?"

The Emperor's smile cooled a little, but he said, "You may."

"Your cousin Vasily Nikolaevich is in Moscow. Won't you see him? For the sake of your old friendship?"

"Good heavens! My cousin Vasily? In Moscow?" The Emperor gave me a startled, and somewhat pitying look. "You are generous, Countess—too generous. Ask something for yourself, not for Vasily Nikolaevich. My cousin has an evil reputation, especially among women."

At first I could not believe that Vasily had indeed done something dreadful enough to make him notorious even by Grand Ducal standards—but then, recalling the very great crowd of imprints that had surrounded him at the séance in Zlata's drawing-room, I could not repress a shiver.

"I think you will find Vasily much changed," I said. "Please agree to see him, sir. I don't require any other payment."

"If he *had* changed, you would know why it is that I warn you against him." Before I could think of a reply, the Emperor bowed his head in assent. "Well, if you insist, you may tell my cousin to present himself at the Alexandria Palace this evening."

# 12

# Chapter XII.

Grand Duke Sergei made me the promised gift—an embroidered purse filled with gold coins, just as though I was a Gypsy fortune-teller in a pantomime. After that I pled weariness and Zlata consented to take me home. This occurred much to the Montenegrins' disappointment, for they were all agog to hear the truth of those screams, and of the ice which they had beheld covering the floor of Militsa's second-best salon.

To Zlata's questions, as we returned home in the carriage, I replied only that the spiritual world was full of mysteries and besides, the Emperor had sworn me to secrecy. In fact, I could not help brooding upon what I had seen today. The poor woman in the Hanwell Asylum had been beset, like Nicky, by horrors she could not banish. Perhaps what her keepers called madness, had simply been the presence of distressing ghosts.

I had always known that madness was a possibility for one such as myself; but now I felt I had a glimpse of what it might really be like. Despite the summer's heat, a thrill of cold fear shot through me. What if Anna, or my father's imprint, had not been so amiable? What if the next departing shade, or the next persistent imprint to attach itself to me, was a horror like Nicky's ancestors? Would I, too, be reduced to a lunatic asylum?

The journey, thank God, was a brief one. I found our lodgings very hot and stuffy, and also empty. I therefore tried to persuade Zlata to leave, but Vasily and Schmidt returned before I could do so, and then of course there was no dislodging her. While Schmidt made tea, I reclined on a divan and said, "You will never guess whom I met today, your grace."

"The Tsar," Vasily responded at an instant.

"Oh! really!" I cried. "That is too bad!"

At that I had the satisfaction of seeing him look absolutely astounded. "What! you mean that you saw Nicky himself? In truth?"

"Yes; he had come to Princess Militsa's on purpose to meet me. Of course I can't tell you about it just now," I added, conscious of Zlata's presence in the room, for she had perched herself on the balcony chair and was looking through Vasily's sketchbook with a frown. "But he has agreed to see you this evening."

At this news, Zlata dropped the sketchbook and exclaimed with pleasure; and Vasily said, "My dear, I could kiss you."

"Not if I see you coming," I retorted, thinking that it was high time—especially with Zlata present—to apply that cold elbow. Alas! the words fell to the ground, for there came a gleam into Vasily's eye which told me he had accepted the challenge.

"Your time with the Emperor was not wasted, Countess!" Zlata exclaimed, clapping her hands. "You must be sure to go to the palace this evening, Vaska. It will be hard for him to refuse you if you are waiting on his doorstep."

"Why should he refuse the Grand Duke?" I asked, confused.

"Ah," said Vasily, his high spirits evidently punctured by Zlata's words. "The truth is, Nicky has an unfortunate habit of telling people what they want to hear and then forgetting about it later. He has always had such a horror of disagreement. Zlata is right: we ought not to count our chickens before they hatch."

"Don't worry, Vaska; perhaps *I* shall be able to put in a good word for you," Zlata said. I could not help a mean-spirited suspicion that she was attempting to position herself, and not me, as the one to whom Vasily should be grateful for his forthcoming restoration to Nicky's good graces. "But tell me about your afternoon. What were you doing while the Countess and I were with the Emperor?"

"Schmidt and I had important business, my dear, which I can't tell you about just now."

Zlata pouted. "Seeing the Emperor is all very well, but it is nothing like as much fun as spending time with *you,* Vaska."

Vasily said something non-committal. Presently Mimi and Nijam returned, evidently bursting to tell us of their visit to the Bolshoi Theatre; but once again the sight of Princess Zlata struck them almost silent. "What news?" that lady asked brightly.

"How hot it is!" Mimi said, rather than answer the question. "If I were you, your highness, I should not spend such an afternoon being broiled alive in a miserable garret."

Zlata did not blink an eye at this outrageous hint; but she dimpled. "Oh! I cannot think why I have not offered you the use of *my* house. It is beautifully cool, and there is more than enough room for all of you."

"I'm afraid that's out of the question," Nijam said, saving me the trouble of explaining that I was quite sure a return to that house would give me nightmares. "But truly, your highness, if the heat is troubling you there is no need for you to remain."

"Princess Zlata has already been of such great assistance to us," I put in, "for she is closely acquainted with the French Ambassador, and has an idea where the Meissonier painting might be. In fact, your highness, why don't you and the Grand Duke go out and call on the Ambassador this afternoon, before going to meet the Emperor at the Alexandria?"

Vasily gave me a reproachful look, but Zlata clapped her hands in delight. "Oh! what a splendid idea! Are you coming, Vaska?"

"Of course he's going," said Nijam, and I added sententiously, "You know what they say about a stitch in nine."

"Yes, but I'm not sure *you* do," Vasily muttered, fetching his hat.

"Is Vasily really having an audience with the Tsar?" Mimi asked the moment the door closed behind him and the princess. "Why? What does *that* have to do with the job?"

I was reminded that Vasily had not made the rest of the crew privy to his designs. "Vasily thinks it's worth seeing if he might find his way back into the Emperor's good graces. We should all be safer without the Okhrana chasing us about as they did in Vienna."

Nijam sniffed. "I don't see that it makes much difference. The Emperor may call off his own dogs, but it was German werewolves who attacked us in London, and they certainly don't answer to the Russian emperor. If Vasily *really* wanted to be safe, the simplest thing would be to fake his death. I could do it with a few pints of blood, a spare corpse, and a bomb. After that no one would chase him about."

This had not occurred to me, but it was in fact a simple and elegant solution. "Well, perhaps that's indeed what he plans," I said.

"I doubt it," Mimi said, with a hard little laugh. "This is Vasily we're talking about. He likes being a Grand Duke too much to give it up entirely. He enjoys the attention. You will see. What *is* Vasily planning, anyway? Confess, Schmidt—you were out with him half the afternoon."

Schmidt reddened. "I can't tell you that! That would betray sir's confidence."

Nijam's lips thinned. "Oh, stop it! You were like a cat on hot bricks all morning. Whatever he's getting up to, it doesn't sit well with you, does it?" Schmidt did not answer, and Nijam put her teacup down so hard that I thought it might have cracked. "I believe that you'd throw yourself off that balcony if Vasily told you to do it."

It had all the hallmarks of an old argument: Schmidt looked frankly miserable, and Nijam as though she might be about to throw her teacup. "Now, now," I said. "I trust Schmidt not to let Vasily do anything that might be injurious to himself or to us, and that's the main thing. And since we've a little time to ourselves, you and Mimi had better tell us how you fared at the Bolshoi Theatre."

"Oh that! Well, we have both bad news and good," Nijam said, glowering. The story she and Mimi told was as follows.

\* \* \*

The front entrance of the Bolshoi Theatre was an imposing

neoclassical porch whose pediment was surmounted by bronze steeds, everlastingly pawing and snorting at the air. This entrance, however, Nijam and Mimi eschewed in favour of the stage door, which admitted them upon a cramped warren of corridors, wardrobes, store-rooms, green-rooms and dressing-rooms.

Not even Mimi had visited the Bolshoi before; for although students at the Petersburg ballet school might occasionally take part in performances at the Maryinsky, they were not usually sent as far as Moscow. All the same, it did not take her and Nijam long to find their way backstage, to that dark and liminal area concealed from the theatre by curtains, wings, and backdrops. On the front stage itself a rehearsal was underway, and the wings were full of people—dancers waiting their turn to go on, stage-hands wheeling about bits of scenery, and severe-looking ballet mistresses and masters muttering beneath their breath. At first no one paid much attention to the intruders, who were able to stroll the length of the dark passage at the back of the stage, craning their necks to observe the workings of the stage-hands above. There in the shadowed heights were fixed a series of rails from which the painted backdrops hung. A gantry accessible by ladders enabled the stagehands to climb up to hang the backdrops, while a system of pulleys and ropes at the stage level enabled them to be raised or lowered without anyone needing to climb aloft.

"I think this will be quite suitable to our purposes," Nijam said, inspecting the mechanism of the pulleys, and giving the ropes an experimental tug. Just then there came the rap of a wandlike staff against the floor, and the two looked up to see an old lady whose rigidly erect bearing and still-graceful figure proclaimed her one of the ballet-mistresses of the theatre.

"And who," she said severely in French, "might *you* be?"

This was Mimi's cue, and she had dressed for the rôle in a dress of diaphanous white muslin whose long, fitted sleeves were surmounted by small puffs. This had been accented with a sky-blue sash and necktie, and a broad straw hat from which white wings and feathers erupted, the whole giving her the look of an exquisite and very fashionable angel. We shall not inquire as to where, precisely, she had found this ensemble. Surely it could not have been difficult; Moscow was, at that moment, *very* full of fashionable young women.

She sailed past Nijam, who refused to wear anything but the severest black, and offered a limp gloved hand to the ballet-mistress. "My name is Adeline Genée," she said. "I think you've heard of me? I am from Copenhagen. And this is my woman of affairs, Miss Nijam."

Nijam made a silent bow. She did not much like having to play a rôle, and arranged matters mostly by looking as forbidding as she could. When anxious, Nijam gave off the strong impression that, although apparently unperturbed, she would nevertheless like to commit a murder or two to relieve her feelings. This had the added benefit, not only of discomfiting her interlocutors, but also of dissuading them from asking any inconvenient questions.

The ballet-mistress, though evidently a woman of strong moral fibre, decided at a glance not to bother Nijam.

"Adeline Genée—I believe I've heard the name," said she, managing to suggest that she had heard it in no good connection. "A dancer in *London,* in fact."

Mimi shrugged. "It's not something I'm proud of, madame,

but it's honest work and it pays the bills."

"And you are here because—?"

"I'm looking for a friend of mine; an Anna Ivanova Sorina."

"Who is this, Madame Christensen?" a haughty voice interrupted them. On the stage, a *pas de deux* had come to its end, and now the dancers came off—a graceful-looking young man, not very tall, and a very pretty young lady in a brassy blonde wig nearly as yellow as her sumptuous costume, which did not quite suit her black eyebrows. It was she who had spoken, holding her head very high and observing Mimi down the length of her aristocratic nose.

"Adeline Genée," Mimi said again. "I'm a dancer in London—"

"I condole you!" said the wigged ballerina. "Yes, yes, be off with you," she said to the young dancer at her side, flapping her hand to dismiss him. To Mimi she added, "I am Mathilde Kschessinska. What brings you here, madame?"

Mimi brightened at the chance to recite her carefully-prepared story. "I'm in Moscow as the friend of Prince Alphonse of Schaumburg-Lippe, who is attending the Emperor's coronation!"

Nijam gave an inward sigh, for it really did sound like a recitation. She distracted herself by doing sums in her head. Yes, she thought, she had indeed included enough phosphorous in her latest invention to create a sufficiently strong burst of light, and she had no doubt that this would come distinctly in handy if their mission took them much longer.

"The world and his wife is in Moscow," said the ballerina, with another dismissive flutter of her fingers. "I mean, why have you come to the theatre? I heard you mention the name of little Sorina."

"Indeed! Anna Ivanova is a friend of mine, and I thought she might be here," said Mimi, sincerely enough. "In fact I'm worried about her. We were unable to find her in Petersburg, and none of her friends have seen her in weeks."

"Sorina isn't here," said Kschessinska, knitting her black brows. "And if I were you, I should take great care around that sly minx, for she only cares for what she can get!"

(In the attic, when Mimi repeated these words, Anna, who had been lolling on the divan, sat up quite straight. "Pardon me! Mathilde said *that?*")

Mimi herself being too surprised to speak, the great Kschessinska flounced away forthwith, leaving only silence in her wake. "How dare she call Anna names!" Mimi said at last, when she was capable of utterance. "I'll set her wig on fire!!"

The ballet-mistress, Madame Christensen, cleared her throat. "It's true, Sorina is not here. But if you want to know, you should ask young Valery Petrovich, one of the dancers. If anyone knows where to find Sorina, it is he."

Nijam shot Mimi a startled look, for neither she nor Oksana had mentioned a young man. Mimi shook her head and desired the lady to guide them. When Valery Petrovich had been extracted from the dressing-room he shared with the other male dancers of the *corps de ballet,* he proved to be a very interesting young man with a shock of fair brown hair, blazing green eyes and a face that might have been painted in raw and slashing lines by an artist of the *avant-garde.*

("What Nijam means," Mimi said, "is that he's *delicious.* Even she knows it, though she won't admit to it." Nijam looked pained. Schmidt, who is also fair and striking, also looked

161

pained. I suspected that Nijam had a type.)

In an empty corner of the corridor, Mimi said, "We're friends of Anna Sorina's. Do you know her?"

At this, Valery Petrovich threw them a darkling glare which could have given Nijam's a run for its money. "Anna never spoke to me of *you*. What do you want with her?"

"She hasn't been heard of in weeks," Mimi said. "And of course I'm a friend of Anna's. We studied at the Imperial Ballet School together. Something's happened to her, and we're going to set it right, but we need your help."

Valery swallowed, hard. "Anna is gone," he said huskily. "That's all there is to it. She's gone, and she ought to be left to rest in peace."

"Then you won't help us?"

"Who do you take me for? Alexander Nevsky?" he said savagely, and then he turned on his heel and went away, and there was nothing left for it, but to find their way out and drive back home.

\* \* \*

"There you have it," Nijam finished. "The theatre itself is perfect for what we have in mind, and the gala performance is only five days away. But we could get no sense out of either Kschessinska or Petrovich."

"That's not important," I said with a careless wave. "What's important is that apparently Anna had a young man, and never mentioned that fact to *me*."

"I *don't* have a young man!" Anna protested.

"She doesn't have him," Mimi repeated, for of course she had not heard Anna's rejoinder. "Perhaps Valery Petrovich is the one who picked up Anna's handkerchief the night of *Cinderella*. He would certainly have been at the academy about the same time as us. But what point would there be in gossiping about it? Didn't Oksana explain how it works? The contract absolutely forbids any liaison between dancers. One lives like a nun for twenty years, or else one takes a lover outside the Ballet, to pay you properly and to pull the strings if there should be any—consequences. He was not her young man—neither of them could have afforded it for another sixteen or seventeen years. Even then they would starve together on a pittance, for God knows the pension is hardly enough to feed sparrows."

"That's why I was trying to cultivate Mathilde," Anna said, sounding as though she was on the verge of tears. "How could she say I only care for what I can get? I *don't* have brilliant connections and I'm *not* a natural dancer—how else am I to live? I would have been a faithful friend to her, all the same! Indeed I would! Why should she call me names? What did I ever do to her? What *could* I have done, when she might have made or broken me?"

I felt sorrier for her than I could say. "I ought to have gone myself," I said in a low voice. "Anna might have helped me get some sense out of Valery Petrovich."

"You can do it tomorrow," Mimi suggested. Then there was a tap at the door, and our landlady brought in the dinner.

This we had barely made any inroads upon, when Vasily returned, this time without Zlata. "You're home early," I greeted him, as Schmidt helped him off with his coat.

Vasily scowled. "Nicky never saw me."

Part of me couldn't help feeling more than a little glad at that; and another part felt guilty, because of what Zlata had

163

said to me in the carriage. And how could I object to Zlata? She was venal and conniving, but so was I. She was able to offer Vasily a path back to the life to which he was accustomed, and I—what had I done, but betray him at every turn?

Dinner ended, the day's oppressive heat began to ebb away through the open windows, and the various members of our crew scattered to their own pursuits. Nijam disappeared into her room to make peculiar smells and bangings, Schmidt picked up a brush and began tending to Vasily's already impeccable coats, and Mimi threw herself onto the divan and was asleep in moments. As for me, I had been meaning to write to my mother; so I pulled out a sheet of paper.

Vasily had not moved from his seat at the head of the table, where he sat drinking tea. "Be careful what you write, little mouse," he told me. "The Okhrana will certainly open your mail and read it."

"Do you think so?"—He gave me a sardonic look. I sighed and laid down my pen. "Somehow I don't feel like writing letters now."

Vasily leaned forward, smiling. "Then put on your hat and come for a walk. What do you want to see? Saint Basil's Cathedral is worth a look, and I'll tell you horrible stories of Ivan the Terrible and his *oprichniki,* the devils in black."

A day or two since, I would have been happy to do so. But I had now had some acquaintance with the terrible Ivan; and I could not quite get Anna's words out of my head. *Grand Dukes don't marry commoners.* Very lightly, I said, "How attentive you're being, your grace! I wonder what you mean by it?"

"I told you, didn't I? It's a confidence trick."

"But what do you mean to steal?"

His eyes laughed. "That would be telling."

164

Perhaps I was weak, but I could not fence with him today. "Well, then," I said, "I'll pretend that I don't suspect a thing."

I did put on my hat, and we went out. Not once did Vasily mention the things we had learned about each other that morning at breakfast, although perhaps one day I should like to; he and I might understand each other a little better because of it. But for explanations, I found that after all, there was no need. There was more to each of us than we had at first known; but Vasily was still Vasily, and I was still myself, and I found that in this matter I could trust him.

# 13

# Chapter XIII.

When my blameless slumber was interrupted about midnight by a commanding rap at the door, I felt a strong desire to pull the covers over my face and burst into tears. Not the Okhrana *again!* What could they want with us now?

"Miss Dark! Sir! Wake up quickly!" The voice echoing from the other side of the door belonged to Alphonse Schmidt. I pulled the covers away from my face to find Anna hovering nearby.

"It's not the police," she told me.

"Then what *is* it?" I inquired, pulling on my dressing-gown. Anna could not answer that question. Vasily and Nijam made it out into the sitting-room nearly as quickly as I did: Schmidt, still fully-clad, was checking his salt-water bulbs and buckling on his revolver. "I'll be there in a moment," he was saying in a low, terse voice to no one in particular. "Just as soon as the others know, too."

"Know what?" Nijam inquired.

"It's Mimi," Schmidt said, tapping his ear. "She's in trouble." I gaped at him. *"Mimi?* Isn't she in bed?"

Schmidt shook his head. "She went out this evening—right before you and sir returned from your walk—and asked me to sit up for her wearing my transmitter, just in case. Something's happening in the streets. She said to come prepared for a fight."

There was a moment's silence. I looked at Nijam and Vasily.

"I'm coming with you," Vasily said, dashing into his room. "You ladies, stay here!"

"If something's happened, Mimi will want a woman with her," I protested. "Nijam can hold the fort."

A moment later the three of us had assembled—Schmidt armed to the teeth and looking very fierce; Vasily and I in greatcoats thrown over our nightclothes. Vasily unscrewed the carved handle of his walking-stick and I glimpsed the gleam of a blade within.

"En avant," he said, but just as we started down the stairs, Nijam—who had somehow managed to get properly dressed, and to equip herself with a carpet-bag—emerged from the attic, locked the door, and came to join us. This was surprising, but we were all in far too much of a hurry to object. Out we went into the perpetual dusk.

"Where is she?" I asked Schmidt, as we hurried into the narrow streets.

"Not far from here, in a street named Petrovka," he replied.

Anna, who had accompanied us, flashed away into the darkness, returning a moment later. "I've found her," she told me. She and I led the others down a narrow alleyway between a row of high tenements; and we found Mimi crouched in the shadows at the far end, looking out upon Petrovka Street.

"Mimi," I whispered, and in a blink she turned upon us. Something glittered upon her clenched fists—the tiger claws to which she had helped herself at the British Museum not long ago.

I stifled a ladylike shriek. "Mimi! Don't be afraid—it's us!"

"What has happened?" Vasily asked, unsheathing his swordstick in one fluidly graceful motion. "Name the culprit. We shall punish him."

"Lord, Vasya, don't be so dramatic," Mimi said, lowering her tiger claws after a long breathless moment. But her eyes were very wide and I thought her breathing was a little too quick, as though she had had a fright. "Nothing has yet happened; but it soon will."

"What's that noise?" Nijam put in, lifting her head like one sniffing the air for battle. It was a faint, insinuating hum that for some moments had been getting into my bones and making my teeth itch. The itch eased a little once Nijam pointed it out, but the sound went on, soft and strangely compelling.

"That's what I called you here for. Sirens! Look!"

Mimi pointed her claws towards the street, and we craned our necks to see. On the opposite side of the street, in the glare of the street-lamps, a gentleman—turned out beautifully from his stovepipe hat to his immaculate spats—was pursuing a somewhat serpentine course along the foot-path. He had evidently dined well. Behind him walked two ladies and two gentlemen, and it was from them that the low humming came. As we watched, the song changed, becoming a little louder, a little faster. The well-dressed gentleman's steps wavered still more; and I wondered whether after all, he had dined as well as I at first presumed.

"We can't afford to act in haste," Nijam said, but her warning was already too late. Snatching a glass bulb from beneath his coat, Schmidt hurled himself into the street. Vasily and Mimi exchanged a glance and followed him.

"They're *mad*," said Anna, disbelievingly.

With a sigh, Nijam began rifling about in the depths of her carpet-bag. Across the street, the siren song ceased, and the ladies shrieked as Schmidt's bulbs shattered against the stone wall of the building beside them, showering them with droplets of salt-water. I heard Mimi bellowing, "Salt-water doesn't *work* on sirens, you *turnip*," and then a general brawl broke out. The gentlemen engaged Vasily with their own walking-sticks, and from somewhere Schmidt received a blow and went tumbling head-over-heels into the road.

In the same moment the song began again, this time loud and piercing. It was the most beautiful thing I had ever heard, and it wrapped itself about me with a horrible, compelling power. It reached into my bosom and plucked out the heart, and there was nothing I could do but follow. Tears streamed down my face as I hurried across the street, arms outstretched to the lovely singers like a moth about to hurl itself into the flame. Self-immolation was the least tribute I might pay to such beauty. Touch them, and I would burn up in a moment's pleasure; but it would be an end worth having.

Schmidt lay in the road groaning; but the song seemed to have the same effect upon him, for he rose gasping to his feet and followed me towards the sirens. Vasily and Mimi had stopped fighting; Vasily gripped Mimi's arm and was making some confounded racket, shouting defiance at the top of his lungs. It was getting in the way of the music, and I felt that I could have throttled him to make him be quiet. The gentleman who had dined well had a similarly hostile impulse. He hurled himself at Vasily, who was forced to release Mimi in order to defend himself; the shouting ceased, the song swelled out in triumph, and Schmidt and Mimi and I threw ourselves at the sirens' feet.

I shudder to think what might have occurred next; but just then a bomb went off in the street behind us.

I call it a bomb—in fact there was nothing in the way of shock, flying debris, and shattered limbs, which one might expect from an explosion. But there was a blinding flash of light, and a roar of sound which together were nearly enough to strike us senseless. The song quite definitely halted, and the sirens went staggering about drunkenly, apparently struck deaf and blind by the blast. In the ringing silence that followed, terror pierced me like a blade of ice. *What* was I doing on my knees? Was this some kind of mesmerism? —I recoiled to my feet, desperate to put some distance between myself and the monsters whom a moment before I had been ready to worship.

"Murder! Anarchists! Help!" the sirens cried, attempting dizzily to remove themselves to a safe distance.

"It's a good thing I *did* come," Nijam said acidly, strolling across the road to join us. She wore plugs in her ears and carried a little canister with a fuse sticking out the top. A similar contraption was still emitting sparks in the road. "For heaven's sake, Schmidt! What were you thinking, running off like that in the midst of our deliberations?"

Nijam's Alphonse had gone white as a proverbial ghost . "I beg your pardon," he said, very chastened. "They were about to drain him. I didn't know what else to do."

Looking about for the sirens' prey, we found the well-dined gentleman lying flat on the pavement beside a weary-looking Vasily.

"What are we going to do with the victim?" I asked, for it was evident that we could not leave him in the street. He was absolutely helpless, and the sirens were still wailing and running into lamp-posts at no very great distance.

"Pick him up and carry him home, of course," said Mimi. "He can't give us a handsome reward if we leave him in the street."

Nijam pinched the bridge of her nose, but all she said was, "Very well," and between them Schmidt and Vasily scraped the unconscious reveller off the pavement and carried him home.

"Did you really call us out of bed just because you saw an opportunity to do somebody a good turn, Mimi?" I asked as we followed them.

"Of course not," she said with a shiver. After a moment she lowered her voice, as though ashamed. "I couldn't stop following them. Didn't you notice how their song gets into your bones? I barely managed to call for help."

I shuddered. Much as I had feared the mesmerism of the melusines of the Schloss Frohsdorf, my assumed identity as Marie-Caroline de Bourbon had protected me from being either mesmerised by them or drained. In that I had been very fortunate—compared to the servants, who had been aged unnaturally before their time, preyed upon by their employers. I did not like to think how many of the citizens of Moscow, like the limp gentleman presently being hurried through the night by my confederates, might be suffering something similar.

It was not far to return to our lodgings, thank goodness, and with some sweating and muttering Vasily and Schmidt got the unfortunate victim of the sirens up six flights of stairs and onto the divan in our garret just as the clock struck one. In the gaslight, we beheld a handsome gentleman of regular features, upon which the advent of middle-age had as yet made few inroads. He had a straight nose, a swooping mustache, and a fashionably pointed beard. Schmidt, with a valet's instincts, had even managed to rescue his silk hat.

"I wonder who he is," said I.

"We can ask him when he wakes up," Nijam answered, ever practical. "And in the meanwhile, Mimi can explain precisely what she was doing on the streets at midnight."

"Indeed!" Vasily said, panting a little. The garret was still warm, and the effort of carrying such spoils of battle up six flights of stairs would tell upon anyone. "Out with it, my dear!"

Mimi, who had been uncharacteristically silent, actually reddened. "You and Schmidt have your secrets," she said. "I don't see why I oughtn't be allowed to have mine."

"It wasn't a man," Vasily said, narrowing his eyes. "You don't need the money, and you aren't the kind to fall in love. It's something else you don't want us to know, presumably because it would affect our business. You asked Schmidt to sit up for you, because you thought it might be dangerous, and because Schmidt is too good a fellow to carry tales. And as a result of all this, had it not been for Miss Nijam's presence of mind, the five of us might now be dead or doddering about in spectacles, having been drained by sirens."

"It really was a *very* impressive display," I said to Nijam. "Was it your phosphorous that went off with such a bang?"

Nijam sniffed. "A reductive way of putting it, but yes. After what happened in London, I couldn't rely upon being able to blow the electric lights next time we fell afoul of monsters.

These canisters provide the requisite noise and light without being actually dangerous. But don't change the subject. Vasily is right: Mimi owes us an explanation."

Mimi went red and pale and obstinate-looking. "All right," she said defiantly, "but you aren't going to like it. The truth is, I've been reporting to the Okhrana."

For a moment her words made no sense to me; but Vasily paled, Schmidt sat down very suddenly, and Nijam's lips thinned, while her face became wooden with shock. I was compelled to believe the report of my ears.

"Reporting to the Okhrana!" I repeated, half numb. Mimi's only loyalty was to herself; all of us knew that. But surely she was too bitter against the Russian Empire ever to become an Okhrana spy! "About *what?* About us?"

"I suppose they paid you well!" said Vasily with a sneer.

"Don't take the high road with me, Vasily Nikolaevich! *You* had the luxury of spying for the Empire for money. *I* have to do it because *they know where my family live!*" Mimi's final words echoed in that small space for a long terrible moment. Then her eyes filled with tears and she repeated: "They know where my family live."

All became clear. "Of course they do," I said, feeling more pity than censure. "They tried to recruit me, too, and I refused them. But then, *my* family is safely in London."

"They tried to recruit *me,*" Nijam said in a low, almost a choking voice, "and they had *my* family in their very clutches!"

I wondered, startled, whether this meant that Nijam considered *us* to be her family!

Vasily gave a death's-head smile. "I blame myself entirely," he said. "I ought to have known it was too good to be true. Of *course* the Okhrana would have someone following me in

Moscow."

"For heaven's sake," Nijam snapped. "The world doesn't revolve around *you*, Vasily Nikolaevich. Can't you see what is really happening? They never set Mimi to watch *you;* they set her to watch *Schmidt.*"

"Me?" Schmidt protested.

"For the sake of the revenants, of course! Pay attention!"

"You should thank me," Mimi muttered. "If I'd said no, they might have set someone else on us, someone who actually wanted to help them!"

"You *are* helping them!" Never before had I heard Nijam raise her voice; never before had I seen her so furious. It was quite different to the last time Nijam thought Mimi had betrayed us for money, when only the Noor-Jahan diamond and our livelihoods had been at stake. "It beggars belief! What! You had Alphonse Schmidt sitting up at night listening to his transmitter, watching your back while you went to report on him to his enemies? *He bought you peppermints!*"

And Nijam clenched her fist upon the flashbang in her hand, half as though she meant to set it off in the unfortunate Mimi's face.

Anna listened with disbelief. "This woman knows nothing of how we do things here. Mimi is right: if she hadn't been watching us, someone worse would have."

I was inclined to agree; but I did not think that it would be wise to repeat the shade's words just now. "There's no harm done, Nijam," I said, catching her wrist as gently as I could. "Mimi has confessed, and we are all still at liberty."

Nijam shrugged away from me, but she stowed the canister back into the carpet bag and crossed her arms, glowering silently at the culprit.

"I knew you wouldn't understand; it's why I said nothing," Mimi said sulkily when the silence threatened to lengthen. "But I told them nothing about Schmidt or *any* of you that they didn't already know. And I'm not the only spy they have watching you, either. No, I don't know who it is," she added, as I opened my mouth to ask. "The landlady, I presume, who's been keeping an eye on the Populists next door. Now I'd better be going."

"Going? Where?" Schmidt stammered. Until now he had been silent.

"Lord, I don't know. To the sirens, I suppose."

"Mimi," I protested. "Don't be silly! No one wants you to go anywhere. We all need our thief—don't we?" I added, turning to the others.

Vasily thrust his hands deep into his pockets. "I vote she stays," he said, scowling. "Police surveillance is the price we pay for breathing the air of this country."

"Don't go, Miss Laine," Schmidt said. "I'd rather my friends were reporting on me than anyone else. Besides, what can the Okhrana do to me, when there's nothing I can tell them about the creation of the revenants?"

"What could they *do* to you?" Nijam broke in. "They could call a meeting of the Kabale and have your memories restored just long enough to extract everything they want from inside your head—that's what they could do to you!"

Poor Schmidt! he went absolutely white. "But I *don't* know how the revenants were made," he said, almost pleadingly. "I *couldn't* have known. That was my brother's work—not mine. Wasn't it?"

Nijam returned his pleading look with one of her own, shuttered and blank.

175

"You wanted to restore my memories," Schmidt said, becoming more agitated. "You would not have wished to do such a thing if I knew—if *that* was in my past."

Perhaps Nijam thought we had had enough confessions for one evening, for to this she made no reply. Poor Schmidt! He turned very white, but he made no further requests.

"It seems that Mimi is not the only one keeping secrets," said I, as gently as I could.

Nijam's mouth tightened, and for a long moment there was absolute silence in the garret. At length she swung around and addressed the erring ballerina in something like her old manner. "If Schmidt doesn't mind what you did, then I won't object to it either. Keep feeding the Okhrana with information that can't hurt us. But next time, think very carefully before you keep something like this from us. And for heaven's sake, everyone," she added, raking us all with a glare, "keep an eye out for Madame Kapanadzy; we can't have her listening at the key-hole while we're discussing business."

So saying, she brushed past us and slammed the door to her room. The sound startled the gentleman who had, until now, remained tidily out of the way upon the divan.

"Bless my soul!" he exclaimed, beholding us all in some bewilderment. His French was faintly accented with German. "Where am I—and who are *you?*"

Vasily turned. "Allow me to introduce myself," he said, all charm. "I am Grand Duke Vasily Nikolaevich. I'm afraid you had run into a spot of trouble with a handful of hungry sirens, so I have brought you back to my lodgings. I don't suppose you can remember what happened?"

The gentleman's brow furrowed. "Dear me, I do remember!" he said. "We dined together with the King of Italy—and then the sirens were following on the way home, and I could not get away from their song! My dear fellow, you've saved my life! Allow me to introduce myself: I am Prince Louis of Battenberg. I don't suppose you'd be so good as to send the news to my wife? Princess Victoria of Hesse—you'll find her at the Kremlin with her sister, the Empress."

Vasily sent me a look gleaming with calculation—and with triumph. It seemed that we had, in fact, rescued the Emperor's own brother-in-law.

"Oh yes," he said, "I do think we might be able to do that."

# 14

# Chapter XIV.

It was due to the happy accident of the night before, that the following day found Vasily absolutely clasped to the bosom of his cousin, the Emperor. A summons had arrived from the Kremlin—the mediaeval fortress at the heart of the city—that morning, and Vasily found himself quickly ushered into the Imperial presence. Both the Emperor and the Empress were present—the latter, Vasily said, a remarkably beautiful girl, although painfully shy and rather forbidding in aspect.

"Alicky and I don't know how to thank you," said Nicky earnestly. The three of them were alone in the gorgeous Silver Drawing Room, with its priceless Gobelin tapestries and oxidised-silver furniture, and Vasily found this informal setting a pleasing sign that they would be free to discuss private family matters. "Poor Louis is of morganatic birth, you know, and ever since Coburg such people have been viewed with suspicion. No doubt the attackers thought only to give him a good fright, and perhaps drain away a year or two of life. Still, if they had succeeded, we should have had a full-blown diplomatic incident on our hands."

Morganatic royalties had always occupied an inferior place in Vasily's world: as the half-caste offspring of royalty and commonalty, they inherited neither their parents' high station nor their monstrous abilities. It was only since the events at Coburg two years previously that such persons had begun to be seen as a threat; for it was their tainted blood which had rendered Vasily toothless, together with the heirs to many of the most important thrones in Europe. Prince Louis could not help his birth; he had probably never dreamed of using his blood as the demure English princess had done, to defang the Kabale itself. Yet he lived in a world where blood was everything; and now more than ever he would be punished for having the wrong sort.

"Don't thank me! Anyone would have done the same," Vasily assured his cousin, with an airy wave of his hand. He did not for a moment mean this, but it sounded appropriately deprecating. "Such times we live in! Better that the royalties of the world should stick together, than that we should turn upon each other with suspicion."

That made Nicky look uncomfortable. "I must apologise for not seeing you yesterday, Vasya. We have been so busy, you know, preparing for the coronation tomorrow. And then, Sergei sees assassins behind every tree, and makes everything so difficult. It was easier when we had revenants. It *is* so nice to see you again! Is it true that you've found a cure for the defanging?"

Vasily had spent a great deal of time on his way from our lodgings meditating upon the best means of approaching his cousin, and he had determined upon judicious honesty. Even if Nicky *was* a practised avoider of difficult conversations, at least he was not the martinet his father had been.

"In fact, I must throw myself upon your discretion, Nicky," he said, adopting the shamefaced look he had been practising in his shaving-mirror before breakfast. "I knew it would be as much as my life was worth to show my face in Moscow without a very convincing set of fangs, but in truth they are false: I'm still sadly toothless. It's been as much as I can do to stay alive as it is, and so I've come back, like the prodigal in the parable, to admit my faults and to seek your protection."

*"Ah,"* said Nicky. The young Empress, who had not spoken since Vasily had first entered the room, looked a little sour. She had been a great favourite with her grandmother, Queen Victoria, and Vasily gathered that apart from Nicky himself, she rather disapproved of the louche and sanguinary Romanovs. He did not think that she was overjoyed to meet with him, let alone that she might urge Nicky to receive him back into the bosom of the family.

Nicky said carefully, "I understand! But you must see how this complicates things. If it were entirely my decision I would offer you my protection at once, you understand."

Vasily blinked innocently. "But who can constrain the Tsar's decision? Is someone pushing you around, Nicky? Best put a stop to that; you *do* mean to be lord and master in this country, don't you?"

"Oh, no one is pushing me around, as you put it!" Nicky reassured him, flushing slightly. "Only Sergei and some of the other uncles do have very strong opinions, and you understand that as the head of the family, and the father of my country, it is incumbent upon me to make the *right* decisions for everyone. You understand that your actions at Coburg were shocking, quite shocking to all of us. I could not possibly think of reinstating you, without some credible guarantee of your behaviour for the future."

Vasily had foreseen this objection; yet he still hesitated a moment before answering, and as stealthily as possible, checked his pockets once more for a stray transmitter. He did not fancy trying to explain the absolute purity of his intentions to the rest of the crew, should they be eavesdropping upon him. Reassured that I had *not* been up to any renewed tricks, he cleared his throat.

"I understand completely, Nicky, and I'm conscious that I must repair my faults if I'm to return to the fold. To that end, in fact, I've secured the services of one of the most brilliant scientific minds of our age."

"Alphonse Schmidt?" How readily the name came to Nicky's lips! It was an unwelcome reminder that the Okhrana ultimately reported to the Emperor; who had, in turn, plainly been reading their reports. "So *that's* why you've been travelling about with young Schmidt, is it? Still, it was one of the last acts the Kabale ever did, to erase that man's memories. It meant dispensing with the revenants, but at that time it was thought that more could be made quite easily, and the greatest need was to prevent any news of that dreadful night's deeds being made public. I'm afraid that we can't restore his memories now. Not without cutting a deal with the sirens, and they have absolutely refused to restore Schmidt's memories; unless a new Kabale is convened and the knowledge is made available to all the members. And of course that doesn't suit Russian interests at all. In the meantime we've had our own men working on the cure for two years without any success. Do you think an amnesiac could do better?"

Vasily himself thought it unlikely; but the slim possibility had been haunting his dreams of late. "I would like to get him set up in a laboratory as soon as possible, and then we might see," he said, evasively. "It would have been easy to do so, were I still in receipt of my incomes—but laboratories are expensive, you know!"

"Then the thing seems impossible," said Nicky. "I couldn't possibly restore your incomes, you know, without a preliminary guarantee. The family wouldn't stand for it."

Vasily sent his cousin a sharp glance. Nicky looked absolutely guileless. Ordinarily Nicky *was* absolutely guileless; except that now for a moment, a gleam of calculation shone in his eye. Vasily was not accustomed to a calculating Nicky.

"Unless?" he prompted, as the silence lengthened.

But I am getting ahead of my story. I did not learn of this latter part of the conversation until, alas! it was much too late.

* * *

While Vasily was meeting with the Emperor, Schmidt and I walked to the Bolshoi Theatre. We had left Nijam furiously at work in the garret, chomping on peppermints. Pleased though she had been with the results of last night's experiments, she said that she now had a better idea for keeping the monsters at bay. It was upon this notion, presumably, that she was now hard at work. As for Mimi, she had hired a troika, done herself up in a splendidly dashing frock and gone out saying that she meant to waylay and charm Vasily's father in the street. Mimi assured me that this was how ballerinas often pursued their liaisons, but I had my doubts as to the result. Mind you, I did not doubt that Mimi's efforts would *have* a result; only I was a little nervous as to precisely which result that might be. Mimi had a great many excellent qualities, but I did not know whether subtlety and tact were among them.

Indeed tact was certainly not among them, I thought with a sigh, casting a glance at my companion. Nijam's Alphonse seemed abstracted, and a faint frown was etched between his brows. "You were very gracious to Mimi last night, Herr Schmidt," I said at length. "But between you and me, are you sure you're comfortable continuing to work with her?"

"With Miss Laine?" Schmidt asked, coming courteously out of his reverie. "Oh, yes. One always knows where one stands with that young lady. She isn't deceitful by nature; only mercenary." And he heaved a regretful sigh.

"Let's hope that Nijam comes around to our way of thinking, then," said I. Nijam had said very little at breakfast, apart from desiring us to pass the butter. I was not quite sure whether this meant she was angry, or lacking in sleep, or wrapped up in thought. Schmidt said nothing, apparently still brooding over his own secret woes. If not Nijam, then what could be troubling him?

"Here's the stage door," Anna told me, pointing. "Rehearsals should finish in about ten minutes."

"Excellent," I said, garnering a startled glance from Schmidt. "Let's loiter for a few minutes, until your Valery Petrovich emerges."

"He isn't *my* Valery Petrovich," Anna said with a scowl. "He's only a friend."

Since their acquaintance was, alas! unlikely ever to proceed beyond friendship, I did not press the matter. Instead, I said to Schmidt, "I suppose it must be unsettling to see me addressing empty air like this."

"Not at all," he said, with gloomy politeness. I was ready to brush my hands of him, but then, at last, he heaved a sigh and said, "I confess to you, Miss Dark, that I'm worried about sir."

"About *Vasily?*"

"Perhaps I shouldn't have said anything."

The events of the past day had quite driven from my mind the question of Vasily's mysterious errands the day before. Now, all my doubts returned in force. "Some secrets," I said firmly, *"do* need to be shared."

Schmidt looked miserable. "It's nothing," he said, thereby proving himself an unskilled fibber. "What sir wants doesn't concern me. But at first, he only wanted a painting. And this morning, he asked me how I fancied settling in Russia for good."

I did not think that Schmidt needed to worry himself too much about this eventuality, at least not where himself was concerned. Nijam would certainly never allow Schmidt to remain in Russia, even if she was reduced to kidnapping.

"Don't you think Vasily might be better off here?" I asked, almost in a whisper.

Schmidt sent me a startled look. "Here? With *these* people? Didn't you hear what his father did to that girl?"

And it was this, more than anything else, which convinced me that I *ought* to worry. All this time I had been telling myself that I must not be selfish where Vasily was concerned; that if he wished to stay in Russia and marry Zlata, it was only right to stand gracefully aside. But if even Schmidt, with no ulterior motive, could see that this life was wrong for Vasily—why, then perhaps my worries were not as selfish as I had taught myself to think.

And he was even now meeting with the Emperor! I

reproached myself bitterly for not having slipped a live transmitter into his pocket, so as to eavesdrop upon that most interesting meeting!

"Vasily can't go back to being one of them; not entirely. Not without taking a cure; and he'll never do that." I bit my lip for a moment. "It doesn't exist, anyway."

Neither of my companions said anything. "You're very quiet, Anna," I observed bitterly. "Didn't you advise me to get Vasily reinstated?"

To my surprise, Anna looked rather sheepish. "I don't know," she said. "The things I've seen since I began to go about with you... I didn't know what these people were really like."

This did nothing to soothe my worries for Vasily. Happily, a moment later, the stage-door opened and dancers began to flock past, distracting me from my thoughts. "Look, there's Kschessinska," Anna pointed out breathlessly as a lovely, dark-haired, vivacious little person emerged in a cloud of fluttering blue silk. "And that lady with her is Olga Preobrajenska. Did you know she was born with a curved spine? And now she is second only to Legnani and Kschessinska." Her excited chatter continued, but I could not help seeing how many of the dancers, especially the men, wore shabby coats and set off at a brisk walk rather than stepping into some beautiful carriage. The world of the ballet, it seemed, was a microcosm of societies everywhere; there were those who ruled, those who served, and those like Anna, who did their best to rise.

"Oh, and that's Valery," Anna put in, pointing.

The young man who paused to put on a cloth cap before starting down the street towards the humbler parts of town was exactly as good-looking as Nijam and Mimi had hinted, that is, if you *like* the fair, raw-boned, passionate type. Schmidt and I followed him at once, crossed the street, and managed to waylay him, a little out of breath.

"Are you Valery Petrovich?" I asked in my most winsome manner. "I am Molly Dark. Anna Sorina sent me."

"What?" Valery snapped, coming to an abrupt halt. His eyes narrowed as he looked from me to Schmidt and back again. "You know Anna? Prove it, then."

It was at this moment that Anna ought to have stepped in to help convince him of my veracity. I waited, confident that the needed help would be forthcoming. Instead, Anna uttered a sound of surprise, just as though she had been sharply pinched.

"Oh!" she said. "Oh, it's all coming back to me now!" —Whereupon she disappeared.

This startled me so much that I could not help crying aloud. "Anna! Where are you?"

There was no reply, but I observed that Mr Petrovich was observing me with grim disapproval.

"I don't know what sort of joke this is supposed to be," he began.

"Wait," I said, making a wild gamble. Mimi had been surprised to learn that Anna had a friend among the male dancers, but in her surprise had let fall some suggestive words. "Anna said you had a handkerchief of hers, which you picked up in a performance of *Cinderella*."

That made Valery catch his breath. "Where is she?"

"Just now? I don't know," I said very truthfully. "But I know what happened to her, and I know it was Grand Duke Nicholas Nikolaevich who did it."

Valery Petrovich clenched his fists, and I perceived that

this fact had been unknown to him. "Of course it was!" he cried. "Who else but royalty could do such a thing with such temerity?"

"Anna is a friend of mine," I said again, more softly. After so much time in each other's company, it was true. I only regretted that the friendship had come too late to do her any earthly good. "Nor is she the only one of my friends who has suffered because of that man. What would you say if I told you that together we might see justice done?"

"I would say that you are asleep and dreaming," he said, with a scornful curl of his lip. But he did not shrug himself free of me and go on his way. Instead, he waited.

Here, at last, I felt rather at a loss for words. How was I to explain to him? I should not believe it myself if a stranger came up to *me* on the street and claimed to be a philanthropic thief.

"A crime doesn't cease to be a crime, only because law and society disregard it," I said at length. "Is it right to let such things go unpunished, merely because there is no judge to hand down the sentence?"

"Ah!" he said. "You are a revolutionary."

"Oh! Dear *me,* no," I cried, with sudden visions of being dragged away once more by the Okhrana, in one of their sinister liquidations. "I'm not a revolutionary! I'm *English,* you know."

But his mouth twisted in a wistful smile. "Naturally," he said. "If you mean that the street is no place for such conversations, I agree with you. But in any case I cannot help you."

And then he *did* brush past me and set off down the street. "Wait," I protested, running after him. "Take this, in case you change your mind." I had written our address on a card, which

I now pressed into his hand. He shook his head, but accepted the card.

"He seemed determined not to help," Schmidt observed pessimistically, as we watched the dancer stride briskly away. "Perhaps we need a new plan."

"Don't give up just yet," I said. "I got further with him than Mimi and Nijam did, didn't I? Let him alone; perhaps we'll hear from him when he's mulled it over for a day or two"

# 15

# Chapter XV.

Schmidt and I hastened back to our lodgings to find Princess Zlata's coachman perspiring idly in the street, together with equally idle horses and equipage. My heart sank, anticipating another tedious attempt to disengage the young lady so that we could discuss our own business. Upstairs, Nijam's presence was evidenced only by a faint burning smell which emanated from behind her closed door, and Mimi was evidently still out fascinating the old Grand Duke Nicholas. But Vasily had thrown himself down indolently on the divan, and Zlata lounged on the armchair nearby; we heard the soft murmur of their voices from the hallway as we let ourselves in. It sounded as though the two of them were exchanging confidences, and my efforts not to feel sulky about this resulted in perhaps a too-bright cheerfulness as I greeted them.

"Your highness, how *good* to see you again," I said. "I'm afraid we haven't much business to conduct today, or I would have called upon you myself. I say, has anyone checked on Nijam? I can smell something burning."

"No, I haven't," said Vasily lazily. "Miss Nijam doesn't seem the sort to burn down a tenement by accident. By design, certainly—but then I doubt whether *I* would be able to stop her! I trust your errand was successful?"

What could he mean by asking such things with the princess listening in?  "Only partly," I said, "for I discovered the milliner's, but it wasn't open for business."

"If it's a new hat you want, I'll send for whichever milliner you like; she won't refuse *me,* let her have never so many other customers," Zlata said brightly.

I wished she would not try to be so helpful. "Oh, I assure you that won't be necessary. I trust your audience with the Emperor was a success, your grace?"

I had thought that this topic was one which might be safe for conversation, but Vasily was no more forthcoming than I had been a moment ago. "As successful as can be expected. I humbly begged Nicky to smile upon me, and he promised to consider it."

"Oh, Vaska!" Zlata clapped her hands. "How splendid!"

After the doubts which Alphonse Schmidt had confided in me, my own attempted congratulations rang hollow: "That will make things a good deal less awkward for you, your grace."

"Oh, Countess, that's the least of it," Zlata cooed. "Vasily was just telling me how the police have been hounding him across Europe."

Was he, indeed! thought I.

"From now on all that is over! If you like, Vaska, I will put in a word for you with my godfather. In the meanwhile, when are we going to steal that painting? The dear old Marquis told me that of course he is going to be attending the coronation, and all the servants have been given the day as a holiday, so the house will be empty. I know it is only tomorrow and not far away, but the moment would be ideal! Wouldn't it, Vaska?"

I sent Vasily a pained expression. Zlata was right, of course; but we had already determined not to attempt the theft of the painting until after his father had been dealt with. We were not in Moscow on our own business, but on Anna's; but Zlata knew none of this, and it was out of the question to enlighten her.

"It would, my dear," Vasily replied, "but I'm afraid that the painting must wait, at least until I have settled things with the Emperor. If I'm caught purloining a painting from the ambassador of a friendly nation, everything will be over."

"And after?" Zlata demanded with an adorable pout. "If Nicky takes you back, you won't need to steal the painting at all!"

Vasily laughed. "If Nicky takes me back I'll buy the painting and you may steal it from me."

"Ugh, no! That won't do at all! I won't be the child you allow to beat you at chess, Vaska."

"Then we'll go to Germany, and you may help me steal the German Emperor's crown jewels," he said indulgently. I had a sudden sharp mental image of the two of them charming their way into a werewolf-infested Prussian drawing-room—and then, with a pang of jealousy, of Zlata soothing Vasily as he coughed blood into a potted plant. "As for the coronation tomorrow," he added, "we shall take the day off to enjoy the festivities, and I will make it up to you for the lack of excitement by acting as your cavalier for the day and escorting you wherever you wish to do. Is it agreed?"

"It's agreed," Zlata echoed, clapping her hands with excitement. I felt rather left out in the cold; and despite everything that Schmidt had said a little while ago as we waited at the stage door of the Bolshoi Theatre, I could not help once again feeling that perhaps it was in this world—in Zlata's company, and not mine—that Vasily truly belonged.

Meanwhile, Vasily rose with a sigh from the couch. "Well, Schmidt! since you have returned, we might as well be about that business of our own."

Zlata pricked up her ears. "What business might that be?"

"Nothing to concern your pretty head," said Vasily smoothly.

She pouted. "How secretive you are! I know that Laine is the thief, and that Nijam is the artificer, and that you and the Countess are the tricksters, but I know nothing of Schmidt. What is he?"

"Schmidt—oh, he is only the hammer. Come along, Schmidt."

Off the two of them went, Schmidt looking no happier than I felt; and off went Zlata shortly afterwards, since the stuffy garret no longer held any appeal for her. Having looked in on Nijam and found her diligently at work, I then retired to my own room, where I curled up with my book. There I stayed, attempting to forget my cares until dinnertime.

Dinner served as a meeting, at which each of us informed the others of the day's doings. Mimi told us that she had successfully thrown herself in the path of Grand Duke Nicholas (the Elder) and I expressed my uncertain hopes that we might in time have the assistance of Anna's Valery. Vasily, however, gave no better account of his meeting with Emperor Nicky than he had done previously.

After dinner, when Nijam and Mimi (whose manner towards each other was still constrained) had retired to their rooms, I seated myself on the window-seat beside Vasily and said, "Herr Schmidt, will you give me a moment with his grace?"

"With *Vasily,*" the Grand Duke corrected me, as Schmidt retired to his own chamber.

"Vasily, then," I said, turning to observe his face. The slow northern twilight had fallen, and the window stood open, allowing a refreshing breeze to sweep through the apartment. Vasily was in his silk robe again, with his shirt half unbuttoned to allow the breeze to cool him. He looked wonderfully comfortable, all soft and rumpled. I wished I was a man, and could adopt such *déshabillé.*

I wished I had not come to know Vasily so well that I knew how he liked to go barefoot indoors. I wished I did not have the sudden, overwhelming urge to lean forward and press a hand to the sliver of chest that was displayed between the buttons of his shirt.

It was, of course, an urge that I resisted. But when I returned my gaze to his eyes, I found him watching me with a pleased, catlike smile playing across his mouth.

"Do you see something that interests you?" he almost purred.

Well, the nerve of the man! First he undressed himself in the presence of a lady, and then he was impolite enough to notice when she found herself staring!

So, instead of blushing and stammering, as I might otherwise have done, I merely took a prim sip of tea and said, "You have forgotten that night at the Schloss Frohsdorf, when you played the rôle of the Turkish Ambassador."

Upon that memorable occasion I had been privileged with the sight of nearly all of Vasily. This had been, I hasten to remind the reader, strictly in the pursuit of business. As magnificent as the sight had been, it made no sense that a sliver of manly bosom *now* should have a more powerful effect upon the feminine mind than whole acres of it *then.* Yet here, in a sense, we were.

"How could I forget it?" Vasily said with a chuckle. "You got your revenge with eucalyptus drops, as I recall."

"And I'll do it again if I must." I gestured to my own bosom. "In fact, I was wondering if you had been injured here, once. The skin is pale and scarred."

At that, Vasily's smile faded away entirely. To my surprise— and, it must be confessed, disappointment—he pulled the shirt closed and buttoned it. "You eyes do you credit," he said. "There was a name tattooed there, once. An old mistake."

I could see that he had little desire to speak of it, and that disappointed me again, for there were none of my secrets now which he did not know. "Did you have it removed, then?"

"No," he said with a twisted smile. "An angry little man peeled off the skin in a locked berth on the Orient Express, somewhere between Paris and Stuttgart. I was a vampire then, so it did not leave much of a scar." My face must have been a study in horror, for he laughed in earnest, although it was not a particularly pleasant laugh. "Did you send away Schmidt merely to ask about my scars?"

"No," I said, finding my voice again with difficulty. "I meant to ask about your audience with the Emperor."

"Did you, little mouse? I wonder why that is?"

"I can't help feeling that there's something you aren't telling us," I ventured, emboldened because although he had told me very little, he *had* told me about the angry little man who liked to flay people alive in trains.

"You're a very observant little rodent," he said, wrinkling his nose drolly. Reaching into his trouser pocket, he produced a crumpled piece of paper and shook it out with an air of triumph. "Look at this," he said. "I saw it lying on Nicky's desk, and I decided to bring it with me."

I accepted the sheet with interest, but quickly found that it held little meaning for me. "It's all in Russian," I said.

"Oh, of course! Well, this is my Cousin Nicky's schedule for the next few days. There's the coronation tomorrow, and then a series of receptions and festivities—meetings with the nobility, the women of the city, and so on—and then, in four days, there is the gala performance at the Bolshoi. The day after, there's a little ceremony out at Khodynka Field so that the peasants can get a look at their Tsar, but then that evening is the great French embassy ball, which is why Montebello brought my painting to Moscow in the first place. What do you think? Our business with my father will be over by then, and the only thing better than burgling an empty house, is burgling a house that's filled to the brim with strangers."

His excitement was infectious, and I wished I could take it at face value. "Then you still mean to steal the painting? But surely the Emperor will return your privileges as a Grand Duke, and all this will be unnecessary."

Vasily's smile faded. "The painting is a contingency, if the other plan should fail," he said. "And despite what Princess Zlata may think, returning to favour is by no means certain. Nicky made it quite clear that there's no return unless I can prove my loyalty somehow." Then the moment of seriousness passed, and he sent me an impudent smile. "The means is entirely up to me, although I know the sort of thing he intends. What do you think, Miss Dark? Should I join the army and stand up to be shot at by the Afghans, or should I build a railway and make a gift of it to him, or should I go into politics and annex Manchuria? Or…should I find a cure for defanging?"

My heart stood still. "I thought you didn't approve of the monsters," I said, when I could find my voice again.

"Oh, I wouldn't take the cure myself," Vasily assured me. "But someone will find a way to create monsters, you know; even if it's only Nijam's and Vandergriff's way, using gadgets and gold rather than blood. *Someone* will profit from human nature; and why shouldn't it be us? What about it, Miss Dark?"

He was laughing at me, only half in earnest; but I did not know which half. And whichever half was the jest, I found it a poor one. If Vasily were a Grand Duke there *could* be no "us", because Grand Dukes did not marry governesses. Nor did they travel about with them, seeking out wronged spirits to redress. This, in turn, left me wondering what Vasily's idea had been in kissing my hand and saying so many absurd and wonderful things to me, if he could so easily abandon me for his former life.

Perhaps the reader may marvel at my fickleness, seeing that I had but lately determined to proffer the wicked Grand Duke the coldest of shoulders; but I do not think I was so very wrong to feel this. Vasily had been my friend and my colleague, and had lately singled me out for such attention that I half expected my father's ghost to demand a clear declaration of his intentions. Moreover, Vasily knew things about me which no other living soul did; and was he now willing to throw off for the sake of his lost fortunes? Once, perhaps, when Vasily was forced to choose between the Noor-Jahan and myself, I *had* been more to him than a stepping-stone to greater things. But there is a world of difference between levanting with a stolen jewel, and being welcomed back into the bosom of a family which wields incomparable wealth and power. Against the first temptation he had been proof, but the second was far greater, and I felt the awakening of old fears.

"If things go wrong," I said in a low voice, "and if you *don't* find a way to prove your loyalty to the Emperor, what then? Everyone knows you are here—not just the family, I mean, but the police, and the Crown Princess of Roumania, and everyone else who might have reason to blame you for what happened at Coburg. Will they spare you merely for the sake of a cure which you cannot give them? And if something happens to you, how shall the rest of us manage?"

Vasily's laughter faded, and he leaned towards me, now absolutely in earnest.

"I know I'm asking you to take the most devilish risks. I swear to you now, on all the honour I have lost, that I will not allow the slightest harm to come to you in my name." His eyes were like green pools, impossible to escape. "Can't you trust me, Mary?"

I caught my breath, for he had never, except in jest, called me by my Christian name. No one did: I was Molly to my friends, and Miss Dark to everyone else.

"My aim is the same as it ever was," he added, "to relieve myself and my friends of the attentions of the police. Don't you see that a chance like this may never come again? It would be folly to miss it, when your life as well as mine might be at stake. I know quite well that I have run all our necks into a trap, which might trip at any moment. But if you can only bring yourself to trust me, I swear I will bring you safely through."

Vasily mocking, Vasily calculating, Vasily angry, and Vasily flabbergasted were all moods with which I was now quite familiar; but Vasily attempting sincerity was new to me, and for a moment I did not quite know what to say.

"If it all went wrong," I said, "and if you had to choose between being a Grand Duke, with all the power and fortune that entails, or being Baron Dragomir Smilets, the diamond thief—which would you choose?"

"I should manage things so I didn't have to choose," he said readily. "And I don't mean to, you know. If Nicky accepts me, I'll stay here only long enough to put everyone off their guard; and in the meanwhile, once I have all my property again in my own hands, I mean to sell it off, or send it away to London or Paris. And then, when everyone is lulled into complacency, one dark night Vasily Nikolaevich disappears from Moscow and reappears in Paris, as good a fellow as ever, but now sinfully rich."

This ought to have set my mind at rest, but for some reason it did not. I shook my head. "Why sinfully rich? What is wrong with being merely comfortably well off?"

For a moment he seemed somewhat at a loss; and then he laughed, and the sincere Vasily was gone, leaving only mockery and facility behind.

"Little mouse, little mouse! I'm afraid I only know how to do things sinfully."

I didn't press him. Vasily was a grown man, and had the right to make his own decisions. I went to my rest that night feeling a little easier in mind regarding his good intentions; but all the same I could not help thinking that it was a very great pity; that the Vasily I had known in London, who did not much care for riches, was in some ways a better man than this one had become.

Early the following day, the day of the coronation, Vasily made himself very splendid and went off with Princess Zlata and Alphonse Schmidt. For our part, Mimi and I put on our finest clothing and went out to partake of the festivities in a humbler way, for all the streets and squares of Moscow were gay with revellers—fortune-tellers, street musicians, circus performers, and Social Democrats distributing explanatory tracts. (As for Nijam, she did not care what she wore and did not wish to leave her work at all.) I recall the day as being full of light and colour, rich with the embroidered blouses and coloured kerchiefs of peasant women, but my spirits were irretrievably darkened. But what else was I to do with my worries—hide in the garret and brood? We stayed out all day, and that evening took ourselves to the balcony of our attic to view the dancing and music going on in the streets below. Sometime after ten, the whole city lit up like magic with a display of electric lights, which had been set up for the occasion throughout the city: and we knew that in the great palace of the Kremlin the coronation ball must be in full swing.

It was odd that Anna did not reappear. Nor, for many hours, did Vasily.

Only Schmidt burst in about midnight, bleeding from a burst lip. "They've taken him," he cried, pale and despairing. "They've taken sir."

His shout interrupted Mimi, who had been hard at work

practising her steps in the living-room; it also brought Nijam to the door of her chamber. I startled awake from where I had been dozing on the balcony in the light of the electrical displays. "What do you mean, Schmidt? Who has taken Vasily?"

"You're bleeding," Nijam observed, alarmed. "Who has done this to you?"

"Vampires," Schmidt said with a sob in his voice. "Two of them, and a young lady. Sir and I were on our way home in Princess Zlata's carriage, when they set upon us before we were aware; and I—I could do nothing to help him!"

His words struck me like an arrow to the heart; my knees failed me, and I sank down upon the balcony threshold. A horrible certainty took possession of my mind.

"A young lady?" I said faintly. "A fair young lady, well dressed, perhaps in a tiara; and not a vampire?"

Schmidt stared. "How did you know?"

"I guessed," said I, numbly. "It's the same lady who set Griff on our trail—it's Marie of Roumania!"

# 16

# Chapter XVI.

At these words Schmidt turned absolutely white, for all of us knew of the Crown Princess of Roumania's vendetta. Uttering a broken exclamation, he took to pacing to and fro, clutching at his golden hair. I fell back against the glass balcony door as a fresh wave of dizziness assailed me.

"Let's not lose our heads," I whispered, but my words did little good. Heads were already being lost. My own was going around and around like a spinning-top.

"We must do something," Schmidt wailed, disarranging his hair to a degree which in better times I might have found almost fetching. "That woman has been after sir for months! Miss Nijam, please—have you no plan?"

"There must be some way to find out where he's been taken," I said, slightly recovering myself.

Miss Nijam frowned, but did not reply. Instead, she took herself back into her room. Mimi, in the meantime, had produced her tiger claws from heaven only knows where.

"Let's kidnap the Tsar," she said fiercely. "They'll have to give up Vasily then."

"No, Mimi, you are not to kidnap anyone!" I protested.

"Why not? I snatched the Noor-Jahan, didn't I?" she snarled, stalking towards the door. Schmidt caught her by the arm. I tried to get up and only brought on another fainting-fit. For a moment, absolute insurrection prevailed—Schmidt pleading, Mimi arguing, me swooning upon the rug.

"Nijam!" I gasped, when I was able to speak again. "Where for the love of all that's good is Nijam?"

"I'm here," she said, once again stepping into the room and depositing her carpet-bag upon the floorboards with an ominous, heavy, metallic thump. The sound, breaking through Mimi's protests, brought her argument with Schmidt to a standstill. All of us gaped, for Nijam was accoutred for battle, in smoked-glass goggles and a belt hung about with the same little canisters which on the previous evening had wrought so salutary an effect upon the sirens.

In that silence, very impressively, Nijam uttered a single word.

"Zlata," she said.

All of us saw the sense in that at once.

"Zlata," I repeated, extending a trembling hand towards Nijam. "Of course! If anyone knows where Missy has ensconced herself, it's bound to be Zlata."

"But can we trust her?" Schmidt protested.

"I can kidnap Zlata," Mimi declared. "Nothing easier! A waste of my talents!"

"We can trust her," I said, overlooking this outburst. "Zlata will do anything to keep Vasily alive; she wants to marry him."

Absolute silence greeted my words. I listened to them with dread myself. Alas! when spoken aloud, they sounded almost like a fairy enchantment, which would bring to pass the curse

202

they uttered.

"Then Zlata will certainly help us," Nijam said, briskly dispelling the enchantment. "Cheer up, Schmidt! We'll get him back, no doubt." With that she strode past him to the door. Schmidt picked up the carpet-bag and ran after her; and Mimi and I followed. I wished I could feel as sanguine concerning our chances as did Nijam; but at the least, I thought gloomily, if I could not free Vasily, then I could see to it that he did not die alone.

It proved that Schmidt had driven Zlata's own carriage to our lodgings after the coachman had been rendered unconscious. He had come to by the time we were ready to set off, but was yet too dizzy to be anything but grateful when Schmidt took the reins and turned the horses' heads towards the princess' house.

The hour was late, but after a brief disagreement with Zlata's butler, which Schmidt won handily in the space of a single upper-cut, we quickly gained admission to the house. Zlata was quickly fetched, the damaged coachman was handed over, the butler was revived and given the rest of the evening off, and Schmidt laid his whole story before the Serbian princess.

"Oh, how terribly thrilling," she said, when she had ceased to press her hands over her heart and utter ladylike shrieks. "Anyone would imagine we were in a sensational novel! But why have you come to *me?*"

"Surely you can help us, your highness," I said.

"Indeed? Well, I *am* terribly glad you came," she said. "I really don't advise going to the authorities; here in Moscow it's Sergei Alexandrovich who is in command of the city, and— well, there's no love lost between him and our dear Vaska, as you know."

I shuddered, for indeed it was out of the question that we should attract any attention from the authorities, whether these were represented by Sergei Alexandrovich or by the police. I had met both the Emperor's gaunt uncle and the bland Okhrana men, and I wished heartily for a more distant acquaintance with both.

"Indeed not," I said. "But can't you take us to see the Crown Princess? You must know where she is staying, and I know the two of you have been friends."

Zlata bit her lip. "I don't know if I can presume upon that friendship, my dear Countess, for it's thanks to Vasily that Missy has lost her fangs. She has revenge in mind, and I don't know that she will give it up even for me."

"Will you abandon him, then?" I asked, as hope failed me.

"Dear me, no!" she said pressing a theatrical hand to her bosom. "Nothing so thrilling has ever happened to me. No; I shall go with you and beg on my knees to share Vaska's fate if I cannot avert it."

I resented her appropriating my own sentiments, but could hardly object to them. Not many minutes later, Zlata and I were knocking at the gate to the house occupied by Marie of Roumania. It was then an hour past midnight, and the manservant who opened the door swore that his mistress had retired and would not be disturbed.

"Tell her it is I, Zlata Milanova," the princess declared imperiously. The manservant reluctantly admitted us to the courtyard of the palace and went away to find his mistress.

I touched the transmitter in my ear. "I do hope your plan works, Nijam. I should have felt easier with one or two of your little devices about me."

Her reply was very clear, for Schmidt had drawn up the carriage not far from the gate. "Out of the question; if anyone was to search you the game would be up. The main thing is to find Vasily; signal us when you do and we'll retrieve you."

"Don't be late," I muttered. In the carriage Nijam had declared there was no time for discussion, merely giving us our orders, but in truth I understood that she did not like to disclose her full plans to Zlata.

"Don't worry," she now replied, crisply frank in the privacy of the transmitter. "Since you ought to know, Mimi's going to create a distraction, Schmidt will go in to bring you and Vasily out, and I will be standing by with the first-aid."

Those last words were far from reassuring, but at that moment the direst warnings could not have dissuaded me from my task. Just then the manservant returned and desired us to follow him; which we did, crossing the courtyard toward the house. Within a small anteroom, the manservant threw open a door to show a flight of stairs leading down, into the dark bowels of the earth.

"The basement?" I said aloud, mostly for the sake of the others listening via the transmitter.

"Madame awaits you within," the servant intoned, lifting his lamp to throw light upon the dank, uneven steps. There was a glimmer of lamplight at the foot of them, and after a momentary silence we heard an exultant, mocking laugh, followed by some sneering words that I could not quite make out.

The malice in those sounds made the hair rise all over my scalp, and for a moment I wanted nothing more than to turn tail and run away. Then I quite distinctly heard Vasily give a laugh of his own, low and bubbling with pain. That stiffened my resolve, and I did not wait for Zlata to lead the way.

The basement, which smelled of cool earth and stone, had perhaps once been used for storage. It had been remodelled since, for the floor had been smoothed and polished and covered with rugs, and a gleaming chandelier hung from the ancient groin vault. A table stood to one side, bearing great silver platters full of fruit and cheeses. There was a carafe of wine, but this had been left untouched; for the room's four occupants—the Crown Princess and her sister Ducky, with the two young vampires Cyril and Boris—had a richer vintage to taste.

At the head of the table, shackled with bright silver chains to a great carved wooden chair, sat a drooping Vasily Niko-laevich. A ring of salt had been sprinkled onto the floor around him, but this was now broken and scattered. I did not know the significance of this at the time. The one thing I did understand, absolutely for certain, was that Vasily was red with his own blood, its stench hot and coppery in the air as it oozed from the bite marks in his neck and his arms. I stopped dead. For a moment I did not know whether I was about to faint, or to dissolve into tears.

Then Zlata stepped out in front of me and said, "Missy, darling, I've brought you a little gift."

At this all of them, with the exception of Vasily, looked up from their business. Missy stood beside Vasily with a little pen-knife open in her hand. The others sat contentedly at either side of the table, the young Grand Dukes with their cousin's blood daubing their faces, Ducky leaning over to Cyril to kiss a taste from his lips.

Missy's face lit up with delight. "Zlata!" she cried. "Can you credit it, the man's a fraud! Look, he's been wearing false fangs—there's no cure at all! Come along and finish him off; it's too late for Ducky and me, but you can still make the change, if we give you the final honours."

They were offering Zlata the kill, so that she might become a monster like themselves! I seized her arm in a sudden terror that she might take them at their word, but she only uttered a hard and silvery little laugh.

"Darling, it's out of the question. I never married a Grand Duke, so I'm not allowed to make the change. Besides, Nicky would have my head if I drained his favourite cousin. You know Vaska's about to be taken back into the imperial graces, don't you?"

"Well, *I've* heard no such thing," said Missy with boundless impudence. "Have you, Boris? No, of course not. Go away, Zlata, if you're only here to spoil our fun. I was just about to find out what makes his eyes so red."

And she brandished the little penknife. I do believe that only the extremity of my terror prevented me from screaming.

"Wait! I have an idea for a little fun of my own," Zlata said, pulling me into the light. "Why don't we have a séance?"

Missy's eyes lit up with an unholy joy, and she seized Vasily's jaw, turning his head towards me. "Oh, my!" she said. "Look, Vasily Nikolaevich! It's your little mistress."

It was only then, I believe, that Vasily saw me. First he went absolutely white, and then he went mad: with a snarl, he snapped at Missy's hand and nearly tore off a finger. The chains groaned as he fought against them.

"Oho! Cousin Vasily's still got some fight left in him!" Cyril gloated. "What's wrong, Vasya? Are you having second thoughts about turning traitor? Maybe we'll drain *her* first, before we finish *you."*

"Let her alone, you cowards!" Vasily shrieked. I will not repeat his ravings here, lest they shock the gentle reader; suffice it to say that of the threats he hurled at them, skinning them alive and boiling the remains in salt-water was nearly the friendliest.

"Be sensible, Cyril," Missy said once Vasily paused for breath, just as though he had never spoken at all. "We all know how precious Nicky is about his French alliance; we can't very well drain one of their countesses."

Boris prowled over to me. The splendid red jacket he had worn to the coronation, with its acres of gold braid and military orders, hung open to expose the snowy shirt beneath, which was all dribbled with Vasily's blood. He slid a hand beneath my chin and tilted my head back to expose the neck. "No one will know or care," said he, "if we just take a nibble."

I closed my eyes, shuddering. *I* would mind, very much! But it was quite plain that in this horrible little cavern, surrounded by people of royal birth, I counted for even less than did Vasily. I felt that I had put that long, shivering expanse of neck very foolishly into a trap.

Oh, where were the others? What was keeping them? Heaven forfend, had something gone wrong? My mind filled with terrible imaginings—they had been captured by Missy's servants, or suddenly seized by the secret police, or else Nijam and Mimi had fallen into a fatal row.

"Don't be greedy! You'll spoil her before we've had a chance to hold a séance," Zlata said, pushing Boris away. "Didn't you hear? The Countess met with the Emperor two days ago and I don't know precisely what happened, but it was quite spectacular. Wouldn't you like to know who is haunting

Vaska?"

There was an intrigued silence. A slow, horrible smile crept across Cyril's face. "Zlata's right," he said. "Let's have a séance."

"No," Vasily sobbed, but his voice had gone thin and reedy after all his screams, and no one paid him any attention.

"Here, girl," Missy drawled. "If you want to keep a whole skin, you had best give us a good show."

Where, oh where, were the rest of the crew? The two Grand Dukes dragged Vasily around the end of the table and I was made to sit facing him opposite, while the spectators gathered about us. Just as had happened at Zlata's house upon that memorable evening when I last held a séance, there was no need to have Vasily call to mind those he had lost. As we took our places they were already pressing close, half lost in the shadows—men and women pale and grisly, bloodied and betrayed. Tonight, even the peasant girl in the embroidered blouse was dripping with gore.

Vasily fixed his gaze upon me. Never had I seen such abject pleading in his eyes. "Don't," he begged me. Oh heavens! he was weeping, who had never been seen to weep before, and I pitied the man's weakness from the bottom of my heart. "Don't force me to remember them."

"You're working for us now, my dear," Missy told me with a sharp little smile. "Report faithfully everything you see."

The truth was that I could force Vasily to remember nothing; the imprints were already here, and I knew well that they were never far from his mind. All the same, my heart wrung for him. I understood that to tell the truth would be in some way a violation.

"I see a fair-haired woman," I said, my voice trembling. "She is not beautiful, but she has a kind face. She holds a little Faberge mouse made of dark quartz, with ruby eyes and a tail all studded with diamonds. It was given to her by someone she loves very much. She does not wish him to be—"

"This is nonsense," Boris said scornfully. "Listen to her heart's beat. She is lying."

"If she won't tell the truth we might as well drain both of them at once," said Cyril.

There was an awful silence. By now, I was so thoroughly disgusted with Missy and her confederates that I would cheerfully have died merely for the pleasure of denying them their perverse little game. But Vasily's life was not mine to give away.

Nor were his guilty memories; but how else was I to save him?

I cleared my throat. My heart was like a stone within me.

"I see a man," I began, purposefully choosing one who hung a little further back in the throng of Vasily's regrets. "He's young and very handsome, and he's wearing a white cravat and carrying a revolver. There's a big, dark, wet patch on his coat, and—oh, now I can see the red creeping across his cravat. I think he's been shot!"

Vasily could no longer meet my eyes, but Cyril whooped with laughter.

"Why, that's young Bulgakov, who our Vasily Nikolaevich shot on a beach one morning in Karelia. Poor Bulgakov! He had a very pretty wife, but she didn't care for him as much as she did for a Grand Duke!"

"They always did ask why he wanted to wear a white cravat to a duel," Boris added. "Of course it offered a target even our Vasily couldn't miss. It's tidier than suicide, at any rate, and more honourable."

I shuddered, knowing that Boris had hit the mark: I had perceived the imprint's feelings and found the same sort of despair that I so often found in unfortunates who had done away with themselves. Perhaps poor Bulgakov felt that he had won honour in the encounter, but as for Vasily—how well he must know what honour might be defended, and what courage proved, by such an execution!

Vasily's chin had fallen upon his breast. I could scarcely tell whether he was still in possession of his senses, let alone mutely beg his pardon with a look for having revealed such a disgraceful thing.

"What else?" Ducky demanded, clapping her hands.

"He's fainted," I objected, but Boris grabbed Vasily by his hair and dragged his head upright. He was limp and sullen, but not unconscious.

"No more excuses," Boris told me. "What else do you see?"

I had to continue, although by now I was beginning to understand that each new secret was likely to be as dreadful as the last. Next I described a short, stocky man with that round, weathered face I had come to associate with the ordinary Russian. He was pale, and his throat had been torn out. For a moment, this stumped them entirely.

"I can't imagine who that might be," said Cyril.

"Could it be a *male* dainty?" Missy inquired, with a wicked grin. "Oh, what a scandal *that* would be!"

"Oh, there's nothing queer about a peasant with his throat torn out!" said Cyril. "Peasants are ten a kopeck, and all our uncles cut their teeth on them. A good, manly hunt is quite different to drinking for pleasure…"

"Then which one is this?" I put in, with a nod of my head

towards Vasily. Both the Grand Dukes reddened.

"Keep a civil tongue in your head!" Boris exclaimed, raising his hand as though to strike me. I flinched; and that must have satisfied him, for he shrugged and added, "Didn't old Nicholas Nikolaevich used to take his sons peasant-hunting with him, even after the emancipation? I suppose this is one of them. You, baroness, or whatever you are! Give us something better this time."

Vasily once again had retreated into his silence. If I had dared I should have reached out and touched him, only to comfort him. It should not have been a point in Vasily's favour that, having once slaughtered peasants for sport, he now remembered them with regret. But I was appalled by the lack of conscience which did not even give Boris and Cyril room for regret.

I had called these people monsters, referring only to their grisly appetites. Only now did I begin truly to understand the depths of their depravity; and I knew in that moment that Vasily could never again have a life among them. Even if he lived to see the morning, even if he was able to prove his loyalty to Nicky, his idea of playing the Grand Duke again long enough to recover his lost wealth was a daydream. Either he must become once more a cruel member of a monstrous family; or he must die.

"Give us a woman this time," Missy demanded. A shudder ran down Vasily's whole body. "There must be a great many of those."

I wanted to protect the peasant girl in the embroidered blouse. She had once been dear to Vasily, and I could not bear the thought of holding her up to the ridicule of these monsters. But at Missy's words all other imprints faded, until only she remained.

There was something different about this girl, something I was not accustomed to feeling in the presence of those who had died violent deaths. I said, "I see a dark-haired girl in a white shirt embroidered with red flowers." Mutely, despairingly, Vasily shook his head: *no, no, no...* Inwardly, I begged his pardon, but I could only go on. "There are more flowers in her hair, and bite marks in her neck. But she isn't afraid, or even resigned. She's full of joy, and hope, like a bride going to her husband."

It was too much to hope that my words would spare her any mockery.

"Ha! It's the milkmaid!" Cyril cried at once. "Did I never tell you that story, Ducky? No? The merest oversight. It's the story of how Vasily Nikolaevich earned his fangs."

"Oh, do tell," said Missy with relish.

"I will *live*," Vasily whispered. As faint as his voice was, it carried with it a concentrated fury that made me shiver. "I will live, long enough to destroy you all if you repeat that infamous story."

"If the story be infamous, whose fault is that?" Boris replied. "But indeed the thing must have been inspired by some infernal genius. Here's the way of it: our dear cousin Vasily was of the age to make his first kill, but he had fallen out with his father and been sent in disgrace to rusticate at the country house in Moldova. There was a very pretty milkmaid on the estate who had taken a fancy to him; and so our Vasily hatched a plan. Having won the girl over with professions of love, he told her the most outrageous pack of lies—that he would make her a vampire like himself, and a Grand Duchess to boot. Believing him implicitly, she allowed him to drain and drink her life's blood, and with the final beat of her heart bestowed upon him the fangs that his father denied him."

"It's a lie," Vasily cried. His eyes were fixed on me. "I loved Ioanna truly. I wanted to ennoble her. It was no cunning plan, only the folly of a lonely boy."

"What, Vaska, are you afraid?" Missy taunted. "Do you think that we'll frighten off your latest mistress? Put your mind at rest. You betrayed your dear countess the moment you made it clear that you had permitted yourself to fall in love with her." She smiled. "I tire of this game. Come, Boris: let's try something new."

I became suddenly aware of a shadowy presence behind my chair—of the smell of blood heavy on the breath that now touched my cheek. I leaped to my feet; but to no avail. The vampire Boris caught me in his arm, with one hand bending my head back to expose the great artery at the neck.

Vasily was speechless: he huddled motionless in his bonds, watching me with sickened eyes. At that moment I could not have explained what came over me as I waited for his cousin to feast upon my blood. All I knew was that if I was about to die for his sake, I would be glad to do so; all I wished to do, at this moment, was to comfort him.

"I believe you," I told him, "even if they do not."

In that breathless moment I am not sure whether Vasily fully understood the words. He only gazed at me, pale and horror-stricken. Before anyone could say or do anything else—before the Grand Duke could open my veins—there was a none too distant muffled boom. The whole earth reeled, and there came the thunderous sound of falling stones.

# Chapter XVII.

The whole basement trembled, and fine streams of dust and pebbles ran from the chinks in the wall. With a cry of alarm, Grand Duke Boris released me. I fell to the ground with a sob of relief. Nijam had come—and not a bare moment too soon!

Above me, the monsters stared at one another, struck into a wild affright. "Anarchists," Ducky wailed, turning pale. "Oh, not again!"

"Stay here," Cyril said, quite bravely considering that he was trembling like a leaf. "I shall go up to see what is happening."

"Cyril, you mustn't! You'll be murdered! Send one of the servants for the police!"

It had scarcely occurred to me that once Mimi had succeeded in engineering our diversion, the monsters might be too terrified to emerge from their stronghold at all. Oh, *why* had Nijam not given me any of her flashbangs?"

Cyril alleviated my worries by saying, "Are you mad, Ducky? We can't let the police know that we kidnapped a Grand Duke, to say nothing of a French countess!"

"Never fear, I shall go with him," Boris put in. "Those

cowardly servants will run away altogether if they are left to themselves, and then who will protect us?"

With that, the two Grand Dukes ventured up the stairs, leaving Zlata and the other ladies clinging to one another in terror. The three of them shrieked as another loud detonation echoed in the courtyard above—one of Nijam's flashbangs, I had no doubt. As for me, I had no time to tremble: I must get Vasily away from these horrors. A key lay forgotten on the table, half hidden between two great platters. Rising from the floor, I seized it and with trembling hands unlocked the chains that held the half-dead Vasily in place.

"What are you doing? Stop that at once!" Missy gasped, hearing the rattle of the chains as I pulled Vasily to his feet. I turned fiercely, in no mood to abide any nonsense from *that* quarter. Marie of Roumania was a princess and had been a vampire, and she was still a perfect terror. But she was a vampire no longer; and I was an English governess, who had dealt with perfect terrors before.

"Young lady," I said in my native language, drawing myself up to my full height, "you ought to be ashamed of yourself. What would your grandmother say if she could see you now? You ought to be given the hiding of your life, and if you raise a finger to stop me I shall see to it at once."

Missy gasped and quailed. Tightening my grip upon the limp Vasily, I considered my next steps. We could not remain a moment longer in this horrible place. There was no sign of Schmidt. My only means of assistance was Zlata, now sobbing in Ducky's arms. Not being privy to our full plans, she did not know that the explosions were our doing.

I seized her shoulder. "Help me," I commanded, but she only wailed with terror and clung more tightly to Ducky.

There was no help for it, and perhaps desperation lent me strength. Abandoning Zlata, I dragged Vasily up the stairs by main force, got the door open, and staggered out into the courtyard. Here, the reason for Schmidt's delay became evident, for he was locked in a struggle with what I judged to be some kind of bodyguard. The man was built like an ox. Schmidt danced about him, dodging his great thrashing fists, dashing in to pepper the giant with blows before darting away again. It was clear that Schmidt could not possibly assist me; I marveled that he had survived the unequal battle for so long.

In some desperation I surveyed the courtyard. Boris and Cyril had evidently fallen afoul of one of the flashbangs, for Boris had fallen to the ground unconscious, and Cyril leaned against the house beside him, rubbing his dazzled eyes. Opposite us, where a few minutes ago the wrought-iron gate of the palace had hung, an immense, gaping breach had been made in the palace wall. As for the gate, that had been wrenched apart like so much wire and was now scattered in hot and smoking pieces about the blasted courtyard.

Cyril blinked at me as I guided Vasily past the pugilists and into the courtyard. "Oh, no, you don't," he snarled, leaving the safety of the wall and advancing upon us. Beside me, Vasily gave a sob and tried to put up his fists. I had other ideas, for I had noticed that Cyril was not in much better shape than Vasily himself. As the vampire approached, I ducked behind Vasily and gave him a sharp push. Caught off his guard, he staggered forward and collided bodily with his cousin; and down the two of them went, for all the world like ninepins.

So much for Cousin Cyril. Next, I turned to Schmidt and his opponent, but I did not think that this was a predicament

I could help to solve, at least not by throwing Vasily at it. Tripping my transmitter, I called, "Nijam! Mimi! Where are you? We need help!"

"Mimi is on her way," Nijam informed me serenely.

"I'm not sure Mimi will be enough!" I protested. "Schmidt's fighting a bodyguard the size of Blenheim Palace, and Vasily…" I glanced down at the two Grand Dukes entangled at my feet. Vasily was on top of Cyril and had got his teeth fixed into the vampire's ear. There was a little bloody spume about his mouth, and his eyes were closed, but he was holding on for grim life and none of Cyril's flailing could dislodge him.

"How dare you bite me, you—you *gelding!*" Cyril gasped.

Just then Schmidt caught one of the giant's blows and flew towards us, landing upon the pavement at my feet. At once he fell afoul of Cyril, who abandoned his efforts to dislodge Vasily and fastened a hand on Schmidt's collar. The giant advanced. I was now the only one of the party still upon her feet. I must do something; but what? —The answer was supplied by a piece of the broken gate, still red-hot at one end and smelling of hot and tortured metal, which lay nearby. Snatching it up, I pressed the hot end gently against Cyril's wrist; whereupon he released Schmidt with gratifying alacrity and a shriek of agony. But it was already too late for my champion to rise. The giant seized Schmidt by the collar, dragging him to his feet. A fist the size of a ham clenched— and drew back to strike.

In that fractured moment I had ghastly visions of explaining to Nijam that her complacency had cost Alphonse Schmidt his life. But a change had come over the giant's face. He gave a queer little cough, and then another. Then he toppled to one side, revealing that Mimi stood behind him with bloodied tiger claws and a look of satisfaction on her face.

At the sight of blood, I must have forgotten Schmidt's recent peril. "Mimi!" I cried, aghast. "You *stabbed* him!"

"Three times," she said, with ghoulish relish.

"But is he all right?"

"Is *he* all right?" Schmidt croaked, disentangling his master from Grand Duke Cyril. "I thought he was about to murder me!"

Without Vasily to keep him down, Cyril made as though to rise. Mimi pounced on him at once, and as Schmidt and I helped the stumbling Vasily through the rubble and twisted iron of the broken gateway, I thought I heard her softly urging the young Grand Duke to give her another opportunity of trying her claws. Poor Cyril! Gifted as he was with inhuman strength and rending teeth, he had had very few opportunities to develop true physical courage, and almost certainly had never been threatened by a claw-wielding ballerina.

No sooner did Schmidt and I drag Vasily out the gate, than Mimi left her station guarding Cyril and joined us in the street. The carriage stood nearby, the horses idle and the doors closed up. "Nijam! Where are you?" I called into my transmitter as the four of us approached.

"In the carriage, of course," she said, and indeed, when Mimi got the door open, there was Nijam, very cosily wrapped up in a shawl, smelling of peppermint and writing in a notebook.

"Nijam!" I reproached her. "Here's Vasily half dead, and you're sitting in the carriage eating peppermints!"

She looked at me over the top of the pince-nez. "Would you rather I spent the time tearing my hair and wailing? Here, pass him up."

Schmidt and I got Vasily into the carriage, but when I tried to extract myself from his grasp, he uttered an inarticulate protest and clung to me like death.

"You're bleeding, Vasily," I protested. "Let Nijam look at you."

Outside, Mimi said sharply, "They are coming after us!"

"Hold tight," Schmidt told us, slamming the carriage door. A moment later he and Mimi ascended to the box and stirred the horses to a quick trot.

"Don't leave me, Molly Dark," Vasily muttered into my shoulder, where he had buried his face.

"I won't," I promised, nodding to Nijam to leave him be. A closer inspection revealed that he was not bleeding too freely, after all; already his wounds had begun to clot, and no doubt he would keep until we had reached our lodgings.

Or would we reach our lodgings? When I glanced out the window, the streets had become unfamiliar; moreover, the carriage was now labouring along nearly at a canter, swinging wildly as we went around the corners. "Good heavens!" I exclaimed, glancing out the small window at the rear of the carriage. "We are being pursued!"

"Thank you; I'm aware," Nijam said, rummaging in her carpet-bag for another flashbang.

I suppose it must have been Boris who had come to his senses and chosen to follow us. Whoever it was, they were using a carriage rather smaller and lighter than our own; and it was only a matter of time before they caught us up. What then? We had done pretty well so far because the young vampires were so wholly unused to any real threat; but they would now be burning with anger and prepared to face real danger.

Just as I was about to give us all up for lost, Schmidt pulled the horses abruptly to a stop. "What is he doing?" I nearly screamed, as he slid down from the box. There was a tall and imposing white wall to one side of the road, with a gate set into it, and Schmidt went hurriedly to knock upon it.

Mimi leaned from the box and cried, "Schmidt, you tallow-brain! What do you think you're doing?"

A wicket in the gate opened, and Alphonse exchanged a few words with the porter. A moment later he turned, beckoning us urgently towards the gate. Nijam and I did not wait, either to protest or to ask questions. If Schmidt had mysteriously produced a tall and strong wall to hide behind, complete with a friendly porter, who were we to question it?

Nijam and I manhandled Vasily from the carriage; and then Schmidt seized him and fairly dragged him in at the little door. Just as our pursuers pulled their chariot to a careering halt in the street, the porter closed the door and shot the bolt.

"What is this place?" I asked Schmidt, as—supporting Vasily—we followed the porter through the shadows of what seemed to be a park. It smelled green with trees and gardens and in the faint dusk I caught glimpses of white walls and gleaming onion-domes.

"Sanctuary," Schmidt answered simply.

Approaching one of the white-walled buildings, the porter opened a door and ushered us within. A few steps more, and we found ourselves in an austere but comfortable room, cool despite the heat that still lingered in the midnight streets. It was evidently a sort of parlour, filled with elegant furniture and a luxurious carpet, as well as a great iron stove to fend off the chill of winter. A crucifix and several large icons hung on the wall, all of them done in the stiff postures and heavy draperies of the Russian church. It was these that told us where we were.

Mimi turned upon Schmidt in absolute bewilderment. "This is a *convent*? Why did you bring us here?"

"Sanctuary!" I cried. "They cannot follow us here, can they? Oh, very clever, Schmidt! But what did you say to make them admit you?"

Schmidt did not seem to know how to answer this. Before he could find the words, an inner door of the parlour opened to reveal an elderly lady in a bath-chair. Both she and the attendant who wheeled her chair wore simple grey gowns and snowy veils. Schmidt stiffened to attention and made a sweeping bow as the old nun was wheeled in; but she had eyes only for one of our number.

"Vasya," the old lady cried, putting a trembling hand over her mouth, and reaching the other out towards him. At the sound of her voice Vasily trembled and started up from the armchair into which he had fallen. For a moment the old nun and the young reprobate gazed at each other with tears welling in their eyes; and then Vasily fell upon his knees before her.

"Mother!" he said. "Mother, it's you!" And gathering up both her hands in his, he burst into a flood of tears.

Only Mimi did not feel the holiness of that moment. "Why, you old liar!" she cried, smacking him over the shoulders. "Why did you tell us your mother was dead? Was that the best you could do to get our sympathy?"

"*Mimi!*" I gasped, but Vasily raised a tear-stained face and gazed in wonder from Mimi to his mother.

"But if Mimi sees you—you are no ghost!" he murmured. "You are alive in truth!"

"See?" I told Mimi indignantly. "Now come away; we ought

not to be here." Seizing her by the shoulders, I removed her firmly to the courtyard, and Schmidt and Nijam followed.

"I don't see *why* we shouldn't be there," Mimi muttered. "I have *questions.*"

"For shame, Mimi! Vasily has just learned that his mother, whom he thought was dead, is indeed alive! There are moments too sacred to be made the sport of onlookers," I told her. Then, unobtrusively, I switched on my transmitter. Schmidt had not noticed me slipping his own transmitter from his pocket, where he had put it for safekeeping; and now, hidden behind one of the cushions on the divan in the convent parlour, it provided me with a means of eavesdropping upon the long-parted mother and son. I could not have said why I did this, except that I was feeling anxious about Vasily—so anxious that I could not bear to be parted from him for an instant. The moment I switched on the device I regretted my actions, for only the sound of deep, racking sobs emerged from the device. I switched the thing off at once; but a few minutes later, when I tried again I could hear the Grand Duchess speaking in soft and comforting French.

"Your father was never happy with me, nor I with him," she said gently. "He was fond of gay and beautiful company, and I have never been either. I learned instead to store up my treasures in heaven, and to employ my time in serving God and His poor. It was hard for such a man to be at ease in my company, and it was hard for me too. It was not merely that he continually resorted to dainties. Not even to please me would he give up peasant-hunting, although he knew I regarded it as a great sin. I pressed him too hard, and the thing came between us. At last I determined to flee his house; but in the pursuit which followed there was a carriage accident, which

223

has left me crippled as you see me. It was this that secured my escape, for to prevent a scandal the Emperor allowed me to enter a convent in Kiev. I am Sister Anastasia now."

"Father told us you were *dead,*" Vasily said in a reproachfully childlike voice.

"I know," she said softly. "I always knew that if I left him I must abandon you children altogether. It was one of the reasons I stayed as long as I did."

"You might have sent word that you were alive."

"I have now. Is it too late, Vasya my dear?"

A silence followed; and perhaps it struck Vasily, as it did me, how strange it was that we should have stumbled upon the very convent that housed his mother.

"I did not come to Moscow for the coronation, you know," Sister Anastasia added. "I came because all of Europe knows that Vasily Nikolaevich, alone of all his kin, chose to strip himself of his dreadful privileges and the place in the world that came with them."

"Oh," said Vasily. There was a silence. "It's not like you think, *maman,*" he said, dashing all the hopes that had begun to rise in my mind. "I'm no great saint. I am only an ordinary man, and, God forgive me! I *want* that place in the world."

Perhaps Vasily really did want to regain his place in the world, and the bloody privilege of fangs to boot! If that were so, I could not bear to hear him say it. Ignorance was infinitely preferable: I switched off the transmitter.

In the twilit courtyard Nijam, Schmidt, and Mimi had found themselves a bench, where they now sat leaning quietly against the wall, half asleep. It must have been very late, but I was not inclined to rest. Instead, I paced to and fro upon the pavement. *Did* Vasily wish, after all, to regain what

224

he had lost? For a little while I had taught myself to think that perhaps he *ought* to be a Grand Duke, and so thinking, had feared to stand between him and his privileges. But in the end I had been wrong, and Schmidt had been right. Vasily did not belong among these people. As a boy, they had oppressed him; as a man, they had nearly destroyed him. If he went back to them now they would almost certainly kill him. For one moment just now, when the Grand Duchess—or Sister Anastasia, as she preferred to be known—had spoken of serving God's poor, and had praised Vasily for giving up his privileges, I had felt the hand of Providence intervening to show Vasily a better way. Yet *still* he still wanted the good things of the world, which would be his if the Emperor took him back into favour?

And how could I blame Vasily if he wanted those good things? It was not so very long since I had been willing to marry Mr Vandergriff for his money. Still, I did not want to see Vasily try to become like his family; I did not want to see him fail, and die for that failure.

Presently, the door to the parlour opened and Sister Anastasia peered out. "Come," she called softly. "Vasily has told me about the family who found him when his own cast him out. Come and make yourselves known to me."

Somewhat abashed by this praise, the four of us filed back into the convent parlour. Vasily sat on the sofa looking pale, and weary as death. We all bowed to Sister Anastasia and introduced ourselves; and it seemed that Vasily had told his mother something about us, for she had kind words for each. "Alphonse Schmidt," she said, "I know all about *you*," and when I rather shyly made my curtsey, she took my hand and drew me down so that she could look into my eyes. "Angelica is a fitting name," she said, and I felt my face grow very warm. "You have all been good to my son, and I thank you for it."

I had no notion what to say; I could only think that I had outwitted Vasily twice, that in Vienna I had betrayed him to the Okhrana, and that more than once I had had the urge to put a spider down his neck.

"I don't know that I *have* been good to him," said I, "except in ways that must have tried him very sorely."

"Which is always our pleasure," Mimi said, only half in jest.

The younger nun, who had wheeled Sister Anastasia into the parlour, now reappeared and spoke a few words to her in Russian or some similar language. "The young men who were following you have been sent away," Sister Anastasia told us, "and now Sister Irene will take you out by another door, where there is a carriage to take you home. Come, Vasily."

Vasily got up obediently and knelt by his mother's chair. "Will I see you again?" he asked.

She put a caressing hand to his cheek. "God knows, my dear, but remember what I said."

Vasily gazed at her with shadowed eyes, and I think that only I heard what he said next. "What will I have, once I have turned my back on my family?"

"What do any of us have, once we have given away this world? Only our souls; but that is a priceless treasure."

After this the young Sister Irene showed us through long passages, dim courtyards and silent cloisters until at last we came to a little gate set in the wall; and on the other side of this was a narrow street and a *troika* cab with a cabman waiting impatiently on the box.

"Do you think it's safe to stay in Moscow?" I asked as we were carried towards our lodgings. "Now that Missy knows about Vasily's false teeth, I mean."

"It will be if I can get at the contents of my box," said Nijam. There was a martial light in her eye which I thought boded ill for any interfering vampires.

"Vasily must look out for himself," Mimi said with a shrug. "But I am not leaving until we have dealt with the old Grand Duke. Can you believe we happened to stumble upon the one convent in Moscow where Vasily's mother was hiding?"

"Not very easily," said Nijam dryly, but she spoke so softly that only I heard her.

"We aren't out of the weeds yet," I said. "Vasily's secret is out. Now even Missy knows that we have no cure, and she won't keep it quiet like Zlata did."

"She cannot expose me without evidence," Vasily said, opening his hand to show the broken pair of dentures, which he must have snatched from the table as we left that horrible basement. "Never fear: people will go on believing in me because they *want* to believe in a cure."

"That's true," I admitted, although once again I felt that our situation was becoming terribly precarious.

"In that case, why don't we try producing a cure?" Mimi asked.

Schmidt started. "My dear Miss Laine!"

"Oh, I don't mean a *real* cure! Only we might take bottled blackcurrant juice, or nettle tea, or some such thing, and sell it for a thousand pounds per bottle."

Nijam snorted. "What a ridiculous notion! I'm sure it would be far more profitable to sell lenses and dentures."

She and Mimi were still debating the venture when we returned home to find the garret warm, but undisturbed. The hands of the clock stood at three o'clock. Mimi stifled a yawn.

"Oh, lord, and the Okhrana were expecting me at midnight! I had better go out and make my report before Cyril and Boris do. How am I going to explain that bomb?"

"Don't," I said. "Cyril and Boris won't; they know Nicky would never stand for them kidnapping a fellow Grand Duke."

That put Mimi at her ease, and off she went. This made me think of another errand that must be run before dawn, and I went into Vasily's room, where Nijam and Schmidt were inspecting his wounds. Poor man! he was covered in bites and daubed all over with blood. Since most of the wounds had ceased to bleed, it was only a matter of sponging away the blood and covering the lacerations with sticking-plaster. While Nijam and Schmidt saw to this task, I brewed a cup of hot chocolate, adding plenty of sugar and a dash of salt. Leaving Vasily tucked into bed with this restorative, I desired a word with Nijam and Schmidt.

"If Vasily really *was* still a vampire," I asked them, "how would he respond to an attack like this one from Missy and the Grand Dukes?"

Schmidt and Nijam looked at each other. "Ask Anna," said Nijam. "She'll know how things are done here, surely."

"I haven't seen Anna in a day or two," I said apologetically. I nearly added *I hope she's all right,* but as a Protestant I was not quite sure whether this might not count as praying for the souls of the dead. "I think a real vampire would storm off at once to Sergei Alexandrovich and lodge a complaint. You had better go to find him, Schmidt, and tell him that your master was abducted by Boris and Cyril and quite shockingly treated. If Missy means to go about telling tales of this night, that should take the wind out of her sails."

With this Nijam agreed, but before Schmidt set off, she said very mildly, "By the way, Schmidt, how *did* we come to seek refuge at the one convent in Moscow where Vasily's mother happened to be waiting for us?"

At this, Schmidt turned absolutely as red as fire.

"Good heavens," I said, "you *knew* about it? You did! Confess!"

"Well," he faltered. "Well, the truth is, I have been quite anxious about sir, as you know."

"Yes, but—"

"It was because of the project he had me working on," Schmidt said. "Sir took me to meet a scientist who works for the Emperor. I'm supposed to help him study blood samples— from sir as well as from his brother Nikolasha, and from a morganatic royalty. Sir seems to think I might be able to remember something of my old knowledge. Of course, even with help, I haven't been able to do anything with the samples; it's like trying to read Greek."

" What are you trying to tell us, Schmidt?" I broke in, in an agony of doubt.

Schmidt let out an unhappy sigh.

"Sir thought that perhaps the differences in the chemical composition of the blood might tell us something useful… He is after a cure to restore the monsters' fangs."

Every word went through my heart like a dagger. "Oh, Vasily," I groaned.

Schmidt nodded. "That is what I thought. And that is why I called Sister Anastasia to Moscow."

"You *what?*" Nijam put in.

"Let me explain," Schmidt said very earnestly. "It first happened in Vienna. I received a letter from Kiev—from Sister Anastasia, in fact. She claimed to be sir's mother and asked after his health. Of course I declined to answer. I did not know the lady, and whoever she was I did not mean to become her spy. But the longer I contemplated the letter, the more it bore the ring of truth. At last, when I began to be worried about sir, I remembered—that is, I thought—." He cleared his throat in some confusion. "In fact, it isn't my place to tell sir his business. Only it occurred to me that sir has very strong feelings when it seems to him that a lady has been wronged. And also I know that sir is strongly opposed to the prospect of becoming in any way like his father. So I thought that, if I were to telegraph Sister Anastasia to come to Moscow, and if she was really his mother, she could perhaps bring him to see reason."

This was the longest speech I had yet heard from Schmidt. Perhaps it was able to go on for so long because Nijam and I were so utterly speechless.

"In fact," said I, putting a hand to my head, "you played sir like a stringed instrument."

"Oh, no," Schmidt said earnestly. Nijam made an inarticulate sound. "Well, that is, perhaps it was a little underhanded of me. Perhaps I ought not to have—but I do fear for sir, if he should remain among these people, and I did not stop to think about whether I was right or wrong—"

He stammered to a halt in the face of my merriment. "Admit it, Schmidt, we've corrupted you," I said.

"I fear I was corrupted long ago, and not by you," he said humbly. Perhaps he was thinking of the revenants.

"You did right," Nijam said with a forbidding scowl. "Don't repent it!'

Then Schmidt went away to visit Grand Duke Sergei Alexandrovich and Nijam closed the door behind him. For a moment she stood staring at the closed door before turning to me.

"Alphonse Schmidt is the cleverest person I know," she said, "and sometimes he terrifies me."

I observed her in surprise, for she seemed genuinely troubled by what he had done. "We are confidence tricksters, Nijam; what do you expect?"

"I don't know," she said, "but who would expect such trickery from Alphonse Schmidt of all people! and towards Vasily of all people!"

I had myself manipulated Vasily on more than one previous occasion; but I understood something of what she meant. I had manipulated Vasily selfishly, because I thought him to be a danger to me; Schmidt had done so with the best possible intentions, because he thought Vasily was a danger to himself.

"Well," said I, "it shows that Schmidt is capable of thinking for himself, at any rate."

"I'm reconsidering whether that's something he ought to do," Nijam said with a shake of her head.

Never one to neglect her beauty sleep, Nijam thereupon took herself off to bed. I attempted to do the same, but my room felt oddly empty without Anna. After all that had happened, I badly wanted someone to talk to. Nor could I be quite easy in my mind until Mimi and Schmidt had safely returned. I remained awake, therefore, until presently I heard soft movement from the sitting-room. Thinking that it might be Mimi or Schmidt, I got up and threw a pashmina around my shoulders before venturing out. The room was dark and I could see no sign of either of my confederates; but finding myself unwilling to return to my bed, I went towards the balcony, the door to which stood open, as usual, to admit the night air. Another soft movement told me that someone was sitting there in the cane armchair. My heart and feet stopped at the same moment, and then the faint scent of pine drifted towards me.

I had hoped to find Mimi, or even Schmidt. The thought of facing Vasily, however, filled me with dread. Who was this man—vampire, hunter, Grand Duke, thief? He had plotted to destroy his father; he had wept in his mother's lap; he had begged me not to expose his secrets; he had, if Schmidt was not mistaken, schemed for a cure to regain his fangs. Never had I felt more confounded by the man. I knew now what he must have promised the Emperor in return for his lost privileges; yet never had my heart yearned over him with greater pity. I could not help feeling that he had betrayed me, yet well I knew that he had not truly betrayed me, but himself.

All these things were true at once; and the trouble of it all was, that I loved him.

The knowledge had been creeping up on me for days without my being in the least aware of it. And how should I? All my life I have been at war with my passions, and all my life I have been the victor. I have felt many things for a great many men and women: friendship, desire, and even infatuation. A leaf which trembles at every breath of wind will not readily believe that the gale has swept it altogether from its parent branch, and so it was with me. Ever since Schloss Frohsdorf I had warned myself against running into the wilderness with Vasily; of losing all grasp upon decency and decorum, upon manners and principle. Nor, even now, did I contemplate such a thing.

And yet I was in love with him. What else could it

be? Pitiable wretch—burning house that he was, I had nevertheless looked into his eyes and found that his very peace of mind was more precious to me than my own life. In the moment at which Boris had been about to drink my blood, my only thought was to spare Vasily pain. The danger I always feared had come upon me, and at the worst possible moment, when we were dancing in the very mouth of the imperial bear. How could I trust Vasily when a word from him might destroy me? Who could say if I could now refuse him anything he asked? For a moment I crushed my hand against my mouth for fear of the words that might escape it.

"Molly Dark," he said softly. "I hoped you would come to me."

I bit my fingers in despair.

"I thought it was Mimi," I blurted out, at the very moment that he, too, said, "I couldn't sleep."

Our words tangled; silence followed.

"Your injuries—" I began.

"The imprints you saw," Vasily said at the same moment. There was something wrong with his voice; it was ragged and nearly raw. "I—I never meant you to see those."

"Of course you did not," I replied, unable to prevent the words from sounding a little embittered. Vasily had never wanted to share his secrets with me; and no wonder, if he meant to return to his former life. Oh, heavens! What kind of monster had I fallen in love with? "In your place I should not."

I was more heart-sick than angry. Vasily could not truly wish to return to his family now; not after the things he had seen tonight.

"I was younger then," he said. "You know that I would never

treat you in the same way."

Still, although I believed him to be sincere, many a man has begun down the road to hell without ever intending to go all the way.

"Does your mother know about them?" I asked, sooner than reply. "Poor Ioanna, and the peasants you hunted for sport?"

*"Bozhe moi,* what you must think of me!" he murmured. "My mother knows the sort of life I must have led. Miss Dark..." He moved, and I felt his hand touch mine before drawing back. "For God's sake say something. Forgive what you have seen, or spurn me in disgust. Offer me anything, but not your *tact."*

I felt almost terrified. I could not tell him that I loved him. I did not yet know how to think of it myself. "You must be weak from shock, and loss of blood," I said. "You ought to sleep, and we can talk about the rest of it in the morning."

"Sleep!" he said, with derision. "How should I sleep?"

There was no help for it. I passed a hand over my weary eyes and seated myself beside him. "The dead appear to me, Vasily. Did you think you could keep me from knowing the things you have done?"

A long silence followed.

"Perhaps I did," he said presently. From the sound of his voice he had attempted a devil-may-care grin.

"In that case you're not half as clever as you think you are," I said. "It isn't that which bothers me."

"But then it's something."

I bit my lip. "A little while ago, I asked whether, if you were forced to choose between us and your family, which it would be."

"This again? Why do you torment yourself with such questions? How can you doubt my loyalties after what happened tonight? Am I to go on proving them forever?"

How could I answer him without exposing Schmidt, or confessing my feelings? And how could I confess my feelings when he spoke to me like this? How could he speak to me like this, when tonight I had nearly died for his sake?

The silence was nearly suffocating, and he was still awaiting my answer. "What is it to you, the things that torment me?" I said at last. He did not answer, and I went on: "Lie to me, if you can't tell me the truth. But for heaven's sake give me something to believe."

"How can I, when you think me a liar?"

"Are you?"

"Of course I am. It is the one thing I have never concealed from you."

I did not answer that. How could I? He wanted to be trusted, but he believed it to be impossible. Since he refused either to accept or to deserve my trust, what could I do?

"Then don't lie to me," I said, now close to tears. "Tonight I have descended into hell for you, Vasily Nikolaevich. You owe me a little truth, at least."

Perhaps that reassured him; for a long silence passed, and then he said in quite a different voice, "What a fool I've been! And what a fool you are, to risk your life for me! My dear, I'm a beast. Here, then, is something that is true: for a little while I have forgotten myself, and priced the world above my soul. Remind me why we came to this place, among these monsters."

"For Anna," I said, perceiving that it was a genuine question.

"For Anna," he repeated, "and to wreak justice upon my

235

father. Very well: then no more dancing attendance on Nicky. If he wants me back he can take me as I am, without any little tests of loyalty. Let us attend to my father."

After this I went back to my chamber not indeed perfectly satisfied, but hopeful that Schmidt's scheme had borne fruit. I rose very late the following morning to find that we had a visitor. Valery Petrovich stood in our sitting-room. "I've thought it over," he declared, "and I'm willing to hear what you propose."

# 18

# Chapter XVIII.

We did little that day except to lay our plans, for all of us were tired from the night before. Nor were we the only ones, for after the great coronation the entire city lay in a stupor.

I think Nijam was the only one of us who proceeded as usual that day, for she was hard at work in her room, from which clanks and whirrs continually proceeded, with an occasional stop as she went out to buy some necessity or other. She would not tell me precisely what she was making. "I don't know yet if it it's going to work, but if we are to remain in this benighted city we shall want something better than the flashbangs," was all she said.

That evening, Zlata came. When I peered through the door to see her on the doorstep, my heart fairly stood still. "Your highness," I gasped, taking the chain from the door and standing aside to let her enter. "Forgive me for abandoning you last night in the basement, but—"

"Oh! You only did it to save Vasily. I pray you will think nothing of it," she said, rushing past me, and coming to a halt when she saw that the above-mentioned Grand Duke was nowhere in evidence. "Where is he? Is he much hurt?"

"He's resting in bed," I said shortly, "for he's lost a great deal of blood." I did worry that Vasily was weak following his terrible ordeal; he was now a mere mortal, and could not return in a blink to life and health after having his blood drained away.

Zlata insisted upon going in to see him, where she cooed and wept over him and pressed childish kisses to his hands. I watched in a dull kind of resignation. Would that I had the courage to kiss and weep over him, or even only to let him lay his head in my lap, and to caress his hair as I had upon the night of Zlata's party! But at that time I had thought myself inured to Vasily's fatal charm, and now I was aware of my weakness.

Having hurried Zlata on her way again, I went to see Vasily myself, and put the little brown Fabergé mouse on the counterpane.

"What's this?" he asked, relinquishing the cup of tea with which he was refreshing himself after Zlata's demonstrations.

"It's your mother's mouse," I told him. "Now that she is alive, you have the opportunity to give it to her."

There was an oddly disappointed look in his eyes. "It was you I gave it to; not my mother. Don't you want it?"

"Vasily," I said, delivering the blow as gently as I could, "I know it was never meant for me—and it isn't the sort of gift I can properly accept from a professional acquaintance."

"Well, I can't give it to my mother," he said, with a flash of temper. "Don't you know that a nun's first vow is to poverty? I suppose it had better go into the rubbish," and with a flick of his wrist he tossed it into the little waste-paper basket that stood in a corner of the room.

Restraining myself with an effort from diving after the pretty little thing, I left him to his sulks—not without a pang of my own. There: the fending-off of Vasily Nikolaevich had been achieved, and now I could breathe more easily.

The following day we were once more ready to act. That morning, to keep up our charade as art thieves, Mimi took Zlata out to conduct a closer inspection of the French Ambassador's house—the splendid Sheremetov Palace, which had been hired for the occasion. But it was in the afternoon that our real work began. Magnificently clad—not only in our own best clothes, but also in some which Mimi had "scrounged"—the five of us called a pair of troikas and set off to attend the regimental races.

Vasily still looked extremely pale, even in the rouge with which Mimi had painted his face, and in the carriage I regarded him with grave misgivings. "Are you quite sure you're up to this?" I asked. "The plan will work just as well if you stay at home."

"What, and show Cyril and Boris that they have conquered?" he asked, baring his teeth. "Never. One cannot show weakness before these people, for they will consider it an invitation to destroy one."

I took this to mean that he had no intention of fainting all over the imperial pavilion. Shortly we arrived at our destination and were admitted to the enclosure, which was bright with gowns and hats and waving ostrich feathers as the noble spectators took their seats amidst much talk and laughter and laying of wagers. To our left we heard voices uplifted in a discussion of the danger presented to horses and good officers by the bloody practice of horse-racing; and to the right a spirited debate on whether the English or the German style of hypothetical and as-yet-nonexistent parliament better suited the Russian condition. Presently Vasily and I beheld the others making their way through the crowds towards us. Nijam was clad in black as always, but Mimi and Schmidt had been transformed into the very image of a fashionable ballerina and her rich protector. Nijam had even fitted Schmidt with her own inventing-goggles. With the smoked-glass lenses turned down, they gave him the air of a wealthy prosthete, very shiny and sinister about the eyes. He and Mimi made a handsome couple. I wondered whether this had anything to do with the air of simmering discontent that hung about Nijam.

Schmidt and Vasily bowed to each other ceremoniously when we met, and I kissed Mimi's cheek. "Has anyone seen my father?" Vasily asked in a low voice.

"Yes, and he's seen you," Nijam said, nodding behind the two of us. Vasily and I turned, and there indeed was Grand Duke Nicholas.

"Why, it's the lovely Countess, in company with my scape-grace son!" said he. His gaze went beyond us at once to Mimi, once again a vision in white muslin and blue ribbons. "But won't you introduce me to your charming friend?"

Vasily at once, with an easy assurance, introduced his father to the celebrated ballerina Madame Adeline Genée and her dear friend, Herr Schmidt, "of the Cologne steam-engine Schmidts."

The Grand Duke paid no attention whatsoever to Schmidt, instead bowing over Mimi's hand. "Enchanted, my dear! Do try to contain yourself," he added, with the most peculiarly satisfied smile. "I have this effect upon all women. It is my blessing, and my curse."

It was not so much this preposterous speech, as the look with which Mimi greeted it, that nearly made me lose my countenance. The urge to laugh departed, however, when a familiar voice broke in upon us.

"Why, Vaska!" Princess Zlata protested, bustling up to us in the company of a gentleman whom I did not recognise. "You never told me you meant to be here. I thought we were partners!"

I felt myself break out into a cold sweat. Nijam sent Zlata a ferocious glare, but Vasily only bowed. "I felt so well this morning that I was able to attend, after all," said he.

Of course, since as far as Zlata was concerned our only business in Moscow was to steal the *Musketeer* and possibly to restore Vasily in the imperial favour, we had not informed her of our plans to waylay Grand Duke Nicholas at the racecourse. This, however, put us into a quandary, for we had just introduced Mimi and Schmidt to the Grand Duke under assumed names.

"My dear Princess," I said, "you're the very person I wished to see! Give me a moment, for I have a favour to beg of you." Looping my arm through Zlata's, I fairly dragged her away from the group. "It's about Grand Duke Vasily," I whispered, when she seemed to resist; and then she followed all too willingly.

We went down to the front of the enclosure, near the ring, just as the gun went off and the horses rushed away from the starting-line for the mile-and-a-quarter race. The air filled with cheers and shouts, and the rolling drum of horses' hooves, allowing us to converse without being overheard. Leaning down to Zlata's ear, I said, "I beg you will show more discretion, your highness! Vasily won't say anything, for he's too much of a gentleman, but really it's as much as all our lives are worth to hint at our being confederates! After what happened at Princess Marie's we are in enough trouble as it is!"

"Where's your sense of humour?" Zlata said, pouting. In her gown of black lace, with a black ribbon about her neck, she looked pale and tragic. "Who are you to tell me what to do? You're only a countess!"

My stomach curdled. Zlata evidently believed our business to be a harmless game, half the fun of which was to hint and gossip at. After the horrors I had endured the other night, I was past finding any such thing charming. All our lives were in her little net-gloved hands—and Vasily's was most at stake.

"I may only be a countess," I said almost recklessly, "but don't think you can set me at naught for all that. I'm the one who has Vasily's ear."

This was taking the gloves off with a vengeance. Zlata gave me a look that was pure murder. I knew she could, if she chose, betray us all and crush me like an insect, and I felt nearly sick with apprehension. Still, I could not help feeling a moment of triumph, for in those resentful eyes I read a consciousness of my own power. It was ludicrous to triumph over such a thing, of course, especially when I was afraid for Vasily's life. I did not want Vasily. If I could have reached into my heart and torn up my love by the roots I would have done so.

"Let us understand each other," I added hastily, seeing that I ought to spin some kind of tale to excuse myself. "Vasily invited me to remain in Russia with him, should the Emperor restore him to his former privileges. Naturally I refused. Paris is the only place for civilised people to live. For the present, however, Vasily is of use to me. You may throw away his life, if you choose, *after* I am done with him; but not before."

Zlata watched me with narrowed eyes. About us, people shouted, cheered, or swore. I gathered that the race had been won—or lost—but could not have said by whom. Beneath the princess' scrutiny I attempted to remain calm. I did not like telling Zlata that Vasily's life was hers to throw away, but the person she had determined me to be would say such a thing. Since she thought me to be her rival in Vasily's affections, I must give her reasons to help, rather than hinder me.

Zlata was still considering this olive branch, when we were interrupted by a troika of very young gentlemen whose fair hair and guttural accents proclaimed them to be Germans.

"Princess Zlata!" one of them said, seizing her hand without waiting for her to offer it. "Where is your friend, the renegade Grand Duke?"

"We heard he was feeling poorly," said another, with a smile that told me poor Zlata was being baited.

"We *heard*," said the third, "that after all Vasily Nikolaevich is only a fraud in false teeth!"

For a moment I was struck dumb with terror, but then Zlata turned to face them. "Who said such a thing?" she cried. "It was that horrible Marie of Roumania, wasn't it? What a liar that woman is!"

I heaved a sigh, understanding that Zlata did mean to help me protect Vasily, after all. Yet the very heat of her denials promised to get him into still worse trouble.

"If that is what you have heard," I told the Germans, "then perhaps you ought to try his teeth for yourselves."

"Maybe we will," their ringleader snarled.

"You wouldn't dare," Zlata declared. "Don't you know who

my godfather is? —Sergei Alexandrovich, the Emperor's uncle and the Governor of Moscow, whose duty it is to keep the peace and see to the security of the inhabitants! If anything at all happens to Vasily Nikolaevich, I will go at once to my godfather and tell him that you are responsible. And I should not like to be in your shoes when my godfather determines that you are disturbing the peace!"

This was not the subtler approach I should have taken, but it certainly had a dramatic effect upon the Germans, who blenched. "Grand Duke Sergei!" one of them whispered with a shudder.

This earned him a look of disgust from the ringleader, who leaned close to Zlata and me, and spoke in a voice that was low and threatening. "You should tell your good friend Vasily Nikolaevich to count himself lucky that we have bigger game afoot than a Russian renegade."

With that the three of them went away, and I found that despite the warmth of the summer day, I was shivering, cold and sick. The gala performance at the Bolshoi Theatre was tomorrow night; we had only to survive another two days in Moscow, at most, before we could flee this dreadful place. But were we already in too deep? With both Mimi and our landlady reporting on us, would the Okhrana allow us to leave? How long before the Germans completed their other business and turned their attention to Vasily?

How I envied Zlata in that moment, for being able to protect Vasily with a few sharp words! There were undeniable advantages to having been born in Brixton; but this was not one of them.

The princess now regarded me with an air of triumph yet more palpable than my own a few moments ago. "I would never throw away Vasily's life," she said. "To you he may be a tool, but to me he is life itself."

The splendid scorn with which she said this was quite at odds with her accustomed childish manner. I sighed, wishing I, too, might have the privilege of declaring aloud how much Vasily meant to me.

"Then for the moment we want the same thing," I said, "which is Vasily's safety."

In a trice, all that scorn was hidden beneath a façade of sweetness. Smiling, Zlata leaned up to kiss my cheek. "Oh, Countess," she said, squeezing my arm. "I knew that we could arrive at an understanding with each other! You really mean to go back to Paris without Vaska?"

I assured her that I did; and having thus buried the hatchet, the two of us returned quite amicably to where we had left the others.

Meanwhile, as Nijam later explained, Mimi's seduction of Grand Duke Nicholas had made a far from auspicious beginning. Mimi's knowledge of feminine wiles proved minimal. Even Nijam knew it would not do to ask the Grand Duke if he had taken a new mistress since the death of Madame Chislova, and moreover how well the position paid if one was interested. Schmidt, who had been instructed to play the wildly jealous lover, did little to improve matters by clearing his throat and uttering infrequent gentle protests.

Then an idea had struck Mimi.

"You did say he believed himself to be irresistible to women," she later explained. "I think he was happy, just once, to be proven correct."

Indeed, upon returning to my friends, I found to my astonishment that Mimi had draped herself over Grand Duke

245

Nicholas rather like a cat over a human it is fond of—rubbing her head against his shoulder and making little keening noises of happiness. Schmidt and Nijam beheld this unedifying sight in a paralysis of astonishment. Vasily was nowhere to be seen, but that had been part of the plan.

"Schmidt," I whispered, jabbing him in the ribs, "what are you doing? Don't forget you're supposed to be playing the jealous lover."

He looked at me in a speechless panic. I had to admit that I did not know what I could have done in his place, either. Mimi locked her arms around the appreciative Grand Duke's neck and appeared to be enthusiastically sniffing his clothing. Happily, it was the Grand Duke himself who put a halt to this. "One moment, my dear," he said, removing his hand from a portion of Mimi's anatomy that ought not to be mentioned, let alone pawed at, in polite company. "Here's Vasily with my winnings."

Vasily approached us, beaming. "I was wrong," he told his father. "It wasn't your horse that won; it was mine. How would you like a fortune in new furs, my dear Adeline?"

He leaned down and gave Mimi a smacking kiss. Schmidt at last saw his chance to act.

"Unhand her, you villain!" he roared, swinging a fist wildly in his master's direction. He missed, of course—and we had made him promise quite solemnly that he should not!

Vasily laughed. "Come, Schmidt," he said, "is that the best you can do?" Schmidt flushed and made a second attempt. This one connected quite solidly with Vasily's body— of course Vasily had particularly begged Schmidt not to rearrange his beautiful face.

"Let that teach you," Schmidt gasped, apparently shocked

by his own temerity, "not to lay hands on—a lady." This was not quite what we had rehearsed, but it would do. "And that goes for you, too, sir!" he added, turning to Grand Duke Nicholas. This time the censure was rather more convincing; but the effect was lost. The Grand Duke was no longer paying attention: he had turned his back on us quite abruptly, and was making his way towards a lady some way off.

Our plan to have the Grand Duke become infatuated with Mimi, only to be warned away from her by a jealous lover, appeared to have come up against an unexpected obstacle. I waved Schmidt and Mimi back and hurried to catch up with the old *roué*.

"Is something wrong, your grace?" I asked. "Madame Genée wished to bid you good-bye, but that brute has carried her away." I had barely time to complete the words, before his hand shot out and seized my arm in a vice-like grip.

"She *looked* at me!" he hissed. "She *saw* me!"

I found myself utterly at a loss. "I beg your pardon—whom?"

"Mathilde Kschessinska!" he cried, "that lady in pink! She is madly in love with me, of course, but she cannot show it in public. She must keep up appearances for the sake of her lover."

"Madame Genée—" I began feebly.

"Oh, hang Madame Genée! I must go to speak with my beloved." With those words he bustled away, leaving me and Vasily to watch his departure in complete bewilderment.

# 19

# Chapter XIX.

"What the devil has happened?" Nijam demanded, stalking into the garret with the rest of us fairly running to keep up with her. "Why did he run off after somebody else?"

"I misread the situation," I admitted, in some chagrin. "I ought to have inquired more closely into his delusions. Nicholas Nikolaevich believes himself to be irresistible to all women, but it seems that he's primarily interested in Kschessinska."

"You mean I've gone to all this trouble and let him molest me for *nothing?*" Mimi demanded. "That decides it! Next time, *you* do the seduction!"

"There, there, Mimi," Vasily put in quickly, "all of us were a little off our game today! Take Schmidt, for instance—we must certainly work upon *his* impersonation skills. I'm sorry, Schmidt, but as a jealous lover you were *not* convincing."

Schmidt reddened, and because I was watching him closely, I saw the look he cast at Nijam. "How can I pretend to be jealous when my heart isn't in it? I'm not in love with Miss Laine!"

"How ungallant!" Vasily murmured from where he had thrown himself on the divan with his sketch-book in his hand.

"Don't talk nonsense, Schmidt," Nijam said. "That's why it's called *acting*. Why, I could have done a better job of it than you!"

There came a moment of silence as we all attempted to picture this.

"*Could* you, though?" Mimi asked, as though the notion fascinated her. "Do you even know what it *is* to be in love, Nijam?"

"Yes," she said forbiddingly. Mimi opened her eyes very wide.

"What! You've actually been in love?"

Nijam did not exactly redden, for her complexion did not allow it; but she flushed a darker hue and snapped, "To be absolutely clear, I've been in love with the same man for years."

Schmidt's mouth opened, and for one fleeting moment a rather stricken look crossed his face. Mimi must have been watching him as well, because she dug her hand into her pocket. "Peppermint?" she asked, but he shook his head mutely, and waved it away. Poor fellow!

Nijam seemed oblivious to this exchange. "The question is, what went wrong, and what should we do next?"

"I think I have a notion," I said, but before I could go on, there came a knock at the door. At first I feared that it was Zlata, but when Schmidt opened the door it proved to be Anna's interesting friend, Valery Petrovich.

"Just the man I wished to see," I declared, leaping up to usher him into the room. In fact it had slipped my mind, but we had made an appointment to meet him here this very day. "Tell me, Mr Petrovich, wasn't Anna in Mademoiselle Kschessinska's dressing-room the day she was attacked?"

"That's right," Valery said, with a scowl. "Kschessinska sent Anna to her dressing room to fetch a wrap, and that's what caused the uproar."

"One moment," said Nijam. "Which uproar?"

"Between Little K and Anna, of course. What—you don't know? When we found Anna, after the attack, she was wearing one of Kschessinska's costumes. Of course it was only Anna's game of make-believe, but Little K, who is the queen of the Maryinsky and as jealous as hell, flew into a rage. She said that Anna was scheming to take her place, and nothing would please her except that Anna should be thrown out of the theatre. Never mind that it was quite evident Anna was not the real target of the attack, Kschessinska would do nothing to help her."

"Oh, I could throttle her!" said Mimi wrathfully. "That's what she meant by calling Anna a sly minx!"

"Well, that settles our next steps," said I. "If it's Kschessinska Grand Duke Nicholas has been after all this time, we can very easily trap him! Doesn't Kschessinska have a *pas de deux* during the gala performance? We could strike immediately after that."

Geelfully, Mimi snapped her fingers. "We will need a few things, Nijam: A wig, a costume, a bottle of whatever perfume Kschessinska commonly wears, and all your false diamonds."

"We'll manage it." Nijam looked at Valery over the top of her steel-rimmed pince-nez. "You understand, don't you, what's required of you? We cannot proceed unless you are absolutely committed to the *rôle*."

"I don't know about the *rôle*," said Anna's Valery with a

shrug, "but someone ought to avenge what happened to Anna."

"Someone should," said Vasily, "but you understand the cost, don't you?"

Valery flicked his hair back in an attitude of splendid recklessness. "For years I have been trying to show Anna without any success that I would die for her. At last, my opportunity has come."

"If *that* was all you wanted you could have cut your throat years ago," Mimi muttered, but she was the only person impolite enough to make such a comment. With our plans completed, Valery took his leave and Vasily announced that he meant to retire for a rest.

"In a moment," I said. "We really ought to discuss the fact that apparently it is now common knowledge in Moscow that you are going about in dentures."

"Oh!" Vasily said, shrugging. "I wouldn't call that *knowledge*. It would be more accurate to call it a *rumour*."

"The point is that they've guessed the *truth*," Nijam said frostily and much to my relief, "and if any of them decides to take advantage of that fact, we shall all be in a great deal of trouble."

"They won't," Vasily said with supreme confidence. "It is as I said: no one wants the rumours to be true. Everyone wants to believe there is a cure, and Missy has no proof that there *isn't*. We can use that. As long as Nicky prevaricates, we have a breathing-space, and I can go into society without fear, and wear my fangs, and convince everyone to believe me. Don't worry, Miss Nijam! Nicky's not like the rest of those horrors; he won't let me come to grief."

"Go into society?" I said blankly; and perhaps my voice

rose a register or two. "You can't really mean to attend the gala!"

"My dear, it's absolutely necessary."

If the imprints did not drive me mad then Vasily would. I wrung my hands in despair. What could I say? I was terrified for him. If he was taken again I would go after him and this time I would certainly die. I was not like Zlata: I could protect him only with my wits and my life. But I could not tell him any of this.

"It's out of the question, that's what it is," I declared. "Please, Vasily, it's too dangerous for all of us. Besides, you aren't recovered. Stay home; we can finish the job without you."

"Little mouse!" he protested. "What are these foolish fears? How can you ask such a thing of me? Here I am, about to destroy the man who crippled my mother and poisoned my life, and you wish me to stay home?"

"*Yes*," I nearly wailed. "We came here to get justice for Anna, not revenge for you. The Bolshoi will be full of monsters. What if one of them takes it into their head to try your teeth? You will be dead, and we shall have no way out!"

"If one of them tries my fangs, others will protect me," he said serenely. "Believe me, my dear, it would be far more dangerous to show fear. Remember that I know these people better than you do."

"Did you know that the Germans would attack you in London?" I demanded. "Did you know that Zlata would recognise you at the Maryinsky? Did you know that Missy would kidnap you at the coronation not two nights since?"

"Missy has already been reprimanded," he said.

I bit my lip. "I can't bear it! You insist upon taking the most frightful risks—your family is willing to drain your blood, and yet you won't keep clear of them! Why, Vasily? Why can't you leave them alone?"

"Because I have unfinished business with them!" Vasily's voice rang a moment in the attic; then he gave an uneasy laugh. "I admit it, my dear: it is difficult, if one has been raised a Grand Duke, to accustom oneself to life as an exile. Perhaps I've had foolish dreams of late, but I have been shot at, and drained, and threatened. I know now that my dreams were nothing but nightmares. I won't take any foolish risks, but we have a task to accomplish, and I am still the only one who knows Moscow society well enough to guide you through it. *You* understand this, don't you, Miss Nijam?"

"I do, but it doesn't please me," she said with some asperity. "From the very first, you've had your own motives in coming to Russia, which I chose to allow because you are useful to the job."

"I swear to be useful to it still," Vasily said earnestly. "Suspect me all you like, but believe that I would never jeopardise my revenge against that man."

"I do believe it—and yes, I know you're worried, Dark," Nijam added, as I opened my mouth to protest, "but if the Grand Duke wants to risk his neck tomorrow night, I'm happy to allow it."

"*Thank* you," Vasily said in tones of relief.

"Only because I trust him to look after his own interests, and if he lets himself be drained he isn't the fox I take him to be," she added. "What do you say, Schmidt?"

"I'm very relieved that sir has made a clean breast of things," he said, "and if he comes with us tomorrow night I promise not to let any harm come to him."

"Well, I *don't* care about Vasily," said Mimi. "I only want

Anna set right, and for that Vasya will be useful, whether or not he gets drained."

And there they were, all arrayed against me. Perhaps the terror and emotion of the night before last was still catching up with me, but I found that I could not speak. Vasily was sick and in danger, and he was determined to throw his life away in one way or another, and there was nothing I could do to stop it.

"If you're all decided," I said, "then there's nothing more to be said about it, of course. Good grief! I'm suffocating in this get-up." With that I made good my escape, retreating to my own room and tearing at the buttons of my elaborate silk afternoon dress. I could scarcely see to undo them. Oh dear! what was *wrong* with me?

Presently a knock came at the door and I halted, hardly daring to breathe. But it was Nijam, not Vasily, who called out to me. "It's me, Dark. I'm coming in."

She closed the door behind her and stood watching me a moment. I did not attempt to hide my tears.

"Something's bothering you," she said. "You'd better come clean."

I had barely admitted to myself that I was in love with Vasily; I could not possibly admit it to Nijam. "It's nothing that matters; only I—I haven't been quite myself, since that night in Missy's basement. And Vasily talks about waking from dreams, but he hasn't told us the things he was hiding from us! He was looking for a *cure.* Did he not care what happened to Anna? How could he have thought, even for a moment, of giving them their fangs back? How can I trust, even now, that he doesn't have other secrets?"

"You needn't worry about that," Nijam said with rough

kindness. "Of course the Grand Duke is the world's foremost egotist, but in this case his self-interest lies in staying alive and helping us complete the job. It was the same in London; nothing has changed."

"Everything has changed," I said dolefully. "We've no contingencies. This time we're absolutely dependent upon him. If he sets a foot wrong we shall all be ruined."

"One could say the same for each of us," Nijam pointed out. "When you brought us to Russia you were hiding things—you feared that your visions were only hallucinations. And what about Mimi? She was reporting us to the *police,* and now she's the linchpin to all our plans. You were very quick to forgive Mimi; why are you treating Vasily differently?"

I bit my lip. I *was* treating Vasily differently—because I loved him and was afraid of what it might lead me to do. Still, wasn't it only sensible to do so?

"Mimi only wants money—that's something we can give her. But Vasily…" I shook my head. "I don't for a moment think that he would intentionally betray us; only there is a part of him that wants something we can never give him, and that may do us more harm in the end. What if Nicky offered him his old place tomorrow? How could he resist? and then what will become of *us?*"

Nijam snorted. "That would be madness," she said. "If Vasily didn't know it before, he knows now that his family would be happy to eat him alive. Let us take it as established that at present he means to help us, just as Mimi does. And he *does* know this world far better than any of us do."

Knowing that she was right, I heaved a sigh. "I don't know what's wrong with me," I said miserably.

"You're like Lady Glencora in *Can You Forgive Her?*" Nijam

said, not unkindly: "you're your own worst enemy sometimes, Dark."

With that she went away, leaving me to my own devices. I tried to think of a contingency—some brilliant plan whereby I might yet snatch my friends and myself out of the trap which I felt closing around us—but my thoughts were in too much of an uproar. I had resolved to trust Vasily; and yet trusting him went against every ingrained habit of my life. Everything was against him. That poor girl, Ioanna, had died because of him; his father was a tyrannical madman stained with the blood of dozens; Mimi had not a single good word to say of him; and in any case, being a Grand Duke, he was not for *me*. The fact that I had unexpectedly and inconveniently fallen in love with Vasily ought to make no difference to my conduct. It *could* be allowed to make no difference to my conduct. I must pull myself together, or I would be absolutely incapable of doing my work. So I washed my face and forced myself out into the sitting-room, where I put on the kettle for some tea. "Forgive me," I told Vasily, as I brought him a cupful of the faintly campfire-scented brew, "you know that I am only worried for your safety, don't you?"

"Little mouse," he said caressingly, "I understand perfectly."

But there was a sort of constraint between us now. Amidst my disappointment, I told myself I ought to welcome it, for it would keep me upon my guard.

20

# Chapter XX.

The following evening found Vasily and myself settling into Grand Duke Nicholas' box at the Bolshoi Theatre, one of six tiers of gilded balconies overlooking the lavish red-velvet curtains of the stage. An expectant hum of voices counterpointed the strains of an orchestra tuning its instruments. Vasily's brothers were both present as well as his father, and the two Montenegrin princesses, who accompanied them, gave me a warm welcome.

Tonight, as usual, Vasily wore his red lenses and false teeth. We found ourselves once again surrounded by vampires: sharp fangs and blood-red eyes hemmed me in on every side. I scented a faint aroma of decay, from whence I could not say; but it made me feel like a rabbit trapped in the fox's den—a small, soft, cowering thing. The elder Grand Duke Nicholas welcomed his son expansively, gesturing with an enormous glass like a brandy balloon, half filled with blood. I did not like to imagine what might happen to *me* when the glass was empty; and thinking to distract myself, I raised my opera-glasses and scrutinised the house. Opposite,

Princess Zlata saw us and blew a kiss from the box she shared with Sergei Alexandrovich and his extraordinarily lovely duchess. The Imperial Box itself was empty, waiting for the Emperor's formal appearance. But there were other royalties in attendance, and my flesh crept as I beheld them.

In England it was considered unmannerly for foreign royalties to display their monstrosity openly, but a different set of rules obtained on the Continent. I saw at once that in addition to the vampiric Russians, a great many of the audience were themselves in "tails", as they had called it at the Schloss Frohsdorf. Besides the vampires, I beheld the shimmering beauty of Greek and Danish sirens, a couple of French or Spanish melusines, a whole party of Italian ogres and even a couple of maned Austrian lindworms. But after the Russian and Roumanian vampires, by far the greatest number of royalties present were German werewolves— great, slavering beasts, part human, part wolf, and all sharp teeth and sulfurous eyes. I shuddered, recalling the dreadful night in London when three of them had tried to kill Vasily; and my hands found the little device which Vasily had given me in the carriage before we entered the theatre.

This was shaped rather like a pistol and came in a little holster which I had tied to my leg just above the ankle. "I had Nijam make you an injector," Vasily had told me hurriedly. "Use it only at greatest need."

Outside the theatre it had been a comforting thing to have about me; but now I was fairly surrounded by the monsters, and the tiny device seemed laughably inadequate.

"Well, sir, are you looking forward to the performance?" I asked the elder Grand Duke Nicholas, when the Emperor and his wife had finally arrived, and the lights had gone down, and the ballet got underway with the Dance of the Pearls.

"Little K is to have a *pas de deux* in the second act," he said with a rather foolish smile. "Of course I could not remain away. It will give her such pleasure to know I am here to see her."

Picking up all my courage, I leaned a little closer. "Speaking of Kschessinska, there is something I must tell you, your grace. You won't imagine to whom I spoke this week."

The Grand Duke put his hand over mine. "How can I, unless you tell me?"

"Do you mean my mother, little mouse?" Vasily put in, reaching out and deftly extricating my hand from his father's. "Can you imagine it, sir?" he added to the elder Nicholas. "All this time we believed she was dead; and it turns out that she has been living in Kiev as a nun! What do you think of that?"

My blood congealed in my veins, and I must have gone as stiff as a corpse. *This* was not in our plans! What could Vasily be thinking, derailing all my carefully laid plans? Did he want his father to turn upon him, and rend him limb from limb? Oh! I *knew* he ought not to have come!

But the elder Nicholas paid no heed to these words. "What do I think of it? I don't think of it at all," he said fretfully. "I thought you had something *interesting* to say."

"Indeed I did," I said in a hurry, but Vasily was not finished. He had gone a little pale, but his hand clenched on mine, halting me before I could go on. I realised with some shock that he was fighting for command of himself.

"Did *you* know, Nikolasha? —that Mother is alive?"

"Of course," said his brother, quite readily. "Father told Peter and me the day we drained our first peasants."

"Why did you never tell me?"

"Well! it wasn't my place, was it?" Nikolasha said, settling back into his seat, and becoming absorbed in the performance.

Vasily did not look at me, but stared at the stage with unseeing eyes. I ought to have been angry, but to my surprise I found that I was sorry for him—that I was filled with longing to kiss away the taut, strained lines about his mouth. Poor loon! did he really think to surprise the old reprobate into a moment of guilt? No such triumph would be ours: even if the rest of our plans ran smoothly, I did not suppose that the elder Nicholas would ever feel a moment's remorse for anything he had done.

I could offer no comfort, save a fleeting pressure of the hand; and then I went on with the plan. "In fact, your grace," I murmured in the old Grand Duke's ear, "I spoke to Kschessinska herself last week, at a séance! You can't imagine how happy she was when she learned that I was personally acquainted with your grace. Her own Grand Duke keeps a close eye on her; but she begged me to arrange a meeting with you, here at the Bolshoi immediately after her *pas de deux*. Then she is assured of being alone in her dressing-room."

At these words, the Grand Duke quivered like a blancmange. "Where is her dressing-room? I will go to her at once."

"No, no, no!" I cried, seizing his arm and laughing. "It must be after the *pas de deux*, or you will be discovered. Be patient, and I will tell you where to go, and when."

Settling back into his seat, the Grand Duke began to fret, and to look at his watch, and then at his programme. I sent Vasily another squeeze of the hand, and he got up and retreated to the rear of the box. I heard the transmitter in my ear crackle softly as he murmured, "The performance has commenced."

"Good," Nijam said. "Keep your eye on the Grand Duke, and the rest of us will be on our way."

On the stage, the performance continued; the first act came and went, and it was time for the *pas de deux*. Under the old Grand Duke's rapt attention "Little K" was winging her way across the boards of the stage, executing feats of acrobatic strength with the assistance of a sinewy young dancer. Behind the stage, quite a different sort of performance was unfolding. I was only sorry that Anna's shade was not here to see it.

"Schmidt and I have taken our positions backstage," Nijam murmured into her transmitter. "Mimi, what's your situation?"

"Valery and I have found everything we need in Kschessinska's dressing-room, and we're coming out now," Mimi volunteered. "Ow! This wig is so heavy! How does she dance in it?"

"Wait a minute," said Schmidt, "there's someone up on the gantry."

"Probably just a stagehand," Nijam said. "Don't worry, Schmidt; he can't stop us meddling with the backdrop. Three minutes until the *pas de deux* ends. You might as well send the Grand Duke on his way, Dark."

My heart was beating quickly. I glanced over my shoulder to where Vasily still stood, silent and brooding, in the shadows near the door of the box. But the box had a new guest: my father's imprint brushed past Vasily and leaned down to kiss my forehead, as was its usual practice at the hour of sunset.

Like most well-behaved imprints, my father's ghost had hitherto visited me only when I was alone. Only recently had it begun to intrude upon me when I was busy with other affairs, and the visitation caught me by surprise. It was as well that the music can come to a crescendo, or my involuntary gasp might have attracted attention. As it was, the old Grand Duke heard me and sent me an inquiring look. With an effort, I gathered my wits and turned my back on Vasily and the unwelcome guest. "The duet is almost over, your grace," I told him. "Go down and wait in the wings on the right; Kschessinska will meet you when she comes off."

Eager and excited, the old reprobate buzzed off; and I nearly laughed up my sleeve at how easy it had been, after all, to deceive him. My sense of triumph was, alas! short-lived. The transmitter crackled, and Schmidt cried sharply:

"That man in the gantry—he's got a rifle!"

"I beg your pardon?" said Nijam, and then, "Oh, so he does."

For a moment our cool-headed leader seemed at a loss; and it was Mimi, ever practical, who supplied the necessary prompt. "The question is, where's he pointing that rifle? At us?"

"He's facing into the audience," Schmidt hissed. "It's an assassination!"

I could say nothing to help them—not in the box, with four vampires listening in. I should be lucky, I thought, if they did not hear the thundering of my heart. Then Vasily's hand fell on my shoulder, startling me. "Stay here and leave this to me," he murmured. The next instant he had withdrawn from the box. Nikolasha and the others sent me inquiring looks, to which I replied only with a smile which I hoped did not betray my inner worries. *One* of us must certainly remain in the box to allay the suspicions of the others. Yet I did not like to be parted from Vasily, either for his sake or for mine.

The moment the door closed behind him, Vasily began

to speak. "Someone's trying to shoot Nicky, which will undoubtedly put a stop to our plans. Can you get up there, Schmidt, and deal with the assassin quietly?"

"Absolutely not," Nijam snapped. "I won't have Schmidt getting shot interfering in imperial business—*Schmidt!* I said *no!*"

Evidently Schmidt had ideas of his own. "I can do it," he said.

"Good man," Vasily said breathlessly. I could imagine him hurrying through the lavish halls of the Bolshoi, pale and perspiring, for he was in no condition to exert himself. "My father's on his way, so the die is cast, and if we don't pull this off tonight we never will. Get into position, Mimi. As for you, Miss Dark, stay where you are and keep an eye on the audience."

Clasping my hands together, I leaned over the parapet of the box in an agony of anticipation. On the stage, Kschessin-ska was spinning on one toe, faster and faster, one *fouette* after another without a moment's hesitation between them. Above, the painted backdrop disappeared behind the swagged curtains of the proscenium. Schmidt, and his shadowy target, were hidden from my eyes; but through the transmitter I could hear Schmidt's quick breathing, and presently grunts and blows. My fingers fastened white about each other.

Through the transmitter, beneath the swelling crescendo of the music, I heard a loud metallic clatter.

"For heaven's sake," Nijam hissed, "don't make so much noise, Schmidt!" And then a moment later, "Watch that rifle— don't let it fall. No," (with resignation) "there it goes."

But if the rifle had really fallen all the way from the gantry to the stage itself, I heard nothing of it, for the crescendo reached a climax and then faded away again.

"We're in position," Mimi reported, "and so is the Grand Duke."

"Good," Vasily panted. "I take it the rifle is out of play, Schmidt?"

"Yes, but—ow! *Would* you?" Schmidt broke off in the middle of whatever he had been about to say, and I understood that his battle was far from being over.

"Keep your eyes peeled, Dark," Nijam put in urgently, "and warn us if anyone in the audience seems to be suspicious."

Dissatisfied though I was at my own enforced inactivity, I did as she asked and cast a glance over the theatre. The attention of the audience, with one exception, seemed absolutely fixed upon Kschessinska. In a box somewhat nearer the stage than our own was an entire party of werewolves, congregated about a good-looking young man in a regimental uniform decorated with so much gold braid and so many medals that one could scarcely see the colour of the tunic to which they were affixed. Some four or five of these creatures now arose from their seats and went slinking out of their box, leaving their merely human friend behind with one or two beastly companions. I had noticed several of these mere mortals scattered about in the theatre boxes, of course. Missy of Roumania was one of them, and I guessed at once that the young man in the gold braid was another of those who had lost his fangs at Coburg as a result of Vasily's meddling.

And now a whole party of them was slinking away! In a flash of intuition I recalled the words I had heard only yesterday at the races—*we have bigger game afoot than a Russian renegade*—and my heart leaped into my throat. Surely it must be the werewolves behind this assassination attempt.

I would bet anything that the gun was supposed to go off during that last crescendo, and since it evidently had not, the Germans were off to investigate. But it seemed fantastic that German werewolves would attempt to assassinate the Russian Emperor at his own coronation gala! For a moment I agonised over what to do. I must of course warn Nijam in case the werewolves *did* go down to see what had become of the assassin; but I could not do so from the box. Vasily had warned me that vampirism bestowed super-sensitive hearing, and at this crucial moment I could not afford being overheard. Accordingly, I rose from my seat and slipped out of the box into the great, curving gallery beyond.

This was illuminated with chandeliers, while great red curtains swathed the exterior windows. I could not yet see the werewolves which shared this curved corridor with me; but I heard them growling together at no great distance, and now and again letting out a gruff *woof* of protest. Hasty paws scrabbled towards me across the shining inlaid parquetry of the floor, and I had barely time to conceal myself behind one of the great curtains before one of them flashed past me at a frantic run. It was followed at a walk by the four others, and at first I supposed that all of them were going down towards the backstage. But then, to my horror, the four of them came to a halt precisely before my hiding-place.

I would have seized upon my injector, but to move would have given me away. Instead I laid my head back against the window-panes and commended my soul to God.

"The game's up," one of the werewolves whimpered in German. "I'm telling you, you should call it off while you can!"

"Don't be a poltroon, Arthur!" another of them growled.

265

"Coburg was all very well for *you!* You people don't care if you're ruled by women or geldings or goodness knows what. Imperial Germany is a different matter! We Hohenzollerns have our self-respect to keep up!"

"I'm not a poltroon!" Arthur protested. "Just imagine the result if we're found out! You will be hanged. The Kaiser will have the war he's always wanted. And I shall face the most frightful scandal!"

The other werewolves snapped and cursed at him for being a coward, and Arthur, whoever he was, lapsed into a muttering silence. I listened to them with the liveliest alarm: whatever was afoot, it clearly had its roots in what Vasily had done at Coburg. How ironic, if after everything I feared, our undoing turned out to be the result of the one thing Vasily had done undeniably *right!*

In another moment the fifth werewolf came loping back, panting from his exertion. "Our man has been waylaid," he gasped, "and he's up in the gantry fighting for his life."

"The devil!" said another of the wolves. "Is it the gendarmes? No? Then why didn't you step in, man? If he's caught he'll be interrogated, and then all the world will know I tried to have my own brother shot at the ballet!"

His own brother! But then—if these were Hohenzollern princes—why, all became horribly clear. I was absolutely speechless. This werewolf must be one of Kaiser Wilhelm's own sons; and his elder brother, who had been deprived of his fangs at Coburg, was about to be murdered in cold blood because Imperial Germany could not be ruled by a *gelding.* I supposed that it made a certain kind of sense—well I could imagine that a werewolf prince might resent his brother for succeeding to the crown without the fangs to justify it—and yet the brazenness of the thing shocked me.

"There's still half an hour of music left," said one of the other werewolves. "There ought to be a second crescendo during the Apotheosis of Neptune and Amphitrite. We can make the shot then."

"In any case we can't let our man be captured and questioned," said the treacherous young prince. "The devil! I suppose we had better go down and deal with that busybody ourselves."

What had we stumbled into? I felt that I was going to be sick, or faint, or fall down dead upon the spot. Here we were merely trying to see justice done for a poor dead ballerina, and we had stumbled upon the most horrible conspiracy. Now five desperate monsters were about to go down to *deal with* my friends, and I did not for a moment doubt that they would murder the lot of us if it struck them as being necessary.

There was only one thing to do, and I dared not waste any time in thinking about it. Even looking back upon that moment from the vantage point of many years, I find myself quite astonished by my own next actions, which were surely worthy of Bess the innkeeper's daughter from Mr Noyes' poem. With the same motion, I swept aside the curtain, stepped into the corridor, and switched on my transmitter.

"Werewolves!" I cried. "Fly at once: you are discovered, and if you are caught there will be the dickens to pay!"

The werewolves turned upon me. In my ear, Mimi breathed, "Werewolves!" and Nijam said grimly, "How many of them?"

I did not answer: I switched off my transmitter, for I did not want them to know that in warning them, I had doomed myself.

\* \* \*

Downstairs, Nijam was far from being alarmed by the news I had imparted. She was primarily worried for Schmidt. The gantry shook and rattled softly now and then as Schmidt and his opponent strove for the upper hand; and let there be never so many werewolves on their way, she did not intend to flee without him. Moreover, the job itself was all but finished: Vasily's father was waiting in the wings, and with Mimi and Valery concealed in the dark passage that ran behind the backdrop, now was scarcely the time to flee.

It was at this juncture that Vasily found her. "Miss Nijam," he gasped, "surely we need not flee at once—my father must pay for his crimes—surely there's time—"

"All the time in the world," Nijam said serenely, picking up a large and heavy pack, and settling it upon her shoulders. It was square and heavy, and there was something affixed to the top that appeared like nothing so much as an immense gramophone-horn.

Vasily stared at it. "What on earth?"

"It's the prototype of something I've been working on," Nijam said, brandishing a little gadget with a dial and several large red buttons, which was connected to the pack by a snarl of wires. "The werewolves can come if they like; I shall be ready for them. You must take over for me; I only need you to climb up *there* and cut *that* line when Mimi gives you the signal. Schmidt!" she added, switching on her transmitter, "can you hold out a little longer up there?"

There came only a strangled sort of sound in reply. Nijam and Vasily, looking attentively into the gloom above them, made out a pair of prostrate figures on the gantry, one of whom appeared to be throttling the other; but abruptly a hand shot out and gave what Nijam took to be a thumbs-up signal.

"Schmidt will be all right," Vasily said with the utmost confidence, "but are you sure that you want to face the werewolves alone?"

"Oh, but I shan't be alone," Nijam said, patting her pack; and off she went, eager to test her latest invention.

* * *

Upstairs in the corridor, meanwhile, I had been obliged to put my back against the wall, for I was surrounded by a ring of horrid red mouths and gleaming bared teeth.

"Who are you?" the werewolves demanded. "What did you hear? What did you mean, fly at once?"

"Quickly, tear out her throat! There's no time to waste!" snarled one.

"Don't!" said Arthur quickly. "I don't want to try hiding bodies at the Bolshoi, and besides, look at her! What if she's *somebody*?"

"I am Marie-Angelique, Countess Dubois de la Motte," I said shakily, since they had interpreted my warning as being meant for them, "and I'm only trying to help."

"Help! What do you mean, help?" demanded the treacherous prince, thrusting his reeking maw close to my face, so that all I could see were his blazing yellow eyes, and all I could smell was his breath, rank with the scent of blood.

"I mean I quite understand what you are doing," I said, for if nothing else I meant to spin out my death as long as possible, so that the rest of the crew might escape. "Believe me, I am

269

French; I know that it is a humiliation to be ruled by geldings! You might as well become a Republic, as we have done!"

"If you're French, what do you care about Germany?" another of them yelped, and then a third said, "For heaven's sake, we can't stand about *talking* all night! We have to shoot Willy!"

"Here," said Arthur, "let me stand watch over the lady while the rest of you go downstairs to take care of business."

"They'll catch you," I said, with a regretful shake of my head.

"They'll catch us anyway if we don't get our man back," said the treacherous prince, and he loped off down the corridor with the others at his heels, leaving me alone with Arthur.

"Come along," he told me gruffly, "you might as well join me in the box, but I warn you not to speak out of turn, or it will be dashed awkward for all of us."

So saying, he ushered me into the box with the German Crown Prince—Willy, as the conspirators had called him—and made me sit down beside him, in the shadows at the back. I sank into the chair all a-tremble with fear. I had been quite sure of my death, and indeed I was yet far from certain that my sentence had not merely been delayed. Any one of these creatures could snuff me out with a single bite. And then, there was poor Schmidt, and Vasily, and the others! I prayed very devoutly that they had done as I warned, and flown while there was time!

The whole affair in the corridor must only have taken a very few minutes, for Kschessinska had only just completed her *pas de deux,* and now preened around the stage, eating up the applause. The Empress must have been the only person in the house not joining in these acclamations. They went on a good long time; and then Kschessinska went off stage left, and I switched on my transmitter to hear Vasily say, "Mimi, my dear, that's your cue."

Ballerinas flooded onto the stage for the grand ensemble dance, but I scarcely saw them; all my attention was upon my transmitter. There was no sound from Nijam, no sign of the werewolves; but I heard Mimi say in a somewhat disguised voice, "Ah! it is you! Come with me, your grace."

We had practiced the scene, and I could imagine how it would unfold: the Grand Duke waiting in the wings for his cue; Mimi, all done up in Kschessinska's wig and negligée and scented with her perfume, brushing past the old *roué* in the dark. She would give him only a glimpse of her back and a whiff of her scent as she whisked into the darkness behind the backdrop, and the Grand Duke would follow the flutter of her silk negligée, and the beckoning of her hand—

I held my breath, paralysed by suspense. For a moment I saw nothing, heard nothing, but the music and the lights, and the dancers darting about the stage like so many colourful dragonflies. Then, lofting high above the strains of music, and shattering the spell woven by the dancers, there came a shout of "Help! Help!"

In the same moment the backdrop trembled—rippled—and began to fall. Dancers scattered. All over the theatre, people started up from their chairs, crying out in fear of anarchists. In great billowing folds the backdrop, painted to resemble the ocean, settled upon the stage, half-drowning the dancers: and there, revealed to all of Russia, stood Grand Duke Nicholas, covered in blood, with Anna's Valery struggling in his embrace!

The Grand Duke lifted his bloodied mouth from Valery's neck and stood utterly astonished, gazing out into the

271

crowded theatre. The orchestra stuttered to a halt. Someone screamed. The Empress put a hand over the Emperor's eyes. After an endless moment, Valery uttered a loud curse and pushed the bewildered Grand Duke away from him. In the same moment Vasily appeared from the wings, dragging a policeman—no doubt one of the guards that had been stationed about the theatre for the safety of the Emperor and his eminent guests.

"There he is!" Vasily cried, with a dramatic gesture. "Arrest that reprobate! My God—" recoiling— "it's my own father!"

The whole theatre was in an uproar. The very people who turned a blind eye when a Grand Duke assaulted a ballerina were now fainting, shaking fists, or crying "Shame!" when the victim was a man; and I could not help but conclude that whatever the source of their disgust, it could hardly be a genuine regard for virtue.

Sergei Alexandrovich leaped from his chair and left his box, gesticulating wildly and calling for the police. This, it seems, awoke Grand Duke Nicholas to a sense of his danger. In a trice he dashed across the stage, seeking to evade Vasily and the policeman.

A tiny figure, improbably arrayed in a towering blonde wig, a bright silk negligée, and a truly dazzling quantity of imitation diamonds, stepped out of the wings and stopped the fleeing malefactor dead at the business end of a formidable-looking carbine.

I perceived that Mimi had found the assassin's rifle.

The gendarmes descended upon the Grand Duke, who nevertheless tried to evade them. "You can't do this to me!" he protested. "It was an honest mistake, I tell you! It was dark! I didn't know he was a man—I thought I was biting a *woman!*" A titter ran about the theatre. "Sergei Alexandrovich! Please!" he added, as the gaunt figure of the Emperor's cousin appeared on the stage. "Don't you know that I only bite women?"

"I think, for the moment, that you had better hold your tongue," said Sergei Alexandrovich, and the gendarmes hurried the old beast away.

In my ear, the transmitter crackled to life. "It's done," Vasily said with weary triumph. "Time for us to disappear, I think. Nijam? Schmidt?"

There was no answer from either. Instead, I felt the most unpleasant sensation creeping over me, as though my head had been suddenly caught in an abominable vice. Beside me in the box, the werewolf Arthur gave a little sigh, turned up his eyes and slipped to the floor. The two beside the Crown Prince started from their chairs with whines of pain and grovelled upon the carpet, scrabbling at their heads with frantic paws. I found myself staring, aghast, at the dark patches of blood that daubed their fur—in fact, they were bleeding from the ears!

Nor were they the only ones in trouble. All over the theatre, I saw vampires, sirens, ogres, lindworms, and others reeling and fainting and shrieking in agonies. I myself felt sick, with a ringing head. For a moment I had not the faintest notion of what was happening; the theatre was again in an uproar, and terror mounted every moment.

Then a flash of intuition struck me, and I switched my transmitter open. "Nijam!" I gasped. "Too much! Too much! You'll kill us all! Whatever you're doing, you need to stop it!"

"What," Nijam responded quite calmly, "can *you* can feel it, too?"

*"Nijam!"* I shrieked in reply.

I heard only a put-upon sigh, but then the awful sensation abated. I staggered to my feet. The German Crown Prince, who at present was the only other occupant of the box to remain on his feet, turned upon me with a face like a mask of terror. "Who the devil," he demanded, "are *you?*"

"The Countess Marie-Angelique du—never mind. I'm going to fetch a doctor," I gasped, for it was the best excuse I could think of, and there would be no better moment for me to make my exit. With that in mind, I fled the box.

"I'm on the stairs, on my way out," I announced through the transmitter as the theatre doors came within view. "Where is everyone else? Schmidt?"

"I'm coming," Schmidt panted. "The assassin was an *Akbar* man. We'd been trained in all the same tricks. But he's bleeding from the ears now."

"Thank goodness for that," I said. "I'll meet you all at the carriage."

Then there came a scrabble of claws on the stair behind me and I whirled about to behold—Arthur, my erstwhile captor, who had evidently regained consciousness only moments after I quit the box.

"You," he snarled. "You're no countess!"

And he pounced upon me.

I made no attempt to dodge him; but I *did* have time to snatch the little injector-gun from my stocking. I pointed it in his direction, only meaning to warn him, but he never gave me the opportunity to speak. His body collided with mine, and I must have pulled the trigger nearly by accident. The next moment I was sprawled across the floor, and—well. Not to put too fine a point on it, there was a man, no longer a wolf, attempting to gnaw upon my shoulder. A man in a certain state of undress, for the shaggy grey pelt which had a moment before clothed him had suddenly disappeared; Nijam's little pistol had defanged him in an instant.

"*Sir!*" I exclaimed, attempting to extricate myself from this highly compromising position, and to put a hand over my eyes, "Is this proper?"

"The deuce!" he exclaimed, and the next moment disengaged from me and attempted to wrap himself up in his own limbs. He went quite pink, all over. "Why, you hussy! What have you done to me?"

You may ask why it was that, having been defanged in the very moment at which he was attempting to murder me, he now reproached me for the manner in which I chose to defend myself. I cannot explain it: some habits are engrained too deep. You might as well also ask why it was that my first instinct was to put up my hands to shield my eyes, and to stammer apologies.

"I *do* beg your pardon! I really had *no* notion what would happen—I say!" I broke off, as I caught a glimpse of the gentleman's head, which was as bald as an egg, and familiar to me from the London papers. "You're the Duke of Connaught!"

He paled. "You are mistaken!"

"You *are!*" I cried, absolutely scandalised. "A *British* prince, and a werewolf! *What would your mother say?*"

"I must insist—"

But his words were doomed to remain unspoken. At that moment the rest of the crew converged upon the staircase. Mimi brandished her rifle at the unfortunate Prince Arthur, and Vasily seized my hand and hurried me towards the door.

"I cannot believe it!" I cried in the not-quite-darkness as

we hurried into our carriage. "That a British prince would stoop so low!"

Vasily pulled the carriage door shut and fell back upon the bench-seat as Schmidt whipped up the horses and we dashed away into the night.

"My dear," he panted, "there are one or two little facts you really ought to know."

# 21

# Chapter XXI.

"What!" I cried, *"all* of them?"

"Yes, every last one."

"But not the Queen herself, surely?"

"My dear, the Queen especially! How else is she to command a family of werewolves? Ask anyone!"

"I cannot believe it!" I cried. "Not the Queen! Not when we English have always prided ourselves on our lack of monstrosity!"

"I assure you that a friend of mine witnessed the transformation with her own eyes."

Had I not witnessed Prince Arthur's transformation myself, I should never have believed it. "And the injector—there was some morganatic blood in there? and it turned him human again?"

"Completely defanged, my dear!"

I pressed a hand to my forehead. "Oh, don't say it! I shall never be able to set foot upon British soil again!"

We had returned to our lodgings in a mood of triumph and some hilarity, but now I began to feel rather shaken. Although our mission was successfully accomplished, I had lifted my hand against a member of the Royal Family, and I knew very well how dangerous *that* might prove to be. Moreover, I had given myself up for dead and on two separate occasions had come within an ace of being bitten by an angry werewolf. I collapsed into an armchair, just about ready to burst into tears.

"Is everyone well?" I asked shakily.

"Never felt better," Vasily assured me, and indeed, having regained his breath he looked remarkably well for a man who had very recently been well-nigh drained by a pair of vengeful vampires.

"Well, of course," Mimi said with a snort. She had relieved herself of her negligée, wig, and rifle, although she was still glittering with jewels. "He's vampire-bitten, now, like me. How does it feel to have some of your old strength back, Vasya?"

"The devil!" said Vasily, in astonishment. "So I *am* feeling stronger. Good God! What an indignity, to regain my strength in *this* way!"

"Schmidt?" I asked feebly. "And Valery?"

Both these looked somewhat the worse for wear, for Schmidt was limping a little and there was a swelling over his cheekbone, and Valery of course was covered in blood.

"Don't worry about me," said Valery, dabbing with a handkerchief at the gashes in his throat. "It's not all real; Mimi doused me with some of the prop blood left over from *Boris Godunov.* As for the rest of it, if I don't have to go into hiding, I suppose I'll become a star."

I do not suppose that there are many men who would willingly accept the stigma of being a male dainty, despite the greater strength and grace it bestowed. "You are a brave man, Valery Petrovich, and very gallant."

"Anna suffered more than I did," he said, "and I knew from the start what I was getting into." With that he took his leave, saying that he ought to be lying low and watching his step for a day or two.

"What about Schmidt?" Nijam put in. "It's he that had the longest battle."

"Don't worry about me: I got the better of the fellow in the end," Schmidt said, reddening slightly. "Who was the assassin trying to shoot, anyway?"

"I do believe it was the German Crown Prince," said I.

"It would be just like the Hohenzollerns, wouldn't it, to murder the heir to the throne because he has no fangs!" said Vasily. "What a shame we have no evidence! It would not be a bad way of getting into the graces of the next German Emperor."

I felt a little stung by this. Could Vasily think of nothing else but how to curry favour with his superiors? "Well, I can swear to it, if you like. I overheard them talking about *shooting Willy.*"

"You overheard them?" Vasily looked aghast. "My dear— think of the danger, had they heard you warning us over the transmitter!! Their hearing is far more sensitive than ours, you know."

I felt that I might be about to go into hysterics. "What about you, Nijam?" I asked, to fend off the evil day. "What on God's green earth did you do to us all, back there?"

"Ah!" said Nijam, with every evidence of satisfaction. "I tested an invention of mine, and it worked."

"A great deal too well, if you ask me!" said I. "What *is* it?"

Fondly, Nijam stroked the enormous gramophone-horn that protruded from her knapsack. "Well, I have been trying to think of some unobtrusive way to combat the monsters. Salt-water and flash-bangs are all very well, of course, but they aren't always effective, and they do rather draw attention to themselves. This, on the other hand, emits a very high-pitched frequency, audible only to the monsters and quite discouraging to them—"

"Discouraging!" I repeated. "My dear Nijam, it had every royalty in the Bolshoi Theatre in convulsions! I saw more than one of them bleeding from the ears!"

"Did it, indeed!" she said happily. "Well, I can do something about that—I can make the tone directional, so as to limit its effects. I say, can you make a detailed note of your observations for me? They might be extremely helpful!"

"I'll try," said I. This change of subject had done me good: I no longer felt in imminent danger of breaking down. Or so I thought: but then a loud report made me leap almost out of my skin. It was Vasily, ejecting the cork from a bottle of Champagne. "Good heavens!" I exclaimed. "Champagne? at *this* hour?"

"Why not?" he asked, pouring it out into the motley collection of tea-cups and tumblers which were all the receptacles available to us. "We have avenged Mimi's Anna, and have thoroughly disgraced that old sinner, my father."

Mimi scowled. "What is there to celebrate in that? Anna is still dead, and what will happen to her murderer? He will be packed off to some Crimean palace, to live in the lap of luxury safely out of the public view. It was worth doing, but I ought to have shot him when I had the chance."

A silence fell upon the company as we all considered this.

I thought of the Anna I had known—ambitious, shameless, desperate for a better life—and dead long before she could mend either her plight or her ways. Sighing, I raised a teacup.

"To Anna," I said, "who deserved better, but who would not have wanted us to waste good Champagne."

Mimi wiped her eyes and smiled. "To Anna," she agreed.

"And now," said Vasily, when the toast had been drunk, "the painting!"

"The painting!" I said faintly. Surely he could not be serious!

"Indeed," Vasily said with the utmost self-assurance. "Tomorrow night is the French Embassy ball; the perfect moment to smuggle ourselves into the Montebellos' place and get our hands on *The Musketeer!*"

He was, indeed, in earnest; but to me it was the final straw to break the sheep's back. "Really, Vasily! How can we possibly steal a painting? Here's Schmidt wanted by the police, and you treading a knife's edge with your family, and to cap it all, Nijam has attacked the entire theatre with a sonic weapon and I, entirely without meaning to do so, have *defanged a British prince!*"

"And *I* bombed the house of the Crown Princess of Roumania," Mimi put in. "Don't forget that."

"Precisely!" I cried. "Anna's job is done, thank goodness, and now we ought to be catching the next train out of Moscow—out of Russia—while we still can!"

"My dear, how impatient you are! We've survived thus far; what harm can one more day do?"

"What harm!" I raised my hands to the heavens, bereft of words.

"Dark is right," said Nijam, before I could say more, or dissolve into tears. "We've done what we came to do, and now that we have defanged a royalty, we really ought to be making good our escape."

"Surely it won't require all five of us to steal the painting," Schmidt put in. He had deposited himself upon the sofa, where he sat looking bloodied and beaten, like the Archangel Michael after a particularly exhausting bout of war in heaven. "If you ladies wish to depart; sir and I will join you in Vienna when we have secured the painting."

"That is *absolutely* out of the question!" Nijam squeaked. Then she cleared her throat and added, in her customary low register: "Don't be a fool, Schmidt. The Okhrana would like nothing better than to keep you in Russia for good; and then if they interrogate either of you, you will almost certainly implicate *us* in the defanging of the Duke of Connaught. No: there's only one thing for it, and that is for all of us to leave at once."

"I beg your pardon," Schmidt said humbly. "I did not think I would be putting *you* in danger, Miss Nijam. But of course you are correct."

*"Et tu, Schmidt?"* Vasily murmured. "Hear me out, at any rate. I'm well aware that the police are watching us; and indeed that is why I think we ought to stay. None of you are native to this country; so believe me when I say that if any of us goes down to the train station in the morning to buy tickets, we will all be in a Butyrka prison cell by lunchtime. It's as I told Miss Dark: the Emperor hasn't given me leave to go, and until he does, none of us will be able to move a mile."

Butyrka—I let out a gasp, recognising the name of the brutal and overcrowded prison which for centuries had served as the tsars' Moscow dungeon.

Even Nijam paled. "How long has this been the case?"

"It was a foregone conclusion from the moment my return became known." Vasily ran a distracted hand through his hair. "Don't be afraid: Nicky is a good man—kind, and loyal. He won't punish us, even if I confess to him that I don't mean to find a cure, after all. At the very least, he'll give us safe-conduct out of the country."

Trapped! We were trapped in this bedlam of a country—had been from the moment we met Zlata upon the train-platform. Vasily had mentioned something of the sort before—and *still* he was enmeshed within his mad dreams!

*"At the very least!"* I repeated in a voice that was small, and vehement, and shaking with despair. *"At the very least* he will give us a safe-conduct—what is that supposed to mean? Do you still think he will give you back all your privileges? Do you still wish to sell your soul to him?"

Vasily had the nerve to look injured. "My dear Miss Dark, I've explained to you that I only wish—"

"You wish too much," I said raggedly. I was shaking with the shock of the words I heard coming from my own mouth. "Ever since we arrived in Russia, at every turn, you've put all of us in danger for your own personal gain—revealing yourself to Zlata, letting her show you off to your family— and now the painting? I can't *live* like this, Vasily! Tonight I offered myself up to the werewolves, just to warn you—I mean to warn *everyone!* And what do I get in return? You are willing to put all of us into greater danger still—and why? Is it the money you cannot live without, or the title, or the f-fangs?"

And with that final word I dissolved entirely into tears.

"Miss Dark, Miss Dark," Vasily cried. "What do you mean— I cannot live without fangs?"

"I meant what I said!" I gasped. "I know you were seeking a cure! I know that was what you meant to trade for your lost privileges!"

Vasily went absolutely white. "My dear, I must *seem* to be seeking a cure, because my life and yours very literally depend upon it."

"Why didn't you tell us?" Mimi asked bluntly. "If you've told the Emperor that you will give him a cure, and if you've been pretending to seek one, then why keep it from us, except for a bad conscience?"

Vasily looked from Mimi to me, and then to Nijam, and finally to Schmidt. Nijam's Alphonse cleared his throat as though he meant to speak, but then he did not.

The silence was excruciating. At last Vasily said, "I *told* you I had been dreaming, but all that is over now! For God's sake, you others, give us the room awhile. I must speak to Miss Dark alone."

"Absolutely not," said Nijam, folding her arms. "She's right, you know. You owe us an explanation."

Mimi snorted. "An explanation! By no means allow Vasya to give an explanation; they're what he does best."

I couldn't bear speaking to Vasily with this Greek chorus in the background. "Oh, by all means, go. Give me a moment to speak to him alone."

They went severally to their rooms—Nijam with a darkling glare, Mimi in scornful triumph, and Schmidt looking excessively guilty. Vasily, who had been standing at my side looking quite distressed, now reached for my hand.

"Mary, my dear—"

I snatched my hand away. "I'm not your dear, and you may address me as *Miss Dark!*"

"Miss Dark," he said, in the same earnest tones, "I had no notion—that is, I take it that you have once again risked your neck to save mine. What ought I to say? Should I scold you for making such a sad bargain?"

Despite everything, he was laughing at me! I had been willing to die for him, little as he deserved it: and he was laughing at me! "Oh, I wish you would be serious for once!"

"Then I really *will* scold you for making a sad bargain," he warned, now laughing openly. "No, no: have your revenge and tell me what I owe you. Spare no detail, but let the knowledge of your goodness crush me to oblivion."

It would serve him right if I told him nothing at all. "It was nothing," I muttered, "only of course the monsters overheard me warning you, and I had to persuade them not to eat me! Had it not been for Nijam's invention, I should never have escaped them. Nor would Schmidt, for they were determined to murder him."

"Miss Dark, Miss Dark," he said ruefully, "why must you do these things? I'm not worth it, you know."

"I didn't do it for *you!*"

"No, of course not; you did it for Schmidt." He reached out as though he meant to touch my cheek; but I drew back and he desisted. "My dear," he said, "isn't there anything you wish to tell me? You've been a better friend to me than I deserve, and there have been times when I wonder…"

I found myself blushing violently. He meant that he thought I was in love with him, of course, but how could he expect me to answer a question like that? If Vasily returned my feelings he would surely have said so. It was his place, after all, to declare himself.

I had devoted some thought to Missy's declaration that

Vasily had fallen in love with me. I did not know about that. Vasily was someone who desperately wanted to feel that he was loved; but whether it was possible for him to feel a pure and unselfish affection for another mortal being, I did not know. Perhaps he had loved Ioanna, and perhaps also that mysterious other woman of whom he had spoken from time to time with such wistful fondness. Still, although he might at times come to me for comfort, surely he was not in love with *me:* there was too much of self-interest in our association for that.

It was one of those moments when a good offence is the best defence. "You can't be serious! How can you and I be friends unless we can trust each other?"

He did not quite flinch at that; but he looked away from me and blinked once or twice.

"Little mouse, you can't really believe that I want my fangs back—not after everything they have done to me, and to you. How can I live among these people, when I hate them nearly as much as they hate each other? But I must get them off my trail."

I found my handkerchief, and wiped my eyes. "If you want them off your trail, why can't you do as Nijam suggested, and stage your death? You might go on then, and live a new life in perfect freedom."

He gave an uneasy laugh. "Ah, but there are other considerations, of course. You of all people know how important money is to a happy life."

"What is *that* supposed to mean?"

"I can remember a time not so very long ago that you were willing to make a very great sacrifice in order to marry money."

I lost my breath entirely for a moment. It was low of him, to reproach me with my foolish pursuit of Warren Vandergriff! "Surely I cannot be hearing this," I cried. "I suppose you mean to marry Zlata, after all, for her fortune! I thank heaven that *I* have no money, or I suppose you would marry me tomorrow!"

At first Vasily looked astonished, and then he gave a rather ugly laugh. "I thank heaven you have no money, or I suppose you would fear me so much that I should lose the right even to pass the time of day with you!"

And he had the nerve to say this, after having proposed marriage to me under false pretences, back in the Schloss Frohsdorf, purely in order to regain his royal privileges—after having told me again and again that he had betrayed every woman who ever trusted him!

"Have you *ever* been made to face the consequences of your own actions?" I demanded.

*"Yes,"* he responded at once, "every day I face the consequences of my actions, and I wish that the last woman to ask me that question was here to witness it!" He walked to the balcony and stood there a moment with his hands thrust into his pockets, staring down into the road. Presently he turned to face me, and something died within me at the sight of his face.

"If we cannot trust each other," he began.

"Wait," I said breathlessly. I knew what he meant to say next: if we could not trust each other then we could not go on together as we had done. We must part ways. Then perhaps he *would* marry Zlata, because even though he loathed her, she offered him everything he wanted.

And that was the one thing I could not bear.

"You truly believe," I said, "that we shall have trouble getting away from Moscow without the Emperor's permission?"

The look he sent me then was weary and utterly without any laughter at all. "Little mouse, don't force me to stake your life upon it."

I bit my lip, because what else could I do? "I *do* trust you, Vasily; only you make it so difficult sometimes. Forget everything I said. You must go to see the Emperor; and if you can manage it before the ball tomorrow then of course we can take the painting when we go."

He swooped down upon me then, and pressed my hands to his lips. "Do not fear. I will see you and the others safely out of this country, I swear it."

With that, we called the others into the room. Nijam was doubtful of the proposed solution, but even she could see that having stuck out our necks so far, there was nothing to do but trust in Vasily to bring us safely through. At last, with a heavy heart, I sought my rest. I did not sleep for many hours that night, brooding over the heavy truth that I had yielded to Vasily, only because I could not bear to let him leave me.

I had reproached him for wanting fangs, but I did not think he truly wanted them, any more than he truly wanted to marry Zlata, or to return forever to the bosom of his ghastly family. No, Vasily wanted smaller things: a painting, a chance to rebuild his fortune, the Okhrana off his trail. They were desires I could sympathise with; but only his family could grant them. Of course they had set a trap for him, baited with all manner of good things; of course he had been tempted, however briefly, to take the bait—to trade his newfound and scarcely-yet-tested principles for money, and safety, and a title, and Lord knows what else! Now he thought that it was possible to escape the trap while only taking a crumb of bait;

and I thought he was mad to imagine it.

Truly did our Lord call the love of money the root of every sort of evil! I felt that it had inexorably poisoned my whole life. It was the love of money which had taken away my father, and had driven a wedge between me and my mother and sisters; it was the love of money which had nearly shackled me for life to the horrible Mr Vandergriff, and now that same pernicious desire was going to be Vasily's undoing, who was dearer to me than life itself.

For many hours these gloomy reflections deprived me of sleep, so that it was mid-morning when I awoke the following day. A desire for the strongest, the blackest of tea drove me from my bed into the sitting-room, where I found a yawning Nijam just pouring smoke-scented elixir from the samovar. Vasily was nowhere to be seen. The morning was warm, and only promised to get hotter, for the sky was a bright hard blue.

I turned to accept a cup of tea from Nijam, but just as I raised the cup to my lips, a horrible sensation came over me. I felt as though I had been shot through with arrows made of ice. I knew without a doubt that I was being watched; I turned to face the window and screamed.

With a spatter of steaming droplets, my teacup shattered upon the floor-boards. Nijam recoiled with an unintelligible cry of alarm, and Vasily burst through his door in a half-tied cravat.

"Dark! For heaven's sake, what's the matter?" Nijam demanded, rushing to mop up the tea before it could sink into the rug.

I could only gesture speechlessly towards the window. The shape peering in through the glass struck horror into my bones, for it was the pale and bloodied image of a young woman. She had died from being crushed, for her body was all blue-black and misshapen, and half her face seemed actually to have caved in, so that one eyeball—but no. You do not wish to hear, and I do not wish to remember. What I do remember, with horrible clarity, is the sensation that washed through me at the sight of her: I could not breathe. I was helpless in a bruising sea of hot and stifling humanity. I was crushed in an awful vice.

At my scream, she had actually flinched; and now she drifted away from the window, hovering uncertainly over the street, as though unsure where to go. Her shadow ought to have lifted from me, but it did not. I still felt that I was suffocated, that I was drowning, that everywhere was blackness and heat and terror... She was a shade, and very recently dead. An imprint would not have responded to my terror. My heart laboured, and so did my breathing, light and shallow. That vice was still about my body.

Something was happening, I realised; something dreadful. The thought impelled me to motion, and I hurried to the balcony. A silent crowd had gathered in the street to watch a sort of procession go by. For a moment I wondered whether the Revolution had in fact occurred while I slept, for there were carts rolling by, and a great many unmoving people within them, like French nobles going to the guillotine. Then a thought struck me, so horrible that at that moment I could not have put it into words, even in my own mind.

I tore open the attic door and hurried down the many flights of stairs, only dimly aware of Vasily following me. The house was quiet; too quiet. Its door stood open onto the street, and beyond this I saw people standing stiff and silent like the watchers at a funeral. I ran out among them, pushed through them—with that suffocating vice about me, every touch was intolerable—and at last got out into the street.

The carts rumbled along the broad thoroughfare towards the centre of the city. One might have been pardoned for thinking that their human cargo was alive, all decked out in festive attire as they were; but no—dead, all of them were dead; mangled, quivering and crusted with their own blood. The street around the carts was thronged with their shades, many of them clad in bright embroidered blouses, the men in flat caps and the women with flowers in their hair. Unlike the living crowd, this one flowed past without touching me. Still I could feel everything they had felt in those awful final moments; agony and despair and wrath. A man walked past me carrying a child in his arms and I let out a gasp at the bitterness of his remorse, that he had brought his beloved child to perish so pointlessly...

Knowing that I ought not to remain among them—that I would go mad—yet I ran after the man with the child.

"What has happened?" I asked him. "Who are you?"

His haunted eyes fixed upon me in disbelief. "You *see* me? But you are one of the living!"

"Tell me what has happened," I begged, plucking at the high neck of my blouse in an attempt to get more air. "Quickly."

"I am Fyodor Ivanovich," he said, "and I came from Smolensk by train to see the Tsar at his coronation."

Other shades pressed close, reaching out their hands to touch me and crying their names.

"I am Katya—I am Sasha—I am Natalya. I came from Tver, from Omsk, from Pskov. I came to escort my grandmother; I came to visit my cousin; I came to see the Tsar at Khodynka.

The field could not hold so many of us. It is Sergei Alexandrovich who made the arrangements, but the ground was dug with pits and trenches where the regiments drill. We were trapped, and packed, and crushed."

"Stand back," I cried weakly, staggering away from them, but they pressed nearer, nearer, and I could not breathe.

"You are alive," they cried. "Please, have you seen my old father? Tell me that my daughter has escaped. Tell my husband that Olga says farewell. Tell the Tsar what Sergei Alexandrovich has done to us. Please, see to it that my father's old silver medal is sent to my brother, Dmitry Igorovich, the schoolmaster at Veshki..."

I was backing away, so blindly that it was a wonder I did not fall beneath the wheels of the passing carts and become crushed myself. Then the wild-eyed shade of a woman thrust herself at me, her broken arms flailing horribly. *"Avenge us,"* she screamed. All her rage and despair pierced through me like a knife, together with the slow horror of the death she had endured. It was too much for my overtasked senses: my head swam, and merciful oblivion followed.

# 22

# Chapter XXII.

I must rely upon Vasily for an account of what happened after. It was he who, having followed me downstairs into the street, witnessed my distracted movements and incoherent cries as the shades overwhelmed me. He said that I cried out to them in English; I cannot explain how the poor souls comprehended my words, unless there is perfect understanding on the other side of death. It was he who, standing by my side, guided me away from the oncoming carts and their grisly cargo. It was he who, when at last I fell into a faint, caught me in his arms.

Schmidt helped Vasily to carry me up into the attic and lay me upon the sofa. "What is it? What has happened?" Nijam demanded, white-lipped. She did not understand the unseen world which I inhabited, and the existence of things beyond her understanding was troubling to her.

"I don't know what has happened," Vasily said, "except that there are corpses being brought into the city on carts, and of course there must be shades everywhere. Mimi, the smelling-salts!"

But Mimi did not move: she stood as stiff and pale as a toy soldier. "They are *here,*" she whispered. "Can't you *feel* them?"

Indeed, Vasily was conscious of something oppressive in the atmosphere: although the attic was awash in sunlight, there lay thick upon the room a darkness of the spirit rather than the eyes. The moment Mimi stopped speaking it pressed in upon the silence, a hush that was made of death and despair.

"Stop this at once," Nijam said sharply. A fine perspiration had broken out upon her brow. "Just because we all feel that something dreadful has happened, it doesn't mean that we're beset by spirits. Go and fetch those smelling-salts, Mimi!"

Almost before the words were out of her mouth, she was interrupted by a shriek and turned to find that I had sat up and thrown out my hands as though to fend off some unseen presence. "No!" I cried deliriously. "For heaven's sake, take pity! I can't help you—it isn't me who did this—go to Sergei Alexandrovich."

Vasily flew to my side, seizing hold of my hands. "Miss Dark," he said, pressing them to his heart, "it's me. Look at me. Feel me. They're only shades, they can't hurt you... *Mimi,*" he shouted, when I did not cease to tremble and stare, "tell me you have some laudanum, I implore you!"

"Make up your mind! Do you want to wake her up or put her to sleep?" Mimi muttered under her breath, but she turned about and took back her smelling-salts in favour of her laudanum. This administered, I soon sank into a restless stupor; and Vasily seized his hat.

"Keep watch over her," he said. "I am going to Sergei Alexandrovich, since he is responsible for this."

Grand Duke Sergei's residence was, of course, not then within the Kremlin fortress itself; it was a palace nearby along Tverskaya Street. It was here, his first port of call, that Vasily found his gaunt cousin in the company of a group of regimental officers and a photographer.

"Vasily Nikolaevich," the Governor of Moscow welcomed him, not very warmly, "to what must I owe this great pleasure?" And he raked Vasily with a scornful glance.

Vasily knew that his clothing was barely arranged—that he had thrown on his coat without allowing Schmidt to brush it, and that his cravat was yet untied. He must appear half mad. He felt half mad, for I was drowning beneath an onslaught of shades and there was nothing he could do to relieve my sufferings. With a trembling hand he pointed his hat in the direction of the street.

"Sergei Alexandrovich, are you aware of what's happened out there?"

"Why, what has happened?" cried one of the officers, blanching. "Don't say it's another dynamite outrage—"

"Lord, no," Sergei said, with ice-cold composure. "There's been some small incident at Khodynka among the peasants who were waiting to see the Emperor. I gather that some of them fell into the drill trenches and injured themselves. It's nothing."

"A small incident!" Vasily was conscious of making a spectacle of himself; ordinarily he attempted to shrug off moments of discomfort with mockery, but this morning he was incapable of such things. "A small incident—why, there must be hundreds of corpses being carried into the city in carts, and all the town is out in mourning to watch them!"

The officers swore under their breath, and Sergei paled a little. His lips pressed together, very thin.

"This coronation is my triumph and the triumph of Imperial

Russia. I won't take it kindly, Vasily Nikolaevich, if you attempt to besmirch this joyous occasion, just to draw attention to yourself! Was last night's disgraceful performance not enough for you?"

"My God!" Vasily cried, well-nigh beside himself. "Here is the blood of hundreds crying out to the heavens—if not thousands—and you reproach *me* for blotting a joyous occasion?"

"Your grace, I know we gathered to take photographs," began one of the officers diffidently, "but owing to circumstances—you being the Governor, of course you will be needed at the Kremlin—"

"There's no reason I should disrupt my day for such a paltry thing," Sergei insisted. "I'll go to the Kremlin as planned, at ten. If anything needs to be done before then, let Count Vorontsov do it; all this is his fault anyway. Do excuse us, Vasily Nikolaevich; you see that I am busy."

Vasily swallowed the retort hovering upon his lips. He did not know a great deal about the workings of shades and imprints, but he did gather that they could be laid to rest if someone was willing to admit their fault. Sergei Alexandrovich, now chivvying his officers into lines for the photographer, was evidently unwilling to do so. Despite the gay appearance of brightly-coloured tunics, gold braid and gleaming orders, the officers' faces reflected something of the dread in Vasily's own heart. There was now only one way to relieve me of my suffering, he reflected, and that was to get me out of the city. Vasily cleared his throat.

"I wish to depart Moscow," he said. "Please, will you give me leave to do so?"

Sergei looked sour, as though he had bitten into an unripe

persimmon. "Naturally I can't give you leave to go; don't you realise that's the Emperor's decision?"

Silently Vasily cursed the inflexible mechanism of autocracy, which could not even grant a tea-merchant a divorce without the Emperor's personal leave. "Then won't you ask Nicky to see me? Today—at the first opportunity. It's a matter of life and death."

"You can't be serious," Sergei said. "The Emperor is busy, you know. There are meetings for him to attend all morning, and this afternoon he must make his appearance at Khodynka, and this evening is the French Embassy ball. Whatever you're after, surely it will keep a few days."

The ball—nonsense! thought Vasily. A disaster of this magnitude could not be hidden, even by Sergei Alexandrovich. The ball would certainly be cancelled. As for Nicky, the Tsar would soon have more pressing matters on his hands—the dead to mourn, and the injured to visit—but Vasily had his own injured to care for, and necessity was for him the mother of temerity. With a curt farewell, he left his cousin and went to the Kremlin, grimly determined to get permission to leave the city, if he must choke Nicky half to death in order to get it.

Alas! he waited and paced in the Alexandria's drawing-room, but never had the opportunity to see Nicky, except once, briefly as the young Emperor, together with his wife and sisters, went out on their way to the field at Khodynka.

"Nicky, I wish you would give me a moment or two of your time; it's a matter of life and death," Vasily insisted, as the Emperor passed him.

"Of course; speak to one of the ministers," Nicky said, and then he was gone. The minister promised to make an appointment for him two weeks away; and then Vasily had nothing to do but return to our lodgings, gnashing his teeth at his own impotence.

It was now the middle of the afternoon, and a punishingly hot day. Vasily found that I had come—not quite to my senses. Nijam sat by my side, looking pale and weary, dabbing at my forehead with a wet cloth. "Don't crowd me so close," I was saying fretfully. "I can't *breathe.*"

"Let her be," Vasily murmured to Nijam.

"It doesn't help; I've tried," she said, resignedly. "When I'm with her she reproaches me for crowding her, but when I go away she cries not to be abandoned in the darkness."

Vasily held out his hand for the cloth. "Then I'll tend her," he said, "Go and work, if it makes you feel better. Where are Mimi and Schmidt?"

"They went out for news," Nijam explained, before escaping to her stuffy little room, where once again she commenced work on her weapon. Vasily sat down and tended to me; in time I slipped again into sleep, and when I awoke again, I was in somewhat better possession of my wits. The shades no longer clustered about me, and the feelings they provoked—their agony and sorrow—had receded a little, allowing me to feel at last my own weariness and terror.

Finding Vasily leaning over me, holding my hand tightly within his own, I let out a sigh of relief. "Have I given you all a terrible fright?" I murmured.

Vasily attempted a smile. "Sergei Alexandrovich will answer for what he has done to you," he said, with a rather murderous light in his eyes. "I regret that I have not yet found the way to make him do so."

"To *me!*" I whispered. "For shame, Vasily! when so many

others lie dead!"

He carried my hand to his lips. "Don't ask me to care for anyone else just now," he whispered. "I've told you what a selfish beast I am."

At the time I was too weary fully to comprehend his words, although they came back to me much later, and then I wondered that I had ever overlooked them. At that moment, however, I caught a glimpse of an imprint, and my heart stopped. My father's ghost sat in the armchair, quietly reading the newspaper as I had seen him do so often in my mother's drawing-room in Brixton. I stared in dismay. What was my father doing *here*, now, when it was still hours short of sunset?

Then the door opened and Mimi and Schmidt returned in a silence that struck me as deeply foreboding. Mimi dragged off her hat; her face was pale with the heat and absolutely bloodless. "Don't ask me," she said, as Nijam came hastening to the door of her room. "I don't want to describe it."

Schmidt cleared his throat. "It's worse than we thought," he said. "Mimi took me to Khodynka. It was bad. There were the Emperor and Empress, and the Governor, enjoying their magnificent ceremony, with orchestra and everything; and there was an immense crowd of people, over half a million of them all packed into that little field, and the smell of blood thick on the air, and the police still hard at work carrying away the bodies from where they had fallen in the ditches."

"Thousands," Mimi said huskily, abandoning her former resolution. "You cannot believe how many bodies there were. There was a cordon of Cossacks around the imperial pavilion, but I managed a look beneath it anyway. They—they'd hidden corpses beneath it. Thousands of them, all heaped up, and the Tsar standing atop them all, with the gilt and the flags and the orchestra and the Preobrazhensky Guards in their red tunics…" For a moment she was lost for words, satisfying herself only with a few pithy expressions in her native tongue.

"*A small incident,* my foot!" Vasily said, between his teeth. "That's what Sergei told me! I knew he must be lying—in this country lies are currency—but this! No wonder he refused to accept the blame. What could he be thinking, allowing so many people to gather in such a small and hazardous field, and not providing any lookouts to manage them?"

He put a hand over his eyes. "My family," he added, with a brittle laugh. "Even when we are not drinking blood, we cannot help being monsters… Enough. We must try to send Miss Dark out of the city at once. Sergei has confirmed my fears that the police won't allow *me* to leave, but Miss Nijam, you must try your luck with Miss Dark. Even if you only make it as far as Petersburg, that will be something."

This filled me with alarm. "No," I cried shakily. "Don't send me away; I'm perfectly well."

"No, you're not," said Nijam with some asperity.

My father's imprint turned the page of his newspaper, as though he meant to bear witness to Nijam's veracity. I was plainly *not* well: I had just undergone the very worst experience of my life, and now something was wrong with my father's imprint, which until now had only ever appeared to me at sunset.

I wrung my hands. "But what about Schmidt—and Mimi—and Vasily? How can we think of going away and leaving them behind?"

Before Nijam could reply, a knock came at the door, striking the words from all our lips. Mimi startled and raised her tiger claws, but then the knock was repeated and a feminine voice called, "Vaska, it's me!"

"Oh, *Gospodin*," Vasily snarled. "I suppose it's too late to say we're not at home; she's heard us squabbling." And he threw open the door. "My *dear* princess, what an unexpected honour!"

Zlata giggled as he carried her hand to his lips. "Vaska, you're making me blush. Good heavens, what do you make of that melodrama at the theatre last night? Do you think they'll send the old Grand Duke away? I can't imagine he'll ever be able to show his face in public again. Fancy being caught with a *man!* He must be quite mad! But, Vaska, do you really expect anyone to believe that you weren't behind it? Why, you *naughty* man, you must have been planning this the whole time, and keeping me in the dark about it! I really am tremendously impressed!"

Her prattle washed over us with a sense of unreality. It was only now that Vasily managed to slip a word in.

"My dear, what a lively imagination you have! Really, I can't imagine how you should suppose that *I* had anything to do with my father's indiscretions. But that's all old news now, surely. You find us absolutely in despair over this Khodynka Field matter."

Zlata laughed indulgently. Shrewd as she was in some matters, I judged that Vasily's jeering truthfulness would absolutely deceive her. "Oh, I heard there was some minor trouble there," she said. "What a relief that it won't stop the ball tonight from going ahead, for otherwise we might have had to give up on *The Musketeer!*"

There was a momentary silence at that; and Vasily sent a glance my way. "In fact, my dear," he said smoothly, "something else has come up and I find myself needing quite urgently to speak to the Emperor."

"Oh, nothing easier," Zlata said with a dismissive wave of her hand. "You can do that at the ball tonight, of course. You have an invitation, don't you? I certainly wheedled the dear old Marquis into issuing one for you, and one for the Countess also, of course."

"But surely Nicky won't be attending the ball, after all that has happened—"

"On the contrary, I have just come from the Alexandria Palace, and it is all decided! The Emperor and Empress will attend the ball, but only for half an hour, in recognition of the misfortune. We might catch them as they leave, and then steal the painting after, at our leisure. What do you say to that?"

Vasily looked mutinous. Nevertheless, I judged that it was my moment to step in, for I was dreadfully sorry for all the things I had said to him last night. To remain at his side I would steal whatever he wanted, let the shades cluster about me never so thick and overpowering.

Besides, there was another thing I must do before leaving Moscow; if only I could think how.

"I say we do it, your highness," I said, sitting up and testing whether my legs would hold me. To my great satisfaction, they did. "No, I know that I have had a trying day," I added to Vasily, as he made some sound of protest, "but a ball is just what I require to lift my spirits. Moreover, the princess cannot fill my rôle tonight, and it's absolutely necessary that you manage to see the Emperor. And of course it would be a shame not to take the painting while it is so close within our grasp. No, I insist! We have laid our plans, and now we must carry them out."

I carried my point against all protest; and then I staggered into my room and with shaking hands managed to splash a little cold water into the ewer. I plunged my face into the water and then came up again.

There was a shade sitting on the end of my bed. A little boy with a torn jacket and mangled limbs, who had lingered when all the other shades moved on. There was a desolately questioning mood about him. *Why* had all those people pressed in upon him so hard, and *why* did his mother not come to get him when he was sobbing her name, before the press became too much even to breathe in?

I knelt before him. "My poor darling," said I, "I promise you that I will do what I can to lay you to rest; only please wait a little, and keep your distance, so that I can have a clear enough head to think what must be done. Will you pass the word to the others?"

He nodded, wiping at his tears with a ghostly sleeve; and with that he got up and drifted off. I turned again and looked into the mirror. I appeared half dead myself; but there was nothing wrong with *me* that a little of Mimi's rouge and a strong cup of tea would not amend. In that I was very fortunate.

# 23

# Chapter XXIII.

At precisely half-past ten, the French Embassy ball got underway as the Emperor and Empress, together with the French Ambassador and his wife, led off the dancing. Vasily and I were there to see them in the shadow of an immense ice sculpture near the door, which had been carved in the semblance of the imperial double-headed eagle. The windows were draped with great swatches of red velvet, which seemed to draw in all the light from the electric lamps and chandeliers. The colour gave a red cast—as red as blood—to the gold-and-cream walls, to the great Baroque mural on the ceiling, and to the pale ivory and blue silks worn by the ladies. Rather than flowers, the room had been decorated with green saplings, whose dark glossy leaves gave the place rather the feel of a perilous forest. It was the sort of forest that might be full of caitiff knights and rapacious beasts—to say nothing of one very tremulous and overwhelmed damsel, unsure whether she was about to be in distress or not. At least Mimi had provided the aforesaid damsel with a marvellous dress. It was made of pure white satin, with a striking black velvet scrollwork unrolling across it, so that the dress stood between me and this teeming wilderness like a pretty ironwork fence; I fancied that it could keep me safe.

From our vantage-point by the door I had a very good look at the faces of the imperial couple. It struck me that the Empress could not have been any older than myself; she had a very pretty face, although it was earnest and unsmiling and, upon that particular evening, drawn with grief. As for the Emperor, he appeared quite pale, though composed, as he guided the Marquise de Montebello across the intricately parqueted floor. I wondered what the imprints of his ancestors had thought of the Khodynka disaster. I suspected they had not been particularly bothered by it.

"Is everyone in position?" Nijam's voice crackled through the transmitter, a little distorted by distance. Once again she had elected to guide us from the comfort of her own room at home, and it sounded as though she had a peppermint tucked into her cheek.

"Vasily and I are in the ballroom," I murmured beneath the strains of music. Neither a Russian Grand Duke nor a French Countess could possibly have been omitted from the Ambassador's guest list, despite the disgrace of the Grand Duke and the purely fictional existence of the Countess. There was a guest, too, who had not appeared on the list. My father's imprint, now clad by memory in his best Sunday suit, had elected to follow us to the ball. I wished it would not. I was all raw and keyed-up from the day's events, and each time I caught a glimpse of my father I could not help receiving an unpleasant little shock.

Etiquette, of course, obliged us to arrive no later than the Emperor himself, which meant that we had half an hour's social gauntlet before us. At the end of that period, Nicky would depart the ball in recognition of the tragedy; and then Vasily could approach his cousin and the rest of us might accost the painting. Full of misgivings, I steeled myself for the ordeal. I had spotted Marie of Roumania with her sister and their cavaliers chattering beneath one of the trees at the other end of the room, and when she caught me looking at her she blew me a mocking kiss.

"Adeline Genée is also here," murmured Mimi from where she promenaded in a gown of midnight-blue silk that accentuated her ash-blonde hair. About her neck she wore the pearls which Mr Vandergriff had given me. These had excited a deal of attention from the masculine attendees of the ball. This was not because of the richness of the necklace, with its rows of pearls and enamelled centrepiece, which may have been almost scandalously splendid for a little ball in London but appeared quite poor and unremarkable among the fabulous royal diamonds, emeralds, rubies, and sapphires on display tonight. It had more to do with the livid marks peeping demurely out from beneath the rows of pearls: the unmistakable scars left by a hungry vampire, which proclaimed Mimi to be at once desirable and available.

"Alphonse Schmidt, behind the drinks table," Schmidt reported. It had been proposed that he should escort Mimi in the identity of a German industrialist, as he had done at the races; but in the end he was happiest impersonating the help. I was not myself sure that *I* would not have been happier mixing and ladling punch, or even tending the samovar in which the blood was being kept warm for monstrous palates, than attempting to make polite conversation with people I had come both to fear and to loathe. The day had worn me

306

to a ravelling, and my worries were a knot of nausea in my stomach.

"Zlata Milanova Obrenovicha is in the ballroom," our sixth conspirator announced through the transmitter with which we had equipped her for the occasion.— "Not so loud!" Vasily hissed.

Zlata responded only with a delighted giggle. "Well?" she whispered, lowering her voice. "What shall we do? Should I show you to the salon with the painting?"

"It would be foolish to show our hand too soon," said Nijam repressively. "For the moment, until Vasily has had his chance to approach the Emperor, please observe the customary social rituals."

"If you want to make yourself useful," Vasily put in, "there's certain to be a detective on every door; you might find the one nearest to the painting and distract him."

"Oh! I can do that," Zlata said eagerly, and I soon glimpsed her sidling up to a plain-clothes man with fluttering lashes and a champagne flute in each hand.

"That poor young man," I observed, *sotto voce,* having switched off my transmitter.

"A princess flirting with him at a ball will give him something to tell his grandchildren about," Vasily demurred.

My father, still in his Sunday best, transferred his Bible from one hand to the other and looked politely attentive. *Why* wouldn't he leave me alone?

"Hullo!" said Vasily. "Is that Mimi dancing with my brother Nikolasha?"

Indeed it was Mimi swooping by us, light as a feather in the arms of Vasily's brother. The two of us stared after them as they went spinning down the room. "Well," I said, "so long as she doesn't stab anyone I shall be perfectly satisfied."

In fact, Mimi was rarely without a dancing partner that evening. For the next hour Vasily and I saw her going to and fro at intervals in the embrace of some sashed and medalled werewolf or ogre or prosthete, and even smiling. No one was stabbed—or clawed, or strangled. I did not understand it at all. Schmidt, however, was enlightened when after half an hour or so Mimi made a stealthy approach to the drinks table.

"Here," she whispered, digging into her pockets, and coming out with fistfuls of signet-rings and tie-pins, "be a dear boy and take care of these for me, will you?" So saying, she dropped them into a pair of tumblers and slid them across the floor, beneath the snowy tablecloth.

Schmidt gaped down at the small fortune at his feet. "I say," he protested, "what if someone notices that they're missing? ?"

"Well, if that happens they'll blame *you,* not me," and with those comforting words she tripped away.

Vasily and I, meanwhile, were quite unaware of this, for we had our own social difficulties to navigate. One young lindworm shook his maned head at us as he passed by. "Why, Grand Duke," he said, "I see that you've cured yourself, and got your fangs back!"

Vasily bared his false teeth in a dangerous grin. "What, did you believe that I would meekly forego the privileges of my birth?"

"I wish to heaven that *some* of us could," said the lindworm bitterly, before slithering off.

Vasily and I stared after the young monster in astonishment. "Well!" I exclaimed under my breath. *"That* I didn't expect!"

"It isn't only my mother who would have been glad to

escape this world," Vasily murmured, looking for a moment very sorry and sad. I wondered whether he was once again thinking of her words—that it was better to lose the world and gain one's soul.

These gloomy reflections were quickly interrupted, however, by none other than the German Crown Prince, who approached us with a gang of werewolf attendants. The creatures fixed their blazing eyes upon me, and one of them said, "Ah! The little French Countess! We have a *bone* to pick with you, madame!"

"Yes!" said another. "It's thanks to *you,* I think, that our friend Prince Arthur is indisposed!"

I trembled, and Vasily stepped before me, baring his teeth. It had not occurred to me—the day having been taken up with other preoccupations—that I should be risking my life by appearing once more in society; but of course the werewolves knew that I was privy to their plot against their own Crown Prince. Perhaps they thought to destroy me by any means possible. Perhaps Prince Arthur was to be that means.

It was the Crown Prince who came to my rescue. "Oh, go away, Friedrich; this is no place for accusations!" said he. "I want a word with the Grand Duke; *alone* if you please!"

The werewolves muttered but departed, one of them with a very menacing look at *me.* Perhaps he meant to warn me against informing the Crown Prince of the plot against his life. I wondered whether, after all, I did not owe it to him to do so. Undoubtedly it would be an excellent thing for Europe if the German empire was *not* ruled by a werewolf.

"You're Vasily Nikolaevich," Prince Willy said in confidential tones, taking Vasily by the elbow. "Listen, they're saying that you're a fraud, and that you don't have a cure at all. But if that's so, then how have you turned your eyes red, eh?"

"That's my little secret, your highness," said Vasily, and if he had been a London costermonger he would no doubt have tapped his nose.

The prince heaved a long, yearning sigh. "Ah, so! You *do* have a cure! Do you know that my younger brothers are plotting to kill me?"

Well, after all the werewolves had not exercised a high standard of discretion. I was grateful for it: they had relieved me of a very ticklish duty.

"You could save my life," Prince Willy said, "and entitle yourself to the German Emperor's undying thanks, if you were to share that cure with me. I'm willing to pay, of course. Shall we say—" and he whispered something into Vasily's ear. "Swear never to let the cure get into any other hands," Prince Willy added, "and I'll double the price."

My hand tightened convulsively upon Vasily's arm, warning him to be careful with his reply. It struck me that the cure might be a hoax, but if Vasily claimed to have one, he would then be like Schmidt, too dangerous to be allowed his liberty. It was bad enough, Vasily being the object of imperial wrath. If he became the object of imperial jealousy things would be infinitely worse.

Vasily's elbow pressed reassuringly upon my hand as he answered. "Why, sir! Such a noble and useful secret belongs to the world, not to a single Empire! I wouldn't *dream* of selling it on those terms! I promise you you shall have the cure, and for free; as soon as I have come to an understanding with my own Emperor about my future incomes. Good evening, sir!"

With that he steered me through the crowd, angling towards the dancers. The press of bodies brought back the day's horrible experiences, and coming on top of our confrontation with the werewolves it was almost overwhelming. "Vasily," I said, "if I spend much longer in this place I shall scream, or faint, or be sick."

"Be strong," he said, with a sharp-edged smile. "We shall be out of it soon, and in the meanwhile off goes Willy, and begs Nicky to reinstate my incomes so that he can get at the cure."

But our ordeal was not yet over. The Crown Princess of Roumania was the next to seek us out. "What a surprise! It's my little friend Vaska," said Missy in her native English, blocking our way just as we were about to break out of the stifling crowd and into the blissful freedom of the dance.

I was glad that Vasily did not touch me; he only put himself between me and Missy. "Have you come to finish your work, your highness?" he asked. "I advise you not to try it with Nicky looking on; he still has a use for me."

There was something wary in his voice, and I knew that he was afraid of this woman, even though she was no longer a vampire.

Missy smiled: she heard it too. "Don't be afraid: why should I go to the trouble and risk of killing you? Indeed, you have done me a favour," she added in confidential tones, taking his arm.

I saw the involuntary shudder which ran through him at her touch, but his voice was steady as he replied, "A favour? Do enlighten me!"

"Well, the Kabale is dead, and Europe can no longer be ruled by a web of royal family alliances. Now it's every monarchy for itself, and we must court the love of our people if we are to remain in our rightful place. That's why I parade my lack of fangs—because defanging is the way of the future. Here are poor Nicky and Alix, surrounded by policemen armed to the teeth because they cannot trust their people. No one in Roumania wants to blow *me* to smithereens. I'll tell you what I'm going to do, Vasily Nikolaevich: I'll persuade Frederick to defang. I'll become a saint in their eyes. I'll be untouchable."

I smothered the words of shock which rose to my lips at this barefaced hypocrisy, the tribute paid by Peter to rob Paul! Like all my countrymen, I was in favour of defanging—or at least, I had been brought up to *believe* that we were—and it shocked me to hear her refer to this sacred cause merely as another way of shoring up her power.

"If you're so grateful, my dear, why did you send Vandergriff after me?"

"Because having taken my fangs away, you then stole my diamonds," she said softly. "Fool me twice, shame on me. Did you think you could play with me forever?"

"I shouldn't dream of it. Shall we agree that I have learned my lesson, and call off our friend Vandergriff? I'll even come to Roumania if you like, and extol the virtues of fanglessness to your dear Frederick."

Missy sent him a laughing, disdainful look that was the mirror of his own. "Call off Vandergriff—why!  are you frightened of a mere prosthete, Vasily Nikolaevich?"

"Not particularly," he said, "but the Countess, here, is a martyr to nerves."

Missy turned to look me up and down; it was the first time that evening she had taken the slightest notice of me. "Ah, yes! the Countess," she said, turning once again to Vasily. "Shall we make a truce? I'll call off Vandergriff if you give me those very fine diamonds around your lover's neck."

"That's outrageous," Vasily said. "Have you any idea how much those things are worth?"

On an evening less fraught with terror, that disingenuous question might have set me off into uncontrollable giggles. Instead, only too glad for the proposed truce, I snatched Nijam's synthetic gems from my neck and held them out to the princess. "For heaven's sake, Vasily! You must not suppose that this trumpery thing is worth more to me than you are!"

I said the words more for Missy's sake than his; and yet Vasily's eyes lingered almost wistfully upon my face. Did he wonder whether I would have made the same statement, had the diamonds been real?

Smiling, Missy clasped the necklace about her neck. "There," she said, preening a little, "now we are quits, and so I shall tell Vandergriff." Off she went, doubtless to find a mirror; and Vasily and I stood regarding each other.

"I wonder," Vasily began, thoughtfully; but before he could say anything, a faint persistent sound struck upon my ear, and I turned to find that the clock's hands had just reached eleven o'clock.

The sight drove all other questions from my mind. "It's *time*," I gasped, pressing the button of my transmitter. "And look—there are the Emperor and his wife by the door, bidding farewell to the Ambassador!"

"Everyone is in place," Vasily murmured with a glance about the room. "Let us begin."

These words had been exchanged in undertones; but now I uttered a ladylike shriek which got everyone's attention. One hand fluttered to my lips, and the other reached out in front of me.

313

"Oh!" I cried, in my best Shakespearean-soliloquy manner, stumbling blindly out into the midst of the dancing. "Shades...shades...shades! All bloody; all mangled; all dead!"

"What the dickens is she blithering about?" someone asked, but everywhere I turned, people were no longer talking or dancing or laughing; the blood had fled their faces and they watched me with absolute terror.

Despite the lies, despite the bodies borne away and stacked where no one could see them, despite the music and laughter and pretense, yet they knew what had happened; knew, and had made themselves accomplices by pretending they did not.

"It's an omen," I cried. Even the orchestra had fallen silent. I lurched towards the tall, gaunt, blazing-eyed figure of Grand Duke Sergei. "You may do your best to hide the bodies, but the dead do not forget! An evil fate is upon you, Sergei Alexandrovich! You will die—you will die as they died, and you will be trampled underfoot as they were!"

"How dare you?" he hissed; and with one swift step forward he actually struck me across the face. Never in my life had anyone lifted a hand to me, even Griff; and I had never imagined that Sergei would. It was a heavy blow, which for some moments robbed me of breath, of speech, of sight. When I knew my surroundings again I found that I was sitting upon the parquetry with one hand spread protectively across my smarting cheek, and Vasily was descending up his cousin with clenched fists and bared teeth.

"*Vasily,*" I screamed, and then, because the show must go on, I swooned gracefully upon the floor.

Dimly, in the midst of my shock, I heard Vasily growl at his cousin even as he raised me up. I am a tall woman, and he did

not attempt to carry me alone. Instead, with Mimi's help—
for the supposed Madame Genée darted from the crowd
to assist—he supported me from the room, into the very
salon where the Meissonier painting hung. Nijam was on the
transmitter, giving directions; I was in too much pain from
the blow to pay much attention to her.

"Bring smelling-salts," Vasily cried, letting me down upon
the sofa, "and water! —No, stay back," he told those who had
followed us to the salon, "she needs air."

There was a confused murmur from the doors as Mimi
shooed out those who had followed us. Vasily tilted my face
to examine the contusion.

"You little fool," he sighed, "why did you do it?"

I opened my eyes with caution. "Why did *I* do it?" I repeated
incredulously. "Ask your cousin! He's the one who struck
me!"

Vasily bit his lip. "Hell!" he whispered, explosively. "If I had
my fangs, no one would ever touch you and live! Don't pay
any attention to me, my dear; I am coward enough to blame
you, since I cannot blame my cousin!"

Indeed I had gone a great deal further than I had at first
intended, when I called Sergei Alexandrovich to account for
the blood that had been shed because he would not spare two
thoughts for the people for whom he was supposed to provide.
I don't know what came over me, other than a great wrath,
which made me reckless. I had had just enough wit not to
point my finger at the Emperor himself. Nicky, I thought, was
almost as culpable as Sergei, for appointing such a careless
person to such a responsible position; but it would have been
impolitic to say so, when we could only leave Moscow at his
pleasure.

Vasily regarded me with an expression of much regret and some awe. "You foretold Sergei's death," he added. "Did—did the shades reveal that to you?"

"Oh, no," I assured him. "I don't know what came over me; only it struck me that it would be poetic, and I thought he deserved a good fright."

Vasily attempted a smile. "You looked as though you believed it. Ah! here's Schmidt with the water; and I had better go after Nicky."

Mimi allowed Schmidt to enter, with a glassful of water upon a silver platter; Zlata slipped in behind him, and Vasily kissed my hand and went out into the ballroom. "My poor little friend has had a shock," I heard him saying, as he closed the doors, "and requires absolute peace and quiet."

The door shut, and the conspirators were alone with the painting (and with my father's imprint, which still refused to leave me). I rose to my feet, nervous energy overwhelming the weariness and the pain which had not been far away all day. The Meissonier painting, depicting a rather haunted-looking Musketeer in a buff-coat and a red sash, hung on the wall near the door. I do not think that Vasily had glanced at it even once. Reaching beneath my skirts, I drew out the long pasteboard tube which I had concealed there. Schmidt took it without a word; and he and Mimi lifted the painting from the wall.

"Your highness," I whispered to Princess Zlata, "a moment of your time, if you please?" She was reluctant to leave Schmidt and Mimi, who were busily engaged in cutting the painting from its frame; but I attached myself to her elbow and dragged her towards the window, where I could be sure of speaking to her without our voices being overheard by

316

anyone in the ballroom.

"Your part is the most important," I told her, "and the most dangerous. When Schmidt and Mimi have cut out the painting we will make our escape through the window, as discussed; but it's your part to remain at the ball—*with* the painting hidden beneath your skirts. When the theft is discovered, they'll think of me at once, and the hue and cry will be raised; and that's when you will walk out and carry the painting off to our lodgings, quite unsuspected. Do you understand?"

Zlata clasped her hands. "Oh yes! What fun!"

"Then here it is," I said, as Mimi came over to us with the pasteboard tube. "Oh, wait—give us your transmitter; just in case you are searched; and Godspeed."

The tube having been attached beneath Zlata's petticoats with the ribbons designed for that purpose, we sent her into the ballroom again and I switched on my transmitter. "All right, Nijam," I said with a sigh of relief, "guide us home."

We did not, of course, mean to leave through the window, even though it was only a short distance to the ground, for the palace was only one storey tall. We were hardly foolish enough to leave the ball by a route the indiscreet Zlata knew about.

I heard the rustling of Nijam's blueprints. "All right," she said softly, "take the door on your right. There ought to be another door in the wainscoting of the next room, which will let you onto the servants' passage."

Most of the time, when something seems easier than it ought to be, there is nothing sinister to worry about. Alas! this was not the case for us upon that memorable evening. Within two minutes of leaving the salon, with its now-empty

317

frame, we had found the servants' passage and passed through it to a busy little corridor leading past kitchen and pantry and servants' hall towards an open door which admitted the balmy night air. "Pardon us," I said haughtily once or twice as we sailed through. Not one of the servants objected to people of such manifest importance wishing to leave the festivities by the service entrance. They only stood aside, bowing; and in this manner we made it through that stuffy passage into the open. The great palace Sheremetov had no courtyard, being placed at the centre of a noble park, but a flat gravelled area stretched from the servants' entrances to the nearby chapel. This was full of parked carriages, and of coachmen amusing themselves with cards and conversations. Our own carriage was not far away; we hurried towards it and took our seats.

And there, alas! we stayed, for there was no sign of Vasily.

24

# Chapter XXIV.

With the *Musketeer* being purloined in the salon, Vasily hurried through the ballroom in search of his cousin Nicky. There was no longer any sign of the Emperor and Empress in the glittering throng which crowded about the ballroom door. Vasily cursed himself for a fool, thinking that he had lingered too long with me when he ought to have been rushing to his cousin. Luck was on his side, however: when he exited the ballroom, he overheard loud, hissing voices from the entrance-hall and beheld Nicky and Alicky standing at bay in a little knot of their attendants, well-nigh surrounded by the towering figures of Nicky's uncles: Vladimir, Alexis, and Sergei Alexandrovich.

"Leave? What do you mean, *leave?*" Sergei hissed, as Vasily hurried to join the stand-off. "This is nothing but useless sentimentality. It took us twenty *years* to bring the French to an alliance, and now you'll spit in Montebello's face for the sake of a few greedy peasants…Oh, *bozhe moi,*" he added with a glare as Vasily approached. "It's the disciple of Robespierre."

The accusation was so ridiculous that Vasily could only

laugh. "And a good evening to *you*, Sergei Alexandrovich. Forgive me for interrupting, Nicky, but before you go, could you possibly give me a word in private? It won't take two minutes."

Nicky looked pale and desperate, and Alicky seemed suspiciously red around the eyes, even for a vampire. Vasily would have sworn the young Emperor would only be too eager to take the opportunity thus afforded, of removing himself from his uncles' hectoring. Instead he said, "Well, I thuppothe I ought to thtay a little longer; for the allianthe." Nicky always *did* have trouble speaking around his fangs.

"That's right," Sergei said, stabbing a finger at the younger man. *"I will retain the principles of autocracy as unbendingly as my unforgettable late father*—that's what you promised when you accepted the empire, and you can't uphold the principles of autocracy if you'll let your actions be dictated by the whims of the peasantry!"

"The *whims* of the peasantry?" Vasily protested. It was all too much. He had not been raised to care much for the peasantry himself; he had killed and eaten his fair share of them. It was only in recent years that he had come to ask himself what Ioanna might have thought of such deeds. He knew very well what a certain other lady thought of them; and then, too, his present confederates had affected his views as well. Nor did he think of himself as a champion for democracy at this moment—still less the revolutionary of Sergei's jibes. Only the past days had filled him with disgust for his family: their cruelty, their egotism, their inability to feel compassion. In Missy's cellar, at the mercy of Boris and Cyril, he had felt for the first time something of what it meant to be *beneath* his family, and his eyes had been opened. Still, perhaps he might have felt the temptation to forget what he knew, to reason it all away as the bad deeds of a few bad eggs, were it not for the blow struck by Sergei in the ballroom just now. Having presided over a tragedy that must have claimed thousands of lives, Sergei had gone assiduously to work covering it up; had blamed it upon everyone but himself—including the very victims—and now insisted that Nicky should follow suit. And, having been charged with his crimes before all of Europe, he had responded with naked brutality, and had raised his hand against one whom Vasily would have died to protect. There was no hope for such a man; but perhaps there was still a little hope for Nicky.

"The whims of the peasantry!" he repeated, now quite losing his head. Over the transmitter my voice echoed in his ears, begging him to make his petition and join us in the carriage; impatiently, he cut me off. "Do you imagine that five thousand men, women, and children perished in agonies purely to inconvenience *yourself*, Sergei Alexandrovich? Do you fail to imagine that any of this could be *your* fault? Nicky, for God's sake, think of all that innocent blood, crying out from the ground. Think how heartless you must look, dancing the night away after such a tragedy!"

Nicky looked despairingly at his wife. "What elthe ought I to do?"

"It's bad enough that you came at all, but listen to reason! You ought to leave at once and go into public mourning. You ought to cancel the rest of the festivities, and above all you should remove Sergei from his post, if you don't wish to be tainted with his disgrace!"

"Disgrace?" Sergei cried disdainfully. "Who can disgrace me, except my Tsar? I wash my hands of everything. This was

Vorontsov's fault—the fool *insisted* upon meddling with my dispositions, and I had no time to waste upon making sure the peasants did not cast themselves into pits!"

"Don't pay any attention to this Jacobin, your majesty," another of the uncles, Alexis, spat. The way he pronounced *your majesty*, it might as easily have been *you cretin.* "No doubt he wants the governorship of Moscow himself, and he thinks to get it by pandering to the revolutionary mob!"

"This is preposterous!" Vasily said. "Nicky, am I to be a Jacobin, only because I don't wish to see you and Alicky suffer the same fate as the sixteenth Louis and his queen?"

No one acknowledged these words. "If you dismiss Sergei," Vladimir said, "then I shall resign my own post at once, and go into exile."

"So shall we all!" cried Alexis.

At that Nicky startled and really began to look desperate. "Pleathe don't thay thuch thingth! I cannot—it ith difficult enough for me to rule thith empire ath it ith! How thall I do tho if you abandon me?"

Vasily could almost have wept with vexation. He did not think that Nicky was a bad man; but he was young, and had no experience, and had suddenly been thrust forth with the powers of a god on the stage of the world. His ancestors and uncles bullied him relentlessly, and yet he clung to them, because he could not bear the prospect of ruling without them. Perhaps, to be a good man, you needed not only good intentions, but also the courage to carry them out.

"We might thtay a few hourth longer. Indeed I think we mutht," Nicky was saying to Alicky, and Vasily knew beyond a doubt that he had lost.

"Remember, Nicky," he said with heavy grief, "that the blood of those people will remain forever a blot upon your reign."

It was neither the bristling uncles, nor even Nicky himself who answered; but Alicky, to his surprise. She went up to him and put a hand on his arm. "Dear cousin, I know you mean well, but you mustn't distress yourself," she whispered. "You forget that Russia is not England. Here we need not earn the love of the people, for they regard us altogether as divine beings. Come, Nicky."

She held out her hand to the Emperor. They were halfway towards the ballroom doors before Vasily could banish his astonishment and recall his original errand. Had it been only his own life at stake, he would at that moment cheerfully have died before begging a favour from Nicky. Yet there was no time for such pride now.

"Nicky!" he cried, starting after them. "I didn't mean—that is, forgive me for trespassing upon your patience! I came here to beg you a favour. The climate here doesn't suit my friend, the Countess, and I'm afraid she will soon be seriously ill. Do give me leave to escort her to Paris."

Nicky, who had been pale, now reddened slightly. "You know I need you in Russia, Vasily. But as for the Countess, of course *she* may depart—"

"As for the Countess," announced a new voice, in tones of clear and ringing triumph, "I'm not entirely sure she's a Countess at all—but she's certainly a thief! Look at this! I've caught her making off with one of the Ambassador's paintings!"

With a thrill of horror, Vasily turned to behold Princess Zlata herself, brandishing the pasteboard tube in the company of a squad of policemen who held Mimi, Schmidt, and myself in their grasp!

\* \* \*

The young Emperor's astonishment quickly gave way to a look of relief. "A theft! Really, I can't stay to investigate; you had better take care of it, Sergei," he said, beating a hurried—and, I thought, a grateful—retreat towards the ballroom.

"Why—you *coward!*" Vasily cried, starting after the Emperor. At a sign from Sergei Alexandrovich, two of the policemen flung themselves upon him, arresting his movement. The Emperor's back stiffened, but he did not turn around; he and the Empress went on through the door, and that was the last I ever saw of the Russian Tsar. Really, I pity the man. He was not strong enough to defy the expectations of his family living or dead. I am afraid that in the end he, at least, lived to deserve the fate which twenty years later was visited upon him.

Such are my thoughts now, of course, but at that moment I could spare thought only for my own predicament. Upon reaching our carriage, I switched on my transmitter to hear Vasily passionately debating politics with his cousins. "Vasily!" I protested. "Now is not the time: we must make our escape!" The transmitter died. I stared at Schmidt and Mimi in silent despair, but there was nothing to do but wait. Presently, after some time had passed without a sign of Vasily, Schmidt decided to venture back into the palace to find him—but it was already too late.

A posse of plain-clothes-men appeared running through the serried ranks of the carriages, searching each in turn. Surrounded as we were by the broad grassy sward of the park, it was useless either to run or hide: in moments the policemen snatched open the carriage door and required us to give ourselves up in the name of the Emperor.

As Mimi and I were haled from our hiding-place, Schmidt had just enough time to touch his transmitter. "We are caught, Miss Nijam!" he cried. "You must fly at once!" The police looked around the place eagerly for any sign of this last confederate; but then, finding that apparently Schmidt had been addressing thin air, they cuffed him over the head in a reproving manner and marched the three of us off to our fate. On the noble front stairs of the palace we were joined by Zlata herself, who appeared very pleased with herself indeed.

"Are you surprised to see me?" she had asked with a smile, having congratulated the policemen on their excellent work.

"I must say that I am, my dear," I said mildly: "You've gone to a great deal of trouble to rid yourself of one who is not in the least your rival."

Zlata's only response to this was a toss of the head and a flick of her fingers as she beckoned the policemen to usher us into the house. Internally, of course, I was fuming. Not merely because Zlata had betrayed us, after all, and more quickly than I had bargained for—but because Nijam's plot to circumvent her would have worked *perfectly* had Vasily been more punctual. What could he possibly have been thinking, getting waylaid at a time like this? I felt bitterly vindicated. I had known all along that Vasily's inability to detach himself from his family would doom us all. Then we reached the great gilt-and-brocade entrance-hall of the palace, and found Vasily with shoulders bowed in defeat watching the Emperor return to the ball. My last hope died.

"Now, what's the meaning of this?" Sergei Alexandrovich demanded, raking all of us—save my father's imprint—with an impartial red glare. His brothers and the Emperor's attendants had followed the Emperor upstairs, leaving us alone with the police and with this dreadful creature.

We were fairly caught—and this time there would be no convincing the police to let us go, for there was a witness to our wrong-doing.

"I have been very clever, Godfather," Zlata said, laughing. Vasily flinched as she reached for his head; but she was only after his transmitter, which she plucked from his ear and ground underfoot until nothing but a few sparking wires remained. "Here is a gang of confidence-tricksters, whom I have tricked as prettily as they thought they were tricking me! All this time, I have been reporting their movements to the Okhrana—just as I knew you would like me to—and now I have caught them in the very act. Upstairs in one of the salons, you'll find an empty frame; and in this tube is the painting the miscreants stole from it."

So saying, she offered the pasteboard tube to the Grand Duke, who motioned impatiently for one of the policemen to take it.

"I can well believe it!" Sergei said, levelling a baleful glare at me. "So, this is what brought you back to Russia, Vasily Nikolaevich—a dastardly plan to thieve from our allies! What do you have to say for yourself?"

"Only this: *why*, Zlata?" Vasily burst out. I was unaccustomed to seeing him in a state of such desperation. With his renewed, vampire-bitten strength he might have broken away from his captors; but the evening's events seemed to have quite broken him down. *"Why? It was you who wanted to steal the painting; I only did it to please you!"*

"You did it to keep me happy," she responded, as quick as a whip. "There's a difference, Vasily Nikolaevich! If you really

326

wished to please me you would have married me when you were asked! *You* might have protected my kingdom from Austria, and saved me from a marriage to a man I hated!"

Vasily blinked, almost as though he had been struck. "I was young," he said in a stifled voice, "and I was not in the habit of considering anyone but myself—which, believe me, I sorely regret!"

I tried not to let my indignation show. What right had I to feel such a thing? If Vasily felt that he had treated Zlata badly, I could not object to it. Perhaps he *had* treated her badly, or perhaps anyone with his upbringing would have found it equally difficult to contemplate matrimony! But Zlata did not deserve to marry Vasily, only because she had badly wanted to. He was too good for her. The moment the thought occurred to me it well-nigh took my breath away, but it was true for all that. That he could repent at all for the way he treated her made it certain.

"It isn't too late." Zlata's next words were exactly the ones I had feared. Moreover, they were melting with longing. "Today you have the chance to restore all the damage you did to me—and to gain everything you want in return. The Emperor offered such terms, did he not, Godfather?"

Sergei Alexandrovich gave a hard little smile. "He did offer such terms at last week's audience, and has not rescinded them. Quite against my own counsel and all rational sense, I might add! My cousin is invited to remain in the motherland, in full possession of all his possessions, incomes, and privileges as a Grand Duke of this great empire, so long as he proves his good faith by accepting Zlata Milanova's hand in marriage. I'd advise you to accept while you still can, my dear cousin," he added, "for it's better than a Jacobin like you deserves, and if you refuse I am to do as I please with you, which means exile in Tashkent or Vladivostok."

So, there were the terms which Nicky had offered at last week's audience—the truth of which Vasily had kept from me, instead plotting mad schemes to annex Manchuria or to find a cure! I did not quite know what to make of this, except that in Zlata's place I should not have been flattered.

"Exile or marriage!" Vasily muttered, seeming to rally his spirits somewhat. "Zlata, my dear, is that pleasing to you? Wouldn't you prefer a husband who *didn't* need to be forced to the cathedral under threat of Tashkent?"

"I find your sentiments to be hopelessly parochial," she replied, quite unruffled. "I'm sure Tashkent is as good a place as any, and I can't imagine a Grand Duke of Imperial Russia being so cowardly as to contract a marriage that would be distasteful to himself in preference to a life in—where *is* Tashkent, anyway? Somewhere in the Urals, isn't it? No doubt one of those places where the governor throws one ball a year, and the ladies attend in their dressing-gowns!"

With that she laughed merrily, but I watched Vasily closely; I watched all hope die for him. When at last he spoke again, his voice was quite hollow.

"And my friends?" he asked. "What becomes of *them?*"

"In truth, I haven't considered it," Sergei replied. "I suppose they'll be sent to prison in Siberia."

Vasily closed his eyes, and I felt a horrible sense of foreboding. "Don't," I begged him in a small voice; but I was not sure he even heard me.

He opened his eyes and spoke lifelessly. "I will accept, on one condition. Allow my friends to leave Russia, and I'll do as you like. I'll marry Zlata, and I'll never speak a word against you again, Sergei Alexandrovich. I swear it."

Did he think it was necessary, dooming himself to save the rest of us? Could he not have a little more faith in Nijam's gadgets, Mimi's claws, Schmidt's fists, and my own feminine wiles?

Sergei looked offended. "You propose that I, Sergei Alexandrovich, should allow four brazen thieves to walk away unpunished? You, who are already so reliant upon the Emperor's goodwill?"

Vasily's gaze was unblinking. "It wouldn't be the first time you bent the rules for a cousin," said he, "and once I am again in Nicky's favour I think you will find it very troublesome if I am *not* on your side."

"That's enough," Zlata said, seizing Vasily's hand. "Who cares what happens to these others? You'll release them, won't you, Godfather, for me if not for him?"

"Very well; I will."

"That settles it, then. Come away, Vaska. I'm sure the Emperor will be pleased to announce the engagement tonight—at once!"

I was in despair. This could not be my last sight of Vasily—not like this, snatched away by a woman he loathed. The policeman attached to my elbow had allowed his grasp to loosen during Vasily's confrontation with his cousin; and now I shrugged myself free and caught Vasily's hand.

I clasped it in both my own. I would have pressed it to my lips if I had dared, but to do so would have been to reveal too much—to him, to the onlookers. His eyes met mine. I had often thought them to be hypnotic and dangerous. At that moment they were neither of those things: only stricken and desperate. Perhaps mine were the same. For a moment that contact lasted—the press of our hands and the electric charge of our gaze, which attempted to say too many things and only failed, in consequence, to say anything at all. Then we were pulled apart. It was an unbearable goodbye after all.

Vasily looked back once as Zlata pulled him into the ballroom; and then he was gone, and Sergei snapped his fingers. "Take them to Butyrka to await sentencing," he ordered the policemen.

Schmidt cried out in indignation: "But, sir, you *promised!*"

Sergei Alexandrovich gave him a scornful look. "I cannot abide disorder," he said, with a peremptory wave of his hand. With that the three of us and my father's imprint were hurried out into the street and put into a black carriage, in which it was impossible to see one's hand before one's face.

The moment we were alone, Mimi spoke. "Has anyone heard from Nijam?"

"Not a word," said Schmidt gloomily.

I said nothing. Vasily had ventured too far into the mouth of the imperial bear; and now those steel jaws had snapped shut upon him, and he had been obliged to give himself up in order to free the rest of us. How perfectly senseless it all was! He didn't need to appease Nicky in order to free himself; he could have taken Nijam at her word. He could have killed the Grand Duke Vasily in a bomb blast and escaped under an assumed name. But no—he wanted the privileges of the Romanov name, without any of its difficulties.

"Do you still have your transmitters?" I asked dully.

"Yes," said Schmidt, "and mine has been receiving all this time, but I haven't heard a word from Nijam since we were caught."

"Zlata would not have forgotten her," said Mimi, as the

carriage got underway. "I *knew* the Okhrana had another spy watching us! I thought it was Madame Kapanadzy! Why did I not think of Zlata?"

"Never mind that; we must act. They'll search us at prison, and take our transmitters," I began, but I broke off with a gasp before I could add what I meant to say, for in addition to my silent father, a shade had quite suddenly appeared in the darkness beside me. I am not sure how the two of them managed to be visible in that thick darkness, unless a little light hung about them, illuminating the interior.

"You've done nothing," the poor trampled little boy said accusingly.

Another shade now appeared. "Did you find my father?" said a new voice. "Have you forgotten?"

"You promised," said the little boy.

"You were terribly shocked and sad," said a third shade—it was the frightful woman who had screamed for vengeance. "But you're exactly like the others. So long as *you're* comfortable, you don't care about the rest of us."

My father's imprint seemed engrossed in his newspaper.

"They're sending me to Butyrka," I protested, on the verge of tears. It was dark in the carriage, hot and stuffy with the lingering heat of the day. I felt the return of the ghastly sensations which the shades never failed to bring with them— the suffocation, despair and agony which told me all too vividly how they had died.

"They're sending *us* to the cemetery at Vagankovskoye!" said the woman mercilessly, and she plunged a hand into my body as though she meant to take hold of my heart and tear it from my bosom. I must have gone into a faint, for after that, I have only confused and horrible memories of that interminable journey. The carriage must have been moving quickly, because it rocked alarmingly going about the corners. I think that Mimi and Schmidt must have been holding onto me to keep me safely in my seat, for I survived it without bruises. In any case the shades rode with me, some of them demanding, some of them pleading for my help, and I wept because I did not know what I could do for them. We had come to Russia to do what we could for Anna, but what could we do for so many people? Having disgraced Grand Duke Nicholas, how could we repeat the trick with Grand Duke Sergei—whose misdeeds had been committed in the open light of day, and were known to the rich and mighty, and utterly disregarded?

At length the carriage came to a halt; the bolts on the door were opened, and our moving prison opened to allow a ray of torchlight to flow in. In that light the shades drew back, and I found myself looking into the face of a young woman, haloed in light. It was then that I felt quite sure I was dreaming, for a shade could not possibly have opened that door, and yet I knew her as well as I did any of my other confederates.

"It's you," I murmured. "You came back?"

Smiling, she reached out; and this time her hands closed over mine, warm and living.

"I told you I was alive," said Anna Sorina. "You really ought to have believed me!"

# Chapter XXV.

"Annushka!" Mimi cried. "Am I dreaming? *Dark!* Why did you tell me she was *dead?*"

"I was being visited by her shade," I whispered, still half convinced I was dreaming.

"I was not dead, but sleeping," Anna insisted, in tones that suggested that she had told me so, and why had I not listened? "It is just as well I did not *move on,* as you so often suggested, hmm? I woke days ago, and came at once to Moscow to find you—and Valery—as soon as I was able to travel. It is just as well that I did!"

There were more surprises in store for us; for at that moment Nijam stuck her head around the opened door and said, "Well, don't sit there forever! Valery needs to get rid of the black maria before the police realise it's missing."

After that I knew for certain that this was no dream. Schmidt assisted me to alight, like the gentleman he is, and a moment later the ominous black carriage rolled away, leaving us looking about a courtyard, yes—but the courtyard, not of the Butyrka prison, but of the same convent, with its white walls and gilded domes, where we had found shelter once before!

Nijam hurried us into the parlour, where a yawning nun was sent to fetch Sister Anastasia. Schmidt, Mimi and I were still in a state of utter confusion.

"All this time you were at large, and coming to fetch us?" Schmidt gave Nijam a reproachful look. "Why did you not *say* so?"

"Too busy doing, to chatter about it," said Nijam succinctly.

She explained that Anna and Valery had just knocked on the door of our lodgings, when Schmidt's message about Zlata's treachery came through. "We had to get to the Sheremetov Palace as quickly as possible. And then we had our work cut out for us dealing with the drivers of the carriage and getting away from the police escort. Still, all's well that ends well."

"No, it isn't!" I wailed, collapsing onto the sofa beside Anna. "Vasily's taken a devil's bargain! Why couldn't he *trust* us?"

Nijam scowled. "We've all been very stupid. Yes, Mimi, all of us but Miss Dark! We ought to have foreseen that Vasily would come to grief in this country sooner or later, and gone while we could! Now I suppose we have no Vasily, no safe-conduct—and no painting!"

"Oh, no, it's not so bad as *that*," said Mimi. "We have the painting, for no one cared to see whether we had given the original to Zlata, or just a decoy." Diving beneath the blue billows of her own skirts, out she came with a pasteboard tube, the twin of the one she had given to Zlata.

This part of our plan, at least, had come off without a hitch. Having prepared two identical tubes, we gave Zlata a decoy to smuggle out of the ball. We, meanwhile, meant to have secured our escape with the real thing. It was a beautiful plan, as I have said, but it foundered because Vasily *had* to try saving Nicky.

Nijam took the painting from Mimi's hands. "Well, one out of three is better than nothing," she said—which was maddeningly philosophical of her. "The question is, how shall we get out of the country?"

"We can't leave sir behind," protested Schmidt. "He doesn't *really* wish to marry that woman!"

Mimi gave an unladylike snort. "Oh, doesn't he? It seems to me that Vasily had any number of other choices before him, and as always chose the one most to his benefit!"

I bit my lip. I had tried to trust Vasily; even now I saw that he was only doing as he had promised, and ensuring that whatever became of himself, we at least could leave Russia in peace. But why like *this*? Surely there were other choices open to him!

"What are you saying?" A new voice broke in upon us, and we turned to see Vasily's mother—Sister Anastasia—sitting in her chair at the door. Her face had gone quite white with shock. "What has Vasily chosen to do?"

In a few words, we explained the evening's events.

"He cannot mean to stay here," Sister Anastasia objected, when she heard. "They'll kill him."

"I'm not leaving him without an explicit order," Schmidt said stubbornly, reaching for his transmitter. But he stopped short with his fingers hovering over the switch. "Oh, drat! That woman destroyed his transmitter, didn't she?"

"Yes," I said, "but that's what I was going to tell you in the carriage—I didn't merely press his hand as Zlata was about to drag him away; I passed him the spare transmitter we'd given to Zlata. Let us pray that one was not discovered." And

I switched on my own transmitter.

"Vasily," I said, "can you hear me? We got clear of the police, and now we're with your mother. Where are you st—"

"Miss Dark," Vasily said in a low, urgent voice, beneath the hum of conversation and the strain of music—he must still be trapped at that ball. "You must all get out of Moscow. Go at once—yes, without me. Tell Schmidt that's an order."

With that, there was a frightful burst of static, and I wincingly pulled the transmitter from my ear. Nijam tapped her temple to silence her own implanted transmitter.

"Doesn't Vasily know how much work goes into making one of these?" she demanded. "I don't manufacture these things so that people can have the pleasure of stomping on them!"

"I knew it!" Mimi said gloomily. "He has what he wanted, and now he's washing his hands of us." Her words echoed in my head. I did not want to believe them; and yet...

"The Grand Duke is right, you know," said Anna. "You should all leave at once. As soon as Valery returns I'll buy you tickets to Petersburg on the morning train."

"Not to Petersburg," Nijam said quickly. "That's where they'll expect us to go. We should leave by a route they don't expect, and try to cross a border that isn't watched so closely."

"They'll watch the Caucasus border too," said Sister Anastasia gently. "Why don't you take the Trans-Siberian Railway to Vladivostok?"

"Because it's on the other side of the world," said Anna, "but you're right, Sister, they'll never think to look for them in the East."

"Then you'd better get us tickets," Nijam said, opening her purse for the needful money, "but only part of the way; let's not broadcast our intentions at once."

I looked at Schmidt despairingly, and he looked at me. I saw at once that he wanted to desert Vasily no more than did I.

"Ma'am," I appealed to his mother, "you can't really want us to abandon him!"

"What more can you do for him than you have already done?" she asked, sadly. "Will you fetch him away against his will?"

I had no answer for that; and we were all sunk in a deep silence when Valery returned to announce that he had rid himself of the stolen carriage.

"We won't return here," Valery told Schmidt. "After what Anna and I have done tonight, we had better make ourselves scarce at once, and that way we can't be connected with you. We'll leave the tickets in an unmarked envelope at the sweet-shop opposite the station; tell the owner that you're my friend Vaslav. Good-bye! I wish you all the best of luck, for you'll need it."

I gave Anna a hug: after her long illness she was still very thin and weak. "Oh, Anna," I said, "you've put yourself into terrible danger helping us like this. I'm afraid it will quite destroy your career."

Anna looked somewhat abashed. "Well, I knew what I was getting into when I came here," said she, "but I've found that although money can buy a great many things, it cannot buy love. I've had false friends all my life, except for Mimi and Valery, and I think I'd rather have love."

She left me and went to hug Mimi, who blew her nose and said, "Schmidt! Do you have those things I gave you?"

"Oh, yes," Schmidt said, patting his pockets absentmindedly. "Here they are," and he handed Mimi a heavy little bundle all folded up in a handkerchief. Mimi handed this to Anna.

"Here's a little something to start you in your new life," she said fondly, "and *do* make sure you get the services of a decent fence, for they're all burning hot."

This was, of course, the loot she had collected earlier that evening in the ballroom! I couldn't help remarking upon it. "Why, Mimi! Such generosity!"

"Now you *sound* like him," she muttered. She was right, of course: Vasily was gone, and I could not help thinking of the things he would have said, were he here.

Our Russian friends having departed, Sister Anastasia pressed us to stay the night in the convent's guest quarters. An attendant came to show the others to their beds; but at the doorway I looked back, and did not follow them.

Sister Anastasia sat alone in her bath-chair, silent and pensive. My father sat near her on the sofa, looking at a book, as I had often seen him sit in life. His presence seemed somehow comforting just now: indeed there was something about the scene, Vasily's mother and my own father sitting together in companionable silence, that pulled painfully at my heart. I wished, just for a moment, that my father was really there—that I had made a mistake, as I had with Anna, and that after all he had been alive all along, and was waiting somewhere to greet me. I thought he would have liked Sister Anastasia.

I thought of Anna's words—*money cannot buy love.* Wise men had been saying similar things for years. *Better a dinner of herbs where love is than a fatted calf with hatred.* Yet Vasily had proven unable to resist the fatted calf. Why—oh, *why* could Anna make good her escape, but not Vasily? Why could he not be happy in what we had?

We *had* been happy together, the five of us, had we not? —And then my heart struck me, because only last night I had accused him of wanting to regain his fangs, and to marry Zlata for her money.

Sister Anastasia looked up at me, and she must have seen the look of sadness upon my face, for she extended a hand and said, "Tell me about it, my dear."

My own mother was far away, and my father was dead; but I knew at once that I could go to this homely woman with all the sorrow that weighed down my heart. "Oh, Sister," I said, kneeling beside her. "So many terrible things have happened today. I hardly know where to begin. First there was the awful tragedy this morning at Khodynka, and now we have lost Vasily, and how can I make any of it right?"

"Are you God, to make it right?"

"Oh, no! I don't mean that. Only, I can't help thinking that I drove Vasily away from me by accusing him of wanting his fangs back. And I don't know how much he told you about me, but I'm supposed to set things right, where I can, for people who have been wronged. I know I'm supposed to do something about what happened this morning; only I don't know what. I *tried*—at the ball, you know. I told Sergei Alexandrovich that those deaths were his fault, and I told him that he would die and be trampled underfoot as they were. But they were only words, you know!"

"Were they?" Sister Anastasia gave me a piercing look. "Why did you tell him that?"

"I don't know what got into me! And it was useless anyway, for it only made him angry!"

"Useless? I should not be so sure of that," she said. "Sometimes it is a very great act, only to speak aloud what has always gone unsaid. If you are indeed someone with the calling to do something about such injustices, then I do not think your words will fall to the ground unheeded."

I shuddered. My fingers were cold as I pressed them against my mouth. "What! You think—you think it will come true? That he will die as I predicted?"

She shrugged, which was reassuring, and then made the sign of the cross, which was not.

"How do you bear it," I whispered, "seeing and suffering so much wrong in this life?"

"I find it helps to be able to *do* something," she said. "To run away from your evil husband, or to spend a day arranging masses and burials for the dead, and food and care for the living." Indeed, she looked very tired; I did not doubt that she had spent much of her day in the work she mentioned. "But no one can do everything that needs to be done. We can only do what we can and have faith for the rest."

"But how can you have faith when it's *Vasily?*"

Her hand brushed back a strand of hair which had come loose from the knot where I had pinned it, at the top of my head. "I think," she said slowly, "that sometimes we must have our dreams, before we can truly know how hollow they are. If Vasily is the man you love—"

I think I might have choked a little.

"If Vasily is the man you love," she repeated serenely, "then he'll come back to you. Already you've done more for him than perhaps you know."

The guest quarters were very comfortable, for the convent was old and wealthy. Miraculously for such an ancient building, there were few imprints clinging to the shadows, and not even the shades had pursued me into this sanctuary: yet sleep evaded me. How could I go away and leave Vasily, perhaps forever, without one word of goodbye—and after quarrelling with him yesterday? The longer I paced that small room, the more wretched I felt. For days I had feared for Vasily; and now that the worst had seemingly occurred, I could not quite believe it. Among his family he had been treated as an outcast; he had been taunted, injured, and at last trapped. No: I could not leave merely because he asked me to. I must have the truth.

My door creaked a little as it opened, and at once there was a sound of movement from the room beside mine. I nearly beat a hurried retreat, for I did not wish to explain to the others what I meant to do. But the door next to mine opened, and Schmidt emerged, fully dressed and clutching his hat.

"Miss Dark!" he murmured. "I thought it was you. It isn't safe to go alone: allow me to accompany you."

Tears filled my eyes at his kind words: but of course Alphonse Schmidt, of all people, needed no explanations from me. Just as the clock struck one Schmidt and I stole out the convent gate and set out at a brisk walk towards Tverskaya Street and our old lodgings. As we passed the Kremlin, I beheld a great shadowy crowd of the dead in the great square before the gates of the ancient fortress.

"Give me a moment," I said, tugging on Schmidt's arm. "There's something I must attend to."

He followed me silently towards the waiting shades. As I approached, one of them turned to see me; and then in a mass they surged towards me, calling in their faded voices for me to fulfil my promise.

This time, I stood my ground in the pool of light beneath a lamp, grateful for Schmidt's solid bulk at my back. "My friends," I said, "I promised to do what I could, and I have. You can see the mark upon my face where Sergei Alexandrovich struck me, only because I accused him of your deaths before all the monsters in Europe. Now his men are seeking me to send me to Siberia, so I ask: will you let me go in peace?"

The crowd pushed forward. I felt their scrutiny upon my bruised face, and shivered as their hands wafted through me. Some made sounds of horror or pity: and that made me want to fall on my knees to them, for they had suffered so much worse.

"Do you think we care for your empty words?" cried the fierce woman who had assailed me twice before. "Where are your deeds, my fine lady?"

But others hushed her. "Be silent, Varvara! Look at her face! She's done what she can, and more than most!"

And another woman, who was clutching the hand of a little shade daughter, said, "It isn't *her* fault that so many of us are dead. Go in peace."

"I should be telling *you* to go in peace," I objected, perilously close to tears. "But how can you, when no one will hold the real culprit responsible?"

"God repays," said an old man. "Grand Duke Sergei will pay for his sins in the next world, if not in this one."

"I cursed him," I said shakily. "I told him that he would die as you died, and that he would be trampled underfoot."

"No wonder he struck you!" said the old man.

"You're a bunch of credulous fools," Varvara sniffed.

"Go in peace," said the old man. "We will watch for your words to be fulfilled."

It felt right to bob them a curtsey, so I did; and then I grabbed at Schmidt's arm and fled up Tverskaya Street. When I looked back the shades were still standing there, eyes fixed upon the great fortress, and I wondered how many long years they might wait, in vain, for the fulfilment of my prophecy. Had anyone told me that within ten short years the Grand Duke would be lying scattered across the pavement of his own fortress in shreds of torn and bloodied flesh, the victim of an anarchist's bomb, I should have utterly disbelieved them. Certainly I never imagined such a thing at the time; but when I read about it in the newspapers I could not help shivering, recalling the rash words I had uttered in the Montebellos' ballroom that evening a few years before.

"They were satisfied?" Schmidt asked presently, as we went up the street. I cast him a surprised glance, and he smiled pensively. "I felt a change in the air, I think. But don't mention it to Miss Nijam, or she'll wash her hands of me."

In time we reached our former lodgings, only to find them dark and empty. Schmidt and I glanced at each other with disappointment. "I suppose we ought to have known better than to expect Vasily here," I said in a low voice. "We might as well gather up our things."

Nijam had thoughtfully packed up and removed all her *own* things from the apartment, but otherwise the place was still strewn with other people's belongings. The samovar had gone quite cold, filled with the tragic remnants of a brewing of tea, and a little heap of peppermint-papers on the table gave witness to the exertions of the evening. Quickly, Schmidt packed his own, while I packed Mimi's and my valise, and changed my white gown for a sensible serge skirt and white shirtwaist. When we were finished, Schmidt carried the bags downstairs to find a *troika,* and I went, as though irresistibly drawn, to the little waste-paper basket in Vasily's old room. The little Fabergé mouse still lay within, a gleam of polished stone and precious metal in the northern twilight. It was heavy in my palm. I struggled with myself a moment. I wanted something of Vasily's to keep with me, but I did not want to remember him by diamonds and platinum. I put it down on the dining-room table instead. Perhaps Madame Kapanadzy would find it and take a liking to it. Or perhaps Vasily would see it, and know—what? I don't know.

It was then that I saw the letter which lay next to a heap of peppermint-papers on the table. It was addressed to Molly Dark, and it was postmarked Brixton; my hands shook a little as I made out the direction in the flickering light of the sole candle with which I had illuminated my activities. Apart from anything else, a letter to Molly Dark from her mother in Brixton was *much* too revealing to be left to the Okhrana's eyes. I tucked it into my valise, together with the final volume of *Can You Forgive Her?* which I found by touch on the sofa. Just then, the transmitter in my ear crackled.

"Miss Dark!" Schmidt called, in a cautious undertone. "Sir has come—but he's surrounded by the police! Try to get out, if you can!"

"Understood," I said, snuffing the candle at once. I opened the door and considered my escape. A small landing provided access to our own half of the attic, while another door opposite led into the Populists' lodgings. The stairwell below rang with the tramp of many feet, and I could see the shadows of men flaring out as they passed the gas sconces at each landing. Had it been the daytime, I might conceivably have tried to hurry past them beneath the cover of a veil; but at the dead of night my presence upon the stairs could not help but be remarked upon. There was nowhere to hide, unless I wanted to intrude upon my neighbours. I withdrew again into the attic, biting my lip with worry. Should I hide beneath one of the beds, or try squeezing into a wardrobe? That would be useless, for the police were almost certainly coming to conduct a search of the premises, and I knew from our "liquidation" in Petersburg how thorough they were likely to be.

Footsteps rang upon the landing. There was nowhere to go except the small balcony outside the window. "If you don't hear from me by daybreak, Schmidt," I gasped, throwing open the French doors and stepping out into the balmy night air, "you had better take Mimi and Nijam, and leave Russia without me."

With that I switched off my transmitter altogether and pressed myself with a beating heart against the wall immediately outside the door. My father's imprint drifted after me—serenely oblivious, as always, to my plight. Voices and the heavy tread of several men sounded from within the attic, and I heard doors opening and closing. My hiding-place seemed an absurdity. They had only to step out onto the balcony to find me. Where could I go from here? The balcony ran all the way along the front of the house, with a wall of thin masonry to divide it from the second attic apartment. I am no Mimi Laine, and have no head for heights; but I was just desperate enough to consider climbing to the outside of the railing and getting around the wall onto the Populists' balcony. But would the railing hold my weight? I had got as far as this when the French door opened a second time.

"I shall be smoking outside, if it please you," Vasily announced, almost in my ear. He sounded weary and apathetic. The policemen within the attic made an indistinguishable sound of assent; and then Vasily closed the French door behind him—turned—and beheld me.

For a moment he seemed to congeal almost to stone. Then he advanced to the railing and struck a match to light the cigarette he carried. I'd rarely seen Vasily smoke before, except the occasional cigar, but his hands were shaking slightly and perhaps the evening's events had left him desirous of steadying his nerves. After the first moment he did not look my way: he only puffed at the cigarette and then said, very softly, "I desired Schmidt to take you away at once. Why hasn't he done so?"

"I'm not a *carpet-bag*," I said, injured. "And Schmidt's not an automaton!"

"So I'm discovering." There came a silence, and I berated myself for antagonising him once again.

"Vasily," I said, inching recklessly closer, "I know you don't really want to marry Zlata. If you're only doing this to get us safely out of the country, then for heaven's sake come away with us now."

Vasily drew a deep breath, but his voice was light and careless. "I'm flattered by the invitation, my dear, but on the whole I think I'll stay where I am."

"Why?" I begged him. "You can't really want to live among these people—I've seen how they terrorise you!"

"Are you accusing me of cowardice?" he asked, laughing. "Or do you really think I'd throw away a chance like this?"

I felt my cheeks go hot, but I couldn't pretend to believe such things. "I know how you feel about these people. I was there the evening of Zlata's party, when you laid your head

346

in my lap."

"You shouldn't set so much store by a few confiding gestures, my dear!"

"Did you make yourself vomit blood, too, that evening, purely as a show? You've seen what I have seen, Vasily. These people can't change—they don't mean to; not even the Emperor. There is a red cloud hanging over this country, and when it breaks, it will rain blood! Why throw in your lot with them? Were you—were you not *happy* with us?"

My voice broke on those last words; my tears overflowed, and Vasily, with a gesture of impatience, ground out his cigarette and threw it into the street. For a moment he stood rigidly before me; and then he turned and swept me out of view of the window, and clasped both my hands in his own.

"All right, all right! Don't torment me so!" he whispered. "Try to understand what I am doing! As long as I remain in Moscow, there's a chance the rest of you might escape without me. But if I go with you I shall bring all the monsters down upon you all, forever. It will be the same as it was in London, and in Vienna before *that*. Little mouse, you can't live like that."

I had been raised not to believe that a broken heart was something one could die of—yet all the same it was as much as I could do not to demand how he thought I would live at all without *him*. As I hesitated, Vasily released me and once again shrouded himself in that awful mask of carelessness.

"Anyway, my dear, it's entirely for the best. I always was a liability, and you ought to have no one on your crew you cannot trust. Tell Schmidt that I commend you most solemnly to his care."

"Why should you imagine I don't trust you?" I protested.

"I didn't mean a word of what I said last night, about you wanting fangs. I *know* you don't! I just don't understand why you are so determined to stay here! Do you think you ought to make Zlata happy, just because you once made her miserable? Do you think it lies in your power to bring any happiness to such a selfish person?"

"I do believe the little mouse is jealous."

"I'm not jealous at all!" I hissed, although it was a lie. The thought of Zlata getting Vasily once and for all into her clutches made me wild, and knowing that Vasily would go unwillingly only exacerbated my very natural feelings. "It isn't Zlata you want—and it isn't our safety, either. Why won't you be honest? Ever since we came to this horrible place, all you've cared for is getting back your privileges—your money, your title. What is so marvellous about being a Grand Duke, anyway? Is it worth your life?"

There was a long silence. At length he said, "You are right, of course. At any moment I could have pretended to dynamite myself, as Miss Nijam recommended. But who would I be then? Plain Mr Basil Nicks? A frightful bourgeois gentleman, who attends church on Sunday in a badly-cut coat?" For a moment I thought he was making disparaging allusions to my father. But then his voice changed. "And what will you give me in return, Miss Dark, for the loss of everything I am?"

The lingering twilight was just dark enough to conceal Vasily's features, but his voice—oh, his voice was oddly pleading. Words failed me. What did Vasily want from me? I could not give him money; I could not give him power. The only thing I had to give him was—love.

"Nothing?" he murmured sadly, as the silence lengthened. Then he released my hands and straightened, and his voice became hard and light. "Don't mourn me, my little mouse. Did I not warn you from the beginning that I was only playing tricks to get your confidence? You've outwitted me twice; and at last I've had my revenge. You gave me your confidence, and now you've helped me to a Grand Dukedom."

I did not know how much of this to believe, but every word was like a blade. At first I was speechless; and then I was outraged.

"Don't call me your little mouse. The only little mouse you care about is the one in there on the table, with diamonds for a tail and rubies for eyes." My own voice was nearly unrecognisable to me, low and shaking with anger. In the echoing silence that followed, I chose my next words the way some men choose their weapons. "I know you loathe Zlata; and I know what will become of you if you marry her. You'll marry her for her money and the Emperor's favour, and you'll betray her because you loathe her, and you'll make both her life and yours a living hell. And at the end of it all…you'll be *exactly* like your father."

He actually flinched a little, as though the words were a physical blow. But then he recovered himself and struck back "A flattering sketch of my character! But what a little fool *you* were, to imagine you could mend such a reprobate!"

"I *don't* imagine I can mend you!" I wailed, quite forgetting that there were police in the house. "Only I can't bear to see it, because I—because I love you so!"

My words rang in the air. Vasily was speechless. There came a sharp word from within the house. Glancing in at the window, I saw that the living-room was empty, for the police must be searching the rooms; and then I knew that I might have only moments to secure my escape. Flinging caution

349

to the winds, I wrenched open the French door, slipped past Vasily's reaching hand, darted across the apartment and flung myself down the stairs.

Shouts and running feet above told me the hunt was up. I slapped at my transmitter. "Schmidt!" I cried, breathless with tears. "Schmidt, they're after me! For heaven's sake, tell me you have a cab waiting!"

He did indeed have a cab waiting, and the cabman whipped the horses into a trot almost before I had thrown myself in a panting heap upon the carriage cushions.

The next half-hour was employed in muddling our trail by means of changing from one cab to another; and then, as dawn approached, we took ourselves to the train station. Here, Nijam and Mimi—having been informed via transmitter of our whereabouts—were already waiting with censorious looks and the tickets. Happily our papers were barely inspected by the conductor, and in a briefer time than I thought possible, the four of us were ensconced in our second-class compartment and on our way east across the vast expanse of the Russian Empire.

"I take it the Grand Duke won't be joining us," said Nijam, when we were alone.

Everyone looked at me. Had it not been for Schmidt, I would not have answered at all; but there was something beseeching in his look, which I found myself compelled to answer.

"Vasily's staying in Moscow to give us a chance to escape," I said. And then, rather bitterly, I added, "At least, that's what he *told* me."

Not even Mimi said anything. The sun rose, painting the countryside gold as we won free of the city. Schmidt, seeing my face, extracted a handkerchief from his pocket and handed it to me. I was not too proud to accept it; and as I did so, a solitary peppermint dropped into my lap, and thence to the floor.

"A peppermint!" said Mimi, pouncing upon it.

"It's mine," Schmidt said, rather dully. "Give it back."

"But Nijam has eaten all the others!"

"She gave this one to *me*," he said, reddening; and tucked it back into his breast-pocket. Nijam sent him a sharp look, which he studiously failed to meet.

"Why didn't you stay with *sir?*" she asked.

Schmidt bit his lip. "Oh, I couldn't possibly. How could I look sir in the face without having seen you ladies to safety?"

"I hope you don't mean to *return* to him," Nijam snapped. Schmidt made no reply. I heaved a sigh and opened my valise in search of a pair of smoked glasses which Vasily had given me, to shield my aching eyes from the glare of the rising sun. My hand lighted instead upon a book, which I drew out in some surprise. It was what I had presumed to be the third volume of my Anthony Trollope novel—but in fact it was Vasily's sketchbook. Listlessly, I opened it up. Then it was as though a knife went through me, for there before me was a sketch of a girl in a white dress, leaning over a theatre balcony with a paper dart poised ready to throw. It was myself. Turning the pages faster now, I saw more scenes I knew—views of the Schloss Frohsdorf, some of the artefacts at the British Museum, a fat London sparrow, the rooftops of Moscow as seen from our attic window—but always among the leaves, *my* features, *my* figure, captured sometimes with loving detail, but more often in a few hasty strokes. I suddenly recalled Zlata picking up the sketchbook and looking through it, and the frown that crossed her face when she saw what lay within; and I understood why she saw me as her rival in Vasily's affections... His affections! Suddenly I could not breathe. Tucking the sketchbook deep into my valise, I leaped to my feet and ran from the compartment.

The viewing-platform at the rear of the carriage afforded me a glimpse of Moscow's spires and onion-domes: the fairytale city where all my own hopes had been dashed. Or had they? I felt myself tormented by doubts. Vasily had filled his sketchbook with portraits of *me.*

*What will you give me in return, Miss Dark, for the loss of everything I am?* Could he have meant—no! He wanted money. He wanted his painting. *You of all people know how important money is to a happy life...*

Where had I gone wrong? Was there something I ought to have said, or something I ought to have refrained from saying, to keep Vasily by me? If this was a fairytale, I had muffed the spell—by a word, a look, an inflection; and now I had only myself to blame.

The door opened, and Mimi, to my surprise, emerged from the carriage to join me.

"Here," she said gruffly, holding out her hand. I blinked through my tears at the little white circle within.

"A peppermint?"

"No, a pearl. Pearls always make me feel better when I'm sad."

I couldn't help laughing. "Thank you, Mimi, it's already done me good. But I'd really rather you kept it."

"Don't be sorry for that blockhead," she said earnestly. "He'll come to his senses."

This surprised me. "But all this time, you've been saying—"

"Oh, it's obvious what Vasya *thinks* he wants," Mimi said with an airy wave. "Back in Paris, he thought he wanted me, and so he got me, and we made each other miserable. He didn't want me, not really."

"What *did* he want?"

Mimi shrugged philosophically. "He's wanted a lot of things. The one woman he couldn't have. A Grand Dukedom. Right now, I think he wants to be a good man; only he hasn't yet worked out that he *can* be." She paused. "Of course, there's no guarantee that he'll work it out in time to save his skin."

She patted me on the shoulder in an encouraging sort of way, and then took herself back inside. Alone with my father's benign ghost, I stood watching Moscow recede behind us; and I thought how both Sister Anastasia and Mimi had told me similar things. Perhaps they were right. Perhaps, after all, my words were not simply a spell that could go right or wrong. Vasily was more complicated than that; and if he was the man I loved—well, he would find his way back to me in time.

Indeed, I was to meet Vasily again, and far sooner than I dreamed. But that is to anticipate another story.

### S.D.G.
Miss Dark will return in
*Dark & Dawn*

353

# Unhistorical Note

At this point I'm not sure why I'm calling this an *unhistorical* note: in preparation for this book I will admit to having consulted: Simon Sebag Montefiore's history of *The Romanovs*, Robert Massey's *Nicholas and Alexandra*, a tome on ballet, biographies of Mathilde Kschessinka and Sergei Alexandrovich's wife Ella of Hesse, part of Marie of Roumania's gushy autobiography, Orlando Figes' history of the Russian Revolution (*A People's Tragedy*, which is approximately the size of a grand piano), my friend Christina's vivid memories of visiting St Petersburg in the 2000s, Nicky II's diary in a Google Translate edition, and an absolutely *fascinating* academic article tracing the influence of the tsarist Okhrana on the Soviet secret police. (Where do you *think* Lenin recruited his best policemen?)

Any errors—which I'm sure are numerous—should be blamed on me.

I'm sure that Grand Duke Nicholas Nikolaevich the Elder, a.k.a. Nizi, didn't actually take his sons peasant-hunting for fun. Nizi, however, seems to have been quite a repellant person. Having personally lost the Crimean War and driven his wife, Alexandra of Oldenberg, into a Kyiv convent, Nizi set about living it up with his mistress, the ballerina Catherine Chislova. After her death, Nizi, already a prolific womaniser, began to suffer from the delusion that all women were in love with him. After mistakenly attacking a male dancer during a ballet performance—though admittedly not during the imperial coronation gala of 1896—he was exiled to the Crimea to live out the rest of his days in seclusion.

The historical Nizi had only two sons, not three; but Nikolasha, the elder, was a colourful and somewhat hysterical personality in the habit of going about armed to the teeth with daggers and a pistol, and indulging in raucous dinnertime practical jokes. During a governmental crisis in 1905, when Emperor Nicky attempted to appoint him dictator for the purposes of putting down a preliminary revolution, Nikolasha brandished his revolver and threatened to shoot himself on the spot if the Tsar did not grant the constitution which the people demanded. In doing so, he may have prolonged the Romanov regime for another twelve years. (His influence over Nicky, however, was not entirely beneficial: it was his wife and her sister, the Montenegrin princesses, who eventually introduced Nicky and Alix to Rasputin.)

The tragic Khodynka Field crowd crush, of course, *did* happen during the imperial coronation festivities. Over a thousand people were killed and many times that number were injured, largely due to the incompetence and neglect of the Moscow governor, Grand Duke Sergei Alexandrovich. Sergei never admitted to his fault and that evening, when Nicholas and Alexandra attempted to leave the French Embassy ball early in recognition of the tragedy, it was he and his brothers who browbeat the pair into staying. It was not the fictional Vasily Nikolaevich, but the most liberal-minded of the Romanovs—the Mikhailovich Grand Dukes Nicholas and Alexander—who warned the Tsar that the disaster would remain a blot on his reign if he did not dismiss Sergei and cancel the remaining festivities.

As I look back on the political climate of 1890s Russia my impressions are somewhat wistful. The Russian Revolution itself was a slow-motion disaster for the country, but in the 1890s there was an awakening civic society with burgeoning ideals of liberal democracy, whether of constitutional-democratic, populist, socialist, anarchist, or anti-colonial nationalist stripes. It is hard not to wonder how much kinder the twentieth century—and even the twenty-first—might have been to Russia had its rulers at that moment been capable of relinquishing the autocracy. Alas: they were not.

Once again, I want to thank my wonderful beta and sensitivity readers for their help—Christina Baehr, W.R. Gingell, Schuyler McConkey, and Marie Lewis. I'd also like to thank the two gentlemen who were seated to either side of me on the plane between Houston, Texas and Charlotte, North Carolina while I was writing the goriest and most melodramatic passages of Chapter 16, for remaining blissfully asleep the whole time. One can hardly work oneself up into a gothic Victorian passion when fellow-travellers are breathing down one's neck.

Suzannah Rowntree
September 2023

# About the Author

Suzannah Rowntree lives in a big house in rural Australia with her awesome parents and siblings, drinking fancy tea and writing historical fantasy fiction that blends real-world history with legend, adventure, and a dash of romance.

**You can connect with me on:**
🌐 https://suzannahrowntree.site

**Subscribe to my newsletter:**
✉ https://subscribepage.io/srauthor

# Also by Suzannah Rowntree

The Miss Sharp's Monsters Series
*The Werewolf of Whitechapel*
*Anarchist on the Orient Express*
*A Vampire in Bavaria*

The Miss Dark's Apparitions Series
*Tall & Dark*
*Dark Clouds*
*Dark & Stormy*
*Dark & Dawn*

The Watchers of Outremer Series
*A Wind from the Wilderness*
*The Lady of Kingdoms*
*Children of the Desolate*
*A Day of Darkness*
*A Conspiracy of Prophets*
*The House of Mourning*

The Pendragon's Heir Trilogy
*The Door to Camelot*
*The Quest for Carbonek*
*The Heir of Logres*

The Fairy Tale Retold Series
*The Rakshasa's Bride*
*The Prince of Fishes*
*The Bells of Paradise*

*Death Be Not Proud*
*Ten Thousand Thorns*
*The City Beyond the Glass*